THE
EXTRADITIONIST

THE
EXTRADITIONIST

TODD MERER

THOMAS & MERCER

Text copyright © 2017 by Todd Merer
All rights reserved.

No part of this book may be reproduced, or stored in a retrieval system, or transmitted in any form or by any means, electronic, mechanical, photocopying, recording, or otherwise, without express written permission of the publisher.

Published by Thomas & Mercer, Seattle

www.apub.com

Amazon.com, the Amazon logo, and Thomas & Mercer are trademarks of Amazon.com, Inc., or its affiliates.

ISBN-13: 9781477806012
ISBN-10: 1477806016

Cover design by Jae Song

Printed in the United States of America

FOR SORAYA

It ain't no sin if you crack a few laws now and then, so long's you don't break any.

—*Mae West, actress*

Just win, baby.

—*Al Davis, Brooklyn boy*

ALUNE

The Logui people live beside a mountain they call Anawanda—"the center of the world"—which is the highest peak of the Sierra Nevada de Santa Marta, the northernmost Andean range in Colombia.

Things happen in Colombia.

Like the Logui being manipulated and murdered by assorted bad actors: right-wing paramilitaries, left-wing guerrillas, narco-traffickers.

I feel the Logui's pain.

Not that the Logui reveal their feelings. They simply observe that there are two kinds of people: Those Who Know More and Those Who Know Less.

The Logui believe it is perfectly fine to commit the occasional sin in order to protect Those Who Know More from Those Who Know Less.

As do I.

I think of the Logui as my family, my sisters and brothers, especially Older Brother and Younger Brother. In turn the Logui revere me as Alune, *their living, loving God, The One Who Knows Most of All.*

But regardless of who or what I really am, I presently find myself in need of a new name, a proper nom de guerre for my own protection. Because, come the dawn, I'm venturing to the outside world to do a little sinning.

I need the new name now, for the sun's nearly up, and soon I will be in Anawanda's shadow—

Hmmm . . .

Shadow?

Perfect.

A FEW YEARS LATER

BENN

You need four things to tell a story: a beginning, a middle, an end, and you can't be dead.

Survival's my ticket to tell this story. No one else is left to contradict it. The other characters have gone to hell and aren't coming back. I tell myself that I'm blameless; that they would have perished whether or not I was involved; that, if not me, it would have been someone else. But, deep down, I know I'm lying.

Because I was not merely an instrument but the key.

Because I ignored lines between good and evil.

Because I recognized the portents from the moment they appeared. Who ever heard of a story with a happy ending that begins with a quadruple-whammy like Christmas, Hanukkah, and Kwanzaa all falling on the very same day that a blizzard just *happens* to blanket the Apple?

No one.

So why was I out in the snow instead of comfortably at home?

Work.

Lucrative, morally questionable work that had me wading through drifts on Police Plaza and climbing icy steps to the entrance of the United States Attorney for the Southern District of New York and, once

Todd Merer

therein, escorted to the conference room of the International Narcotics Bureau.

It was cozy there, and pin-drop still. Tea for two, without the tea. Me and the INB chief. Our relationship was best described as a mutual abomination society. He thought I was unethical and grossly overpaid. I thought he was self-righteous and envious. Probably we were both right.

I shifted in my seat and recrossed my legs.

He sighed theatrically. "Today of all days? You drag me out for . . . *this?* For Christ's sake, your guy's a fucking CPOT."

I simply nodded, though acronyms annoy the hell out of me. Unfortunately, I labor in a system that's an alphabet soup. At this very moment, an AUSA, or an assistant US attorney—the INB chief—was reminding me that the DOJ—Department of Justice—had authorized the DEA to designate my client a CPOT, or Consolidated Priority Operational Target. CPOTs tend to grow old and die in jail, which was why I'd made the government a hard-to-refuse offer:

My client Fernando Ibarra (aka Fercho)—facing life sentences on indictments here and in the Southern District of Florida—pleads to a concurrent five-year bit. In exchange for this extraordinary laxity, Fercho gives up evidence on the Colombian government's murderously corrupt antidrug czar. A huge takedown that would ignite the career of the prosecutor who initiated it. A bonfire of the vanities that would prove irresistible. I hoped.

"*If* I authorize this—I'm not saying I will, but *if* I do—my ass is on the line," the chief said. "You better not be fucking with me."

For most SDNY prosecutors, the job was a stepping stone between a top-ten law school and a top-ten firm partnership. The chief was an exception. He was a career prosecutor. He'd taken the subway to law school and now was riding the rails toward Main Justice. A hard case who trusted nobody. In that respect, we were alike.

"Fucking you would be fucking myself," I said.

He eyeballed me, parsing my obscenities. I understood his concern. Was I expressing a shared worry . . . or mocking him?

"We're in this together," I said. "I want this to happen as much as you do."

"I bet you do. All right . . . *if*. How long would it take?"

I shrugged. "You know how these things go."

"Do I ever." He sighed again. "Okay, bring me the head of General Uvalde."

"Funny," I said, although it wasn't.

I wished the chief a very merry, happy whatever, then buttoned up my overcoat and went to try to find someone to warm me during the cold night ahead.

For sure, it wasn't going to be my ex-wife, although she remained my one true love. The last time I tried—and failed—to mend fences with my ex, she'd punched me in the mouth. And while I was spitting blood, she said nasty things about my moral compass, to the effect that I was an abject slave to a risky business.

She was partially correct.

Yes, I was consumed by my work, but there was little danger in my doings. The sins of my clients ranged from personal betrayals to crimes against humanity, but never had I felt the slightest twinge of fear. Not because I was brave or reckless, but because I did not lie or steal, and I played well with others.

But why quibble?

The real reasons she left me? Not how but with *whom* I played. Also, that I wasn't a one-woman man. She was right about both.

* * *

Mere hours after arranging to bring a mass murderer to justice in exchange for a lesser killer being wrist-slapped, I was pleasantly inebriated in the back of a hansom cab fondling a snow-stranded Avianca flight attendant, the treetops glistening and the two of us listening to the sound of our horse clopping through Central Park . . . me, about to instruct the top-hatted driver to end the journey at my place, when—

"Let's go see the tree at Rock Center," said my date.

"Sounds like fun," I lied. I hated group jollity but was a big believer in patience earning rewards. Right I was. After a few freezing minutes amid a jam of sniffling tourists, she shivered and pressed against me.

I said, "Umm?"

"Mm-hmm."

My place. We shared a joint and popped a cork and lay by the fireplace. In the flickering light, her body glowed like honey and tasted even sweeter. It was one of those glorious moments when you think life can't get any better.

But then it did.

As I was about to close the books on what already had been my personal-best year, a trifecta of new clients suddenly emerged from the free-fire zone of the war against drugs: three major criminals willing and able to pay XXX-size fees for top-notch legal representation.

Modesty aside, that was me.

It went like this . . .

CHAPTER 1

By the following morning, the snow was dirty. Reminded me of the recent extremes of my life: sprinkled with fairy dust at night; sooty and littered by day. I walked to my office in an old mansion off Fifth, one of the few Upper East Side buildings not yet renovated, its ambience midway between faded glory and louche.

Alongside its faded marble entrance hung bronze plaques bearing the names of its tenants: a private financial consultant, an art dealer to the crème de la crust, the New York representative of a Swiss firm. The fourth plaque denoted yours truly:

BENNJAMIN T. BLUESTONE
EXTRADITIONS

The double *n* in my given name is a testament to my mother's quirkiness. The ingenious specialty *Extraditions*, a tribute to my own. I'd considered *esquire*, *lawyer*, and *counselor at law*, but no longer saw myself fitting any of these descriptions. *Extraditions* was more accurate, as well as vaguely innocuous, in keeping with my deliberately low profile. My top-floor office was modestly shabby chic: old armoire, worn leather couch, threadbare Caucasian rugs, walls lined with sketches of juries I drew back when I actually tried cases.

I neither sketched nor tried cases anymore.

I took on very few cases. Solely extraditions in which I led my clients—mainly deep-pocketed cartel chieftains—down the yellow-brick road of cooperation. Except for my driver-factotum—a loyal fellow named Valery—I ran a private one-man shop.

My phone rang. When I answered, a man spoke in Spanish: "Good morning, Dr. Bluestone. Felipe Mondragon here."

I'd been leaning back with my feet atop my desk, but now my soles hit the floor. Courtesy of my ex-wife, Spanish is my second language.

"Good morning to you, Doctor," I said, standing. Colombians call lawyers *Doctor*.

Felipe Mondragon was a connected Bogotá lawyer who referred well-heeled clients to a despicable clique of Miami Cuban lawyers. I'd crossed paths with Mondragon, but we'd never acknowledged each other. Until now.

"Sorry to trouble you during the holidays," he said.

"Not at all. So busy here, I'm still working."

"Not too busy to meet a person, I hope."

"As a professional courtesy, never too busy. What jail?"

"He's not yet incarcerated. He is considering a negotiated surrender. You'll have to travel to meet him. Someone will deliver expense money shortly. Yes?"

"Perfectly fine." I figured Mondragon's guy was a fugitive from an extradition-generated capture order. Meaning a hefty fee for negotiating his surrender; another fee after he surrendered.

"The meeting will be three days from now, at noon, in the cathedral of the city among the three volcanoes."

I knew the city. I'd find the cathedral. "I'll be there."

We exchanged the usual courtesies and terminated the call, leaving me once again marveling at the unpredictability of my business. Fifteen minutes ago, Mondragon was just another hole in a world of asses. Now he was my great olive-skinned hope. Which got me wondering . . .

Why hadn't he referred the case to one of his usual Miami Cuban attorneys? Could be they'd stolen a buck too many. They were like that. Or maybe Mondragon had overreached from them. He was like that, too. Everyone liked money much too much. Except me. Well, actually, I *loved* money; it was the making part I was sick and tired of.

But I had no choice.

In my years of lawyering, I'd earned fortunes, but subtract from them the sums of my unholy trinity—drugs, drink, divorce—and the subtotal was troubling. Now, like a shark needing to keep swimming to breathe, I needed to keep working to maintain my extravagances. My fees, although sizable, were a fraction of what I needed to retire in the manner to which I was accustomed. I was all alone in the world and wanted the kind of nurturing only big bucks could buy.

The other day while online, I was required to select my date of birth by scrolling down a numbered wheel. I watched the years pass, thinking how quickly they had gone. My next birthday was a year ending in zero, and I didn't want to go on working until I ran out of juice. *Couldn't*, because sooner or later, the whole rotten-drug-lawyer monopoly game was going to crash, and a lot of players would be drawing cards that said *Go to Jail*. I planned to be long gone by then.

Because I had a dream . . .

I'd snag a client named Biggy who would deliver unto me the mother of all scores. I knew that my Biggy existed in the realm of possibility. In fact, he might even be Mondragon's guy. One never knew—

My phone rang, the second of the day's three momentous calls.

The caller was requesting FaceTime. I accepted, and there was my pal Foto, smiling with all thirty-two pearly whites. "Benn, old boy," he said. "I've got a proposition: come spend the holidays here."

Here was Panama City. "I'll try, but I may be elsewhere. Work."

"Try hard. There's work for you here, too."

Foto's mirrored shades reflected several young women in bikini bottoms, lounging about his penthouse terrace. He was a so-called *comisionista* who introduced certain people to certain people, then took his fee and stepped from the picture. The smart thing to do. Career drugsters have a life expectancy akin to World War II bomber pilots flying missions over the Third Reich. Most end up shot down by the law of averages. But Foto went on flying.

"*Very* serious work," he added.

"In that case, I'll be there."

We settled on a day, and I clicked off. I'd juggle and manage. You learn to in a business that's totally unpredictable—months without a peep of new work, then two cases in two minutes. The work itself, however, was totally predictable: same old, same old, researching and developing deep-throat information Uncle Sam deemed significant—drugs by the tons and seizures in the multimillions of dollars—then horse-trading it for minimal jail time my clients could do standing on their heads.

Being the keeper of such secrets entailed great responsibility—and, if one were careless, a fair amount of risk. I reduced that hazard by maintaining constant vigilance and trusting no one. The password to my password-keeping app was *PARANOID.FLOYD*, and along each step of all my ways, I buried vital paper trails—insurance policies of a sort that I sold to myself, being the natural-born salesman I am.

And the extradition business *is* all about selling. A shining example of my craft was the line I used in my standard client rap:

Walk with me . . .

Uttered alone, the words sound like a cheap imitation of Christ, but in circumstances requiring faith, they rang clear as a bell to prospective clients. Besides, it was true. My clients *did* walk with me . . . at least as far as the departure terminal of the plane extraditing them stateside.

Ping!

The third call of the day was actually a texted message from a Colombian lawyer named Paz: URGENT YOU COME SOON! STAND BY!

Decoded, Paz had a case for me.

Three new cases. If I was dreaming, I didn't want to wake up—

Bzzzz!

My visitor was Mondragon's Mr. Green, bearing my expense money. Entering, he lowered his hoodie, removed his Yankees cap, and shivered.

"Maldito frío afuera."

His countrified Dominican accent was typical of those who deliver me manna: gofers in the street crews that distribute product for the Mexican transporters who buy wholesale from Colombian drug-trafficking organizations—DTOs, in DEA parlance.

He handed me a brown paper bag. From its heft, I figured it held five thou in small bills. Tens. I've handled greenbacks for so long, I can count them by sound, so I proceeded to do so, taking out a banded pack and riffling it at my ear . . .

I paused and looked at the bills.

Not tens, but Ben Franklins.

Five hundred of them. Fifty thou.

Who the hell pays fifty large up front just for a meet? I didn't ask, just tucked the money under my horseshoe paperweight while wondering: *Is Mondragon's guy my Biggy?*

Mr. Green handed me a throwaway phone. When I put it to my ear, a guy with a Colombian accent said, *"¿Todo está bien?"* Voices have a nasty way of becoming incriminating, so I just grunted affirmatively.

The guy hung up, and I *guessed* way down south he'd be collecting $60,000 from my unknown benefactor, which included a 20 percent charge for moving cash outside the system. *Guessed*, because this was pure drug-money laundering—but only if one participated knowingly— and I personally knew nothing from nothing. I'm a law-abiding citizen. As spotless as a Good Humor Man's shirt. Pure as the snow that enabled my night with the Avianca flight attendant . . .

Her scent still lingered, or so I imagined. Delicious.

After Mr. Green departed, I retried making sense of the deal. Mondragon and *moi*? I looked at the Franklins beneath my horseshoe paperweight, a gift from my ex that reflected my history. The horseshoe was gold plated but hardly visible within an acrylic slab badly scratched on the surface. In my good old bad days, I used to razor-chop and snort lines of coke off its surface.

Now my ex was gone, and my clients were world-class drug dealers. What else is there to say? I am what I am.

I slid open a wall panel, revealing a small safe. I slipped ten thou in my breast pocket and stashed forty in the safe. Any half-assed burglar would spot the panel, and the safe was as easy to open as a can of tuna, and the burglar, thinking he'd found my fortune, would depart in ignorance of the more subtle places that hid my major money. I kept cash in many places because I'm a believer in the world as we know it ending—sooner rather than later—and I wanted to be mobile when chaos and anarchy reigned.

More on that later.

Right now, it was Biggy time. I had no doubt he was out there. Or that I could make him mine. It was simply a matter of getting him to . . .

Walk with me.

Tsk. Why, if I had one dollop of sincerity, I'd utter the words with an addendum tattooed on my forehead: *Walk at your own risk*. Another reason why I needed to leave the business. I was tired of bullshitting. Very tired.

And yet, there was no escaping the truth.

As much as I wanted to quit the game?

I cannot deny that I *loved* playing it.

CHAPTER 2

I lived a few blocks from my office. Dollar-wise, the neighborhood's triple-A. My apartment is a brownstone condo nestled between grand edifices owned by hedge-fund billionaires I ranked by their acquisitions as the Greater and the Lesser, although both were equally greedy. But who was I to judge?

My relatively austere apartment was absurdly overpriced, although it boasted certain necessary amenities: the lobby was manned 24-7 by a concierge—one of three look-alike Serb cousins who all went by the name Viktor—and my full floor was accessible only via keyed elevator.

I'd added a few improvements: several cleverly concealed safes, a super-king-size round bed, and a sleek kitchen kept well stocked by my driver's wife, Sonia, who—although I'd never met her personally—checked off the laundry lists of my wandering existence.

After hurrying the few blocks from office to pad, I opened my closet, which was neatly lined with crisp sets of both my uniforms. Work was navy suit, blue shirt, and silk tie with hand-stitched loafers. Civvies were blue blazer, blue jeans, and blue-suede loafers. I was a regular Little Boy Blue, with a dash of Lord Fauntleroy. In a moment, I had my carry-on packed and was ready to go off into the wild blue yonder.

Val's Flex was idling at the curb. Val had a smoker's lined face, buzz-cut straw-colored hair, and deep-set eyes. He wore dark suits, a white shirt buttoned up, no tie. When he unloosed his gruff, middle-European accent, he sounded as scary as a killer for hire, but if he accidentally stepped on an ant, he'd probably cry.

He handed me the tickets that Sonia's sister, who worked in a Greenpoint travel agency, obtained, always getting me seat 1-A, my customary private windowed corner, offering first-on, first-off access.

First, I had a stop to make. "Brooklyn."

Val nodded. In our jargon, *Brooklyn* usually meant the federal courthouse or jail. But Val picked up on another Brooklyn from my tone: East Flatbush, where I'd lived my first seventeen years. A study in deterioration since. Gone from lower-middle class to bad to badass. At our destination, Val pulled over in front of a tenement. Its front-door lock was broken. I went up two flights to a rear apartment, where I knocked three times and whispered low. A lock turned, and the door opened a crack, enough for me to smell Bea's Chanel No. 5 and hear her girlish giggle.

"Benn, you can't come in just now. I look a mess."

"Baloney. You're always gorgeous." Through the crack, I palmed her ten Franklins.

"Oh, Benn, you can't . . ."

"Just paying more of what my father owed your husband." A lie. My old man owed no one; people owed him. Bea had been my mother's best friend. Loyal to the end. This was my way of payback, Bea's "monthly installments."

On the way out, I nearly ran into a young guy. The landing light was out, but I recognized him. The guy's hoodie was black, and so was he. He wore a Brooklyn Cyclones cap. His eyes, slightly buggy, no doubt had seen some things. Me, I'd seen plenty of guys like him, baby velociraptors that thrived in the hood. I'd known him for years, before he changed his name to Billy Shkilla, lead singer of The Shkillas.

He juked sideways. I juked to the left. Then we grinned and exchanged high fives.

"Soon I'm gonna come see you, Mr. B."

"Don't find a reason why you should."

"Yeah, you will. I'm gonna need a lawyer to negotiate my record. "

"Not an old white guy who's not into rap music."

"You will be once you hear ours."

"Maybe. Keep a close eye on Bea."

"I keep an eye on all my girls. Later."

I was worried about Billy. He was a good person whose world was filled with bad things. He'd survive. Maybe. I was even more worried about Bea. My ma's five-decade windowsill neighbor had no relatives left. No friends. Just me. That Bea hadn't greeted me all decked out and rouged was a bad sign. Her world was beginning to close. Happens to all of us. Sneaks up quick. Which is why I wanted *out* now . . .

* * *

Scant hours later I was on my way to Miami, drinking vodka while browsing my daily web reads: *Insight Crime*, the *Colombian News*, *El Tiempo Bogotá*, and the latest press releases from the US Attorneys' offices in New York and Florida. A common thread was speculation about a mysterious drug lord said to be the biggest of the big. Right now, he was simply known by his aka:

Sombra . . . Shadow.

He was the drug-lord flavor of the year but still in the larval stage, his face and name yet unknown. A legend to the Indians in his mountain lair, the messiah for whose return they'd prayed for the last five hundred years. The chosen one who would unite the Indians and mixed-blood peasants against the white Spanish, yadda, yadda, yadda.

In my experience, tales of the moral principles of drug legendaries are bullshit. On the opposite end of the spectrum, stories of their violence are underestimated. This *Sombra* character supposedly was greatly feared by both the establishment and his rival narco-traffickers. It was said he neither paid bribes nor extorted officials. Had no partners and made no alliances. He was a lone wolf. Sometimes it was rumored he was dead, or about to be arrested, or negotiating his surrender. More bullshit. The only thing all agreed upon was that *Sombra* was the richest man in Colombia. And the most dangerous.

For a moment or three, I self-indulged a fantasy—*Sombra* as my Biggy—then began reading a new blog called *Radio Free Bogotá*, penned by someone named L. Astorquiza. The subject matter grabbed me:

> General Oscar Uvalde, who portrays himself as the archenemy of drug traffickers, in reality is a corrupt pig who feeds at the trough of their money. He claims to be a warrior for justice, but he is both partner and protector of these bandits who are destroying our beloved country. Soon proof of his crimes shall emerge, and when it does, we will be rid of this traitor. Viva Colombia!

Shit! Someone else was looking to trade time for Uvalde. I'd hoped my guy Fercho had the exclusive dirt, but apparently, he was in a rat race to deliver the general. And if Fercho lost, I'd get no bonus . . .

Then again, Fercho would likely win, it being a long shot that L. Astorquiza—probably the alias of an angry young man in Bogotá's bohemian Candelaria neighborhood—would have the proof, or the cojones, to go public against a monster like General Uvalde.

I gave a little shiver, realizing that Uvalde wasn't going to like me much, either.

CHAPTER 3

I dozed off and when I awoke, I saw below the chain of lights that was Miami Beach. Ahead were the jumbled blocks of Brickell high-rises, and beyond them the vast grid of the city. My second home, ever since I'd received a sprawling penthouse in lieu of a legal fee.

A very nice score to start, and a gift that kept on giving.

Whenever New York got too gray, I'd escape to Miami. Binge on sun and sin, and in between visit a client in jail or break bread with a source of work or some such. Enough to write the trip off as a business expense and the condo as my branch office.

The next morning, I put on my work uniform and went off to slay dragons. In New York, I got around in Val's Flex, or my relatively under-the-radar Mini. In Miami, where extravagance is the norm, my ride was a Bentley GTC. I put my shades on and cruised in the sunshine. Palm trees flashed by. I raced over a causeway above a turquoise sea. Nearing an exit, I downshifted, and with a satisfying growl, the big car slowed as I neared the Miami Federal Detention Center, the pretrial jail.

Jails.

A highlight of my life are those moments I leave them. I estimate that over the years, my jail visits have added up to more than ten thousand hours. Round that out to four hundred days. With a reduction for good behavior, that equates to about a year inside. Could I do a year?

No way. I'd never make it past a month. Kill myself, or go mad. Yet to my guys, a year inside is a trifle. They're made of sterner stuff than I.

Inside the FDC, I showed my ID, filled out a visit form, and in short order was escorted through a metal detector and an air lock into the visit room. It was about the size of a high-school gym, only with a high console from which correctional cops kept an eye on things as a spectator stand. In the center of the room were tables occupied by lawyers and inmates. Other than the clients wearing jail tans and the lawyers' ice-cream-colored suits, they looked equally disreputable.

A cop addressed me: "Counselor, your guy's in the SHU."

Not good. Of all the acronyms in the business, the SHU—Special Housing Unit—is the one I hate most. A guard escorted me through another air lock and a steel door to a sally port, where we got onto an elevator that deposited us at another corridor with cinderblock walls, bare but for a picture of Miami FDC, taken from a distant low angle.

Framed by palms and blue sky, the jail looked like one of the thousands of high-rise condos studding Miami. But instead of an airy, bright apartment, the door I went through left me in a narrow, windowless space. Fluorescent light, plastic chairs, a Plexiglas divider, on the other side of which my client Fercho Ibarra sat, smiling.

"Hello, Benn," he said through a circle of small holes drilled in the Plexiglas. "I been thinking. It's true, what you said at the beginning."

"Everything I say is true. Which thing are you talking about?"

"'Walk with me.' I close my eyes, I see me walking with you."

"You okay, Fercho? They put you on meds, or what?"

"Nah. Just that you see all kinds of things when you're locked down in an eight-by-ten. Another thing I keep seeing? The prosecutor in New York saying yes to my giving them General Uvalde for the deal we want."

"Basically, you saw it exactly as it was."

Fercho grinned. "My man, Benn."

"*Tranquilo.* One day at a time."

18

I was low-keying the issue because nailing a major player like General Uvalde was at best a long shot. Still, if anyone could pull it off, it was Fercho. He'd survived a past that was like a walking history of the drug wars, starting out with the Revolutionary Armed Forces of Colombia—FARC—guerrillas when they were idealistic and prospering with them as they transitioned into trafficking. Along the way, he began dealing with Autodefensas Unidos de Colombia—AUC—paramilitaries, guys who'd originally signed up to fight the guerrillas but, like them, become traffickers.

"Wait and see," I said. "What about the other . . . ?"

He whispered: "Go see my Panamanian friend."

I nodded. Excellent. Helmer Quezada, who was helping Fercho cooperate, lived in Panama. Since Fercho was paying my expenses, no point in mentioning I was already planning to go there to see Foto about a case.

Fercho's preternatural smile—naïve and knowing at once—returned. "You'll be in the neighborhood, anyway."

I cocked my head, trying to read that smile. Did Fercho somehow know I was headed to Panama? Or by *neighborhood*, was he referring to the city among the three volcanoes, also in Central America, give or take a few hundred miles? Either way, hard to figure how Fercho knew, and pointless to ask because he'd tell me only if and when he wanted.

"Your new client?" Fercho said. "He's a toxic piece of shit."

My only new client was Mondragon's guy. I didn't even know his name yet but long ago had ceased being surprised at how news gets around in the drug business, and how facile Colombians are at working the jail grapevines. I waited for Fercho to elaborate, but he didn't, and I knew better than to push him.

I got up to leave.

"Benn?" he said.

I looked back.

"Be careful."

ALUNE

At last, after so many years, the endgame is in sight. From now on, I shall maintain close, constant surveillance. I expect all to proceed as planned, but even if something unexpected should occur, it will not prevent achieving my final goal, for I am ready, willing, and able to, as the Americans are fond of saying, roll with the punches.

Ah, the Americans . . .

So knowledgeable, and yet so malleable. They make me think of clay being shaped while spinning on a potter's wheel.

Well, not all. Benn Bluestone's an exception.

I'm really looking forward to seeing him.

CHAPTER 4

My flight angled into its landing approach above a pale tropical sea speckled with vessels awaiting clearance through the Panama Canal. The plane continued banking, and the view changed to an orange ball of sun sinking into the western sea. Then we leveled off, and I saw a shoreline that seemed a wall of fire: miles of glass towers reflecting the setting sun. These were new luxury condos, mostly owned by absentee foreigners escaping home-country taxes. Then the plane banked still again, and I saw downtown Panama City and felt a familiar rush.

A perk of my job was traveling the Caribbean Rim, and Panama City, or PC, sitting astride the neck of the Americas, was its geographic center. PC was twenty-first-century creature comfort amid a boomtown culture that was the legacy of the old Spanish Main. The city offered criminals, and their money, and women.

What else could a man like me want?

I was a premium guest at my boutique hotel. Upon arrival, I placed calls, setting up my agenda. Then I wound down with a well-oiled manipulation by a lithesome Thai masseuse. She offered to continue her company, but I declined in favor of a lonesome blue Valium. Nothing like a good sleep between crisp sheets.

I awoke to birds cawing outside my balcony doors. I breakfasted on a patio beneath palm fronds gently rattling in the heated breeze. Over a second cup of coffee, I read my usual narco news, but nothing much was happening. The yearly holiday truce had begun, and both cops and robbers were enjoying family time.

But not L. Astorquiza. The dude's *Radio Free Bogotá* blog was still rocking.

Today's rant was that legalization was the only solution to the drug problem. He bemoaned the fact that opposition to legalization was powerful: not only from corrupt politicians who were protecting traffickers but also from tens of thousands of people gainfully employed in the criminal justice and penal systems. Cops, guards, clerks, judges . . .

According to L. Astorquiza, the worst were the lawyers:

> These doctors, be they Colombians or Americans, are leeches who swim in the same cesspit as General Uvalde. They, too, must be brought to justice, and relieved of their ill-gotten gains. Viva Colombia!

Upsetting, because it was true. Eventually, L. Astorquiza's voice in the wilderness would be joined by others, and they would swell to a majority chorus for legalizing drugs, and it would be the beginning of the end of the drug trade, including the machinations of my profession. That's why I needed Biggy so badly: to grab all the cash I could carry, then head for a hill where I could live clean.

Taxis were queued in front of the hotel. I grabbed one that soon became trapped in a traffic jam. PC defied any and all attempts to ease vehicular traffic. Traffic lights were ignored. Pedestrians blocked crosswalks, tan and brown and black masses yearning to be elsewhere, streaming beneath election posters of candidates with white skin and European features.

As my taxi inched forward, I saw ahead a perfect example of the way I viewed Panama City: a wildly modernistic glass tower whose twisting façade had earned it the nickname *El Tornillo*, The Screw, which was fitting in more ways than one. Its exterior design was incompatible with its interior workings, making the elevators inoperable. The structure was literally screwed, but no one seemed to mind. The Screw fit in a town where appearance was as important as substance.

The taxi dropped me at an upscale mall, where I strolled the luxury shops. When I was certain no one was following me, I left the mall by a different exit than I'd entered, hailed another taxi, and crossed town to Casco Viejo, the original colonial section of PC. I loitered until the taxi was gone. Then started walking.

There are two parts of Casco. The gentrifying part was cool at night and hip by day. The old part was a jumble of tenements and ruins between mosquito-breeding puddles. That's where I walked. The store-fronts were shuttered for siesta. I squared a block, saw no one behind me, then ambled along a quiet street that meandered between faded pastel buildings and a seawall, beyond which the blue-gray Pacific shim-mered in the waves of heat.

I had no Bond-like pretensions. I was known in certain circles and didn't want to chance anyone observing me with the man I was meeting on Fercho's behalf.

Helmer Quezada was an ex-CTI—Colombian Judicial Police officer—who was still plugged in to a good-old-boy network of corrupt cops and politicos running a protection racket in which the victims were criminals. The traffickers who paid fortunes in protection money were unaware that their contracts had expiration dates: Helmer and his pals sold information on these traffickers deemed newly expendable to former traffickers who—like Fercho—were jailed and cooperating in the States.

My job was in the middle of the merry-go-round: passing info on new targets to the feds. Of course, the law required cooperation to be from the cooperator's own knowledge. Purchased cooperation was not only unrewarded; it was illegal. Did I know the cooperation was purchased? Stack your Bibles, and I'll swear I know nothing from nothing. I wasn't the only prevaricator: if and when it suited them, federal prosecutors and agents turned a blind eye to sources of important information.

Bottom line: everyone lied.

The windows of the old houses were black rectangles in the pale walls, but from the darkness within, I sensed eyes on the unlikely sight of a mad gringo out in the noonday sun. Past the seawall, through the heat haze, was the distant outline of a gray ship I knew was an American Coast Guard cutter on Canal Zone patrol.

I envisioned its dark radar rooms, where green lines moved across black screens: the zigzag routes of go-fast boats ferrying cocaine from mangrove swamps on the Colombian Pacific coast to Central American coves. There, the loads would be transferred onto trucks for the voyage north to Mexico and divided into shipments bound for the States.

I sensed someone behind me, turned, and saw the cropped gray hair and seamed face of Helmer Quezada, an unlit cigarette between his blunt fingers.

"A light, please, *señor*?"

I'd glommed a hotel matchbook. I struck a match. As he cupped his hands around it, he murmured, "Parasitic torpedoes."

I didn't reply. Parasitic torpedoes were cylindrical containers filled with cocaine, ballasted to stay submerged just below the surface while being towed by a fishing boat. If the fishermen ran into law enforcement, they cut the torpedoes loose; equipped with automatic buoys and location transmitters, they could be easily reacquired when the cops were gone.

"Good day," Helmer said, walking on.

It wasn't until I was chilling in a cab that I unfolded the wadded paper he had palmed me. It was a map of Colombia's *Departmento de Chocó*

Pacific shoreline showing the coordinates of an inlet where the torpedoes were assembled.

When I got to my hotel, I photographed the note and warehoused the photo in my cloud. Then I tore up the original and flushed it away. Then I took a long shower, followed by a short nap. I wanted to be ready for the night.

I was going to Foto's place.

CHAPTER 5

People who knew Foto by reputation thought him a fashion photographer and notorious pussy hound. People who knew Foto casually thought him a pimp for narco-traffickers. People who knew Foto well thought him an informer. The real Foto was all of the above, as well as a world-class hustler.

His penthouse resembled a club: bass-thumping music, mirrored bar, polished dance floor, potted palms between private couches, great-looking young women, and extremely rich older guys.

I wasn't interested in the couch people. The buzz between them was champagne, Cialis, and coke.

The buzz that interested me was cold cash.

I saw Foto talking with a short, fair-haired man whose arm candy was a tall blonde with a perfect, round ass. Foto cut his eyes to me and winked, then went on listening to whatever the guy was saying.

I became interested in the blonde. *Very* interested.

There were plenty of knockout females about, but she was special. No implants or veneers or lifts. Maybe she hadn't been born blonde, but neither had Ms. Monroe. Actually, she reminded me a little of Marilyn, projecting the kind of vulnerability that is catnip for men. Her body left little to the imagination in a clingy raw-silk dress above long legs, smooth as heavy cream.

Now, I like all types of female flesh—white or dark meat, necks, thighs, breasts—but come down to it, I'm a leg man. Hers were off the chart. When I looked up from them, she was looking at me with hazel eyes easy to read.

Hello, they said.

Before I could reply, the fair-haired man shook hands with Foto and cupped the blonde's elbow. As they turned, I saw the man's face: Botox-smooth, pale eyes, thin lips. For a moment, I thought he glanced at me. As they walked away, Foto love-tapped my arm.

"Who is she?" I asked, staring after her.

Foto motioned me to follow, and we went out to the terrace. Quiet there. The city lights bled into a starry sky; the black sea was salted with shipping lights. We were alone.

"*She,*" Foto said, "is with a man you don't want to annoy. Pussy aside? Jilly can't meet with you just yet."

"Jilly?"

"Your new case, *amigo.* But not to worry. Thanks to my efforts, consider yourself already hired. Your fee is one million. To start."

"One million," I repeated. "To start."

"The case is an extradition to New York. They'll pay you there. In regard to my end, will that be a problem?"

I kept cash in Miami, where Foto often visited. After I got the mil in New York, I'd give Foto his 20 percent referral from that stash. "No problem."

"Most excellent," Foto said.

"*¿Qué?*" a woman asked.

She had appeared silently, a petite brunette. Her nose was strong; her mouth wide. She wore a white dress that hugged her body. All in all, a very attractive woman.

"Ah, Laura," Foto said. "I was just saying life is excellent to my dear friend, the eminent doctor Bennjamin T. Bluestone . . ." Foto's brow knit. "I always meant to ask, Benn. What does the bloody fucking *T* stand for, anyway?"

"The *T* doesn't stand for anything at all," I said.

Laura cocked her head as if conversing with herself, then spoke in Colombian-accented Spanish. "Is that true, Mr. Bluestone?"

"Benn. The naked truth."

Foto giggled, but Laura just nodded. "I get it," she said, switching to unaccented English. "*T*, like the *S* in Harry S. Truman."

I raised a brow. I figured Laura was about thirty. Remarkable that a Latina of her generation knew such arcane trivia as Truman's middle initial, let alone who Truman was.

She grinned. "I think maybe you have a middle name."

I smiled. "That's the trouble with Harry."

Foto asked, "Who's Harry S. Truman?"

"Who the buck stops with," Laura said.

"I'm from Missouri, too," I said.

"No," Laura said, "you're not."

"Correct," I said, "I'm not."

Foto's head swiveled between us as if watching a tennis match. I was thinking it had just begun, and the score was love-love.

"Not eminent, either," she said.

"But definitely prominent," I said.

"So long as you're continent," she said.

I laughed. I couldn't recall a woman so perfectly tuned to my weird wavelength. Foto didn't get any of it, but it was obvious that Laura and I had connected. "Praise be to God," he said. "A match made in heaven by his faithful servant, Foto. Benn? Laura? Name your first son for me. I'll leave you now."

"Stay, Foto," Laura said. "I'm the one who must be leaving. Work tomorrow and all. But I have a wonderful idea. Invite the doctor to your New Year's party."

"He's invited," Foto said.

"I accept." I was thinking Laura was the type who made love with her eyes wide open: look at me looking at you; intellectual mind-fucking, that kind of thing. Tomorrow I needed to be in the city among the three volcanoes, but afterward, I could hop on a flight back to Panama City. As my client in Miami had observed, it was in the neighborhood, after all.

"Good night," Laura said. She stood on her toes and pecked Foto on the cheek. Then gave me a smile and a business card while coming close enough for me to inhale her herbal scent, sort of a cross between orange blossom and gardenia.

We watched her cross the room, her small butt swaying sexily.

"I'm thinking," Foto said, "it must be very nice."

"What must be?" I said.

"Fucking a woman it's actually interesting to talk to. Of course, the things we talk about are best left unsaid. Let's have a drink."

At the bar, Foto drank Scotch. I kept to Bison Grass vodka and got a mild buzz on. People drifted by. A lot of women. I paid them no mind. Any other night, Laura qualified as one of my ten most wanted, but tonight I was riding the crest of a blonde tsunami. Not sure how to put it, but the blonde was one of those rare girl-women that gets into your head and, like heroin, forever remains a yearning.

I drank some more. Picked up on people. A Mexican-telenovela leading man. An ex-DEA gone PI who hustled cases for an unsavory Miami lawyer. A man with an altered face whom I took five seconds to recognize as a notorious informant. A graft-tainted Colombian politician. A Venezuelan opposition journalist. A tableful of loud guys I knew were pilots, all of them wearing platinum Rolexes. Not surprising. In this part of the world, pilots made out like bandits.

Actually, they *were* bandits.

Foto went off to hit on a woman. I finished my drink and ordered another. I was feeling pretty good. Good old Foto had just added eight hundred large to my retirement fund. One new case in the bag, and two to go . . .

Funny how sometimes you drink and don't feel it, then there's a little *click*, and things connect. Like—*click!*—and all at once, I was totally tuned in to the music, a rapper telling a chickadee to forget about her boyfriend and be with him.

Exactly the sentiment I wanted to convey to the blonde: that it should be *me* plumbing her depths. I finished my drink and got a refill. The rap music pounded louder about the girl being a healthy type. I pictured the blonde in silk and lace . . .

Man, I was feeling it. Shaken *and* stirred.

Somehow, I'd become a corner of a square of people humping to the beat: me, two women who either were twins or used the same plastic surgeon, and a guy my age with inky hair, white suit, and gold chains who danced like an escapee from *Saturday Night Fever*. One of the women put her hip against mine.

The rapper told his girl what he planned to do to her. The beauty next to me seemed to like the idea. The gold-chained man opened a vial and tapped powder atop his knuckles. The women tooted.

The rapper said something about enjoying a gushy twosome.

A white-topped knuckle appeared beneath my nose.

Blow. Good, glittery, prime, fish-scale blow . . .

The rapper wanted to freak. I did, too—

But I froze, forcing myself to remember the bad days that followed the good nights, back when I used to disappear up my own nose . . . And then . . .

I turned and ran away as fast as I could.

Forget the elevator, I took the steps.

On a landing, a girl was giving a man head. I brushed past them. At the street door, a security guard turned, alarm on his face, reaching for a holstered weapon. I couldn't have cared less.

I burst through the door—

Outside was heavy, wet heat, but I was trembling. I'd been inches away from starting back down the too-familiar road that always ended

30

at the same washed-out bridge. I leaned against a palm and vomited green: Bison Grass and bile.

I returned to my hotel, still spooked.

I needed to calm down. Alcohol was a relatively controllable problem, so I had a nightcap from the minibar. Sweet, dark Panama rum. I had another and got mellower. A third, and it was sleepy time. Tomorrow was another travel day. When I put my wallet on the dresser, I noticed a business card sticking out of it. Laura's card. It said:

RADIO FREE BOGOTÁ
LAURA ASTORQUIZA

I laughed long and loud. My wise friend Foto had put it exactly right: It must be nice, sleeping with a woman who was interesting to talk to.

CHAPTER 6

The next day I flew to Guatemala City. My taxi's AC was broken, and the city flooded in through its opened windows. Music, blaring horns, hot air blue with exhaust. But half an hour later, Guaty was gone behind, and we drove between low mountains. Cool here. Another hour later, we came around a bend, and ahead lay a town whose grid was lined with low buildings, a thousand little pastel sticks in rows below three cone-shaped peaks.

This was the city among the three volcanoes: Antigua, the colonial capital of Guatemala until it had been destroyed by the earthquake and eruptions of 1740.

A plume of smoke, or perhaps a small cloud, hung over one of the volcanoes: *Volcán de Fuego*, the Volcano of Fire. The volcano loomed taller as we neared Antigua. As it did, I had a growing apprehension that suddenly appeared like an uncharted asteroid. I visualized an explosive eruption. Felt the earth beneath my feet tremble. Saw and felt super-heated gas rushing downhill like a tsunami—

Amid chaos, I heard a voice, commanding as a prophet:

Save yourself, fool. Leave the business. Get out. Now.

I thought weakly: *I will, I will . . . soon . . .*

On my hotel's shadowed patio, an ice-skimmed vodka calmed me. Then I went for a stroll. I'd been to Antigua before. A once-upon-a-time capital city of avenues lined with magnificent facades. Cathedrals and monasteries and convents. On a warm evening in the eighteenth century, suddenly collapsing to rubble behind the still-standing facades. The quake had educated the locals—build low—and present-day Antigua consisted of low, modest buildings within walled compounds whose gardens were fragrant with tropical plants.

Nowadays, Antigua was a small town centered around a square block of park, the *placita*, where I sat on a bench across from the cathedral. I set my device atop a knee and pretended absorption in it. I wore wraparound shades that hid my sideways glance so I could check the scene unobserved.

I saw Lonely Planet types, Indians peddling junk to tourists, hippies of the species found in Ibiza or Marrakesh, and a very big middle-aged guy who wore a spotless white suit. When I looked his way, he averted his eyes.

I picked up on another guy hiding behind a newspaper. Extremely small fellow, a couple of centimeters above midget-size, wearing a pale guayabera. Something else strange about him, too . . . the way he held the paper? No, his fingers caught my eye. They made his hands resemble paws, having been chopped off at the uppermost joint. The Colombians referred to these as permanent manicures, and the kind of guys that receive them never work alone.

A little distance away, another guy was wearing a similar guayabera. Then I spotted another; altogether a foursome whose opening game plan was working hard at not looking at me. No doubt they were here on behalf of my putative client—who only wanted to talk surrendering, meaning he was far from committed—to make sure I wasn't a decoy for law enforcement.

I stretched and unkinked my neck, lingering a moment on each of their ugly mugs. *Come on, caballeros, check me out to your black hearts' content.*

It was hot. My watchband slid on my damp wrist. An hour and five minutes had passed. I run my watch five minutes fast. It reminds me to be on time. The people I meet rarely are themselves. Except for hit men like *Los Guayaberas*, early risers, hoping to catch a worm.

I recrossed my legs. I might be here all day. Maybe all day tomorrow or until some moron paid attention to business. A too-big chunk of my life was spent waiting for my Godots. The trick to dealing with them was to think of something else. Or someone.

I thought about the blonde. Where her long legs joined her butt entwined with me and my junk. Wet, slick saltiness and—

Heels clacked. I looked up as a young woman on platforms teetered by. Pretty face, improbably large bust, impossibly enormous butt. She paused at the edge of the park, gave me a come-hither look—or so I thought—then crossed the street, went up the cathedral steps, and entered.

Silent as a snake, a man sat on my bench and read a newspaper that blocked his face. All I could see of him were cuffed trousers and square-toed shoes, but I knew he was the same big man I'd spotted a few minutes ago. Felipe Mondragon, Esq. He spoke from behind the newspaper, and from the sound of his voice alone—too smooth, too ingratiating—I didn't like him at all.

"Good morning, Doctor," he said. "The client is running late. To be expected. He's cautious. Doesn't even trust me. But he will appear, of that I'm sure."

I grunted affirmatively. We waited. The young woman appeared in the cathedral doorway. She looked at me, then withdrew.

I stood. "The client is here."

We entered the cathedral.

I like churches. No better places to think. This one was dim and cool and smelled of incense. Its stone floors were worn smooth. Dust motes danced in sunlight shafting through a high window. No one was in sight. I thought maybe the young woman was kneeling in prayer, so I walked along the pews, but she wasn't there—

There was a faint rumbling, and I looked through the church door: in the brilliant sunlight, the volcano, framed against the sky, was smoldering heavily.

Mondragon whispered: "Doctor, this client is a very serious man. More than you can imagine. Therefore, his fee is substantial. One million dollars."

Right. I kept my hungry mouth shut.

"I don't want a referral," he said.

My jaw nearly dropped. One mil? With no kickback? No way. Guys like Mondragon don't give ice in the winter. This was too good to be true. There had to be a kicker, but forewarned is forearmed, so I'd take the money and, if necessary, run later.

"I accept," I said.

Mondragon raised a wolfish brow. "However, should things go well, there will be a very large bonus. *Very.* As to that, I would expect, say, forty percent?"

Aha. The name of the game was pay-as-we-go, and Mondragon would contend the balance was a bonus. A battle to be fought another day.

"Twenty," I countered.

"Thirty."

"Done."

Of course, it wasn't done. Right now, Mondragon controlled the source of money. Until I managed to. First order of business was getting money on the table. Second was waiting for the drug dealer to blink, then swipe it off the table. After which I'd do the dictating as to what constituted a fair referral.

The young woman peered from behind the altar. She withdrew as we stood. As we went down the nave, I felt like a sailor inexorably being drawn to disaster on the rocks. It was a recurring feeling, and I mumbled, "Siren ahead."

Mondragon paled. "Siren?"

"I should hope not."

We continued to the altar. Behind it a rectangle of daylight shafted through an opened door. Outside was a courtyard between the rear of the cathedral and a facade on the next street. It was littered with overgrown rocks and stones. The centuries-old remains of the quake-destroyed cathedral. Amid the rubble, the young woman was locked in an embrace with a stocky, balding older man.

"Dr. Bluestone," Mondragon said. "Don Rigoberto Ordoñez."

Don? Scumbag was more like it. I knew about Rigo Ordoñez all too well: boss of a cartel that had metastasized out of Medellín and was rapidly climbing up the narco ladder, an organization composed of former paramilitaries, *autodefensa* units gone rogue and ruthless. *Los Hachos*, they were called—the Hatchets—for reasons whose details you'd rather be spared.

There was a reason why I'd followed Rigo's career.

His was an up-and-coming cartel in the group collectively known as the North Valley Cartel, the same thugs who'd murdered the only client I'd ever considered a friend: Nacho Barrera, my first and only Biggy. After killing Nacho, they'd killed his family. Colombians in the drug business tend to have large families. Difficult being a force without your blood protecting you. Nearly two hundred of Nacho's family were hunted down. Cousins fifth-removed, three-generations-old family trees, women, a special little girl.

A man only known as Rigo had been among the suspected killers. Rigo, for Rigoberto, a lot of those around.

"Papi." The girl clung to this Rigo. She could have been his granddaughter, but nothing was paternal in the way he held her, or the sweet, dirty things he was whispering in her ear. He needed for her to know

that their separation would be brief. That it was the first step toward the new life they would share. Did she understand?

"*Sí, mi amor. Yo entiendo.*"

"*Te amo, mi Estefania.*"

I was thinking, if this guy was the same Rigo who'd offed Nacho, then I'm out. But *was* he the same Rigo? If not, I'd be walking away from a million-dollar score. The smart move was to wait and see. I could always—

From the church came sounds and movement. Then half a dozen guys—gringos, for sure—wearing jeans and sneakers and carrying handguns appeared.

"Nobody move," one said.

Fuck me. I'd landed right in the middle of a freaking DEA takedown. I wasn't doing anything illegal, but in the future, I'd be wearing a scarlet letter:

D for dirty.

That was, *if* I had a future, because for sure, Rigo would think I'd set him up. Didn't matter that he intended for me to negotiate his surrender; that was in the future. This was now, and the lawyer who'd betrayed Rigo could never show his face in Colombia again.

Maybe not anywhere.

I was finished.

Fried.

CHAPTER 7

The agents surrounded us. One was a burly guy with Indian features. The badge around his neck was not DEA gold and blue, but the silver star of a Guatemalan *federal*.

A DEA agent winked at me, and in Nuyorican Spanish said, "How you doing, Counselor?"

How was I doing? Praying this was a bad dream was how. And processing the fact that if the agent knew I was a lawyer, then the DEA had known I was going to be here, and God only knew what else they might know about me, fee-category-wise. *Fuck*. I'd just taken a giant step toward a criminal tax investigation.

As Rigo was cuffed, Stefania wailed. The Puerto Rican agent turned to Mondragon. "Tell her to chill, Felipe."

Felipe? Had Mondragon set up the takedown? That'd normally be kept secret, yet the agent was open about it.

Mondragon put a reassuring hand on the young woman's shoulder—

"Take your fucking hand off her," Rigo said.

Mondragon's hand jumped as if burned.

"Make nice to your lawyer, Rigo," the agent said.

"The *señor* is stressed is all," Mondragon said.

"Welcome to the club," the Guatemalan agent muttered nervously. The DEA agents had holstered their weapons, but his remained out. That bothered me. We were on his turf, and he knew it best.

Mondragon seemed nervous, too. "Sorry to put you to work during your Christmas, Gus."

Gus was the Puerto Rican. He grinned. "*No problema*. Rigo's my Christmas present."

In my mind, a lightbulb came on. Rigo wasn't being captured; he was surrendering by prearrangement. But arranged by *whom*?

"Our work is done," Mondragon said to me. "Let's go."

I said, "Agent, a moment with my client?"

Gus handed me a business card that said *Gustavo Romero, Special Agent, Drug Enforcement Administration*, and below that, the Eleventh Avenue address of the Manhattan DEA office.

"Not now, Counselor," he said. "Arraignment's in the Southern District of New York, bright and early January second. Have a nice New Year—"

The air shuddered, and I heard a pop.

A pink mist erupted from the Guatemalan cop's head.

Pop! Pop!

Gus shouted, *"Down!"*

Pop! Pop! Pop!

I hit the flagstones and rolled toward the cathedral, confused but aware of Gus and the other agents kneeling, guns out, firing—

Bam! Bam! Bam!

The Guatemalan cop lay next to me, the top of his head gone. I frantically crawled away from him, only to find myself entangled with Rigo doing the same thing—

Pop!

Bam! Bam!

Rigo and I lay face-to-face, blinking at each other distastefully, like the post-sex glances between a drunken slob and a disgusted whore.

"Clear?" Gus said.

"Clear."

"Clear."

"The package okay?"

"Alive and kicking," an agent said, hauling Rigo to his feet.

No one helped me. Just as well, I was busy not puking.

Gus said, "Get the fuck out of here, Counselor."

I didn't have to be told twice. Up and out I went.

Outside the cathedral, a crowd had gathered. Weak kneed, I sat on the same park-side bench. The same man as before sat next to me; his face was drained of color.

"A terrible thing," Mondragon said. "Terrible."

"Fuck you, terrible. You *knew*."

"Absurd. If I had known, I would never have . . . a bullet struck just inches from me. I was nervous, yes, because certain . . . people don't want our client to cooperate."

"Why didn't you tell me you'd set up the surrender?"

"Gus said I shouldn't tell anyone. Not even you. It's all right. Apart from the *federale*, who probably was corrupt, and the assassins, no one was harmed. But not to worry. Your fee is, as they say, in the pipeline. I will see you in New York."

A car pulled to the curb. Mondragon got in, and it pulled away, leaving me with a feeling that something had . . . *changed*.

I no longer felt in control. Too much I didn't understand. Why invite me to Mondragon's party? I didn't know. Possible Mondragon had set up Rigo for a hit? Maybe. Options? Get paid, and decide later.

I considered that and laughed aloud.

I was thinking of money again.

Nothing had changed.

Except that the volcano now belched ominously dark smoke. I heard a rumble like a subway train under a Manhattan street. A roll of distant thunder, and the ground trembled.

Ten minutes later, I split town. I figured to puddle-jump over to PC and usher in the New Year with Laura Astorquiza at Foto's place. But because of the eruption, people were ditching Antigua, and the airport lines were long. I found myself staring at a TV screen. A news program. I blinked.

The footage was familiar:

The immediate aftermath of the cathedral shootout. The camera lingered over a body. A man wearing a blood-soaked white guayabera. I'd been right: the guayabera guys were hit men—*sicarios* in Colombian-speak—and no doubting they were Colombian—

I got a text from the Colombian lawyer Paz:

COME NOW.

I wrote back: Sí.

CHAPTER 8

It was raining when I emerged from the airport terminal and ducked beneath the umbrella held by Diego Castrillon, head of my Bogotá Department of Transportation, established when a satisfied customer gifted me a Caddy Escalade. Deal was, I let Castri use the Escalade as a hired car when I was away, so long as he and it were mine when I was in town. Castri was a wise old face who'd been around lots of places and people. The fact that he'd survived was a testament to his true grit as an hombre who knew how to keep his mouth shut.

We climbed into the Escalade, and its double locks snapped shut. The truck's previous owner believed in double locks, triple-layered shatterproof glass, and four-ply-thick Kevlar bodywork. Like a tank, we sallied forth from the airport.

"You appear well," Castri said.

"I am," I said. "You?"

"Good, thank you."

That was the extent of our conversation. Castri got that I wasn't in the mood to talk and just did his job, dropping me at the hotel I favored: Casa Medina, a small, elegant place that catered to wealthy businessmen and bigwig politicians. I was the only American lawyer who stayed there. My competitors favored Bogotá's flashy new hotels, the better to see and be seen, but I liked staying under the radar, conducting business in the hotel's enclosed patio, where gas flames burned amid lush flower beds.

I had my bag sent up to my usual suite and went to the patio. The headwaiter greeted me warmly, and led me to a corner table where I could see but not necessarily be seen. I ordered a light dinner—not wanting to overwork my digestive tract while getting accustomed to Bogotá's nine-thousand-foot elevation—adding a couple of aspirins for dessert.

A few minutes later, Paz appeared: small, dapper in a suit, starched white shirt, wide tie, and the square-toed shoes Colombian lawyers preferred. He was among the better Colombian lawyers, or at least not as bad as most.

Paz sat and handed me an envelope containing an Eastern District of New York—Brooklyn—indictment: bare-bones, three pages of legal boilerplate accusing a person of various narcotics crimes.

Paz leaned close. "You understand?"

I shrugged. "An indictment. So?"

"The defendant's name," he hissed.

"FNU LNU," I said. First name unknown, last name unknown. Goddamned acronyms. "It might be a help if you told me the person's name."

"I don't know it. No one does. He's called *Sombra*."

I just nodded, but my neurons were blinking like the Rock Center Christmas tree the Avianca flight attendant had dragged me to.

Sombra . . . aka Biggy.

"The gentleman is a pragmatist," said Paz. "He believes someone will cooperate against him soon. Once his true identity is known, it is only a question of time until he is captured. He wants to negotiate from a position of strength while he still can. He can give up all the cartel chiefs and guerrilla leaders and corrupt officials in Colombia. *All*. And for the lawyer who can negotiate well for him? There is a *large* fee."

"How large is large?"

"Millions. *Many*."

Did I have any particular reason to distrust Paz? No. Did I distrust him? Of course. He was no different from Mondragon. *Many* was an open-ended number controlled by the man in the middle. Him.

"*How* many?" I asked.

"I want to clarify our arrangement. This case is so big, it will preclude future work. Putting it another way . . . after *Sombra* talks? No criminals will be left."

Did Paz think he could con a con man? Oh sure, after a big bust, there'd be a shortage of clients for a month or two. But soon enough the hidey-holes would open, and the criminal underworld would reboot, a new class graduating to its top. No more criminals? Paz was inventing leverage to bargain.

"It's really true," he said. "You have no idea."

"No criminals? What would we lawyers do?"

"Precisely. Me, I will retire. Thirty percent."

Twenty points was standard, but *Sombra* was a Biggy. We went back and forth before settling on 25 percent, then shook on it.

Then I said, "Now tell me . . . how many is *many*?"

His voice dropped an octave. "Twenty million."

I drew a breath. "When do I meet the client?"

"Tomorrow," he said. "In Cúcuta."

Things were happening fast. Maybe too fast. The mere thought of $20 million was a drink spiked with knockout drops. Left you lustful but dull. I forced myself to examine the downsides:

No one ever paid that kind of money unless something far beyond the call of duty was expected in return. Cúcuta was a bad sign. The town was a shithole near the Venezuelan border, rife with cops and robbers and, most dangerous of all, cops who were robbers. Was I walking into a potential disaster? Maybe.

But the price was right.

I watched Paz leave, an unobtrusive man to whom no one on the patio paid the least attention. But he had just turned my life upside down.

I'd have to tread carefully.

If *Sombra* cooperated, big people on both sides of the law would be going down, and as his lawyer, I'd find it impossible to show my face in many places . . .

But after Paz's cut, I'd have fifteen mil in pocket and no longer any need to go to those places. Fifteen mil meant I had a new normal. Freedom, travel . . .

I was getting ahead of myself.

Thus far, the only thing on the table was a possibility. A nibble. Could be there were other Colombian lawyers out there trying to match *Sombra* with other Mr. Rights. Could be Paz himself was shopping the case, looking to cut a better deal for himself.

CHAPTER 9

Paz texted in the morning: a ticket in my name would be waiting at the airport counter servicing the flight to Cúcuta. The counter person handed me an envelope. There was no ticket inside. Just a note:

Look to your left.

I did. At another counter, people were checking in. Paz was among them. When I approached, he accidentally-on-purpose bumped into me, in the process palming me a boarding pass. Not for the flight to Cúcuta.

To Cali.

We sat in different rows. I kept my face turned to the window. The flight path from Bogotá to Cali crosses the Cordillera Central, the middle range of the three Andean spines that trisect Colombia. The view was otherworldly, the between-peaks flight path heart-stopping.

I was amped.

Emerging from the Cali airport terminal, by smell alone I'd have known I was in the Cauca River valley. Here, big-pharma smokestacks belched fumes that blanketed the valley floor between the facing peaks of the Cordillera Central and Cordillera Occidental. It was warm. Cali's a mile lower than Bogotá, and only a few hundred miles above the equator. I followed Paz to the cab line, and we each got into one of the ubiquitous tiny *amarillo* taxis that buzz like flies in every corner of Colombia.

Before leaving the airport, the cabs turned into a deserted cargo area. Paz hustled from his cab into mine and told the driver to go, fast.

Outside the airport, the road was narrow, and we whizzed close by people and horse carts on the shoulder. We sped through tall cane and crossed a span over a muddy stream where a boy watered a cow. Ahead, a white city sprawled across the foothills of the Cordillera Occidental.

The taxi dropped us at the Ritz, but after it left, we crossed the street to the Intercontinental. Paz had reserved a room there. He didn't speak in the elevator or the corridor. When we were in the room, he double-locked the door, then led me onto the balcony.

Even there, he whispered. "I'm waiting for a call. Maybe soon. You know how these people operate."

I sure did. On Criminal Standard Time.

Paz didn't reply. He was looking to the distance where the Cauca River was a silver thread weaving through the city.

Cali. I had memories here. In the ultraviolent period between the death of the Cali Cartel and the birth of the North Valley Cartel, the river became a favored human-waste disposal. Far as I knew, bodies no longer bobbed in the current. Southwest Colombia wasn't as wild as it used to be. Outwardly. These days the DTOs settled their quarrels in private. But the civilians still clung to their old ways. In the distance, a line of ant-size people crawled up a hill atop which stood a huge Christ on a cross.

Paz crossed himself. It occurred to me how little I knew about him beyond our common goal. What was his life like? Did he still fuck his wife? Did he like his kids? Have grandkids? A girlfriend? Was he thinking about how his referral fee might change their collective futures? Or did he intend to take the money, then live footloose and fancy-free?

His phone rang. He said, *"Sí,"* listened, then hung up, face flushed. He said, "Time to go."

Cars for hire were lined up outside the hotel, but we walked by them. We continued walking for a few blocks. Paz kept glancing across the street. I followed his gaze to a man wearing jeans and a tee. The man reached a corner and turned right.

So did we.

Soon we were out of the hotel district and in a neighborhood of littered streets and shuttered storefronts. It was growing dark. The streets were desolate. In many sections of Cali, one does not stroll at night. This was such a section.

The man we were following turned a corner.

When we turned it, he was gone from view.

The door of a parked car opened.

"Get in," the driver said.

We got in the car, and it pulled away. It was a midsize that needed a wash. Paz and I sat in the back. Up front were the driver and the shotgun. Normal-looking types, but if you were in the business, you weren't normal. Driver kept flicking his eyes to the rearview mirror to see if we were being followed. Shotgun kept twisting around, looking all over. I snuck a glance:

Warehouses faced rutted streets.

No people, no other cars.

We squared a block.

Driver suddenly accelerated into an alley. Shotgun opened a door for us to get out. We did. The car headed down the alley and was gone. The alley was dark and quiet and smelled foul.

What next?

I thought maybe another car. Wrong. Light suddenly flooded the alley as a door opened, and a man leaned out and motioned for us to enter.

We did.

The door closed behind us. For a moment, it was pitch dark, then flashlights beamed in our faces. From behind the lights, the man told us to raise our arms.

We did.

Hands patted us down. An electronic wand passed over us. Our phones were taken. "An understandable precaution," Paz said nervously. The flashlights went out, and the door opened and we were told to go.

We did.

A van waited in the alley now, its rear doors open. We climbed in the rear, and the van started off. A curtain obscured the driver. Through my window, I watched the neighborhood recede, and then we were back in downtown Cali. I thought we were headed for the hillside neighborhoods, where gated homes were few and far between, but instead, we turned onto a highway.

Soon Cali fell behind us. On both sides of the road, mountains outlined a moonlit sky. I knew we were going through the valley but not in what direction. We passed a sign with an arrow pointing to an exit—Yumbo—but all I saw in that direction were fields of tall green cane . . . another sight from my past.

There had been a time when my ex-wife and I called ourselves Children of the Cane because of a man I sometimes met in the middle of a Yumbo sugarcane field in a ramshackle bar with the unlikely name of The Sahara Club. My ex and I had had private names for everything, back when we were in love and she thought well of me—

Forget the man. Forget her thoughts. Forget her.

The van hummed along.

It was growing dark but still very warm. Paz had taken his suit coat off. His shirt was damp. I pulled up a mental map of Colombia. After thirty minutes we didn't reach the airport, so I figured we were heading south, away from Cali down the Cauca Valley, which went all the way to Nariño.

Made sense. Nariño was guerrilla territory, and *Sombra* reputedly bought *coca* from guerrilla factions engaged in perpetual strife with the government. Was *Sombra* bringing us into a war zone? Then again, the meet might not be in Nariño, because the river valley intersected dozens of smaller valleys, and these were veined by hundreds of no-name canyons. All secluded, remote, *Sombra*-type lairs.

So, maybe we were headed to Popoyán, the City of Cathedrals.

Perhaps, like Rigo, *Sombra* intended to meet me at a church—

Paz leaned closer and quietly said, "Jamundí."

Something caught in my throat . . . another memory. This one cut deep.

What goes around comes around.

I had returned to Jamundí.

CHAPTER 10

Flashback: twenty years ago.

Mady is my new bride. We're not only joined at the hip; she is also my accomplished paralegal. We are deeply in love and best friends and workmates. Our future is bright and limitless. My professional star is rising. I'm just a couple of years out of law school, not yet thirty, but already I've become a hell of a trial lawyer. My ascent begins when I work some courtroom magic, get lucky at the same time, and win a no-win case. For a Colombian. He sends his friends to me. His friends send friends.

One day I receive a call from a man with a hoarse voice. He is extremely polite. Reserved. Would I consider an expenses-paid trip to Cali to discuss a case?

"Yes," I say. "With my paralegal."

"Of course."

But I have reservations about bringing Mady. Maybe even concerns about myself. Colombia doesn't have good press. This is the wild nineties, and bad shit happens there. Enough for the State Department to issue travel warnings. But Mady wants to go. Growing up in a Spanish household, she heard good things about Colombia. She admires the country's writers and poets. But I'm not into fiction or fantasy. I'm uneasy—

Until a Mr. Green appears with first-class expense money for two *and* a $25,000 retainer for my time. Two hundred fifty unissued Franklins.

Outside the Cali airport terminal, a small convoy awaits us. Dark-windowed Chevy Luminas. Ours is the middle van. Our driver and his assistant do not speak during the trip, which is south through the Cauca Valley.

To Jamundí.

We leave the highway for secondary roads that grow smaller until we are on a narrow path through dense jungle. Dappled sunlight flickers through the dark windows; in the light, Mady is changeable: beautiful and more beautiful.

The vans emerge from the trees to a vast green in the center of which is a large, modern glass-and-steel building. Mady asks the driver what it is.

"The training center for *America de Cali.*"

I'm impressed. This is a world-class soccer team the Cali big boys are rumored to own. Was the man with the hoarse voice one of them?

"Look," says Mady.

Behind the building are three or four perfectly groomed soccer fields, on each of which uniformed teams are playing. When we get out of our Lumina, we can hear their cries across the turf. The sky is deep blue, the day warm and breezy, the colors so bright . . .

I remember as if it were yesterday.

We walk along the sidelines.

I see a player who seems familiar. When he grins and waves at me, I recognize him as Mr. Green, who fetched my fee for several Colombian clients. *Small world,* I think.

Even smaller than I imagined.

In short order, I see half a dozen other Colombians I've met: a bail jumper, another fugitive, the brother of a client, the husband of another client, an unindicted coconspirator, still another Mr. Green. Some are spectators, some are players, one a referee.

Why are they all here? Am I dreaming?

Until that moment, I had dismissed references to Colombian cartels as law-enforcement hyperbole. But now it dawns on me. If all these seemingly unconnected people know one another, it can only mean one thing:

Yes, Benn, there is a cartel.

And so there was. Their CFO turns out to be the man with the hoarse voice. Nacho Barrera. He is bespectacled, modest.

"The problem is my brother, Max," Nacho says.

Max, short for Maximilian, had been recently arrested in New York. Max ran Nacho's money-laundering enterprise, each day sending a jet-liner nose cone filled with drug money from New York to Cali. For this service, Nacho charged the other Cali bosses fifteen points to the dollar. Brother Max also ran a kilo-distribution operation out of Queens, where he blended in with the Colombian émigré community.

"I'll do anything to help Max," Nacho says.

"If there's a way, I'll find it," I say.

If. I didn't make promises that couldn't be kept. I told the truth, come what may. Nor did I pretend my clients were upstanding citizens. I knew what they did, but it didn't matter. Some people sold weapons; they sold a product the system deemed illegal. So what? In those days, I and everyone I knew used blow. Except Mady, who was—as she had been so often in those days—looking at me strangely.

"Money is not a problem," Nacho says. "Whatever it takes."

Nothing better in the world than being well paid for something you love doing. I'm thinking this when Mady turns and says, "Hello, who's *this*?"

A little girl has appeared. She has long brown hair that cascades around her shoulders, hair the same brown as her eyes, which are large, like a child in a Keane painting. She is gravitating toward Mady, but her eyes are fixed on me. I wink, and the girl giggles.

"My daughter," says Nacho. "Sara."

Sara looks to be about seven. Mady and I quickly bond with her. For some reason, the kid is fascinated by me. Few people understand my humor. Not only does this kid Sara get me, in no time at all she's speaking English like a New Yorker.

"She wishes we weren't married," Mady says.

"Why is that?"

"She wants to marry you herself."

Sara is only one nice aspect of all that follows, which truly is—forgive the cliché—the best of times. Nacho puts the word out, and I become the go-to lawyer of all Cali. I am making serious money. Blizzards of Franklins. I expand my offices. Hire lawyers to do my grunge work. Every day is court, jail, eat, sleep. Every month, we travel to Colombia. We meet with Nacho at one or another of his properties, sometimes in a bar amid the cane fields, in The Sahara Club.

Max's case is a slam dunk for the prosecution. When Max goes down, I will suffer the ignominy of being dunked on. There is no way out unless he cooperates against the big guys, but this is before extradition, and since the big guys never leave Colombia, there are no big fish to cooperate against because they send only workers to the States. Back then, the Colombian DTOs functioned vertically, handling everything from growing to street-peddling. If a worker got busted, his family, although technically hostages to guarantee his silence, would be well taken care of. Merely bringing up the subject of cooperation was enough to get your throat slit.

But to my surprise one night in The Sahara Club, Nacho brings up cooperation. I remember the moment clearly. Despite its shabbiness, The Sahara is stocked with crates of world-class wine. We are working through a third bottle of California's finest cabernet—Nacho loves all things American—and the mood is mellow when, in that raspy voice of his, he says, "Perhaps there is one way to solve all our problems."

I take a sip, look at him.

"Cooperation, Benn. We give the federals things in return for Max, yes?"

"Things?" Meaning other people and their money. Meaning I'd be on the wrong side of a lot of angry narco-traffickers.

"Pablo's things."

Brilliant Nacho. His Cali cartel was at war with Pablo Escobar's Medellín cartel. Pablo's forte was brute force. Nacho's was brainpower. He had spies in Medellín who knew the specifics of Pablo's people and operations.

And so Max did what at the time was unthinkable for a Colombian. He became a *sapo*. A rat. And I became the messenger between him and Nacho, bringing Max information on Medellín drugsters, who in turn fed it to the DEA.

This was shortly after credit for cooperation became codified in federal law, ushering in a new era in which prosecutors had loose guidelines about sources of cooperation, their primary focus being results. Which meant guys could literally buy their way from jail by selling out others.

I don't mention any of this to Mady. It's high-voltage stuff, no need for her to walk beneath live power lines.

Nacho finances an organization called People against Pablo Escobar. PEPE. A rare acronym that earns my seal of approval. In point of fact, PEPE is one big *sicario* hit team.

Soon Pablo goes down. Cali is victorious. Nacho reigns.

Max's sentence is reduced from thirty years to fifteen. Nacho delivers a huge bonus. Despite his newly elevated status, he is humble. As a boy, he escaped a poor barrio by the only route available, much like American robber barons for whom criminality was a stepladder, men like Joseph Kennedy Sr., who made his first fortune as a bootlegger.

To my surprise—and I think to Nacho's—we become friends.

Life is good. I have money, Mady, a future. All is well.

But then all of a sudden, it isn't.

Nacho owns hundreds of properties: *fincas*, mining tracts, Cali high-rises. His life is a moveable feast among them. On one trip, we meet at a grand mansion on several thousand acres near Jamundí known as Toylandia. A private resort for Nacho's DTO, it features a shooting range, billiards hall, several gyms, a soccer field, golf course, horse barns, cockfighting arena, a lake stocked with game fish, and bathing beauties galore. Nacho even has a personal chef named Maestro.

One evening, we are enjoying Maestro's fare when Nacho gets a call that makes him frown. He excuses himself for a moment, leaving us with Sara. The moment becomes an hour, then two. Night falls. Maestro leaves. The three of us are alone. The vibes are negative.

The lights go out. From the darkness come gunshots. They grow louder, closer.

I scoop Sara in my arms, take Mady's hand, and we leave. Outside, none of Nacho's people are around. I find a car with keys in the ignition. We get in, and I drive from the property. Sara is crying. She knows something bad is happening.

I'm not sure which way to go. Behind us flash the lights of other vehicles, gaining on us. Then I realize we are passing cane fields. The Sahara Club. I pull in, cut the lights, kill the engine. The pursuit cars pass. We sit in the dark, empty bar, waiting.

Much later, Sara and Mady are asleep when I hear sounds. I slip through shadows to the entrance. From outside, footsteps. Low voices. Two men. Looking for us. I look around for something to defend us with. But there are just wooden wine cases . . . atop which lies a crowbar.

The door slowly edges open.

I flatten against the wall, sure the intruder can hear my beating heart.

A man enters. He holds a gun. I come up from low and behind and place the crowbar around his throat and yank—*crunch*—and he goes limp. I know he's dead but don't care—no, I'm *glad* there's one less of them to deal with. I am operating on an automatic pilot I never even knew existed.

I bend for the fallen man's gun as the second man enters. Without thinking, I point and shoot. The muzzle flash is blinding, the shot deafening in the shack.

When my faculties return, I see both men lying still and hear Sara's sobs. Mady is holding her tight, rocking her.

"Stay here," I whisper, and leave.

I don't know whether the two men were alone, but surely, their comrades cannot be too far away. I move their car deep into the cane, where my own car is already hidden. It is dark, and it would be insanity to drive with headlights on. But I will remain outside, so if others come I can lead them away from The Sahara Club.

Hours pass. Nothing. Dead quiet, but then:

From the cane: "Sara. Sara. Sara . . ."

The voice is hoarse. Nacho's?

Before we can stop her, Sara bolts.

We go after her, but she is gone in the cane. And then comes another cry. Not Nacho, but Sara. Her voice is fearful, calling for me by my middle name, a name I never use but one Mady had playfully shared with her.

My seldom-used name echoes, a cry . . . but from where?

Then another shot rings out.

Then all is silent.

We stay there until late the next afternoon when, hopefully, it will be safe to leave. Mady cannot bear being in The Sahara with the dead men, so we wait in the car. It must be a hundred degrees inside it, but it's even hotter outside. I sit behind the wheel. We do not talk. There is nothing to say.

I know she is thinking about Sara. So am I.

I know she's thinking about the dead men. So am I. But my regrets are solely about Mady's reaction. Myself, I'm not rueful in the slightest. If I thought one of the fuckers was still breathing, I'd go back inside and pinch his nose until he stopped. I'm glad I reacted the way I did and won't brook any criticism. After all, who can argue with the fact that I'm the last man standing? I'm also pissed as hell. Angry that Mady doesn't appreciate my defending us. What, she'd have preferred being murdered?

I mutter, "It was them or us."

Mady does not answer.

It is not until we are back in Cali that we learn Nacho and his people and his extended family all have been murdered by a newly formed alliance of smaller cartel bosses.

During the flight home, Mady gives me the silent treatment. As we land, she says she's done working. I nod understandingly. My present clients are gone. But, I add, there will be new ones. There always are.

"You don't understand. I don't want to do this work anymore."

"We can't just quit. I'm a lawyer. This is what I do."

"I'm not a lawyer. You do it without me."

"Look, I know this was a bad—"

"You killed two men, Benn."

"Them or us . . . and Sara."

Mady wipes a tear. "I know that. I'm just sorry—no, I'm *angry* that I was there."

"I had no idea what was going to happen—"

"I'm not angry with you, Benn. I'm angry with myself. You preferred not seeing things, but I couldn't do that. I've been thinking this way for a while. Maybe from the beginning. I don't want my life to be helping criminals."

I give Mady my JFK Sr. rationale. What else could a poor boy in Colombia do? Her answer is that I'm not a poor boy in Colombia. I have no answer for that.

"Things aren't always black and white," I say. "It's not as if the government is always the good guy. Prosecutors are lawyers, just like me. And lawyers care only about winning. They all cheat and lie if they have to."

"Like you, Benn."

I figured after a few weeks that she'd come around. And that my work would all but vanish. I was wrong on both counts. Dozens of elements that had been part of the Cali cartel were operating on their own now, and new work flooded in. And Mady stayed away from the office, leaving me to soldier on alone. We didn't see each other much. I'd come home, she'd be sleeping; I'd wake up, she'd be gone. She went back to school. Good for her, but bad for us. Out of sight, out of mind.

I started getting high. With other women. We divorced a year later.

A big part of me vanished with Mady. I'd met her when I was a law-school intern and she was a paralegal student. For a year, we eyeballed one another but no more. Then I became a state-court public defender, and she went to work for pretrial services and the inevitable happened. Man, those were the days. Growing the business by day, growing closer by night.

I received the final papers the same day I learned the names of Nacho's killers. The Cali Cartel had been replaced by the North Valley Cartel. It wasn't just the name that changed. The NVC bosses were an ugly crew of violent freaks. The Amputee. The Double-Aughts. The Butcher, who, when not drug dealing, enjoyed castrating cattle at one of his many grand *fincas* that had once been Nacho's.

Rigo, they called him.

CHAPTER 11

Post-Nacho, Jamundí became infamous when one Colombian elite counternarcotics force working for a cartel murdered eleven members of another elite counternarcotics force working for the FARC guerillas. The battle was one of many over the spoils of Nacho's kingdom. Those blood feuds from the old days continued to simmer today. I wasn't looking forward to driving through Jamundí at night.

My worries were misplaced.

The van exited the highway and circled the town proper and proceeded along a single-lane blacktop. Ahead, a jagged ridgeline stood like dark teeth against a starry sky. Other than the van's headlamps, the countryside was unlit.

The roadway tilted and became winding as we drove higher. Coming out of a bend, we slowed, entering the crowded dirt street of a town populated by Indians wearing purple ponchos. Which got me thinking of the legend of *Sombra*—the mystical figure who protected the Indians, who in turn protected him.

Then the town was gone, and we were on the winding road again, climbing higher and higher. We came out of a turn, and abruptly, the van slowed to a stop. I leaned closer to the rear window.

Armed soldiers were gathered around a jeep.

"Retené," Paz whispered. Roadblock.

We heard voices from the front of the van: our driver exchanging pleasantries with the army officer. The voices lowered, and I guessed pesos were being passed, because then both men laughed and bid each other good night.

The van continued on, but slower now.

By the sound of the tires, we were on an unpaved road. After a few more miles in the middle of nowhere, we stopped. Our driver got out and opened the rear door, and we got out.

As my night vision adjusted, I became aware of men in the shadows. Burly men with Indian features, wearing bandoliers and carrying rifles.

Sombra's Praetorian Guard?

There was a small house. A candle flickered within. A large man stood outlined in the doorway a few steps above us. In the dimness, I stumbled—*ow!*—the misstep tweaking my bad right knee. Happens sometimes. Hurts like hell when it does, but this was a time to suck it up.

The large man had Indian features. Jet-black hair. Neither young nor old. He wore a white cotton peasant shirt and trousers. He reminded me of Brando in *Viva Zapata!* No doubting his word was the others' command. But was he a step or two above them, or was he at the top of the ladder? Was he *Sombra*?

His eyes were obsidian. They drilled into mine, and I had the queer sensation of his inspecting my mind. Checking nooks and crannies for my secrets. The Indian turned his gaze to Paz and nodded. Paz addressed me.

"Doctor, you are expert at negotiating with the American government, yes?"

"I have some experience."

"The *señor* may wish a negotiation. For that, he wants to establish a relationship with you now. For your expenses, please accept this."

The man who might be *Sombra* snapped his fingers, said, *"Enano."*

Enano means *midget*. He was addressing the short man, the guy with the missing fingertips who'd led the posse that tried to take out Rigo in Antigua. A thought crossed my mind like a black crow: *If Sombra were behind the attempt on Rigo, I might be next on his hit list.*

But all *Enano* did was hand me an envelope that, by shape and weight, I guessed held a brick of money. If it was US currency, I figured it was fifty large. A nice-enough number, but from a guy like *Sombra*, a too-small token of appreciation. A fucking tip.

"Now I say thank you?" I muttered.

Paz said, "Sorry, I didn't hear . . ."

"Tell him thank you," I said.

"I'm informed the gentleman has a question," Paz told me instead. "Doctor, in your experience, what drug-interdiction capabilities does the United States have in the far north Pacific?"

A question that came out of left field, and one I preferred not fielding. I assume these conversations are recorded. Therefore, my habit is to respond in words that could not be construed as how-to advice about criminal activity.

"I don't really know," I said. "If I had to *guess*, I'd say very little, if any at all. From what I understand, the United States' resources are already stretched thin patrolling the southern ocean routes from South America."

"And the interdiction capabilities of other nations in the area?"

I figured *Sombra* had designs on the growing market for cocaine on the far side of the Pacific Rim. "Again, I don't know. My *guess* is none."

Zapata gave me another long look. An evaluation, I supposed. But whether thumbs-up or thumbs-down was impossible to tell. Then he stood aside, and *Enano* came toward us. He went into his knapsack and took out an automatic pistol. It looked awkward, held in his shortened digits, but I saw that his finger was able to curl around the trigger.

I took an involuntary step back—

But *Enano* walked by me, raised the pistol, and shot it point-blank into the face of the van driver. The man dropped where he stood. *Enano* stepped over the body and got behind the wheel of the van.

I was too stunned to run, and where the fuck could I run to, anyway? Besides, Big Chief Motherfucker didn't want to hurt me; he just wanted me to observe what happened to anyone not a team player.

"A necessity," Paz whispered. "The driver could not be trusted to know the *señor*'s whereabouts." Disturbing.

When we got back into the van, our phones were on the seats. As we drove off, I tried making sense of what had occurred. Clearly, *Sombra* had wanted to check me out before his next move . . . but the meet had been so perfunctory, I doubted anything would come of it.

"Let me see the envelope," said Paz.

I gave it to him. As I'd expected, it contained fifty in Franklins. He began counting, but I was more concerned about the bigger picture.

Would there be a sequel? Or was I merely one of many attorneys summoned for *Sombra*'s inspection? Was the fifty a door prize for unlucky contestants?

Paz whispered, "Fifty. An indication that you'll be retained."

"Why fifty thousand? Why not millions?"

"It was already agreed beforehand."

"*Sombra* didn't say word one."

"That's the way he is. Quiet. An observer. It's said that he and his family have a magical ability to converse when they're apart. So long as one of them is present, they all are as well."

"Too bad they didn't sweeten the pot."

"God in his ways," he said, pocketing his share and handing me mine. "My wife requires an operation. This will help pay for it." He opened his wallet to a photograph of a young woman. His eyes were teary. "Of course, that's an old photograph. Time passes so quickly."

I was thinking the same thing. Years go by, and most lawyers don't even get an opportunity to snag a Biggy. Unfortunately, I sensed that I'd whiffed; *Sombra* was passing on me.

Paz and I caught the last flight back to Bogotá.

It wasn't until the wee hours that I slumped into my suite. My knee was hurting enough to limp, which in turn triggered my bad hip to creak, and it in turn inspired my lower back to scream. I gulped aspirin, thinking I'd stuck my neck out for a relative few bucks and a pointless meeting that also cost a man his life.

But at least I could make it to Foto's New Year's party.

Wrong. The next day I learned New York was in blizzard conditions. I could get to Panama, but there were no open flights from there to New York until January 3.

Problem was, Rigo's arraignment was January 2.

The counter agent pecked around. "Hmm. I could get you to New York on January 1, but it won't be a direct flight. You'll have to lay over the night of December 31 in another city."

"Whatever," I said. "Which city?"

The person told me which.

I felt a sickening lurch in my gut as I confronted the true source of my greatest forebodings. Not the inability to outrun a volcanic eruption. Not the deadly surrender. Something much worse. Putting it another way?

Of all the cities on the old Spanish Main, I had to walk into . . .

ALUNE

I am a chess master. My life is an elimination tournament in which only the winners remain alive. In my first few games, I was ignorant of the players and their moves, but fortunately, my defense was unlike any my adversaries had seen. I did the opposite of what was expected. No fakes, no feints, no false attacks. Instead, I revealed all. I exposed my flaws and vulnerabilities . . . and, very slowly, my naiveté lowered my adversaries' guards, my helplessness a magnet they could not resist. Then, when they set caution aside and entered my space, I locked the door behind them.

The king is dead. Long live the queen.

As one opponent breathed his last, he called me a Venus flytrap.

Younger Brother thought that hilarious. "It's true," he said.

At least, it was back then, when my only weapon was deception—pretending to be what I'm not—in order to survive. It not only worked but to my astonishment also quickly carried me to the very top of my business.

A perilous journey. I had no choice but to take risks. To expose my identity to those who might one day betray me. To personally make deals rather than let others be my face. Worst of all?

I mixed business with pleasure.

Somehow I survived, thanks to my brothers. It was like having six eyes, six ears, three brains. The drug business was a maze; the key to escaping was to know what was true and what wasn't. We made all the right choices. We were invincible.

Was this a God-given miracle? The power of human nature?

Or are we really the People Who Know More?

When the American lawyer left, we agreed he was the right man for the job we had planned. We had no delusions. He had no stomach for violence, but he was money hungry. Despite our failed attempt to kill the dog Rigo in Antigua, the lawyer remained on the case. Clearly, he was frightened, but greed oiled his decision.

The failings of lawyers never cease to amaze me. They are consumed by dreams of large fees, but they let their money lie fallow. Buried in a box in a suburban backyard, neatly banded in a temperature-controlled vault, a memorized number of an otherwise-anonymous bank account.

But not this lawyer.

I know this lawyer.

He pretends to be normal while lurching through time and space. He lives for the pleasure of . . . pleasuring himself, no matter the cost. Hence, his ceaseless hunger to earn more. Simply put: he can be bought.

He has another flaw that might prove useful: he lives alone, shuns relationships, and yet he has a weakness for women.

I look at my brothers and see they are smiling. Agreeing.

Money and women. The poor lawyer has no chance.

CHAPTER 12

"Welcome to San Juan, Puerto Rico. All of us at InterCarib wish all of you a Happy New Year."

I stirred in my cramped economy seat. I was in a foul mood. What a shitty way to approach the new year. *Sombra* wasn't meant to be. Rigo was a promise. Same with Foto's case.

Worst of all? I was headed to a city I didn't want to be in, never, ever. The familiar route to the city from its airport ran parallel to a lagoon. Reflected neon from the far side pulsed on the dark water. I sensed energy coming off the hotel strip. The clock was ticking toward the New Year: the high rollers would be swarming the casinos, the discos growing louder by the minute.

Then across a bridge, and the last of the hotel lights receded behind, and my taxi started up the narrow peninsular road that led to the old city. Viejo San Juan. The road ran along a seaside cliff. Below it, the ocean was lined with the pale crests of breakers, rolling in from the Atlantic inexorably, like moths to a flame. Like me to Viejo San Juan. The city and the song whose lyrics always touched me: *One day I will return to Viejo San Juan, to search for my love, and dream again.*

I am foolishly sentimental.

We passed one of the sixteenth-century forts that enclose the old city. Drove uphill along the old cannon-notched battlements. That narrow street was Calle Sol. That one was Calle Luna. Sun and Moon. I'd seen them last . . . what, five years ago?

Who was I kidding?

Five years, three months, three weeks, two days ago.

VSJ looked the same. Always does, always will. VSJ was a historic district. Frozen in time. Traditional. New Year's Eve being a family night, the streets were empty. Good. There were people who would recognize me, and I didn't want my presence known.

In the Guaty airport, I'd squatted in a corner and recharged my device while trying to book a room in Puerto Rico. The Isla Verde hotels were closest to the airport. They were sold out for the holidays. I tried the beach hotels, but they were likewise sold out. I forced myself to try Old San Juan. El Convento had a room.

I hurried into the hotel with my head down. Thankfully, I didn't know the desk clerk. The elevator bellhop seemed familiar, so I took the stairs to my floor. Along the corridors, oil lamps flickered on balconies. It was quiet, except for the rustle of fruit bats in the ancient *níspero* tree in the courtyard, and the occasional chirp of a coqui. These frogs are native only to Puerto Rico, and their cries brought back more memories: tropical nights, whiskey, music, *amor* . . .

Centuries ago, my room had been a nun's cell, but now it was sleek and modern. And claustrophobic. I opened the balcony doors and stood there, looking at planted rooftops. The stream of memories was fast becoming a river. I went with the flow—

A whistle shrieked, followed a moment later by a *whump*.

Above, a rocket burst, a junior version of the New Year's fireworks show. I looked at my watch. Ten before midnight. What was I doing feeling sorry for myself while the best view to watch the great show was steps away on the hotel terrace?

I hurried up the tiled staircase to the terrace floor, passing no one and nothing but carts filled with bottles of champagne on ice. I started toward the terrace, then stopped short.

No wonder the champagne.

It was intended for the hotel guests gathered on the roof for the same reason I had come. Doubtful any of them knew me, but I wanted to be alone. I reversed course, grabbed two bottles of the bubbly, went down the stairs, ducked out a side entrance.

I hurried up Calle Cristo and turned onto Calle San Sebastian, a cul-de-sac at whose end was an overlook. I stopped there.

Below, a row of residential houses ended at the gates of La Fortaleza, the governor's palace. Ahead lay the dark waters of San Juan Bay and the distant lights of the far shore. To the right was the great lawn sweeping up to *Castillo del Morro*, whose turreted mass was dimly visible against the darker sky.

One minute to twelve.

I didn't want to be here, but I couldn't bring myself to leave. I was my own audience, trying to understand my character.

A cat scampered past the row of houses below.

A few desultory rockets burst on the far shore.

Thirty seconds. *Fucking Viejo San Juan—*

Up and down the long reach of the far coast, rockets began bursting, and all at once my gloom was gone. I undid wire from a cork. I'd drink champagne to resolutions I would make happen. I swore that.

Five . . . four . . . three—

So help me God.

Two . . .

The solitary rockets fused to a stream of bright explosions, moments later followed by echoed *whumps*.

From below the overlook came closer sounds: a door opening, water splashing. Another New Year's tradition observed in VSJ: throwing water out at the stroke of midnight. *Out with the old. The fucking irony of my life—*

The opened house cast an oblong of light on the wet, gleaming cobblestones. A man and a woman appeared. His hair was silver, his suit dark. The woman's legs were slender. I blinked hard but still saw the same thing: beautiful people in a still photograph from an old noir film.

I drew a breath so sharp, my heart felt pierced.

I drowned the pain in champagne. In one long glug, a whole bottle poured down my upraised throat. Rivulets ran into my hair, down my chest. I emptied the bottle, opened the second—

Was the woman's gaze now focused on me?

I jerked back out from view. From below came the sound of the house door closing. My heart was hammering. I guzzled half the second bottle. Gasped for breath. The booze had me now. I spread my arms to the explosive-stained heavens above.

So fucking what?

So I'd been caught looking. No big deal. I was in a public place . . . No. My problem was not that I'd been watching, but what I felt about what I'd seen . . . a man and a woman in love. Which triggered a realization:

My life was loveless. I lied about not caring that I was alone, but I *did* care. I lied about loving my work to conceal its sordid reality. My braggadocio about being a ladies' man was the biggest lie of all. The Avianca flight attendant was a one-night stand. All my affairs were. Because I feared a woman seeing my faults? Whatever. The fact is that I was alone. No lovers, no friends . . .

Boo-hoo. Poor me. I'm drunk as . . . a . . . what the fuck is that?

An apparition had appeared in the bay. A spaceshiplike enormity lit by a million pinpoints. It glided across the water. A beautiful close encounter. The little moving things on its deck were people waving hello. I raised the bottle—*hello*—and drank.

The cruise ship's white-swirling wake swept away my dark thoughts.

It was a new year, and I was the old me again.

Benn T. Bluestone, aka Johnny Bipolar.

When I got back to my room, I realized my device was blinking. The fireworks had deafened me to message pings. Many of them. Now I read and nearly wept for happiness.

Because I wasn't alone after all.

There *were* others out there thinking of me: thirty years' worth of grateful clients wishing me a Happy New Year. So what if criminals were my only friends? Forget what that says about me. What's important?

I'm remembered.

The next morning, I was on my way to New York. I didn't want to watch the junk that passes for movies and had nothing to read, so I pulled up a drawing app on my device and free-associated, letting my fingers do the working—

"Wow," the woman next to me said. "That's really good."

I'd been absently drawing what I always drew. My ex.

"You must love her very much," the woman said.

"No," I said. "She's a figment of my imagination."

CHAPTER 13

New York in the grip of midwinter. Fifty shades of grime. Depressing. I had a voice mail that made things worse. It was from my young friend Billy. Bea was in the hospital. When I returned the call, it was too late. Bea had passed last night. Billy had been the only one with her. Indigent, she'd been cremated.

It hit me hard. Except for Billy, I was the only friend or family Bea had. A lonely end to a poor life. Then it hit me harder:

Bea was the only person *I* had.

Fuck it. Time to work. I wanted face time with Rigo before he was arraigned, so I headed downtown early. Since 9/11, the Manhattan federal courts, US Attorney's Office, and adjacent federal jail have been a no-vehicle zone whose perimeter is guarded and patrolled 24-7. These buildings compose the premier federal district in the country, the Southern District of New York, archenemy of jihadists, far right loony-tuners, lone-wolf Unabomber types, and, praise be, drug kingpins.

The SDNY courthouse address was 500 Pearl, but the Pearl Street entrance fell within the no-drive zone, so Val dropped me off outside the perimeter at the intersection of Mulberry and Worth streets. The old heart of Little Italy, when I first began. Part of ever-expanding Chinatown now. There was only one constant in my New York:

The frigging courts, baby.

Security people with attitudes. Money. Stressed lawyers lugging paper. Money. People with problems trying to go unnoticed. Money. Lights, camera, action; close-up on the money.

I went through security, down a long marbled hallway, and up an elevator to the fifth-floor hallway. On the way, I passed two or three dozen people I knew or knew of. About half I'd be afraid to turn my back to. The other half, I couldn't care less about. I wound among them.

On one end of the fifth-floor hall was pretrial intake, where new arrestees are pedigreed under the watchful eyes of agents, a collective from acronym heaven. FBI. DEA. ICE. USPO. USM. ATF. SS. Pretrial was where I met with new clients on the verge of being swallowed by the system. On the opposite end of the fifth-floor hall were proffer rooms, where assistant US attorneys met with me and my client cooperators taking their first baby steps toward freedom. It was for this journey across the fifth floor that I was paid so well.

I loved the fifth floor. Today I headed not to either end but to the center, the magistrate's courtroom, where new arrestees were presented. Mag court was empty except for a clerk. I handed him my notice of appearance. He glanced at the defendant's name, shrugged.

"Not yet, Counselor. Try again in half an hour."

Perfect. I went down to the fourth floor. Above a reinforced door, a camera looked down at an intercom. I pressed the intercom and raised my face to the camera and said my name and my client's name.

"Wait, Counselor."

I waited. The other end of the floor was the SDNY US Marshals office. Its anteroom was decorated with wall hangings. My kind of art. Criminal realism:

The latest FBI Most Wanted list, replete with mug shots.

A poster-size drawing of a gaunt marshal: ten-gallon hat, behind him a gallows. A caption identified him as Marshal George Maledon, executioner for Isaac Parker, the Hanging Judge. Beneath his name was a bold-lettered declaration: ***Let no guilty man escape***.

I weighed that against the proposition that we're all guilty of something. I know I am. I sometimes imagine myself being caught. Doesn't matter for what—taxes, perjury, obstruction of justice. Deep down, I know that one day I *will* be caught. Begging the question of why not quit before it's too late? Easy answer:

It's the money, Stupid.

Maledon eyed me.

Not today, Marshal.

I moved on to an enlargement of an old black-and-white newspaper photo of marshals wearing long overcoats and fedoras, escorting Julius and Ethel Rosenberg. Behind mustache and eyeglasses, Julius's expression was numb. Ethel looked as if she'd just had a bad conversation with an oncologist.

I paused to admire an old photograph of the first woman marshal. In it, she was leaning against a car holding a revolver. Her legs were shapely—

The voice said, "Take number four, Counselor."

The marshal pens are twelve-by-six spaces partitioned by steel-mesh screens. In Antigua, my first take on Rigo was short, dark, and ugly. Now, although the screen slightly blurred his features, his scowling features beneath the harsh overhead fluorescence confirmed my impression.

"You okay?" I said.

"Here? How the fuck can I be okay?"

"I'm referring to the incident in Antigua."

"*Incident?* They were trying to kill me."

"Mind telling me who is *they?*"

"I have to educate you? *They* are people afraid I'm going to sit on them."

Sombra, I thought. "I know that. I was asking *who* they are. If you're cooperating against people, I need to know who—"

"You'll know when you have to know. Let's be clear, Doctor. I'm the one in the cage. I'm the one who decides who I sit on and when. No more questions, okay? Just do your job. Okay?"

I needed to grab the controls. "Okay. Whatever you say. All I ask of you are two things."

He cocked his head on his short neck and squinted at me.

"One? Take care of our business. Now."

"Your fee has been authorized."

"Two? I need for you to . . ."

I flattened my palm against the screen. Usually at that point, the client anxiously presses his palm to the other side of the screen from mine. One for all and all for one, but Rigo didn't seem to give two shits about ritual bonding. I continued my act, anyway.

"Walk with me," I said.

"Gus is here?"

"Gus?"

"Gus, the DEA."

Ignoring my palm was bad enough, but *Gus*? That pissed me off. Newly arrested guys are like newborns who fall in love with the first nipple they're offered. Usually, the nipple is mine, but not so this time. Thanks to Mondragon's overreaching machinations, the case had begun without me being anointed as master of ceremonies.

"Gus may or may not be here," I said. "From now on, Gus is unimportant. He's just a worker for the prosecutor."

"On the plane, Gus said you'd arrange for me to have commissary money. And phone calls and reading material."

I nodded pleasantly. Chores this motherfucker's people should be doing. I wasn't a fucking caregiver. Whatever. Once my fee was in pocket, our relationship would shake out my way. The door behind Rigo opened, and a marshal leaned in.

"Time, Counselor."

When I returned to mag court, Gus Romero was sitting in the first row alongside a black guy wearing a conservative suit and button-down shirt. He was Rigo's prosecutor, Assistant US Attorney Barnett Robinson. We'd done a case together some years back, during which I'd scored a rare litigated win: not a jury trial but a hearing, convincing a judge a search had been illegal, the case then getting tossed. The client was an illegal alien, though, subject to automatic deportation. Still, after acquittal, he'd languished for long months in immigration jail. Communicating with the immigration jail meant floundering through an endless menu of numbered options that invariably ended in an unanswered ring, a dropped call. Immigration court was the worst. Anyway, I'd known that one call from Robinson would get the gears in motion. I'd e-mailed him, asking him to intervene, reminding him my client had not been convicted. His reply had been in caps:

ACQUITTED DOES NOT MEAN INNOCENT.

So it goes. My client did an unnecessary eight months in immigration jail because Robinson, a straight-as-a-ruler-salesman honest man, was also a lawyer. Lawyers can't deal with losing. He needed to dole out some punishment.

Rigo's case was called.

In the well, Robinson and I exchanged a brief handshake as Rigo emerged, flanked by a pair of court cops. The proceedings hardly took a minute. Although Rigo had surrendered, technically he was illegally in the States, meaning there was an immigration hold on him, meaning he could not be allowed out on bail. So in one run-on sentence, I waived a bail hearing, waived a reading of the indictment, and entered a plea of not guilty.

As Rigo was led back inside, I whispered that I'd visit him tomorrow, so as to begin planning his cooperation. He shook his head. "Not yet. Dr. Mondragon is planning everything."

An unlikely pairing, I thought, not for the first time. In Antigua, Mondragon had been disparaging of Rigo, who in turn seemed contemptuous of the lawyer.

Outside the courtroom, Barnett Robinson and Gus Romero were waiting for an elevator. I told Robinson, "My client will want to come in from the cold. Letting you know now, but I'd like to put it off a bit. Until I'm satisfied he's ready to proffer."

"We're on the same track, Benn," Robinson said. "Prior to his arrest, your client supplied us with certain information we'd like to check out before we sit down with him. I'll give you a heads-up soon as that happens."

They got on an elevator whose door slid shut, leaving me with the realization that everyone in the case was on the other side of a stone wall from me. I rode solo down in the next elevator and left 500 Pearl.

Felipe Mondragon waited outside the courthouse. "Ah, there you are. For the next few days, I shall be meeting with our client privately. Nothing to do with his case here: that's your responsibility. My conversations with him concern his properties in Colombia."

"You might remind him my fee is due."

"Not to worry. It's in the process."

"Right. Will you be meeting him mornings or afternoons? Whichever you choose, I'll visit him the other to discuss his cooperation."

"I will be with him both mornings and afternoons."

"I understand," I said, although I didn't.

CHAPTER 14

At my office, I received a voice mail from Foto, telling me to call Jilly at a given number. I made the call, and a man with a Slavic accent answered. *Hmm.* Clients sent by Foto were invariably Latin. But I shouldn't have been surprised. There's no corner of the world that isn't the territory of some criminal organization. Crime is crime, and in the crime business nowadays, the white powder is king. Russia's a big country, got to be at least a couple million people there who like a toot now and again. Or so I assumed.

"We come bring Jilly now," the man said.

"Say, in an hour. My office is—"

"We know where." He hung up.

While waiting, I read Laura Astorquiza's latest *Radio Free Bogotá* blog:

> Extraditing Colombian citizens for crimes they committed in Colombia is another form of colonialism. In their arrogance, the gringos ignore our judicial system and judge our people by the laws of their own country. The latest example is the extradition of Rigoberto Ordoñez. Undoubtedly, this thug will use his resources to buy cooperation

that will result in his early release, but he should
be judged by his crimes against the citizens of our
country. Justice will belong to us. Viva Colombia!

I agreed with Laura. Extradition in its present, body-count-driven
format was sorely unjust. But fuck that. What struck me was that Laura
had singled out Rigo. Had she known I was his lawyer? I'd filed my
notice of appearance just a few hours ago, so it couldn't possibly have
already been posted on the case docket. Unless she knew someone who
knew before—

The cage elevator whined to a stop outside my office. I heard its
door slide open and floorboards creaking. No one had buzzed me from
the street entrance, so I assumed the footfall was that of my neighboring
tenant, S. Stephen Sonnenberg, a private financial adviser to the kind of
people Page Six noted as having dined with so-and-so in a downtown
restaurant. Since I had no standing in that crowd, Sonnenberg ignored
me, although, ever the gentleman, I always greeted him politely by the
diminutive of his first name. He didn't appreciate that because *S* stood
for *Solomon*, which he hated. Hence, I called him Solly, which he hated
more.

Solly's footsteps didn't fade toward his door as I'd expected but
advanced toward my door, followed by a knock.

"Enter," I said, and the door opened.

It was Solly all right. His usual dashing self: camel cashmere coat
draped over shoulders, shades propped atop spiked hair.

"Hello, Benn."

"Solly."

Uncharacteristically, he ignored my jibe. "As I was entering the
building, a visitor was about to ring your bell. I informed the visitor
that you were my neighbor, and it would be a pleasure to show the way."

"You on Ecstasy, Solly?"

"My Ecstasy is beauty." He stepped aside and gallantly waved an arm for the person with him to enter my office.

"Thank you," the visitor said, entering.

"No, thank *you*," said Solly.

Solly closed the door, leaving me staring at a pair of hazel eyes that looked even better now than they had in Foto's penthouse where I'd last seen them.

Hello again, they said.

CHAPTER 15

I'm not often at a loss for words, but at the moment, I was speechless.

"Mr. Bluestone?" Her voice was whispery.

"Please, call me Benn."

"I'm Jillian," she said demurely, adding a surname that sounded like *Shenolt*. "Everyone calls me Jilly."

"Oh. I thought Jilly was . . ."

"That I was what?"

"A man. I mean, you aren't a man, are you?"

She laughed, pink mouth, white teeth perfect but for a slightly crooked upper incisor. Hey, perfection is boring. That night in Foto's apartment, she'd seemed purely beautiful. By day in my office, she was still beautiful but no longer pure. Something about her aura seemed damaged. Out of nowhere, a thought struck me: she was, or had been, a drug addict. I was sure because it takes one to know one. And let me tell you something: to a former addict, there's no woman more desirable than the one in your lifeboat.

"Not important. Please, sit. Take your coat?"

She sat but kept the coat on. It was some kind of coat. Dark mink with a silver fox hood; a vision of a legend in Blackglama. I eyeballed her coat's cost as about the same as a Mercedes S-Class with all the options. The silver fox framed the lower half of her face and tangled with her hair. I wanted to cross around the desk and lift her from the chair and lay her on a Caucasian rug and take her goddamn fast and furious right fucking now.

"So, Ms., ah, I'm sorry, I didn't catch . . ."

She repeated the name sounding like *Shenolt*, adding, "I suppose you know why I'm here."

"My impression is you have a problem."

"Not me," she said quickly. "Someone I don't even know. I don't even know why they wanted me to visit you. I'm not very good at talking to lawyers."

"Don't blame you," I said. "We're a motley crew."

Her laugh was sudden, there and then gone. She glanced away and drew a breath, then turned back and looked me in the eyes. "I have a . . . business associate is the way to put it, who wants to help a friend. The friend is the person who has the problem. I'm told this explains it."

From within the coat she took out a skin bag, whose worth I rated as a fully equipped Honda, and from it took some papers that she handed to me.

It was an Eastern District of New York indictment captioned *United States of America v. Joaquin Bolivar*. It was just three pages, bare bones and minimal, alleging the defendant conspired with unknown others to import more than one ton of marijuana into the United States.

Huh? Foto was referring me a pot case? Way back when I was an up-and-coming mouthpiece, I'd done plenty of pot cases. But for a long time since, the big fees had been in hard-drug cases. Still, Foto had said the fee was a million—to start—so there had to be more to the matter. The indictment was nine months old, probably unsealed when Bolivar was arrested in Colombia. I turned to the third page of the indictment and again was puzzled: the predicate acts of the indictment took place six years ago.

Hold on. The drug-conspiracy statute charged in the indictment expired after five years. But apparently, Bolivar had been arrested after the statute of limitations had run. I had an inkling of how and why but left the thought for now.

"Tell me about Mr. Bolivar," I said.

"Like I said, I don't know him. I'm just here for the person who knows about the case. Could you please meet with him?"

"Your business associate?"

"My . . . yes, him."

I figured the associate was Joaquin Bolivar himself. Again, I wondered if he were a fugitive. "When does he want to meet?"

"Now. He's waiting."

I took that to mean Bolivar didn't want to go public. Which answered my question:

Fugitive.

Jilly's ride was a lead-gray stretch limo with a customized grille resembling a bulldog with an underbite. It rode heavily, as if armored. The driver sat behind a shuttered panel. Jilly sat looking out the window. Her fingers, long and lightly tanned, were clasped in her lap. On her marriage finger was a faint, pale outline where a ring had been. I wondered about that story.

We drove down Fifth and turned west on Central Park South. Horse carriages were lined up across from the hotels. Just a few days ago I'd been in one with the Avianca flight attendant.

"I love horses," she said. Unscripted, her voice had a touch of country.

"I used to like the ponies myself." How fucking true. The second time I'd gotten wealthy, it had stayed in Vegas.

"Where I grew up, lots of kids had horses," she said.

"I never touched one until I was seventeen."

She wasn't listening to me. "We couldn't afford a horse."

"We couldn't afford a TV to watch them." *Did I just say that?* I was totally out of control. This one was so gorgeously perfect, I was shaky. A guy with my voice said, "Where did you grow up?"

"Not far from Tulsa."

I used to love this country song—"You're the Reason God Made Oklahoma"—about a full moon over Tulsa and a rancher's daughter. I pictured the rancher's daughter like Jilly: perfect skin and hair and teeth and the effervescence of a girl enjoying being a girl.

She smiled.

I wanted to move on her, badly. But she was already with a man that Foto feared—Foto, who never worried about anything farther than his enlarged dick and probably held the world's record for having been chased naked down the most fire escapes by angry husbands waving weapons. Besides, maybe the man who had her also had my fee.

Bad idea. Forget it.

We passed Sixth Avenue and then Seventh. Ahead, outlined against the white winter sky, stood a jagged skyline of new one-hundred-plus-story condos whose price tags were far more than the getaway money I yearned for. Not for the first time, I thought I was in the wrong business. But what was the right business? The kind that allows so many people to afford those kinds of prices?

The bulldog entered Columbus Circle and stopped in front of a new building known as the Kursk Needle. A while ago, it had been in the tabloids because its namesake was a Russian oligarch with links to organized crime.

The Needle's lobby was nouveau Trump. Doormen uniformed like Ruritanian generals. Mammoth marble atrium dominated by an odd work of art: an actual battle tank, bronzed like a baby shoe. A plaque identified the tank as a T-34, the legendary battle horse of the Red Army that had gone toe-to-toe with German Panzers in the greatest tank battle of all time: Kursk. As in, the Kursk Needle.

The elevator had two buttons: "Lobby" and "PH." My stomach dropped as it whooshed up. Jilly stood facing the door. She was visibly nervous. My stomach caught up with me as the elevator slowed to a stop and slid open, and we entered the point of the Needle.

Impressive, I had to admit. The glass was cut in layered panes, forming a sheath that covered the vaulted ceiling. Glass and marble and minimalist leather furniture. Plus two black-suited thugs.

"Welcome, sir," one said. "My name is Andrey. This is Kyril."

I recognized Andrey's voice as that of the man who'd spoken over the phone. His accent was sort of like Val's: Mitteleuropean, but thicker, more eastern. He was thin as a blade and smelled faintly of Vitalis. Kyril was small, bespectacled, with a shaved head. He looked me up and down without so much as a nod.

We followed Andrey through another room that was empty except for a tripod-mounted telescope pointing out at the city. We passed the scope and went down a ramp that looked stolen from the Guggenheim.

The lower level was empty except for a thin man seated in a chair. He wore an Adidas tracksuit and was using a chopstick to scratch an ankle. His color scheme matched the décor: black eye patch, paper-white face, black yarmulke. He worked the chopstick beneath a blue plastic ankle bracelet.

I revised my forecast.

The bracelet was an electronic monitor worn by people under house arrest. Joaquin Bolivar wasn't a fugitive. He was already a defendant.

I was wrong again.

"I'm Nathan Grable," the man said, his Russian accent like Andrey's but the voice higher, reed-thin, like his seemingly undernourished body. "My friends call me Natty."

"Nice meeting you, Natty."

As we shook hands, I saw a crudely inked tattoo on Natty's wrist: a hammer and sickle enclosed by a red star with barbed borders.

"Now we are friends," Natty said. "Friends are only important thing in a man's life. Me, I am friend of Joaquin Bolivar." He pointed at his leg. "This fucking bracelet I wear? Like Joaquin, I am falsely accused by the feds. For me, they fabricate lies that I manipulate commodity sales. Gasoline. For Joaquin, the lie is that he conspires marijuana.

Ridiculous. I have a lawyer, but Joaquin does not. I want to help my friend. Why, you wonder, yes?"

"Tell me if you like," I said. "Or not."

"Because I believe. Loyalty. *Friends*."

When my clients talk about friendship, I keep my trap shut. I've seen the things these types of friends do to one another, and they ain't pretty.

He motioned in the direction of Andrey and Kyril. "These are friends, too. Why? Because we went through hell together. You know *Spetsnaz?* Special forces of former USSR? My unit fight so many Afghan blackies, you wouldn't believe. Kill plenty but always plenty more. Like cockroaches. Finally, politicians say war cost too much. We go home leaving behind Marek, buried under rocks near Jalalabad. The two Leonids come with us, but in pieces. Little Leon, no more arms, no more legs, sips vodka from a straw, and pisses himself. Big Leon, in a sanitarium with black mold on the walls. We still help them. Why? Loyalty. *Organiskiya*. You understand, yes?"

"I think I catch your drift."

"Ask how I came to call you. Go on, ask."

"How did you come to call me?"

"I want my lawyer to represent Joaquin, but my lawyer says he does not do narcotics cases. He says for narcotics the number one man is Bluestone."

I smelled a referral coming on. "That was very nice of your lawyer. What did you say his name was?"

"Not important. Here is the thing. Joaquin is going to be extradited from Colombia. We want you to defend his case. We want for you meet with Joaquin. But first, business is business." Natty snapped his fingers, and Andrey handed me an envelope. There was a check inside. Certified, drawn on a Swiss bank. The checking account title was Murmansk-54 Imports, Inc. The check was made out to me.

For $1 million.

Be still, my heart.

"Okay?" he said.

"Fine."

"Tell Joaquin we are finding property for his bail."

"It may not be necessary. If he's a Colombian citizen, after extradition he's technically in the United States illegally. That means there'll be an immigration detainer—a hold—on him, which means he's ineligible for bail."

"Passport no problem," he said. "Maybe Joaquin American citizen."

"That's good," I said, although bail was still a long shot, because someone being extradited surely would be deemed a flight risk. "Hopefully, we'll get bail."

"Hopefully?" Jilly said to Natty. "I thought it was certain."

"Please, no talk," Natty said. "Be good girl. Go."

For a moment, Jilly stood there, helpless. Then she left the room.

Natty smiled benevolently. "Beautiful lady, yes?"

"Yes," I said. "About the bail?"

"I know about bail," said Natty. "They didn't want me to have bail, but my lawyer got it for me. You can do the same for Joaquin."

"If it can be done, I will—"

"You can do," Natty said, resuming working the chopstick. Andrey was thumbing his device. Kyril was looking at me. The message was clear: *Say goodbye, Benn.*

"Goodbye," I said.

No one saw me out. I went up the ramp. Jilly was at the window, looking through the telescope. Apparently, my reappearance startled her, because she quickly stepped aside. Averting her face from me, she headed back down the ramp. I watched her descend. Nice. Perfect posture. High breasts; long neck; thick, golden hair. V-shaped torso and perfect, pert ass and those legs . . . I swore to myself that if ever I had another chance with her, I would not pass it up.

Passing the telescope, I paused. I always like a good bird's-eye view and was curious what she'd been looking at. I put my eye to the scope. It was pointed high in the skyline all the way downtown, where it was focused on a building topped with a statue that shone golden in the sunlight.

I recognized the building. It signified nothing to me.

I held the check up to the light and peered at it. It signified the same as a moment ago: made out to me for $1 million.

I pocketed it and left.

CHAPTER 16

As I made my way back to my office, I thought about the Colombian-Russian link. I didn't consider it all that unusual. Colombians produce and deliver their product to others, then step back and wait to get paid. Didn't used to be like that; in the old days, the Colombian DTOs operated vertically, each cartel doing everything from growing to street selling. But they soon learned the streets were too dangerous and sold their vending franchises to lesser criminals. Dominicans, Mexicans, Puerto Ricans, and apparently Russians. Such connections were predictable. Underworlds are conceived in jail.

But forget the *hows*. Concentrate on the *whos*.

After an hour of Internet searching for anything resembling the woman—Jilly, Jillian, sounds like *Shenolt*—I realized my attempts were futile. She was a cipher.

PACER was the official US federal courts database in which all docketed cases could be found. I entered PACER, linked to the Eastern District of New York, and queried *United States of America v. Joaquin Bolivar*. There were only two items on the docket: the indictment, which I already had, and an attorney's notice of appearance entered by the prosecutor, AUSA Kandice Kauffman.

Fuck. More on Ms. Kandi Kauffman later, none of it good.

Again I searched for *Jillian Shenolt* but got nowhere.

I went back into PACER and queried *USA v. Grable*.

I got a hit. According to an indictment, Nathan aka Natty Grable and a dozen-odd codefendants had conspired to defraud American investors in nonexistent gasoline. The amounts were in the tens of millions. Most of the defendants had already pled guilty except for Natty and two others. Judging by the motion practice, the three were well on their way to trial.

Natty was represented by Morton L. Plitkin.

Surprising. I'd disliked Morty Plitkin for many years. He was a shark, but he knew I was a killer whale and made sure to keep a wary distance from me. No way he'd recommended me for a drug case like this, because Plitkin did all the drug work he could scare up. Even more surprising that he hadn't called me in advance to secure the request for a referral fee I was sure would be forthcoming.

I took a closer look at Natty's case. He'd originally been denied bail, but because of a medical issue that could not be properly treated in jail—its specifics redacted from the docket—Natty had been allowed house arrest with exceptions for medical treatment, legal consultations, and religious observance, pending trial.

Natty was as fishy as a Baltic herring. I thought it wise to have some b.g. on him, so I rummaged in my bookcase and found a slim volume titled *Russian Criminal Tattoos*. I skimmed through it until I found a tattoo identical to Natty's. The tat was self-administered by prisoners in the Soviet Gulag, specifically a camp named Murmansk-54.

That got me to wondering which came first: the camp, or the company of the same name. And that in turn got me to wondering whether the check written by Murmansk-54 was any good. And that ended with me wondering how a world-class beauty like Jilly got mixed up with low-class slime like Natty . . .

I reran my memory tape of when she'd introduced herself. So beyond beautiful, her breathy pronunciation of *Shen-olt*. A foreign-sounding name. A romance language: extended, lilting . . .

Shen-olt.

I needed to disassociate. Let my mind wander elsewhere. I opened my device. Last I'd used it was in the air-sketch app, and the face of my ex-wife now appeared. Classic-shaped face, both lips the same width, symmetrical brows above large eyes—

But to hell with her.

What about Jilly?

Shen-olt?

Uttered aloud, the name was vaguely familiar. Someone I know? Knew? No. Someone I knew of? Maybe. Wait, wait, wait . . .

Then I got it.

I'm into old war films. Black-and-whiters I used to watch on obscure cable channels when I was getting high, doing all-nighters. How many times had I made cocaine-fueled love while staring at *Thirty Seconds Over Tokyo*? Or chain-smoked and drank tequila while glued to *Gung Ho!* as a girl or two snored next to me? *God Is My Co-Pilot* was my favorite. The legendary Flying Tigers, P-40 squadrons led by Raymond Massey, playing General Claire Chennault—

I searched for *Jillian Chennault*, and up popped entry after entry on:

MRS. JILLIAN CHENNAULT III

The entries were a series of articles from the same source, the *Ozelle News*. I searched *Ozelle News* and found it was the newspaper serving a small town on the Pacific side of Washington state's Olympic Peninsula. The articles were chronological; the first, four years ago:

A wedding announcement. Groom Sholty Chennault III, CEO of Chennault Industries and son of Mr. Sholty Chennault Jr. (deceased) and Mary Chennault (nee Debevoise) of Palm Beach, Florida. The bride was referred to as Jillian Chennault (nee Randa), but she dominated the photograph. She wasn't platinum then but a natural dark blonde, a Miss America if ever there was one. Alongside her, Sholty was older, bland behind thick eyeglasses.

I sat up straight when I saw the next article. The headline said it all:

SHOLTY CHENNAULT III SLAIN

Entries unspooled like frames in an old black-and-white thriller:

DA SAYS WIFE A PERSON OF INTEREST
Chennault Family Calls Wife Black Widow

More stories about the investigation followed, gradually becoming repetitious, smaller. Then nothing at all until two years ago:

CHENNAULT INVESTIGATION CLOSED
Wife Awarded Inheritance

The prosecutor's announcement was brief, although the Chennault family was more verbose, maintaining that Jillian was the killer. But apparently nothing came of that, because no articles followed. Made sense to me. I couldn't see Jilly as a murderess. Nor could I see her as the wife of Sholty Chennault III. Nor could I see her with the man she'd been with in Panama City, much less with Natty Grable . . .

On the other hand, I could definitely see her with me.

But I was straying off topic. What about my money?

I searched *Murmansk-54 Import, Inc.*

Zilch.

I noodled around variants. Murmansk Export. Murmansk Import/Export. Nothing. I searched Murmansk businesses and firms, but all I found was stuff on Murmansk itself. During the Second World War, it had been the principal Russian port receiving supply convoys from the States. I pulled up a map and located the city of Murmansk, on the

Russian Arctic coast, more west than east by far, right next to Finland, in fact. A port city connected to the Artic Sea by a wide bay and river, ice-bound excepting for a few summer months. What cargo came into Murmansk in the warm months was easily rerouted west to Scandinavia or through the Baltic Sea to the Baltic republics and Eastern Europe.

I was straying again.

I searched for the Swiss bank that had certified the check.

It was a real bank in a Swiss city whose main business was moving money. Which inevitably meant some of the money was dirty. Which was why I had once visited the city in connection with a money-laundering extradition. I remembered gray buildings by a gray lake under a gray sky. Was the check also in a gray area? What if it bounced? Depositing a phony check for one mil reeked of con. I needed to ensure that it was clean.

I went into the US Treasury Department Office of Foreign Assets Control website. OFAC had a Specially Designated Narcotics Traffickers list—aka the Clinton List—and all American citizens, including lawyers, had to obtain an OFAC license before doing business with a listed trafficker. A lot of midlevel nobodies were on the list, and a lot of big traffickers were not. The list was a perfect example of the state of the war against drugs: off center due to its being half-assed.

Murmansk-54 wasn't on the list. Nor was Joaquin Bolivar. Nor Nathan Grable.

I needed to confirm the check was real, but because of the time difference, it was night in Switzerland, and the bank would be closed. Doubtful the gray bankers would tell me anything, anyway.

Okay then. Supposing the check was real?

Then I pocket a million shekels, and it don't matter who's paying. For sure it wasn't Natty Grable. He might go to extraordinary lengths to help his brethren, but who was Joaquin Bolivar to him? Doubtful it was Jilly, despite her inheritance. She had no apparent interest in the case, and I was convinced she couldn't break a plate. On the other hand, she'd referred to "business associates," ostensibly meaning Natty or Bolivar . . . and, more chillingly, she had been suspected of murder.

No big deal. The criminal life was my milieu, and the prospects of my two other would-be Biggies were fading. Besides, this was my year of living dangerously

I shut my computer and left.

After I deposited the Murmansk check at my bank, Val jumped some red lights and I caught the last available seat on the last flight to Miami. By chance, 1-A.

I was on a roll.

I thought.

CHAPTER 17

Fercho was tanned. He'd been rotated into a different SHU cell through whose slit window each day came a short hour of sunlight. He had with him a plastic legal file I'd given him, its cover embossed with my name and number. Prisoners are allowed these, and the inmates take notice of one another's legal representation. Those who respect my guy see my name, and instantly, I become a possible go-to lawyer. Trick of my trade.

Another reason I give my guys files?

To pass things without having to worry about them being read by the correctional snoops. What I do—did—was request the privilege of opening the window between us so that we could better confer. During which conference I took from my files a printed copy of Helmer Quezada's map showing the coordinates of the parasitic-torpedo assembly site. Fercho casually slipped it into his file. Tonight he'd memorize the data, then flush it away, prepared to state the information had originated with him. I'd give another copy of the map to Fercho's DEA case agent, who currently was stationed in Bogotá.

"You're absolutely certain the information is accurate?" I whispered.

Fercho smiled enigmatically. "One hundred thousand bucks certain."

I didn't reply. The subject of buying cooperation? I know nothing.

"How does Rigo like New York?" Fercho asked.

I hadn't realized when Fercho had called my new client a piece of shit that he already knew it was Rigo. Clearly, there was bad blood between my clients. More remarkable was Fercho's up-to-date knowledge of my work. I'd always known the Colombian jail grapevine was rich. I wondered if Fercho had gotten his intel via CORRLINKS, the e-mail correspondence available to federal inmates. Perhaps a prisoner in Manhattan had mentioned Rigo's presence via a CORRLINKS message, and the word had spread to the Miami lockup.

When I didn't respond, Fercho motioned me closer, whispered, "Rigo's trying to cooperate against General Uvalde. I need for you to fuck up his process. Uvalde is mine."

My nod conveyed receiving his message, although I was not acquiescing. Until now, I had no inkling Rigo was trying to give up General Uvalde, but if it was true, then I was being asked to help one client by betraying another. I liked Fercho and had an aversion to Rigo, but no way I'd choose sides. Let the chips fall where they may. Whoever nailed Uvalde got the credit, period.

"Word on the street is that Uvalde sent people to kill Rigo," he said.

I nodded vaguely, though I knew otherwise: it was *Sombra* who'd tried to take out Rigoberto Ordoñez. In addition, Fercho's theory made no sense. DEA wouldn't work with Uvalde if he was putting their agents in the line of fire.

As if reading my mind, Fercho said, "That's just the street. I also heard DEA"—he pronounced the acronym *day-ah*, as Colombians do—"thinks the attack came from another source."

I waited for him to elucidate, but he changed the subject to one I liked more.

"Someone is bringing you a little something for expenses."

Fercho's "little something" was usually fifty large.

When I got out of jail, there was a message on my device from Mondragon: Rigo's family was awaiting my arrival and prepared to pay my fee. Perfect.

I called my bank. The Murmansk-54 check had cleared.

I headed back to the airport, smiling like a cat invited to a canary convention. Rigo had to have many millions stashed away. As did the Natty-Bolivar team. So maybe I was trolling a Biggy after all.

Maybe . . . *two?*

CHAPTER 18

In Bogotá, I slept with the blinds up so I could rise with the sun and get a jump on the day before it jumped on me. Over breakfast, I checked my device. Last night I'd texted Paz to let him know I was in town, taking a long shot he might convince *Sombra* to take a second look at me. But Paz hadn't responded. Nor had Mondragon. And I had other business to attend to.

Today Castri was driving his wife's Chevy compact. Bogotá's monstrous traffic mandated a *pico y placa* system: even-numbered license plates allowed on even-numbered days, odd on odd. Didn't help. The traffic jams—*trancones*—were still curb to curb.

Bogotá wasn't much of a town to look at, but in every direction steeply forested mountains loomed above the city.

Mountains fascinate me.

They're the ultimate physical barrier. It never ceased to amaze me that a handful of Spaniards—many of them Jews the Inquisition had rendered penniless outcasts—had morphed into soldiers of fortune in the service of a nation they despised and a God that wasn't theirs, crossing mountains up and down the long length of both Americas—

A sudden rattle of pebbles against the underside of the little Chevy as Castri swerved onto the road shoulder and accelerated past the *trancon.* He turned into an alley that widened to a street of quiet homes before dead-ending at the high walls of the US Embassy.

The embassy compound is square-blocks huge and ringed with sensors and guard posts. We stopped, and I made a phone call to a DEA agent named Dave, who worked inside. Easier for him to come out than for me to enter. The place was protected by security air locks, and it could take a half hour for a civilian like me to go through.

"Five minutes, Counselor," Dave said.

Dave was a *Zero Dark Thirty* type. Polite, but no bullshit. In exactly five minutes, he appeared. I handed him an envelope containing a copy of the map I'd received from Helmer Quezada. Dave studied it intently.

Across the street a woman was walking a black Lab. Comes to animal husbandry, Colombians are brilliant. Their beloved *vacas* and *paso finos* are tops of their breeds, and their dogs are the finest in the world. The woman's Lab was long legged and heavy boned in the way good Labs are, and as I watched his wagging trot, I felt a pang that my lifestyle did not permit me to have a guy like him. A friend. A pal—

"We'll see what we see," Dave said. "I'll pass the information to Special Ops. For whatever it's worth."

"Seems to me torpedoes are worth a lot."

"Fair to middling is more like it. Just cost two or three thousand to make. What we'd appreciate more are the people who send the torps. Why do I think we might nab a worker or two, but there won't be a *jefe* in sight?"

I one-shouldered a shrug. We both knew the torpedo-factory seizure was a setup, but destroying it would add to DEA's numbers—the drug-war equivalent of Vietnam's body count—and Fercho's AUSA would then add the torpedoes to his cooperation letter, the endgame document, with which I'd argue for a sentence reduction based on quantity, as well as quality, of cooperation.

A siren screamed nearby.

A trio of unmarked vehicles flashing purple lights entered the embassy compound. In the center of the little convoy was a polished

Lincoln with Colombian flags atop the front lights. Through a dark-tinted rear window, I briefly glimpsed the silhouette of a man wearing an oversize officer's hat.

Dave spit on the sidewalk. "General Fucking Uvalde himself. He's being honored today. Jesus. They're making a thief like Uvalde an honorary DEA because of his contribution to the success of Operation *Los Hachos*."

Los Hachos was Rigo's nasty cartel. Uvalde claiming credit for the takedown underlined how big a player Rigo was.

"Really?" I deadpanned. "I didn't know *Los Hachos* were major."

Dave grinned. "Funny, that. How was Antigua?"

I grinned back at him. "Beautiful town."

"Don't yank my chain, bro. And watch your ass. Rigo is on a hit list."

"I learned about that firsthand."

He grinned. "Gus said you nearly pissed your pants."

"Fuck Gus. Do you know whose hit list?"

"If I did, I wouldn't tell you. If you knew why I wouldn't tell you, you'd get into another line of work."

"What's that mean?"

"It means stay well, Benn. Gotta go now. Always nice seeing a man who lives the good life."

"Same here, Dave. I really mean that. See you."

I got back in the car and checked my watch. Almost nine. I was on schedule for my next stop. On the way, I thought about what Dave had said about watching my ass. Worrisome. But although Colombian lawyers often get whacked, I'd never heard of an American lawyer even being targeted.

At 9:30 a.m., Castri dropped me off at a building Colombians call the Bunker, although its proper name was *La Fiscalía de la Nación*, aka the Office of the Attorney General. Fifty percent of Colombian prosecutors were, in my well-informed view, on the take. The other 50 percent spent most of their working hours creating documents that no one read.

When I got to the Bunker, I located a CTI exterior guard named Leonidas, who, for an American fifty-dollar bill, happily deserted his post to assist my bypassing the time-consuming formalities of obtaining the legal pass—*boleta*—required to visit an inmate in a Colombian jail.

While waiting, I looked at the distant peaks. Nothing up there but forested highlands above which condors wheeled. Little wonder *Sombra* chose to live in the mountains.

Hearing a burst of laughter, I turned and saw some lawyers I guessed were American because their shoes weren't square-toed like those favored by Colombian lawyers. Apart from their shoes, American lawyers and Colombian lawyers look the same: guys with fixed grins wanting to bond with well-fixed bad guys.

Too little, too late, boys.

I'd been lucky. When I first went to Colombia, there had been only a few gringos with the cojones to work there. Coke was just becoming the next big thing, and the first-generation kingpins did business like gentlemen—relatively speaking. You could shake a man's hand and be reasonably certain to get all ten fingers back. But no longer. Everyone cheated everyone else. Everyone was game, fair or not. Everyone went down. Everyone ratted.

Fucking time to get out of this business. Fast.

Leonidas returned with my *boleta*, and I left. As I descended the steps, horns blared and brakes screeched, and I looked up and saw Castri's wife's little Chevy cutting across the three-lane roadway. It wasn't like Castri to drive recklessly, and I wondered why as he pulled curbside. As soon as I climbed in, he swerved back into traffic and accelerated.

"What's the rush, Castri?"

"*I'm* in no rush, Doctor. It's the way *you* came from the Bunker."

"What are you talking? I did my business and left, was all."

"You were *running*. Like you were being *chased*."

"Yeah, well," I said. "Take me to jail."

CHAPTER 19

We drove along the ring road atop the mountainsides surrounding the metro area. It was crossing a crazy quilt of centuries. Here, a mile of smooth roadway flanked by new condos. There, a field where trash fires burned and goats grazed. Then a sweeping view of the Bogotá savanna. The ruins of a stone village. Slums and wilderness and luxury. We raced past a horse cart; a Mercedes raced past us. Schoolgirls in pleated plaid skirts walked on the shoulder. At a roadside stand, Indian women wearing derbies cooked arepas over a charcoal fire. I realized that I was going to miss Colombia.

Abruptly, the road descended through switchbacks that leveled out on a plaza dominated by a grand old church. Below its steeple stretched miles of tin-roofed shantytowns. Then we turned into old Candelaria, where I'd first imagined L. Astorquiza dwelled.

Laura.

I'd been so enamored of Jilly the night I'd met Laura I hadn't thought much about the bold blogger. My bad. In retrospect, she remained incredibly attractive. But my attraction to her was more than physical. Our brain waves were tuned on the same length; we shared a mental compatibility—

My stomach lurched as Castri guided the little Chevy through another steep swoop, and then we emerged from Candelaria smack into the heart of swarming south Bogotá. Windowless shops whose goods spilled onto sidewalks. Crippled beggars and peddlers and jugglers at the red lights. Along the Spanish Main, *costenos* smile and laugh a lot. The faces in Bogotá were sour.

Again, my inner voice rose up:

Get out before it's too late.

"Castri," I said.

"Yes, Doctor?"

We were now out of Bogotá proper on a littered suburban highway between bare brown mountains, their spines adorned with makeshift shacks whose tin roofs winked sunlight. Above the road ahead rose a cluster of buildings I knew well.

"Nada," I said.

We turned off the roadway and stopped at a gate beneath a sign that said **Instituto Nacional Penitenciario y Carcelario**—INPEC—the Colombian equivalent to FBOP, the US Federal Bureau of Prisons. The Colombians had caught acronym fever from the gringos.

That wasn't all they aped. INPEC's older prisons resemble medieval dungeons, but its newer prisons were exact copies of American lockups, and not by coincidence. One of the many benefits Colombia receives for being so kind as to allow the United States to conduct the war against drugs on its soil is that American money pays for the construction of Colombian prisons designed by American penologists. This particular jail was *La Picota*, which housed defendants awaiting extradition.

Visiting ended at eleven thirty. I glanced at my watch: 10:30 a.m. Cutting it close. Entering a Colombian jail meant going through half a dozen checkpoints, each requiring stamps and signatures and thumbprints, a process that could literally take hours. But a couple of pesos in the right pockets opened doors, and fifteen minutes later, I was in the visit room.

It was a cavernous space whose raw concrete walls exuded damp-ness. I chose a corner table and sat back to the wall, so as to see the other lawyers and defendants.

There were a lot of both. Now that most everyone cooperates, car-tel personnel turn over quickly, so more and more extraditions occur, and more and more fees are paid to American lawyers, often with the very same Franklins that arrived in Colombia as sold-in-America drug proceeds.

Round and round the money goes, and although much of it sticks to palms along the way, it doesn't matter because the money keeps on coming. A steady stream of money. A river. A Gulf current. You have no idea how much. Actually, no one does, although I had an informed opinion, having moved in drug-money circles for so long. I thought the amount of money was well beyond the highest estimates.

"Dr. Bluestone," a prisoner said.

He was tall and lean with angular, weathered features. I made him about forty. A handsome white devil with a few drops of Native American. Humor in his dark eyes as if he were amused at the absurdity of his situation. A cool customer.

"Joaquin Bolivar," I said.

He sat across from me and spoke in English. "Here, everyone has an alias. I'm called Indio."

"Indio who speaks colloquial American."

His white smile was relaxed. "Grew up in the US of A. Must have made a good impression because they seem determined to get me back."

"Why, Indio?"

"I lived with the Logui."

I nodded. Bored hours leafing through flight magazines had imparted to me many touristic facts, including those about the Logui, the so-called Lost Fifth Tribe of Indians who centuries ago retreated from the invading Spanish to the remote Sierra Nevada de Santa Marta mountains, where it's said they still remain, insulated from the rest of the world.

"Those Who Know More," I said.

He smiled. "I'm impressed. Your religion, Doctor?"

Back in the days when I represented generic American miscreants, at various times I'd professed belief in Jesus, Buddha, and Mohammed. On occasion, I've been an atheist, and once I was a Rainbow Person. Lately, I allow my clients to think I'm Jewish because Colombians believe the Chosen People are super-smart warriors. Similarly, among DTO kingpins, it was in vogue to employ Israeli mercs to train one's own house guard.

I said, "I believe for every drop of rain, a flower falls."

Bolivar laughed. "I'm big on first impressions. I saw you sitting here and knew right away you were going to be my lawyer. I understand you already are, fee-wise?"

"Yes, I've been retained."

"Good. We can dispense with that bullshit. Here's the way it was. Six years ago, I ran a boatload of weed from Cartagena to New York. Or tried to. The load was seized, but me and my crew escaped. A lawyer educated me as to the federal statute of limitations. If there's no indictment within five years of a drug crime, there can't be a prosecution. Right?"

"Right," I said, thinking no way Bolivar was simply running weed: the trip was a test run to learn if the sailboat ploy was a viable route for tons of blow.

"So for five years, I stayed far away from the modern world. I lived in the Sierra Nevada with the Indians. Five years passed, and I wasn't indicted. I believed my problem was over. Only it wasn't. Why?"

Indians? An imitation of the legendary *Sombra*'s life among *los Indios*? A tribute to it? Or was Bolivar dropping a hint that *he* was *Sombra*?

I said, "Because a guy who owed you money from a load way back contacted you. He said he was flush now and wanted to pay the old debt. You'd forgotten about it and didn't need the money, but you thought, why not? Problem was, soon as you agreed to take the money, the old conspiracy came back to life. From a legal standpoint."

"None of this was in my indictment. How'd you know that?"

"Modus operandi of the prosecutor who indicted you in the Eastern District of New York. Loves making historical cases on dealers. Like Maledon said, 'Let no guilty man escape.'"

"Who's Maledon?"

"Doesn't matter. All you need to know is that conspiracies are like zombies. Some stay buried beneath gravestones in the form of statutes of limitations. But lift the gravestone, and the zombie climbs back into the world."

"What do you do when that happens?"

"Pick up a stick and kill it again."

"So then. You'll win my case?"

My nod was noncommittal, but Bolivar let it go at that. A smart guy, I figured, not wanting a lawyer who lies. Also a control freak who'd insist on running the case. For sure, his agenda already included Plans A, B, and a big chunk of the alphabet. In the final analysis, he'd end up cooperating, but only after making a show of fighting the system.

Thirty seconds passed without a word, so I kicked it up a notch. "*If* anyone can beat your case, it's me. *If*, meaning I'm good at what I do."

He looked around the big room. "American lawyers talk to these people as if they're children. Tell them what they believe they want to hear. One of them promised he could get me back to Colombia inside a year. Possible, Doctor?"

"Call me Benn. Impossible."

He nodded. "Who's the prosecutor who indicted me?"

"Her name is Kauffman."

"A woman. Nice looking?"

"There's nothing nice about her." I didn't want to upset Bolivar prematurely, but no point in denying what would soon become obvious. For too many reasons to mention, Kandi Kauffman was the nastiest prosecutor I'd ever dealt with, and very possibly the worst person I'd ever had the misfortune of knowing.

He checked his watch. "Don't want to keep you."

"You're not. I get paid to talk to you."

"I want to make the morning Mass."

"*Mass?* No more forces of nature?"

"I'm no longer among Indians. I'm thick with thieves." His handshake was strong. "Today's a good day. I met my brother from another mother. See you in New York."

Sometimes jails remind me of X-rated movie houses. Filthy but lucrative enterprises. I left *La Picota* dwelling on the links between a Colombian cocaine supplier and a Russian gangland distributor.

As Castri steered the Chevy back to Casa Medina, I went into my device and looked up the native people of the Colombian Sierra Nevadas. The largest remaining tribe, the Logui, didn't worship the usual earth mother or father in heaven, but a living human, The One Who Knows Most of All. I looked up from my phone and considered *Sombra*'s rep as a standup guy for the downtrodden native peoples. It was a nice public-relations gimmick, but Joaquin Bolivar had supposedly been there and done that six years ago.

The crazy thought flashed again: *Maybe Bolivar really was* Sombra.

Nah. Zapata had to be the man. Two good reasons why. First, Paz had auditioned me in front of him. And *Sombra* wouldn't personally be doing something as dumb as a trial coke run in a sailboat. Bolivar either was family to *Sombra* or possessed knowledge enough to get *Sombra* indicted if he flipped.

I closed my device. Time to savor the best part of my job: the getting-out-of-jail-breathing-free-air-and-having-a-drink part.

ALUNE

Today the lawyer appeared. Clearly, he was the right choice. In his world, he is as capable as any. When the moment comes, he will act forcefully, driven by self-preservation and greed.

He is a loner, a peacock, his life a series of episodic survivals.

In all likelihood, he will never realize he's acting on behalf of Those Who Know More in their endless conflict with Those Who Know Less.

One issue remains unresolved. The lawyer's fate. Live or die?

It depends on whether he becomes one of Those Who Know Too Much.

CHAPTER 20

The next morning my knee was sore. I limped the half block from Casa Medina to Harry Sasson, a joint frequented by Bogotá's who's who. Mondragon had said he'd be there to introduce me to Rigo's family, but when I arrived, they weren't there yet.

I'd figured as much and green-lighted Castri to score some referrals by pointing clients my way. With *Sombra* a fading possibility, I was open for business. Castri had friends in low places, and when he put out the word I was in town, they came flocking.

Over an espresso, one lawyer pitched me to take on his client, but the fee didn't even amount to admission to the bleachers of my ballpark.

Over a second cup, another lawyer wanted me to visit his client, who he swore had big bucks, but the guy was locked up in *La Modela*, a horror show of a dungeon where even payola visits take hours of meandering through mazes lined with windowless, cavelike cells from which defendants lying atop old mattresses curse and spit at passersby. Scratch going to that zoo. Just the thought had my leg shaking, although maybe it was the coffee.

Over a third cup, I met with a north-coast DTO boss willing to meet my price to represent one of his lieutenants. The DTO boss made it clear that my mission was to make sure the lieutenant wasn't going to sit on him. I chose not to accept it. No matter what I did, the result would be disastrous. Fight and lose the case, and a year later I'm in appellate court trying to convince the black robes I had prevented the client from flipping to protect the boss. The alternative was for me to actually help the client flip; problem was, if I did that, the boss would make me meat.

"In all respect?" I told the DTO boss. "At the moment, I'm too busy to take on a new case. It wouldn't be right for me to accept a fee for work I don't have time to do properly. Having said that, please know that if you personally find yourself in need of my services, no matter how busy I am, I would make time enough to solve your problem."

The boss liked that. "I've been speaking to a lot of lawyers, but you're the only honest one I've met. If—God forbid—I ever have a problem? You're my lawyer."

I figured the boss would become my client in about a year, for a fee double what I'd have charged for the lieutenant. It was like dealing in futures. Better a bird in the bush than one in the hand.

Over a fourth cup of coffee—I had the caffeine shakes by then, but they felt good—I chatted up a lady lawyer who had a client she wished to refer to me. I'd flirted in passing with this *doctora* but never had had an opportunity to follow through. Now seemed an opportune moment. But before we could set a time and date, the waiter interrupted, handing me an envelope, and said, "A gentleman said to give this to you."

Inside the envelope was a note—typed, not written—from Mondragon saying the meet with Rigo's family had been changed to Medellín. He included an airline and flight number. It left in two hours.

Medellín. City of guns and roses and, for years, the murder capital of the world, reluctantly surrendering the title to San Pedro Sula, Honduras—predictable because so many Medellín killers had relocated there. Dating back to Nacho, I had issues with Medellín. Trepidations about the people I'd facilitated Max to cooperate against. Whenever he'd cooperated successfully, I'd been elated: *Ka-ching! Winner!* Now, looking back, I was ashamed of myself. What was left of my soul was screaming to escape . . .

"I'm so sorry," I told the *doctora*, but something had come up, I had to leave immediately.

"Business is business." Her knowing smile was greedy. I was glad to leave.

It was a beautiful day as Castri started off to the airport, but it was pounding rain when we arrived. The route to Medellín is over the Cordillera Central, peaks even higher than those on the route to Cali, an insanity to attempt a crossing in bad weather. I waited out the rain on an airport bench, where I left reality and entered my device.

The weather in New York was sunny and cold, and the Dow was off three hundred points. I didn't give a shit because I didn't own stocks—*couldn't*—because all my money was in cash. I didn't care about the news, either; it's either bad or worse, so why bother? All I cared about was my own little world.

Laura Astorquiza's blog was now on my reading list as number three with a bullet, almost neck and neck with *Insight Crime* and within striking distance of *Colombia Report*. I scanned the latter without anything catching my interest, then went into *Radio Free Bogotá*, and found this:

> Our nation is in the grip of suspense. The hunt for *Sombra* is a soap opera watched by all. But do not be preoccupied with what transpires next: instead, go back to the past in order to unveil the true mystery. Citizens, ask yourselves how it was possible for *Sombra* to have evaded capture for so long. Better still, ask the question to the man whose job it is to capture *Sombra* . . . a soldier whose modest salary somehow allows him to acquire grand houses and *fincas*. Very soon evidence beyond doubt will emerge, proving General Uvalde is a thief, and a traitor to our nation. Viva Colombia.

Laura, Laura, Laura. You brave, foolish girl. You think you're safe from General Uvalde because you live in Panama. But no one is safe from a man like Uvalde. One word from him, and you become another of the disappeared ones—

Wait a sec . . .

In her previous blog, Laura mentioned Rigo. Now she'd mentioned Uvalde and *Sombra*. All three shared a common denominator: me.

The coincidence factor. Again. Fool me once, even twice, but *three* times?

No. Someone was telling me something. But what?

I had no idea. Nor did I have an iota as to what proof against Uvalde she was referring to.

The PA squawked: My flight was called.

I boarded the aircraft, wondering: *Medellín: guns or roses?*

CHAPTER 21

As I emerged into the terminal, two thugs greeted me. A *gordo* and a *flaco*. They escorted me to a Ford F-150 with oversize tires and a four-door cab. I got in the back with *Gordo*, and *Flaco* climbed behind the wheel.

A third guy was riding shotgun. Hefty, with narrow eyes and prematurely thinning hair. Picture Rigo at twenty-five, and that was him. The same surly manner as his *papi* as well.

"I'm Omar," he said over his shoulder. "You'll answer to me. Clear?"

"Absolutely," I said. "We need to be clear about everything . . . including our business arrangement."

"My family pays its debts, Doctor."

That settled, I sat back and enjoyed the ride. Hot Cali's altitude is lower, and chilly Bogotá's altitude is higher, but Medellín's altitude is midway between, perfect as a California dream.

The airport highway meanders through the high country around Rio Negro, passing estates of the famously rich and secretly wealthy, before dipping toward the sprawling metro area in the bowl-like valley where sprawls Medellín, the heartland of Antioquia, a province whose homeys have *paisa* accents. They consider themselves above their countrymen because—unlike the rest of Colombia, which shares some amount of Indian blood—most Antioquians are of European stock, or get plastic surgery to make them appear so.

I've represented people from every corner of Colombia but never really clicked with the big guys in Medellín, probably because I'd been with Nacho during his war with Pablo Escobar, a sainted figure among the *paisas*.

That was fine with me, because *La Oficina de Envigado*—Envigado being the municipality adjacent to Medellín—produced some of the cruelest killers of the drug wars. When they weren't killing rival cartels, they were killing one another. If I were a wagering man, I wouldn't have bet a peso on my fellow travelers' life expectancies.

Instead of heading toward Medellín, we turned toward Envigado. It was late afternoon, and the sun had fallen behind the mountains when we turned up an unpaved road that wound through a forested hillside. It was dim beneath the trees, but twice I saw men with shotguns and had no doubt there were more of Rigo's *Los Hachos* nearby.

We emerged from the trees to a hilltop compound—a huge main house, several smaller but impressive homes—and an array of stables, all surrounded by lush grass, compared to which the Yankee Stadium infield was a weedy lot. Little wonder, for a small army of landscapers was tending the grounds. Another army of ugly types armed to the teeth prowled everywhere.

The F-150 stopped near the stables. I got out and took a deep breath of fresh air slightly tinged, not unpleasantly, with horse manure. People were gathered at a paddock railing. Omar motioned for me to follow him there.

As we neared the paddock, I heard the rhythmic tattoo of a *paso fino* high stepping atop planks, then saw a fat old man astride a husky little mare huffing and puffing beneath the load.

I swallowed hard.

The fat man was one of the infamous Ordoñez-Ochoa brothers—widely known and feared as the Double-Aughts—who in their heyday partnered with Pablo Escobar and afterward threw in with the North Valley Cartel. Both of which were Nacho's blood enemies. Ordoñez was a fairly common name, but now I was almost certain that my suspicions had been correct:

Rigo Ordoñez was the Rigo among Nacho's killers.

The old man's eyes—narrow, like Rigo's and Omar's—cut to me, and I wondered if he knew I'd been tight with his old archenemy, Nacho. That worry spawned another:

Had Mondragon enticed me here so the Ordoñez could settle old scores?

But I was thinking like a conspiracy wing nut, because these people don't kill where they live, and among the people at the railing stood a woman Omar offhandedly introduced as his mother.

"Sandra Milena," she said pleasantly, offering her jeweled hand. She was a handsome woman of a certain age who in her younger days probably looked much like her husband's current squeeze, Stefania. "How is my husband, Doctor?"

"Well," I said. "He sends his best regards."

"How do you see my father's case?" Omar asked.

Before I could reply, Mondragon appeared between us. "Dr. Bluestone is already making progress. The prosecutor is very pleased with the *lanchas*."

Lanchas, also known as go-fast boats, are big, super-powered speedboats that, even loaded with thousands of kilos of *cocaína*, can easily outrun Coast Guard cutters. So Mondragon's pre-extradition dealings for Ordoñez with the government were about information leading to *lancha* seizures. Probably what AUSA Barnett Robinson had been alluding to when he said the government was checking out previously supplied information.

"I was asking Dr. Bluestone, not you," Omar said to Mondragon.

Clearly Omar didn't like Mondragon. Probably not me, either.

"It is my understanding things are going well," I said blandly.

"Results," Omar said. "You've been paid. Where are the results?"

"Paid?" I said. "I received a small deposit for my expenses."

Omar frowned, but Mondragon was unruffled. "There was a difficulty paying cash in New York. But I have Dr. Bluestone's money with me."

He crooked a finger for me to follow him, and we walked to a parked Mercedes. He popped the trunk. A large suitcase lay inside. He opened it to reveal banded bricks of brightly colored Colombian currency: hundred-thousand-peso notes—each worth about fifty bucks—so the suitcase held the rough equivalent of $1 million US currency.

"Your fee," Mondragon said. "Not to worry about carrying it safely. Omar's people will accompany you to Bogotá."

I wasn't worried about the trip to Bogotá, rather how I'd get the suitcase into the States. Even if I was crazy enough to try to carry it through customs, and even if I tried and succeeded, no way I could explain the amount to a currency exchange. Surely, Mondragon knew all this, and it pissed me off that he was making an offer I had to refuse.

"Of course," he said, "if you wait a little longer, we can arrange payment in New York."

"How much is a little longer?" I said.

He shrugged. "A week. Two at most."

Omar had followed us. "Acceptable, Doctor?"

"No more than two weeks," I said.

"Results," Omar said, stalking off.

"When you return to the United States, the major cooperation begins," Mondragon said to me. "Give this to Mr. Robinson, Doctor." He handed me a small object: a thumb-size flash drive.

"What's in it?"

"I'm sure you'll see for yourself," Mondragon said. "Well, then, you should be off. You've got business to attend to."

I bade the family farewell from a distance. Sandra Milena put up a hand, and Omar nodded solemnly. Old man Ochoa glanced an acknowledgment.

Descending from the compound in the twilight, the bright grid of Envigado shone below, and beyond that Medellín, and beyond Medellín, dark against a purple sky, were tall mountains, mysterious as ever.

But another mystery now had my full attention:

The contents of the thumb drive.

CHAPTER 22

Once in my hotel room, I double locked the door and pressed the "Do Not Disturb" light. From the bar I took vodka minis and lined them atop the writing desk. I opened one but did not drink because I wanted to be clear about what I was about to see. The minis were for post-viewing because I had the uneasy feeling I was about to shock my nervous system with a secret revelation. A mass execution of captive combatants? A tortured confessional?

I inserted the thumb drive into my device.

It was a video, all right. A nondescript room. A shaded window and two men at a table. I knew one and knew of the other. Rigoberto Ordoñez and General Uvalde.

They didn't speak and didn't have to.

Obviously, the subject of their meeting was the opened suitcase between them. It was not unlike the one Mondragon had shown me at the *finca*, crammed to the brim with money.

Rigo closed the suitcase.

He moved it to Uvalde.

They shook hands.

Cut to black.

I swallowed hard. If Uvalde learned I possessed this evidence against him, I was fried. I ejected the drive and dropped it into my breast pocket. Best to keep it close, so if push came to shove, I could swallow it. I was furious and frightened. Rigo was putting me in harm's way while playing games with my fee. Insult and injury. And once I turned the evidence over, Rigo was well on his way toward a cooperation agreement for which I would no longer have the leverage to collect my fee.

Additionally, Fercho would be screwed out of nailing Uvalde, and in turn I'd be screwed out of Fercho's bonus. No way I could give the evidence to Fercho, but just maybe Fercho could, ah . . . piggyback on it.

Hmmm.

A free ride. Why not? I tell Fercho about the video—not that I have it, only that I saw it—and Fercho then tells the INB chief he personally observed Rigo bribe Uvalde . . . in fact, he himself had shot the video. After Fercho conveyed that tidbit, I'd give the evidence to Barnett Robinson on Rigo's behalf *after* he paid me. Ergo, Rigo gets his deal, and Fercho gets cooperation corroboration brownie points.

Not bad. It could work . . .

No. It wouldn't fly.

The geniuses in the SDNY attorney's office wouldn't buy it. I could picture their eyes rolling over Benn Bluestone's miraculous coincidence. Two for the price of one.

Find another way.

At the very least, I had to tell Fercho that Rigo had beaten him to the punch. Of course, it was unethical for me to tell him, but I owed the guy that much . . .

But did I really?

Fercho wasn't my blood, or my friend. I owed him honest work for his money, but no more than that. My first commandment was "Thou shalt not cross lines," aka "Step on a crack, break your back." So fuck Rigo and Fercho. Fuck them all. I uncapped a mini.

Drank it in one swallow.

Had another . . .

The last thing I recall before passing out was leaving a message for Sonia to book me on the morning flight to Miami.

CHAPTER 23

An hour after touching down in Miami, I was in a doctor's office—a medical doctor, not a lawyer. His practice was concierge: no insurance, all cash. He was a tax gonif. Not that I didn't live in the same glass house. Anyway, Doc Concierge was well worth it: no waiting time, and scripts for all the Valium I desired.

He usually dispensed the script by phone, but I saw him sporadically, whenever my problem trio acted up: knee, back, hip. All three were barking now, ever since I'd stumbled approaching the man who might be *Sombra*.

Self-inflicted wounds. Story of my life. Years ago, while playing hide-the-blow from my then-wife, I'd torn a meniscus retrieving a gram that rolled beneath a couch. Arthroscopic helped, but over time the knee became wobbly, and one bone rubbed another until my hip was declared replaceable—which I'd been putting off for years. Favoring the hip led to lumbar problems, which also require surgery—which I'd likewise avoided.

My temporary solution was steroid injections that alleviated pain. Until they wore off. Which was when I saw Doc Concierge. I'd asked if it were true that too many steroid boosts could have serious consequences.

He'd inserted a hypodermic into my knee and said, "Life has serious consequences. We start aging the moment we're born, and eventually, we circle the drain and disappear. If it's not steroids that do you in, something else will. So stop worrying and enjoy."

This time he said, "Something serious we need to discuss."

Serious? Not good, coming from my doctor.

"My fee has increased," he said. "Doubled."

"No problem. So long as I feel better."

"For now," he said. "But no one gets out alive."

With those words ringing, I went to seek sex. My mission was soon accomplished, but it felt far from satisfying. I didn't know how my sex partner felt because I left her place immediately afterward.

I kept a hidey-hole in my Miami pad. I emptied it—two hundred thou, exactly the number I owed Foto for the Bolivar referral. Then I bought a throwaway phone, dialed a certain number, and made arrangements to be at a certain place. The scenario was a dead drop. After it went down, I texted Foto a question mark. He replied with a smiley face.

Then I went to visit Fercho.

For whatever reason, the powers that be had released Fercho from the SHU into general population. While I was waiting for him to come down, a drug lawyer named Dreidel paused at my table.

"Been down south lately?" he asked.

I bit my lip to keep from telling him to mind his own business. Dreidel was a kiss-up, kick-down type who had spent most of his working life as an AUSA. He had been a two-faced prick as a prosecutor and as a defense lawyer was a prick of many faces. But he was a lucky prick. His turnaround from cops to robbers gained him publicity he amplified doing media interviews about how he'd jumped the ship of state because he could no longer bear the human tragedy bobbing in its wake. Despite the fact that he'd been a top-ten-most-cruel inquisitor, the sanctimonious jerk actually picked up a few extradition cases.

"How you doing with Rigo?" he asked when I didn't answer.

The bad aspect of PACER was that it was easy for lawyers to know what their legal brethren were doing. I shot him a look that meant *buzz off*. But instead he buzzed closer.

"Reason I'm mentioning it?" he said. "I got a nibble about representing a *Los Hachos* guy."

My gut churned, but I kept a poker face. If Dreidel were talking truth, then Rigo's DTO was seeking other counsel, and they really were playing games with my fee.

I spotted Fercho and blew Dreidel off.

Fercho sat. "I don't like that lawyer."

"He says one of Rigo's people contacted him."

Fercho nodded. "Word is that there's problems in *Los Hachos*. General Uvalde's on the hunt, and people are scattering."

I recalled what Dave the DEA agent had told me outside the embassy in Bogotá: that Uvalde had decimated Rigo's DTO to prove his cojones with the Americans. Undoubtedly, it was a double score for the general: getting praised by the gringos and paid for the operation by Rigo's enemies to boot. Were the enemies Fercho's people? Maybe.

"Aldo the Barracuda?" said Fercho. "He met with *Sombra*."

The thought that an inept lawyer like Aldo had stolen my Biggy hurt.

But wait. Fercho's knowing look was a reveal: he knew I'd been flirting with *Sombra*. But how? That couldn't have been on the grapevine. Could it have?

I shrugged. "I hear the man's met with lots of lawyers."

"Aldo's saying *Sombra* is his. Don't worry. You still got a shot at *Sombra*."

I looked at him, waiting for more.

"Just saying," he said. "Another thing. It's strange Mondragon put you into Rigo's case, since he works with the Cuban lawyers. The other day, he came with Aldo to see a client."

"They've done lots of cases together. Maybe it was one from back when."

"No. The guy they came to see was just now extradited."

That reopened the question of why Mondragon had referred Rigo to me rather than to one of his usual cronies. Another reason to believe I was getting screwed.

"I gave the DEA the parasitic-torpedo coordinates," I said.

"Good," said Fercho. "What's up otherwise?"

I figured *otherwise* meant Uvalde. I wondered if somehow Fercho knew about Rigo giving up Uvalde. Yet Fercho's expression was as guileless as a choirboy's.

I'm a snoopy kind of guy. My business is other people's secrets. Come to Fercho, though, it was give-and-take. So I fed him a morsel. "There's a video of Uvalde being bribed by Rigo."

Got him! His eyes had narrowed. "You have this video?"

"Mondragon is relaying it to the government. It goes without saying, you didn't hear this from me."

"Who's on the video?"

"Just them."

"Interesting."

"You're not disappointed Rigo beat you to Uvalde?"

"What can you do? Where did the bribe take place?"

"A hotel room, far as I could see."

"That's your trouble, Benn."

"What is?"

"How far you see."

CHAPTER 24

When I got back to New York, I phoned Barnett Robinson and told him about the video.

"Sounds good," he said. "Gus Romero mentioned Rigo was working on something along those lines. When do I see it?"

"I'm e-mailing it as we speak."

"Thank you, Benn."

I thought Robinson seemed rather cavalier given the seriousness of the subject matter. I e-mailed him the video, expecting a quick response. But the week passed, and he didn't call. Nor did I get a visit from Mr. Green, so I visited Rigo.

Instead of coming down to the visit room, he sent a message that he wasn't feeling well. Avoidance was a bad sign. I tried calling Mondragon but got a recorded voice saying his mailbox was full.

I received notice that Joaquin Bolivar had a reserved seat on the next extradition flight from Bogotá. That lifted my spirits. Action at last. Just for a change of pace, instead of going from my pad to my office along Madison, I walked down Fifth Avenue.

Beyond the bare treetops on the far side of Central Park, a tall building glinted in the sun like a needle—the Kursk Needle—which got me thinking of Jilly again.

As I lowered my gaze from the Needle, I noticed a pretty young woman on the other side of Fifth. She stood there, either waiting to cross or waiting for a taxi. She seemed familiar. After a moment, I realized she was Rigo's paramour, Stefania. I wondered what she was doing in New York—

A man came up behind her. He was small, slightly shorter than she. *Enano?* Before I could process that thought, he'd put an arm around her. They stood like that a moment and then he lowered her to the sidewalk, snatched her shoulder bag, and quick-walked away.

A lot of people were passing, but none noticed, or at least none wanted to notice. Then a woman screamed, and all at once people rushed to Stefania. A pool of blood spread from beneath her throat: her face was ashen, eyes staring.

I felt an urge to join the crowd but knew she was beyond help. And why put myself on a witness stand? I went to my office and poured myself a stiff one, the liquor tamping down my shock and allowing my mind's gears to mesh.

Enano, *Sombra's* *sicario*, who had tried and failed to murder Rigo in Antigua, had just murdered Stefania. This was in keeping with *Sombra's* vendetta against Rigo. But something troubled me: *Enano* had also taken Stefania's bag. Why? What was in it?

Forget that for now. More importantly: Why had Stefania been on Fifth? On her way to see me? Or on her way to the Kursk Needle?

Ping!

A CORRLINKS message: Rigo complaining that he wasn't receiving medical attention. Poor Rigo. The whining pig who'd dragged a girl into the bloody chaos of his existence wasn't feeling well. But for the sake of maintaining a paper trail, I e-mailed the jail and requested Rigo be examined.

The jail didn't reply. Figured. So I went to see Rigo. Again, I was told Rigo was too sick to see me. I tried reaching out to Mondragon. Another useless exercise.

A few days later, Barnett Robinson called. He was ready to proffer Rigo. We set the date for the following week. I figured by then Rigo would be okay. I was done trying to reason with him. Let the hardhead walk into a proffer cold without my prepping him; he'd emerge worrying that he'd get no cooperation agreement at all.

As if summoned by my uncharitable thoughts, a Mr. Green visited, lugging many bricks of US currency—at a glance, enough to pay all or most of Rigo's fee.

"Dr. Mondragon sends regards," Mr. Green said.

When he was gone, I bent to inspect my treasure—

"Oh my God," a woman said.

Mr. Green hadn't closed the office door properly. It had swung partially open. My neighbor, the fine-art dealer Gracie Loeb, was staring . . .

At me. On my hands and knees. As if worshiping a pile of money.

I mumbled something about nothing and closed the door securely. Then went back to the suitcase and—

Damn! The money was small bills. Fives and tens in $5,000 bricks. Ten lousy bricks of filthy street lucre. Fifty thou. I was still short nine hundred grand. I tried calling Mondragon. He was not available.

I simmered. They want to play games? Fine. Soon enough the case would heat up—*What do we do now, Doctor?*—and I'd leverage the answer to get my fee.

I hid ten in the steel safe set in a faux supporting column, then went home and stashed ten in the safe faced like a wall oven, then deposited twenty in my legal account.

I noted the transactions in PARANOID.FLOYD, then lingered over the bottom-line numbers. Not counting the Miami condo, I figured I was worth about three mil. I would neither starve nor run out my days idly rich. But I'd need a lot more to live in the style I was accustomed to.

I'd whiffed on *Sombra*, but I'd score a Biggy. I had to. One way or another. Aboveboard was fine. Below board was no problem. Catch me if you can. I'm a survivor. All these years, and I'm still standing.

Little did I know I was about to be floored.

CHAPTER 25

I was in my office when the street bell rang. Anticipating my lunch delivery, I buzzed the visitor in. A minute later, a knock came at my door. I opened the door.

A woman stood there. I knew her well. *Very* well. She was the woman whose face I'd sketched on the flight from Puerto Rico.

The same woman I'd watched throwing water at midnight on New Year's Eve in Viejo San Juan; the same woman I'd watched hug a handsome, silver-haired man.

The same woman named Madaleina Andaluz, before and after she was Mrs. Bennjamin T. Bluestone. My ex-wife.

"Hello, Benn."

"Hello, Mady."

My voice sounded far away. Maybe because it was lost beneath the strings of my heart, zinging. For those who can't read electrocardiographs, here's what Mady looks like:

Large eyes, strong nose, wide lips, firm jaw. One-of-a-kind impossibly gorgeous: slender yet full-bodied, perfect butt, long legs. Light-olive skin, light-brown eyes, light-brown hair with an undertone of auburn. Her habit was to let her hair hang free, but when working, she pinned it up. She had it pinned up now.

"Please, sit," I said, pointing at a chair near mine.

She sat but on the other side of my desk. She wore a wildly over-priced cashmere coat I'd bought for her during a weekend in Paris. "No matter what," I said, "we'll always have Paris."

Her smile was pure sunshine. "It's the only warm coat I own. This is the first time I've been out of Puerto Rico in years."

It occurred to me that Mady had seen me skulking on New Year's Eve. So, in addition to being back in her sight, apparently I was also back in her mind. Be still my heart.

"You were there over the holidays," she said. "You should have called."

"I didn't want to intrude. I saw you had, ah, company . . ."

She looked puzzled. "You *saw* me? I didn't see you. Diego told me you were there."

Diego? Ah, right. The Convento bellhop had seen me after all. "So, how's it going?" I asked, lamely.

"Really great. You?"

"Couldn't be better."

She looked around, as if doubting this. Made sense. Last I'd seen Mady, I was in my old Midtown offices, a plush suite populated by my employees. I said, "Big change, but for the better. I'm no longer in the defense-lawyer business, at least not the way I was."

"I was wondering about that. The sign downstairs says 'Extraditions.' Meaning?"

I wanted her to know the things that had kept us apart were no more. "I only do two or three cases a year. One of them pays as much as I made in a year, back when I worked nights and weekends."

"I'm glad for you, Benn."

"Not only are my hours normal; I've crossed the aisle and enlisted in Team America. I'm with the good guys now. What I mean . . . I've come to see the error of my ways, so to speak. Morality-wise. The thing is, you were right, and I was wrong."

Mady simply nodded. She always was a cool reactor, one of her many qualities I'd loved so much for so long.

"What I'm trying to say," I said, "is that I'm no longer living and breathing ways to beat the system. I work with the agents and prosecutors now, not against them. And you know what?"

"What?"

"I sleep better knowing I'm on the right side of the law."

"Sort of like what you tried to do with Max."

"Exactly."

"I'm glad you've found your way, Benn."

Right back into your loving arms, baby, I wanted to say but didn't. Better not to come on too strong. Better that Mady come to me in her own good time.

"Benn, I've been thinking . . ."

I nodded sympathetically, realizing it must be hard on Mady, humbling herself by coming to me. From her bag, she took a paper and set it on my desk.

A legal document. A quitclaim deed conveying the house I'd seen her emerge from on New Year's Eve. I looked at the deed, remembering the night we met.

We'd walked the cobblestoned streets of Viejo San Juan for hours, holding hands, nuzzling, talking. At two in the morning, with the city dark beneath a crescent moon that shone like a silver blade above the black bay, we sat on the ramparts of the city wall. Behind us stood a lovely old house, one that since she was a little girl she'd wanted to live in. *Casita Azul,* she called it: Little Blue House.

The next day, I bought the house from its reluctant-to-sell owner, price be damned. How I loved making Mady happy. We weren't married yet, so I put the house in my name so I could write it off as a business expense for doing cases in PR. We shared some wonderful times there, and when things turned not-so-good, Mady lived there alone. When we divorced, I was tailspinning into one of my nutty periods, and to avoid confrontations, I gave her everything in both our names I hadn't yet depleted: what was left of the bank accounts, stock, and art.

I meant for her to have *Casita Azul* as well, but I was in dire need of deductions to minimize my taxes. I thought when my tax liabilities stabilized, I'd sign the house over to her. But the next year I put it off, and by the following year, I deemed it unimportant. Mady'd said she wanted to live in *Casita Azul* for the rest of her life, and since I had no desire to live there, or sell the place, I left her my share in my will, so it would be her home forever.

"Please sign," she said. "I want to fly home today."

"Today?" I said. "Why?"

"I can't afford a hotel."

"You can stay with me—"

"Don't go there, Benn."

"A hotel, then. I'll get you a suite. Stay as long as you like. Just like I have, the city's changed, for the better. I'll show you around. We'll go shopping. We always had fun shopping, remember?"

"Thank you, Benn. But I really can't stay. I just want you to sign the deed and leave. Please do it now."

"Why now?"

"Why do you need to know why?"

"I don't need to know. I'm just asking."

"Fair enough. Why now? Because I want *my* house in *my* name. As I recall, our divorce provided for me to get everything, which wasn't much, by the way. I believe *Casita Azul* fits within the definition of *everything*."

"Actually, everything in *both* our names was to go to you. *Casita Azul* was in my name. It doesn't fit the definition."

"You're saying it wasn't clear *Casita Azul* was to be mine alone?"

"It was clear. All I'm saying is, it's still in my name. You want to discuss my transferring it, fine. I'm just curious as to why now, after so long."

"Please don't try to control the situation. Keep it simple. If you're willing to sign, do it now. If not, say so."

"Is this about the house, or are you here because you wanted to see me? If that's what it is, I want you to know something. Ever since you left, I think about you every single day."

"Honestly, Benn, I just came about the house. Not to discuss our history, or how you've become one of the good guys. But, if you must know? Why *now* is because I didn't learn that *Casita Azul* wasn't in my name until now. Okay? So, let's get it done."

She stood and came around my desk and snatched my pen and put it to the deed, making a small *x* alongside the conveying party's signature line. Then she thrust the pen into my hand.

"Sign, Benn."

I looked at her long, smooth fingers, avoiding her eyes. No matter the jerk I'd been—I wasn't in denial—when it came to money and material things, I'd always been true. All she had to do was ask nicely, and I was butter. But no, that temper of hers, always explosive, always shoving things down my throat.

"Say please," I said.

"What did you say?"

"I said, say please."

Her nostrils flared. "You haven't changed at all. You're as pigheaded and arrogant as ever. There's still nothing but money on your mind, and blood on your hands."

"Blood? That's not true. I'm *helping* the government—"

"The only one you ever help is yourself. Sign."

"No."

Her eyes flashed. *"Do it."*

"You still haven't said please."

Someone knocked at my door.

"Tell them to wait," she said.

"Come in," I called.

Mady snatched up the deed and started out as the guy delivering my lunch entered. She smacked into him, and the delivery went flying.

I heard her heels hurriedly clicking down the stairs.

Then the echoed clang of the street door, closing.

I stood at the window and watched her cross the street, her hair undone now and blowing in the wind. She reached the corner of Madison and was gone.

I ran a sleeve across my teary eyes. Something small and white lay on my desk. A grain of rice. I looked at it stupidly, then said, "Supposed to throw rice when you get married, not when . . ." My voice broke.

"I'm so sorry, boss," the delivery guy said, looking at my lunch, which had exploded all over the office.

Something red and white lay amid the mess of curried rice: a white napkin with a red heart. It was Valentine's Day.

"Me, too." I picked more rice from my hair. "Me, too."

CHAPTER 26

That night I drank to numb myself. Deep down, I'd always nurtured a spark of hope that Mady and I might someday get back together. Now that slight ember was extinguished, replaced by an alcoholic resolve.

Fuck it. I was meant to fly solo.

And in my style. If I wanted a woman, there was plenty of love for sale. Plenty of the best of everything money could buy. And since I had expensive taste, time to get serious about business.

First, Rigo.

Tomorrow, he was proffering. The cheap bastard thought he'd played me perfectly: the video nailing General Uvalde would surely lead to a cooperation plea, so he didn't need to pay a million-dollar lawyer. Wrong. Robinson was a pro who knew to keep cooperators on edge. Rigo could give him a dozen videos, and Robinson would tell him he still needed to vomit up more. There would be a tense moment in which I'd deliver my ultimatum: pay me in full right now, or I'm history . . .

Maybe he really was ill. If so, I hoped his last days were painful. *Fuck you, Rigo. Here's to you, Nacho. RIP.*

I shifted focus to Bolivar. Nothing to ponder there.

So I daydreamed about *Sombra* . . . Zapata.

A criminal genius but a moron in real life. Thickheaded as a cigar-store Indian. Imagine not seeing the difference between a half-Jew New

York mouthpiece and a Miami Cuban lawyer who lights candles on the anniversary of the Mariel boatlift. But given the opportunity, I'd teach *Sombra* the difference.

I drank to that.

Besides, who needed *Sombra*, anyway? There's were plenny of fish in the sea. It was just a, ah . . . quesshun of getting the fish to, shwim . . . *walk* . . . wish me.

The next morning, my head hurting but clear, I arrived at the proffer my usual five minutes late. As per standard procedure, AUSA Barnett Robinson suggested Rigo and I review the proffer ground rules privately beforehand.

When Rigo and I were alone, he seemed to crumple. "Doctor, a terrible thing happened."

I didn't reply. No way was I going to bear witness to Stefania's murder. Far as I knew, Stefania was on a beach taking selfies while getting a pedicure.

"I've been poisoned," he said.

It was true that Rigo appeared sallow and bloated, but I doubted he'd been poisoned. More likely jail food and stress, the deadliest of combinations. Once-powerful men in jail are prone to conspiracy theories. I hedged a response that I'd do the best I could to help him, but I doubted anything would come of my request, because BOP sets the go-to-doctor bar high—in the vicinity of plague and other near-death aliments.

"I'll get you a doctor visit."

"When?"

"Today. Soon as you pay me."

"Mondragon—"

"Wipe your eyes and listen up. Today's proffer has rules—"

"I already know them. I know you think me a stupid man, Doctor, but I studied the rules before I was extradited. Lucky I even made it here, after the piece of shit Mondragon set me up."

So I'd been right about Mondragon's involvement in the attempted hit. He was working for *Sombra*, then. But why had Mondragon referred me Rigo—

Then I got it.

Mondragon wanted to taint me with *Sombra* by having me represent *Sombra*'s enemy, Rigo. That way, Mondragon nudges *Sombra* into hiring one of his Miami Cuban lawyers.

"Mondragon tried to kill you," I said. "But you kept him as your lawyer. Why?"

"None of your business."

"Why did you let Mondragon recommend me?"

"If you must know, I wanted him to think I was doing as he said. I keep my enemies close. Forget Mondragon. We need to discuss—"

"My fee."

"Repeating yourself. Trying to get paid twice?"

"What? You owe me nine hundred thousand."

Color patched his neck. "Mondragon, he—"

I grabbed a fistful of his shirt collar and spat words like nails into his face. "You killed Nacho Barrera's family."

"No, I was against that. Others—"

"Pay me, or you'll rot here, you son of a bitch."

Rigo forced a smile. His teeth were pegged and yellow, like those of a jaundiced child. "I will authorize your fee immediately, but you better do right by me. Now let's talk importance. You received the video?"

"Yes."

"You gave it to the prosecutor?"

"Yes."

"What did he say?"

"Nothing, yet."

"That's normal?"

"There is no normal."

"Do your job properly, and you really will be paid twice. We don't like one another, but we can still do business. You watched the video?"

"Yes."

"It's good, me giving them Uvalde, yes?"

"It's very good."

"Uvalde is nothing," he said. "I am going to give them *Sombra*."

I didn't respond, but my suspicions were correct: Mondragon had sabotaged me out of the *Sombra* sweepstakes by handing me Rigo's case. For if Rigo cooperated against *Sombra*, I was automatically conflicted from representing the mythic kingpin. Not that it mattered, now that *Sombra* had passed on me.

"*Sombra*'s on the video," he said.

Was Rigo a whack job? Or was he saying that *he* was *Sombra*? Or that Uvalde was? These possibilities were off the charts.

Or were they?

Why couldn't Rigo be *Sombra*? In the alternative, Uvalde made for a perfect Mr. Big, one who deflects heat by creating a legend called *Sombra*.

"I am ready to proffer," said Rigo.

CHAPTER 27

Rigo nodded impatiently as Barnett Robinson introduced himself and the rules of engagement. "Do you understand everything?"

"I understand everything," Rigo said. "Did my lawyer explain that I require medical attention?"

"He did. We're going to request you be examined. Anything else before we begin? Gus? Benn? All right, let's do it."

"Okay," Gus said, "how'd you learn about the *lanchas*?"

"From persons I sent my lawyer to," said Rigo. "Everything my lawyer did was at my direction."

Robinson said, "This is your Colombian lawyer, Mr. Mondragon?"

Rigo nodded. "Him. He paid no one for information, just as I instructed."

Rigo's spiel was so textbook, it was a joke: no one was being paid for information; all cooperation was from his personal knowledge; whoever assisted him did so at his instruction. Not that anyone was laughing.

The opposite. They were working. Forget probing Rigo's ways and means, Robinson was on his device, Gus on a keyboard. The drug war had been lost for so long that even the good guys go along to get along.

"Your information resulted in the seizure of two *lanchas*," Robinson said.

"Twenty-four hundred kilos, Rigo," Gus said. "Thirty percent pure. Worthless crap."

Rigo blinked rapidly. "I have no way of knowing the quality—"

"You're lying, you dumb, fucking asshole," Gus said. "The loads were deliberately diluted to save money because you created them."

Rigo shook his head. "The shipments were not mine."

"Well, then," said Robinson. "Whose were they?"

Rigo sat up straight. This was the moment he'd been waiting for. He flashed his pegged-tooth smile and said, *Sombra.*

Gus exchanged looks with Robinson.

"The video your lawyer provided?" Robinson said. "When did you meet with General Uvalde?"

"About four years ago."

Gus said, "Where?"

"In the mountains."

Robinson said, "Only one meeting?"

"Yes."

Gus said, "The videotape is brief."

"Such meetings are brief."

Robinson said, "Who else was present?"

"The video speaks for itself," Rigo said.

"The audio's erased," Gus said. "What was said? By whom to whom?"

Rigo nodded. "In return for this information, I expect to be freed from jail and allowed to stay in this country."

"You're in no position to bargain, sir." Robinson looked at me. "You may want to talk to your client, Benn."

Robinson and Gus left the room. I shook my head.

"What? What do they want you to tell me, Doctor?"

"That you're a fucking moron who doesn't understand you're in no position to bargain. Don't play games with these people."

"Not games. Strategy."

"Strategy? You need some advice about strategy. Pay me, and I'll show you the way to go home. Right now, before you lie your way into a hole too deep to climb out of."

"Ask them if they liked what they saw. Tell them soon I will show them things they will like even more."

That made me pause. Maybe it explained Rigo's strange remark about *Sombra* being on the video. Could the video Mondragon gave be a truncated version?

"I know how to deal with government people," Rigo said. "Feed them a little bit at a time so they stay hungry."

When I emerged from the proffer, I had a new voice-mail message.

"Passing through, saying hello. Later," said Laura Astorquiza.

CHAPTER 28

I thought a lot about Laura. She hadn't been blogging lately, but that wasn't the reason. It was sex. I wanted to have and to hold her. She was a vixen, and I was a fox in heat. Been too long since I burrowed into a warm den. But Laura had passed by, and no one else caught my eye.

Female-wise, the times couldn't have been worse. Until they were.

I was telephoned by a woman who spoke in whiney up-talk—*Like, everything's a question?*—compounded by an unpleasant Long Island accent.

"Mr. Bluestone? AUSA Kandice Kauffman?" she said formally, although we'd been knowingly disrespecting each other for years. "Your client, Joaquin Bolivar?"

She paused for my reaction, so I deliberately kept silent.

Indefatigable, she continued. "The presentment is tomorrow, at ten?"

"What judge?"

"Trieant."

Two five-hundred-pound safes had just fallen on two heads—Bolivar's and mine—in the forms of AUSA Kauffman and Judge Charleton Trieant, the man for whom a word had been coined: *curmudgeon.* This was seriously bad news. At the same time, it was a familiar good feeling. I was up for a fight.

"I assume your client wishes to cooperate," she said.

Assume? Bile rose in my throat. Kauffman—or Kandi, as everyone calls her, although there's nothing sweet or girlish about her—was an unethical bully in the pulpit of the US Attorney's Brooklyn office of the Eastern District of New York. I despised Kandi for many reasons, but my deepest anger was irrational: her presence desecrated Brooklyn, my hometown, where Flatbushers of my generation spoke about *dis* and *dat*.

"Don't assume nuttin'," I said.

"What?"

"I said—"

"I know what you said. You have a responsibility to discuss cooperation with your client."

"Thanks for the free ethics. You're going to like my client. I bet you're salivating over his mug shot."

"You're a pig, Bluestone. If your client chooses not to cooperate, I'm leaning toward a superseding indictment, charging a crime far more serious than marijuana importation."

I wasn't concerned. Kandi's modus operandi included empty threats. Still, another charge was possible. "That crime being?"

"Like, the real motive for his marijuana-smuggling operation?"

I felt a pang of headache behind my eyes. Kandi knew the weed run was a cover to map out a coke route. *I assume your client wishes to cooperate.* The witch was right. Bolivar would opt to preserve his ass by netting old pals in old conspiracies. The only thing to do in these cases. Why bet your life at trial when you can do a couple of years by cooperating? Cooperation was fine for lawyers as well, being a tenth the work of trial . . . and yet, I missed trying cases. The joys of victory and agonies of defeat and all that jazz. I'd like to try another case before I'm out of the business. Against Kandi.

Like, it would be fun?

"Still there, Bluestone?"

"No, I'm on Mars."

She hung up.

CHAPTER 29

The next morning Val drove me south along the FDR. Natty's phone was off, and Jilly's disconnected. So much for Bolivar's bail package. The day was clear and cold, the Manhattan skyline like Alps against the blue sky.

Mountains.

For a moment, I recalled the sulfurous reek of Antigua's volcanic air . . . the earth spewing blackness above old ruins spattered with fresh blood . . .

I willed the image from my mind. We exited onto the Brooklyn Bridge ramp and zoomed past a sign:

WELCOME TO BROOKLYN
Like No Other Place in the World

Amen. There are two provisions in my will: Mady gets *Casita Azul* and all my worldly goods, and my funeral procession travels the mean streets of my boyhood.

The federal Eastern District courthouse fronts a street closed to vehicles since 9/11. I got out a block away and crossed Cadman Plaza Park to the courthouse. Wind in the open space numbed my face. The courthouse windows reflected pale sun. Twenty years ago, the courthouse had been a small, five-story cube. Shortly after, it was enlarged into an adjoining space, three times larger. Shortly after that, it was replaced by the new tower. All in all, a half billion of the trillions wasted in the war against drugs.

And so my world turned.

It stopped when the elevator opened onto the third floor and I spotted Assistant US Attorney Kandice Kauffman together with several agents in the corridor outside Judge Trieant's courtroom. Made me want to spit.

It's a reaction based on events of long ago, when I was representing Nacho Barrera's brother Max. I'd already cooperated his potential life-with-no-parole sentence down to twenty years, and was then seeking another cooperation-based resentence. Kandi had called and said she believed Max had valuable information in a major case she was investigating. Was Max interested in helping himself by helping her? Naturally, Max was interested. I thought if I could get him down to ten years, less good time and time served, he'd be out in a year or two. So Max was taken from his comfortable mid-security-level jail to an eight-by-ten SHU cell in MDC. Best he was there, Kandi said, for his own protection.

SHU was hard time. Six cement surfaces with a bright light on 24-7. A food tray passed through a slot and, every third day, a shackled walk along the cell block. No radio, no books, no nothing.

Except for me. Max shared Nacho's likeability, and I visited him regularly. He was an optimist who saw the path to freedom and walked straight down it. In a flurry of proffers, Max gave up a lot of heavy information I was sure would result in a substantial sentence reduction. Videos and affidavits confirming the president and extended first family of a Caribbean nation were deeply involved in the drug trade. Soon, North Valley Cartel guys Max had fingered were being arrested. A few at first, then a stream that became a torrent, then the dam burst and the North Valley Cartel washed away.

Kandi let Max languish in solitary for a year before sending him back to complete his sentence without according him *any* credit for the new cooperation. I was stunned. Kandi's rationale was that Max had been working in New York; therefore, he hadn't had personal dealings with the Colombian-based guys he spoke about. Hence, no personal dealings, no value as a witness, and besides, plenty of guys were lining up to testify against those Max had first pointed at. He'd been the goose that laid the golden egg that cracked into pieces like Humpty Dumpty.

"Max was the first to kick the can down the road," I had protested. "Isn't valuable intelligence cooperation?"

"We already knew his rap. He just corroborated what others said."

"No, the others corroborated *him*. Corroboration is cooperation."

"Good point." For a moment, I thought she was serious, but it turned out she was just toying with me. "Thing is, it's a judgment call. I judged not."

"After keeping him in the hole for an entire year?"

"If you can't do the time, don't do the crime."

Fortunately, the conversation was on the phone, or I would've punched her lights out. Hitting a woman? *That* woman? You betcha.

In any event, our disagreement soon was moot. Faced with the evidence, the Caribbean president was allowed a golden parachute that dropped him in a prosperous country that welcomed all stripes of wealthy men. And even as I was preparing a long-shot motion for the government to be directed to reward Max's cooperation, a North Valley *sicario* had murdered Max in jail.

At this moment, Kandi was working two phones at the same time, talking on one and texting on the other. Despite her many faults, she was totally dedicated to her job. The problem was how she performed it. In the past, she'd been sanctioned for hiding discovery evidence and behaving inappropriately with counsel: rude and aggressive to those who dare fight; overly generous with those who kiss her ring.

She glanced my way, then turned her back.

Fine with me. I didn't mind not looking at her. In her salad days, Kandi was pretty in the zaftig way Long Island princesses can be, but that was then: now she's more Botox than flesh, and her face is plasticized into a permanent frown, as if she's wondering who farted.

I know I sound immature, but I truly detest this woman. Not only is she a liar; she's totally corrupt. While proffering cooperators, she wins them over with homemade cookies, then covertly name-drops certain lawyers—like her old former-prosecutor buddy Dreidel. If the accused switches lawyers to Dreidel, a kickback winds up in her purse. Too bad I couldn't prove it, so I just had to grimace and bear her.

One of the agents—tall, pale hair, pitted cheeks—flashed me a horsey smile. He seemed familiar, but I couldn't make a connection.

"Mr. Bluestone?" he said, approaching with another agent. "Charles Scally. Call me Chaz. This handsome guy is my partner, Nelson Cano. Say hello, Nelly."

Cano grunted. He was a stocky Latino in jeans, sneakers, and a parka. Given his look, he probably worked the streets and wasn't happy wasting a morning in court.

"You're the case agent?" I said to Scally, slightly surprised. I figured he was on the far side of forty, an age when most agents have become group supervisors. Then again, Bolivar's case was six years old, so probably Scally's presence was a vintage rerun. He'd begun the case and now would finish it.

He chuckled. "You know how it is. Just when you think you're out of the business, they pull you back in."

Kandi held her palm out to Scally, snapped, "Pen."

Color patched Scally's cheeks. His lips formed an unspoken word: *Bitch*. Cano leaned between them and gave Kandi a pen.

I thought this was odd. Kandi usually was close with her agents—often *too* close, openly flirting with them. I remembered a proffer during which she'd referred to a couple of young agents as Mr. September and Mr. October. Clearly, it wasn't that way with Scally. Maybe Scally didn't fit her teenage fantasies. She sure didn't fit his.

The courtroom door opened, and a clerk leaned out. "The judge is ready."

We entered the courtroom. The clerk handed me Bolivar's pretrial report. I quickly scanned it: he was forty-one years old, in good health, no US address. The rest of the fill-ins were blank, including his citizenship. Maybe he'd declined to answer; guys often do that.

The pen door opened, and marshals led Bolivar out. Even in jailhouse blues, he managed to appear dignified. Two of the marshals were women. I heard one say to another, "TDH, definitely."

True, Bolivar was tall, dark, and handsome. I flicked a sideways glance and caught Kandi checking Bolivar out. I went before the bench. Bolivar stood at my right, Kandi on my left. Her perfume was cloying.

"All rise."

Judge Trieant doddered to the bench, then slumped behind it. He was a mean bastard when I first started lawyering and since then had become meaner. He still wore his trademark waxed handlebar mustache: the one that had earned him the nickname Oilcan Harry when he was a prosecutor. Nowadays, Trieant didn't talk much, and when he did, it was unpleasant.

The clerk called the case, and Kandi entered her appearance. I entered mine, waived a formal reading of the indictment, and entered a plea of not guilty.

"I'll hear the government as to bail," Trieant said.

Kandi went into a boilerplate rap about the defendant having been a fugitive, that it was likely that if released on bail he wouldn't return, blah, blah, blah.

I still hadn't gotten an update from Natty Grable as to a bail package. I said, "The defendant consents to an order of detention but reserves the right to argue bail at a later date."

"Discovery?" Trieant barked.

"Will be provided soon," Kandi said. "Within the month."

"Moving on," Trieant said, setting a motion schedule and a trial date of July 6. He banged his gavel and stood.

"All rise."

Trieant doddered from the bench. Bolivar was led away. Kandi said, "Let me know when your client's ready to proffer."

"Whip up a batch of cookies," I said. "Hit the tanning salon. Then stand by your Shalimar, and wait for my call."

She smiled. "I'm going to destroy you, Bluestone."

"Wear black. Makes you look thinner."

Unbelievable how two grown-ups, professionals both, can behave so childishly. I left the courthouse.

When I'd entered, the wind had been at my back. Coming out was like leaning into the teeth of a gale. Head down and hands deep in pockets, I crossed the park, and as I climbed the gray stone steps in front of the Brooklyn War Memorial, I realized why Scally seemed familiar:

He was a dead ringer for Marshal George Maledon.

Let no guilty man escape.

I shuddered but not from the cold. As I hurried from the park, I saw the Flex idling in the street, but as I headed toward it—

CHAPTER 30

I stopped short to avoid colliding with a woman coming toward me. The sun was in my eyes, and in the glare I couldn't see her face, only a surround of silvery halo. She spoke in a soft voice nearly snatched by the wind.

"Did I come too late for court?"

I moved to get the sun out of my eyes and saw, within a hood of silver fur, Jilly's flawless face. "I'm afraid you did."

"Oh no. What happened?"

"Not much. Too cold to talk here. Where's your car?"

"My car? Oh. I took a taxi."

"Come." I cupped her elbow and helped her into the Flex, then got in myself. When she was done shivering, I told her the court appearance had been brief, a formality. "What happened with the bail package?"

"Natty said to say he's working on it. He asked me to go to court so I could tell you."

"And to spy and see if I was any good."

"No, it wasn't like that—"

"Only serious. Tell him I was great. And get yourselves a pair of working phones, will ya?"

She forced a smile. We drove in awkward silence. City light through the windows striped her face with a repetitious shadow: one moment she was luminous, the next a shadow, over and over. We'd been crossing the Brooklyn Bridge, whose girders threw the shadows. We slowed for traffic in a shadow. In the dimness, her mouth was opened like a night flower. I was about to put my lips on hers—

Val said, "Where to?"

She replied to Val in the same soft way she spoke to me. A bit of charm, a hint of flirt. It was a country thing, I supposed. Val had been a war refugee and mistrusted attractive women; they were users. He'd seen them twist commanders and commissars alike around their little pinkies. Bread for bed. He'd clearly initially disliked Jilly but had softened now that she'd acknowledged him. He kept cutting glances at her in the rearview. Couldn't blame him, she was so insanely beautiful.

She leaned against her window, looking up as we came off the bridge. I followed her gaze up forty stories to the colonnaded top of the Municipal Building, where a golden statue of a woman gleamed in the sun.

The same statue she had viewed through Natty's telescope. As we passed the building, she turned to keep it in sight. Her eyes were moist. She caught me looking at her and averted her face.

Val turned west on Houston. The address Jilly had given him was on the border of the West Village and SoHo. A trendy joint.

"Here we are," I said, but she didn't move. "What's wrong?"

She shook her head. "Nothing. I just feel . . . low."

"Been there, done that a few hundred thousand times and still counting. In the mood to talk?"

She chewed her lower lip with that ever-so-slightly crooked upper incisor, then gave me a faint smile.

"Take a girl to lunch?"

CHAPTER 31

The hotel restaurant's lunch crowd was typically downtown: swinging dicks and great-looking women.

But Jilly turned heads as we entered. The seating person deferentially led us to a corner booth. I swept my hand for Jilly to sit facing the room, but she chose to face the wall. I asked what wine she preferred, and she said whatever I liked. I ordered a top-of-the-list Super Tuscan. We didn't speak until the wine came, but after a sip, Jilly leaned across the table and spoke softly.

"I don't have a single friend I trust," she said. "I mean, a friend I can *really* trust. But I feel, I don't know why, that I can trust you. Can I, Benn?"

I thought the question weirdly sudden, perhaps the opening to another chapter. *Can you trust me?* Oh yes. *Do you trust me?*

"Absolutely," I said.

Her fingertips touched atop my hand. She took another sip of wine. "The only friend I ever trusted was my momma. She had me when she was real young. Raised me all by her lonesome. While I was in school, she wrote her memoirs. And at night, I'd tell her what I learned, and she'd read me what she wrote. Between you and me, her memoirs were kind of scrambled. Didn't really matter, because the title said it all: *I, Centerfold.*"

I understood. In my trophy hall of memories are two Playmates and a Pet. Unsettled women, all. Damaged. Understandable. Pipe-smoking Hef and gold-chained Bob were the reasons why I never wore pajamas or jewelry.

"Momma's claim to fame? Voted the best Miss April, ever. The day after high-school graduation, I told Momma I wanted to go see the world. She cried a little and made me promise to always use a condom. So I got on the Greyhound and waved goodbye to Filly, and two days later I was here in the big city."

"Your mom's name is Filly?"

"Filly, for Filomena. Was."

"Sorry."

An awkward moment, but then Jilly's phone rang. She fished it from her bag and looked at the screen and put a finger to her lips for me to keep mum. I could hear a man's voice but couldn't make out the words. She flashed me a brittle smile, then spoke into the phone.

"I'm having lunch," she said. "Of course, I'm alone."

She hung up the phone but wouldn't look at me. I wondered if she was talking to Natty. Or the man she'd been with at Foto's party. Painful to think of a woman like this with men like that—

Speaking of which, a guy with curly hair and cupid lips appeared at the table. He leaned over me and double air-kissed Jilly.

"Hello, Rafe," she said. "Benn, Raphael Borg."

I knew of Borg, one of my dirtier secrets being that I read Page Six, in which Borg's publicist made sure he was regularly mentioned as a model-dating, mogul-baiting, bad-boy super lawyer. But the real skinny in the legal community was that Borg couldn't lawyer his way out of a paper bag. He wore a leather jacket collar-up over a muscle tee and had a smart-alecky attitude that made you want to slap him. At least, I did.

"Sorry," he said. "Didn't catch your name."

"Rafe, this is Benn Bluestone," Jilly said.

"*The* Benn Bluestone?" he said. "Oh wow. I'm in awe. We got to get to know each other, man. Break some bread, whatever. But right now, me and Jilly have some important things to bat around. You stay, enjoy your wine, hit on a model. You want, I'll introduce you to one."

"That's okay."

"Sure. Another time." He winked at me, then turned to Jilly. "C'mon, sweetness."

"Give me a minute," she said.

"Give you thirty seconds, honey."

Rafe went to the bar. We didn't speak, but Jilly read my face. "Rafe's really not the way he seems."

"Depends on what you mean by *seems*."

"He's just protective of me. He handles my investments. So many documents they make my head swim. I mean, I can't even keep track of my laundry tickets. If it weren't for Rafe, I'd be lost. Look at him, waiting. I know that look. Business to discuss. Papers to sign. Thank you for the wine, Benn. I'm so glad we're friends."

"To the end and thereafter," I said.

I left Jilly to her other lawyer.

On the way uptown, Val said, "I can say something?"

"You will, anyway. Go on."

"For fifteen minutes, that woman stands in cold, looking at court. When you come out, she pretends to walk there. Not so. She waits for you the whole time."

"You saw her arrive in a taxi?"

Val shook his head. "No taxi. She come in gray stretch with a front grille looking like the face of some kind of dog. A, ah . . ."

"Bulldog," I said.

CHAPTER 32

When I got back to the office, I called Foto and asked why he hadn't told me who Jilly was from the start.

"I didn't know from the start. You doing her?"

"None of your business. No."

"Good. Keep it that way."

I sat at my computer and researched the golden statue of the woman that crowned the Municipal Building—the one that had so captured Jilly's attention through the telescope. Turned out to be a strange and sad story. The real-life model for the statue had been an actress named Audrey Munson. Well known in her day, she was a beautiful woman who'd come to the city in search of fame and fortune but, despite the golden statue that became her legacy, had come to a bad end. Made me wonder if the woman reminded Jilly of herself.

The next day Val drove me to MDC, the Brooklyn federal jail.

It's located on a spur of Sunset Park bounded by the Gowanus Expressway and New York Harbor, an isolated neighborhood of enormous old warehouses erected during World War II, back when the area was known as the Brooklyn Army Terminal, Uncle Sam's round-the-clock man-and-materiel point of embarkation to the European Theatre. Now, it was mostly vacant but for a scatter of light industry, and after dark its only inhabitants were the staff and inmates of MDC's two jails, which sat side by side on a street dead-ending at an old pier jutting into the harbor. The old jail was a converted terminal warehouse; the new jail a concrete box whose slab face was lined with slit windows.

Val pulled into a spot in front of the new jail. When I got out of the Flex, the wind blowing off the water nearly knocked me down. The flag above the jail entrance was snapping furiously, its lanyard clinking hollowly against the pole. I hurried up the front steps and came in from the bitter cold.

Better. Unlike the lonely place that was FDC Miami, MDC Brooklyn was my home turf. Same familiar lobby, same friendly guard.

"What's up, Bonesy?"

"Nice tie, Counselor."

I filled out a legal-visit form and signed in the attorney-admissions book, scribbling my and my client's names unintelligibly, the better to veil my doings from other defense lawyers, ever eager to poach.

I passed through a metal detector and got my hand stamped in invisible ink. Entered an air lock where the jail brain—CONTROL— was hidden behind a dark window. Set below the window was a black light. I put my hand beneath it, and the invisible stamp of the daily password glowed fluorescent green.

How many times had I done this? A thousand? More? No matter, the ritual never changed. What did change was the daily password, and the hand that was stamped. One day the left hand; next day the right. As often as not, the stamp is applied poorly, leaving a green florescent smear instead of a password. But so long as there was a visible glow, CONTROL loudspoke its approval.

Today my hand stamp glowed as a readable password: BARN. I'd always wondered who comes up with the passwords, and why: Was BARN a random choice, or a private joke referring to a place where animals are kept—

CONTROL squawked: "Good."

The inner air lock door clicked open, and I entered the visit room. It was similar to the one in FDC Miami: space in the middle for social visits, vending machines and glass-walled visit rooms along the walls, an elevated guard desk overlooking all. I walked along the visit rooms in search of an empty one.

The next-to-last attorney room was unoccupied. As I entered it, I glimpsed the last attorney room, double-size to accommodate codefendant meetings. There was a sign on its door that said **RESERVED**. Its walls were stacked with dozens of document cartons—no doubt containing discovery evidence—amid which several lawyers and inmates were seated. The inmates were white guys whose pale, haunted look made them seem recent arrivals to the States. Italians, I guessed, or maybe Albanians. Two of the lawyers I'd seen around but didn't know. The third was Morty Plitkin, who represented Natty Grable—

Shit. Plitkin had seen me and gotten up. I steeled myself for a request for a referral for Joaquin Bolivar's case as Plitkin left his conference room, grinning.

"Bennie, my boy," he said. "How's the pot case going? Kandi breaking your balls?"

"You know," I said.

"Ha. Do I. Tell you what, though. When Kandi first came on the scene, I wanted to boff the ass off her. Unfortunately, she's aged like cheap wine. Not like this PR gal I keep stashed in the Bronx. Going on forty but with the tits of a fourteen-year-old. But, hey, who am I to tell you about Puerto Rican women? Your wife was some kind of beautiful back in the day, and I bet my ass she still is. Am I right?"

I managed a nod.

I caught a whiff of cigar as Plitkin moved closer and quietly spoke in my ear. "Between us? I was pissed Natty didn't send me the pot case. The selfish son of a bitch wants me to concentrate on his case. See the piles of discovery in there? There's three times more boxes still to come, and Natty wants me to check every page. But what the fuck? He's paying a fortune, so who am I to complain? Still, it killed me not doing the pot case. Yeah, I know, the fee's just chump change. But I wanted to make a run at the eye candy paying it. Some piece, that Jilly. Am I right, or am I right?"

"Uh-huh."

"Just 'uh-huh'? Guys like us, we can't stop bullshitting. The check's in the mail. I won't come in your mouth. Am I right?"

Plitkin love-tapped my shoulder and went back into his room. I sat in mine. Plitkin had a nose for money, but apparently, he knew nothing about the retainer I'd received for Joaquin Bolivar's case. Like Jilly, who claimed to know nothing about Bolivar's case at all. Like Bolivar, who didn't know anyone. Three liars. I already knew that much about Plitkin. Sad to think that about Jilly and Joaquin, though they made a handsome couple. I intuited that they were and that it was she, the wealthy widow, who'd fronted my million bucks to Murmansk-54 Imports, which wrote my retainer check to veil her participation.

I thought this way because creeps like Natty Grable don't shell out a million clams to help strangers. Who was Bolivar to him, really? Not a fellow ex-Soviet soldier or gulag survivor, that was for sure—

Stop. Back up to Plitkin. Maybe he wasn't looking to wet his beak because he *hadn't* recommended me. Maybe Natty had been lying; maybe it was Foto who'd first recommended me.

So what? Keep it simple. All that needed knowing was if and how I was affected. Natty Grable meant nothing to me; he was just codefendant to a couple of white guys who couldn't jump bail. But Natty could jump bail. Would he, if his case turned sour? Probably. Would Bolivar jump if I got him out? Definitely. Believing this, would I help him?

Of course. There's no belief system in my line of work.

Beyond the glass wall, a social visit was in progress. I smelled popcorn and chicken wings heating in microwaves, observed inmates bouncing kids on their laps, their women clucking approval. For all its minuses, jail offered some pluses. Given the class of people, family domestic life could be volatile, if not downright violent, but once the men were jailed, all was peace and love. And the women liked knowing where their males were at night. In fact, an unusually large number of the visiting women were pregnant.

The inmates' door opened, and a batch of prisoners emerged.

I didn't see Bolivar but recognized another man among them who had been—until recently—an up-and-coming drug lawyer. With a lot of work and a little luck, he might have made it big, had he not gotten too involved in a client's drug conspiracy. Every so often, one of my professional brothers crashes. Like this guy. Like another I knew, now doing a hard sixteen for advising—or, as the government put it, *conspiring*—to murder a witness. Another, doing twenty for being the point-out man for a crew who robbed drug dealers.

The list goes on.

I myself once had a close call when I was picked up on a client's wiretap, and some bright-boy agent claimed my idle chatter was conversation coded to conceal money laundering. In truth, my conversation was about my client's money, albeit in the form of a fee passing from him to me. Nevertheless, it ignited an investigation that ultimately went nowhere but whose sleepless nights left permanent bags under my eyes, daily reminders in my shaving mirror that triggered my mantra:

Get out, get out, get out before it's too late—

The door opened, and Bolivar entered.

His handshake was firm. "You good?"

"I'm fine. What's with you?"

"One day closer to leaving this shithole. I'm right that the lady prosecutor would want to meet with me?"

"I'm sure she'd be interested in hearing what you have to say."

"Exactly the way I figured. Go ahead and set up the meeting."

"Slow down. First, tell me what you can cooperate about."

"Crimes and criminals. What else is there?"

"Which crimes? Which criminals?"

"Lots of both. Long story."

"I'm in no rush."

"Benn, with all respect? I know how things work. I understand about cooperation being first party, and the need for total truthfulness and providing substantial assistance. I got everything nailed. Just set up the meeting."

"I will. But tell me, anyway."

"You got paid a lot of money for my case. Things work out right, you'll be paid a whole lot more. I appreciate you wanting to do things by the book, but I'm a piece of literature you've never read."

"Proffering is not an automatic pass. The first thing the prosecutor will say is that just because you're talking, that doesn't mean you're getting a cooperation agreement. Especially from *this* prosecutor. Bounce your cooperation off me. Think of it as a rehearsal. We may want to tweak a few things."

He flashed a white smile. "Okay, my lawyer. Ask away."

"Most foreign weed is transported by land from Mexico. How come you go-fasted a load all the way up to New York?"

"Not a go-fast. A sailboat. Black-hulled. I called her the *Swan*. Old but built beautiful, the way they used to build them. That boat was a woman, I'd've married her."

"Smuggling all that way via sail seems weird."

A shrug. "I like weird."

"Sailboats don't fit the maritime drug-running profile."

"You're spot-on."

"So why not run cocaine, where the real money is?"

"I don't like blow. Weed, I love."

"I don't think she'll buy that."

Bolivar cocked his head. "You have a better story?"

"Try this one for size. Weed, not coke, because you were dipping your toes in the water. Making sure the route was cool. Worst-case scenario, you get tagged and dump the pot. No great loss, investment-wise. But, if things go well, you go to stage two, in which the load is coke."

Bolivar smiled. "You're good."

"I'm not finished. There's a problem. Conspiring coke exposes you to more time than pot."

"You'll find a way around that."

"Bear with me. I'm correct that stage two—running loads of coke—never progressed past your innermost thoughts?"

"Of course it—"

I held a forefinger in front of his mouth. "Listen carefully. You never actually *did* anything about stage two, right?"

"How could I? The route was blown—"

"You never spoke to *anyone* about it, right?"

"Aha." He gave another brilliant smile. "Never."

"Because the scheme existed only in your head. Because conspiracies are like tangoes. It takes two to dance."

"Exactly the way it was. In my head."

Perfect. Without directly saying so, I'd conveyed Bolivar's position to him. "Good. I'll set up a proffer."

"In the courthouse?"

"No. In the US Attorney's office, just across the street from the courthouse."

"So they'll probably take me in an unmarked white van, the same as when they first took me to court, yes?"

"That's how they do it."

"Take me in the morning? Or afternoon?"

"Depends whether the meeting's in the morning or afternoon."

"Bet they got unmarked cars following the buses, huh?"

"I believe so. Randomly. At least some of the time."

"They say every third day. Cops operate according to patterns. Like when they stamp your hand when you visit. Left, right. *Pico, placa*, like in driving in Bogotá. Odd, even."

"Who told you about the hand stamps? Jilly?"

"Who's Jilly?"

"Never mind. Why all the questions about how and when they take you? You planning an escape, or what?"

Bolivar grinned. "A: that's impossible. B: why should I try? I got me a lawyer who's going to spring me legitimately. The reason I'm asking questions? Because if you're done proffering after the noon bus leaves, you wind up waiting for the late bus, without lunch, in a holding pen filled with bad criminal types."

I grinned. "As opposed to good criminal types."

"You get the point."

CHAPTER 33

When I got back to the office, I kicked my feet up and did my daily reads. Laura Astorquiza had a new entry on *Radio Free Bogotá*:

> Citizens: According to General Uvalde, the woes of our nation arise from the mysterious personage of the bandit known as *Sombra*, whose imminent capture or surrender has been announced for nearly a year. But could it be that *Sombra* does not exist? That he is a myth perpetuated to deflect attention from the *real* drug lords, whose wealth is shared with General Uvalde?

For once, Laura was wrong. There was a real *Sombra*, and I had fifty thou to prove it. I wondered why well-informed Laura would posit such a dubious possibility.

My phone rang. I answered.

"Me," a man grunted.

"How are you?"

I knew the caller well. He was a long-term client of mine and extremely circumspect, as befitting a most-wanted personage. I kept his file stored in a fold of my brain labeled *PF*, as in *Permanent Fugitive*.

PF called me every once in a long while, and when he spoke, I listened, because he paid me a lot of money for very little work.

"Read," he said, and hung up.

I left the office, walked a few blocks to Lexington, went into a copy shop that rented computer terminals. I bought some access time and hunched close to a computer screen so no one could see over my shoulder. I opened a certain Hotmail account and read a brief message. Just three words:

THE BAD PLACE.

The following day, I was ensconced in 1-A on a southbound flight. I napped for a while, and when I awoke, I saw five miles below the green flatness that was Florida giving way to shining sea. I could not help but look eastward, in my mind's eye seeing the ocean breaking on the rocks below the city walls of Viejo San Juan, one thousand miles away.

Drug agents refer to Honduras as *downrange* and its Mosquito Coast as *battle space*. Those were compliments compared to Honduras's San Pedro Sula, aka the world's most violent city. I'd been there before but always been lucky enough not to have stayed overnight. Downtown was a traffic circle amid bad vibes. The Hilton, supposedly the best place in town, was a dump.

It was late when I arrived, and I was hungry. Dinner was a buffet. The meat looked suspect and the chicken undercooked, so I went with the fish, which I was assured was fresh off a local boat. Snapper. Their pupils were black and they smelled briny, so I acted according to tropical rules: eat fresh or don't eat. I was cleansing my palate with a beer when a man sat across from me.

"Anything?" PF said.

PF was an elegant man, although at the moment slightly threadbare. Understandable. He'd been living in the boonies ever since the Justice

Department's Narcotic and Dangerous Drugs Section had indicted him in DC for running the Central American branch of a large DTO.

He had a big problem.

If he surrendered and cooperated, he'd have to testify against his family. If he didn't cooperate, he'd have to go to trial, which was a sure ticket to a life of hard time. Therefore, he was a fugitive, and my job, which I chose to accept, was to periodically update PF on the continued availability of witnesses against him. Unfortunately, these particular rats in waiting had long sentences, so the chances of them being unavailable were nil.

Before flying down, I'd checked with the BOP's inmate-search site. The witnesses against PF remained in general population, alive and well.

"The same," I said.

"Fuck," he grunted.

PF was well educated. When I first met him, he spoke a pure, eloquent Spanish. But years of life on the run in solitary places had reduced his vocabulary to single-syllable sounds.

He poured himself a glass of wine and drank it in one long swallow. Then dipped a napkin in a water glass and wiped his teeth. The napkin came away blotched purple.

He put the napkin down, looked at me for a moment, then smiled the way he used to. "Look at us, drinking swill like this. How are you, Benn?"

"I'm good."

"As befits a man intelligent enough to live on the proceeds of crime, without suffering the consequences of being a criminal."

I smiled at PF's return to his old style of diction.

PF sat back, finally relaxing a little. I was not only his sole link to the civilized world, and the possibility of his returning to it, but also a life preserver offering him a grip on sanity. A cultivated discussion over dinner and wine—simple human contact—was a vacation from the madness of his everyday life.

In truth, I enjoyed our visits, too, PF being as close to me as anyone. He knew my history, my ups and downs, the way I'd once been and now was.

It was late when he stood to leave.

"*Sobrino,*" he said.

This was a reference to his nephew, who would pay me seventy-five large for my trip. I figured the trips earned me roughly two thou an hour, including sleep time—easy money for a day of discomfort—but on this trip, I earned every penny. It rained all night, water running down the wall of my room and puddling the floor. Lightning knocked out the power, and the AC went off. The windows didn't open, and the room became a steam bath. My dinner fish decided to escape, so I spent five or six hours hugging the toilet bowl, counting water bugs between retches.

I slept on the flight back home, and when Val picked me up, I curled up in the back seat, slept some more, and as soon as I got home, I crawled into bed.

But the next day, everything abruptly improved.

First, Paz called: *Sombra* was seriously considering me. Second, Rigo's son Omar called: the family was putting my fee together. Third, PF's nephew delivered 750 Franklins, the fee for what had been little more than a social visit to my old client and friend.

Who said money doesn't buy happiness?

CHAPTER 34

One thing worried me. If Rigo truly could cooperate against *Sombra*, I was conflicted from representing *Sombra*. But then again, Rigo was a nutjob, and AUSA Barnett Robinson would not buy either Rigo or Uvalde as *Sombra*.

I considered this while riding shotgun with Val as he steered the Flex beneath the elevated tracks columns on Brighton Beach Avenue in south Brooklyn. Natty's man Andrey had gathered the people with the property for Bolivar's bail. Not that it was necessary, since Bolivar was going to cooperate, but that fact was not something I could reveal. Better to go with the flow.

It was a bitterly cold night, but the street was bustling with Russian speakers, for whom it might as well have been spring. Ahead, red neon glowed above a restaurant. Val pulled over, and I got out and entered the Red Star.

They were expecting me.

Behind the street door hung a heavy velvet curtain. It parted—a brief din of crowded diners—then closed as Andrey appeared, slicked hair gleaming. He raised a hand in greeting, and on the inside of his wrist I glimpsed the same jailhouse tattoo as Natty's: the Murmansk-54 mark, a red star within barbed wire.

Andrey led me upstairs to a narrow corridor with two doors. One door had a Star of David and some Hebrew lettering painted on it. The other door was unmarked. We entered it.

The room was dusty, dim. Stacked cartons, filing cabinets, cleaning supplies. A single light above a small table, at which eight people were seated. Four men and four women. They stopped talking when we entered.

Andrey introduced them by Russian names that sounded alike. Broad and fleshy faced, they looked alike, too, as if they came off the same Soviet-era assembly line. But that was then and this was now, and they had become naturalized American citizens: four married couples who jointly owned several buildings, including the one that housed the Red Star, and had the tax returns to prove it.

I asked if any had ever been convicted of a crime. Eight heads shook as one. I asked if they all knew Bolivar, and in return got eight nods. I asked if they understood that should Bolivar skip, they would owe the government the amount of the bail.

The men answered: *"Da. Da. Da. Da."*

"You're still ready to pledge your property?"

They all nodded and replied as one: *"Da."*

I turned to Andrey. "Bolivar's passport?"

"His Colombian lawyer has it."

"Who's the lawyer, and what's his phone number?"

"We're in the process of speaking to him."

They were wasting my time, not to mention their own. Without a US passport, I couldn't prove Bolivar was an American citizen. On the other hand, Kandi had the burden of proving Bolivar an alien, and since his pretrial report had left nationality a blank, doubtful she had proof.

"I'll arrange a bail hearing," I said. "Let you know where and when."

When we left the room, I expected to follow Andrey back down the stairs, but instead he knocked on the other door, the one with the Star of David and Hebrew lettering. It buzzed open. I went through, but Andrey remained outside.

The room was small. A couple of folding chairs and a table draped in burgundy velvet, atop which several throwaway phones and a half-filled bottle of vodka sat beneath a menorah. There was an opened cabinet housing an object that might or might not have been a Torah. I supposed the room was a synagogue, but the man seated behind the table was no rabbi.

"Hello, boy," Natty said. His drawn face seemed fragile as a communion wafer, his black eye patch standing out in sharp relief. "Welcome to my shul."

I had to laugh. Beautiful. I thought I'd seen every bail-condition beat scheme there was—from phony doctor visits, a la Tony Soprano, to sham marriage ceremonies—but this was genius. Natty was tracked by his ankle bracelet, but his bail conditions allowed him to attend religious services.

"The bail package is good?" he said.

"Very professional."

"So, you going to win bail?"

I shrugged, although I was beginning to think it possible. The sureties were impeccable. The case was pot, not heavy drugs. The alleged crime took place six years ago, suggesting a lack of factual evidence. If there was a passport, bail was a winnable fight. Of course, there was the problem of Judge Trieant's progovernment tendencies, but if he denied, I'd go up on appeal, and the appellate judges were fairer than Trieant.

"We need talk private," Natty said.

"Aren't we doing that?"

"Come."

There was another door hidden behind the religious paraphernalia, and we went through it to an even smaller room: no windows, bare ceiling light, folded towels atop a table. Clothing hung from a peg. On the floor, paired rubber clogs. Natty was unbuttoning his shirt.

"We take *schvitz*."

My nerves were jangling with that old familiar but not unpleasant feeling of being about to walk the fine line—the classic unwired conversation in the steam bath.

Disrobed, Natty revealed a pale, bony body. A tat of a satyr anally fucking a woman covered his chest. He must have been heavier when it was inked, because now the horned creature was shrunken, and the woman's breasts drooped. He grabbed a towel, stepped into clogs, went through another door. I unpeeled my duds and did the same.

The steam was as dense as a foggy night in London. Draped in the towel, Natty sat hunched atop a tiled bench. I sat across from him. I waited for him to speak, but he didn't say anything. I wished he would get to whatever his point was because the steam was hot. Already, my body was oiled, and I felt my lungs heating—

Something landed at my feet. Leaves? Yes. I'd sweated out many a hangover and recognized a *venik* when I saw one. Someone laughed.

I turned and saw two more men. The smaller one was totally bald with a twisty smile. Kyril.

The other man had a towel draped over his head. He idly swatted a *venik* across his back as he spoke in short sentences whose syntax screamed *foreigner*.

"New oak leaves," said the mystery man. "Smell like forest. Open pores. Remove toxins. Bring blood up. Cool body off."

"Sure, why not?" I swatted myself, but the movement only made me hotter.

"I am businessman," he said. "I want something, I buy it. What I want? For you to do what I ask. For that I pay you. Deal?"

I wiped sweat from my eyes. "Depends on what you ask."

"For you to make free Joaquin Bolivar."

"I'm already retained to represent him."

"I want to be sure. So now I meet the master lawyer in person. But still I don't know how smart he is. Is he smart enough to take our money, do the job, and keep his mouth shut?"

His towel lowered enough to allow a partial view of his face. He was fifty, give or take. Thin, but well muscled. A graduate of the Putin School of Masculine Ideals. I thought I'd seen him before, but where? Didn't matter. I didn't care if I never saw him again, either. This guy's aura was quicksand.

He stood and pulled a chain, and water showered down on him. "Take care of yourself. Stay strong," he said, and left the *schvitz*.

Natty and Kyril had left, too. I stood beneath the shower and pulled the chain. Icy water shocked me alert. I felt raw, inside and out.

When I left, they were gone. I went back down the stairs. The curtain was parted, and behind it, the Red Star was booming. A waiter blocked my way. For a moment, I thought there was a problem, then realized he was giving me something.

It was a frosted bottle of pale-green liquid. Bison Grass.

I started to ask a question, decided not to, and left.

In the Flex, I wondered: *What did they really want? Who were these people? Russians, a Colombian, Jilly . . .*

I needed to clear my mind. Nothing better than a long, slow ride through the stomping grounds of my days of yore, to view the world through my eyes when I was young and innocent. Hard to believe, but I was.

Once upon a time.

I told Val not to take the Belt Parkway back to Manhattan, but to drive the long way through the streets of Brooklyn. He started to say something, but I held up a palm.

"Not now, Val. I need to think."

And drink. I opened the bottle and swigged. I wondered how these people knew I was into Bison Grass. What else did they know about me? What did they expect of me?

As I swallowed, I remembered the days when my life was simple.

CHAPTER 35

The Flex hummed along. Behind was the dark water of Sheepshead Bay. Ahead the long reach of Bedford Avenue, bisecting Brooklyn. There was Voorhees Avenue, where in the shadows beneath the Belt Parkway overpass decades ago on another cold night in a thirdhand car, I took and lost virginity. I don't remember the girl's name but still remember her scent, as if it had seeped into my memory, like permanent ink.

I took another swallow of Bison Grass.

We passed Brooklyn College, and I recalled a late afternoon: a professor's voice droning, sun slanting through ivy-bordered windows, me sketching a nude girl.

I swallowed Bison Grass.

We passed a housing project on the very spot where Ebbets Field had stood, home turf of the original Dodgers: Jackie and Pee Wee and Roy and Duke and both Carls—Oisk and Furillo—and all the other lost boys of summer my father told me about before he, too, was lost.

I took another swallow.

I was fairly drunk now.

Wondering who I was.

Or not. I was not Joe Perfect. Not JQ Public. Not like anyone I knew. I was a loner, a master of the universe of the white-powder bar, possessed of a criminally oriented genius for solving problems, a manipulator who found seams between regulations, who oiled the hinges of sealed doors.

I drank deeply.

That direction led to my old hood. I thought of Ma and Bea and Billy. That direction lingered and slowly fell behind . . .

And there was the Brooklyn Museum, where I'd idled away so many hooky hours wandering the replicated Egyptian tomb, dreaming of becoming an archeologist.

I drank more.

There was Grand Army Plaza and Flatbush Avenue, and then we were crossing a bridge above black water, and then downtown Manhattan. That street there, third house on the left, fourth floor window? My first pad.

Midtown. A white-brick apartment-building penthouse where I discovered the joy of sex while high. Beginning to make good money then. Spending like a bandit with bandits' money.

Uptown. Big apartment over there I bought when Mady and I got married. Good years. Then the apartment was gone. And Mady, too.

Question: How did I let such a thing happen?

Answer: I was way too high to notice.

Irony. Drug addict to drug lawyer.

"Mr. Benn?"

"What? Oh."

I was home.

Usually, Val gets out and holds my door open, but now he just sat, waiting for permission to speak.

"Yeah, Val?"

"They say the Red Star is owned by mafia."

I nodded farewell and stumbled to my place.

First thing inside, I pissed Bison Grass. Second thing, I unpeeled my clothing. Third thing, I fell in bed and closed my eyes. Fourth thing, I got out of bed and turned on my device and let my fingers do the walking.

And this is what I learned:

The Kursk Needle, whose lobby art was a bronzed T-34, the legendary tank that saved Mother Russia in the battle of Kursk, was erected by a man who'd renamed himself Kursk. Evgeny Kursk.

A long lens shot showed Kursk emerging from a private jet bearing an EK logo. Another depicted a liner-size yacht with the EK logo on its bow. Another a snow palace in Courchevel, the snowcapped French Alps beyond.

One close shot of Kursk showed a pale face, sandy hair—

I recognized the man who'd been with Jilly at Foto's.

The same man in the *schvitz*, who'd offered an additional fee.

Where did Kursk fit in? With Bolivar? With Jilly? If he was hooked up with Natty, why hire me instead of Plitkin to rep Bolivar?

I called all of Foto's phones. No answers.

I made another call to another man.

ALUNE

We are the Logui of the Kingdom of Tayrona. We are the fifth tribe of the Sierra Nevada de Santa Marta, the last family still unsullied by the outside world. We exist within the circle of life in which the past is the future present. Our life springs from the pure joy of being among Those Who Know More, of being one of the believers who follow The One Who Knows Most of All.

We are lovers and also warriors.

Long ago, when the whites came, we repelled their cruelties and resettled in remote Tayrona. When they followed us, we killed so many, they left us alone for the next half millennium.

Forty years ago, the whites returned to the Sierra.

They enslaved the other four families. Then they moved against us. So many of them. First the drug traffickers. Then the guerrillas, who spoke of good but did evil. Then the paramilitaries, who wanted the guerrillas' treasures for themselves. Then the government soldiers, who were the worst of all.

We fought them all.

One day, a man appeared. This was forty years ago, a time when the Sierra Nevada was a major source of marijuana. The man was one of the traffickers who operated here, but unlike the others, he treated us with respect. He was a powerful man who protected us from other traffickers, the paramilitaries, the guerrillas, the army. At first, we thought him just another avaricious white, but over time, he became our friend and benefactor. Without him, we would have been exterminated before The One Who Knows Most of All existed.

After a long, bloody war, we prevailed. But then the other narco-traffickers killed our friend and protector. But using the weapons and tactics he'd gifted us, we fought on until our enemies left the Nevada.

All this I know, for I am Alune, The One Who Knows Most of All.

CHAPTER 36

The next day as I approached my office, a man got out of an idling taxi. I expected a visit from the man I'd phoned last night, but this man was rumpled and unshaven as if he hadn't slept for days, pinned eyes and dried saliva in the corners of his mouth betraying a binge on stimulants. It took a moment before I recognized Raphael Borg.

"Benn, man," he said, "I gotta talk to you."

Without waiting for a reply, he accompanied me inside. The cage-elevator ride was short, but long enough for me to get a contact high. Once in my office, Borg set down a green-skin designer briefcase, stuck a cigarette in his mouth, fumbled with a match.

"No smoking here," I said.

He put the match away but kept the butt between his lips. "I'm a little nervous is all. Freaked by what's been going down . . . I can trust you, can't I, Benn?"

"You asking or telling?"

"Hoping. Can I?"

"Give me a dollar."

"What? Oh. Right." Despite his present condition, Borg's legal training kicked in; he recognized I was asking for a token retainer, making me his lawyer, so our conversation was privileged. He sorted through crumpled bills, set down a five spot. "That okay?"

I nodded. "You've got five minutes on my meter."

"Jilly is crazy about you. She says you're a rock."

I would've liked to hear more about Jilly's feelings for me, but the visitor I expected was due any moment. "Cut to the chase, Rafe."

He looked around as if others were secreted in the corners, then leaned closer and spoke in a low voice. "Certain people are threatening me unless I walk away from Jilly."

"Which certain people?"

"I can't abandon her. Without me, she'd be eaten alive. They've already ripped a fortune off her. She's still wealthy, but they want the rest. If I don't stand aside, they'll kill me. Jilly needs me, big time."

"I'm sure you charge her, big time."

Borg wiped his hands across his face. Looked me in the eye. "I'm a good lawyer, Benn. I've got problems, but who doesn't? I'm worth every cent Jilly pays me, because I really care about her. Not like those fuckers."

"Which fuckers?"

"The Russians and the Colombians. All of them. *All.*"

"What is it you think I can do about it?"

"Call them off me. Christ, it's like I'm being *hunted.* Tell them I'll deal. Just let Jilly keep a decent-size piece of what her husband left her, maybe throw a crumb or two my way. That's all I ask."

"Why don't you tell them yourself?"

"Because . . . where's the bathroom?"

I pointed the way, and Borg beelined there. A minute passed, and then another. I figured Borg must be adding to the junk circulating in his system. But before I could knock on the bathroom door, the building entrance door buzzed, and I pressed the entry button—

Borg rushed from the bathroom, nostrils white-rimmed with coke, eyes wide with fear.

"You *called* them!" he cried.

"Take it easy, partner."

"You're *with* them."

He ran from the office as the elevator cage opened. He let out a shriek, sidestepped around the man coming from the cage, and plunged down the stairwell. The man stood looking after him, then shrugged and entered my office.

His name was Traum.

"Friend of yours?" he said.

"Lawyer."

"Figures."

CHAPTER 37

Traum knew the way my mind worked; he knew all my ways and some of my secrets. Traum had put in twenty years as an NYPD detective before retiring and going private. Our relationship was based on a compact: in return for him keeping his lips zipped about a certain attorney crossing lines, no one got to see a security-camera video of Detective Traum being bribed by a bodega owner who sold grams on the side.

How it was, way back when the bodega owner's son was my client, a kilo dealer, the owner gifted me the video in case I wanted to extort the crooked cop. I had no such desire, but it was the kind of thing I kept around, just in case.

Sure enough, a few years later, Traum barged into my office, flashed his blue-and-gold detective buzzer, and said, "The other night you were observed entering a beauty parlor on One Twenty-Two and Lex, where you received forty-nine thousand dollars cash. A few minutes after you left, the beauty parlor was raided. Several persons were arrested, and three kilos of cocaine were seized. Three into forty-nine thou is roughly sixteen thousand. The same number as the wholesale price of a kilo. If one of the people arrested confirms you delivered the kilos, that'd kick off an investigation that most probably would lead to an indictment.

Yours. I'm the commanding officer of the unit that hit a certain bodega a few years back. You following me?"

I was. The money had been for a case fee, and we both knew it. We also both knew that my fee had been fifty thou. A grand had magically disappeared, and I had no doubt my client would say anything Traum told him to, the truth be damned. I could easily go down on a dealing beef. And even if I beat the rap, the stain would remain forever. I didn't reply, but my silence spoke volumes.

"I'm informed you have a certain video," he said. "Give it to me, and your presence in the beauty parlor never gets to the file."

I didn't trust him, but I had no choice. Reluctantly, I gave him the video.

"I'm retiring," he'd said. "Going private. Maybe we'll do business."

And so it came to pass. Whenever I had a problem beyond my reach, I called Traum. He was a natural networker who knew the right people to learn about wrong people.

I related what I knew about Jilly, Natty, Joaquin Bolivar, and Evgeny Kursk. "I want to know who's hooked up with who, and why, and whatever else there is about them. This case is hinky."

"Who put you into it?"

"Ah, Jacobo Velez."

He smiled. "Foto?"

When I nodded, Traum belly laughed so hard, the floorboards squealed. When he was done laughing, he shook his head and looked at me as if I were a child.

"Benno's got a feeling he's in the dark about things that might bite him in the ass. Am I right?"

I nodded. "Right."

"Also, Benno smells money and is wanting to partake of some."

I didn't reply.

Traum grinned. "As always, I will find answers to Benno's questions. But first, I want to ask him a question."

I nodded.

"You actually thought you could trust Foto?"

I started to reply, then shut my mouth.

CHAPTER 38

I called Kandi and told her I wanted to set up a bail application for Joaquin Bolivar. She wasn't pleased.

"You go for bail, there's, like, no way I'll *ever* proffer your client."

Bull. The quintessential Kandi. In your face like a tough guy, threatening this and that. But I knew better. Bolivar's case was triable. Maybe, almost. But enough for her to worry she'd lose to me at trial. So when she won the bail argument, she'd gloat until I called, requesting a proffer. Which would earn me a lecture, followed by a reluctant agreement to proffer, so long as my client and I understood it would end at his first lie.

"Shall I arrange the bail hearing, or do you want to?"

"Your application, your call, Mr. Bluestone."

"Right." I dialed up Judge Trieant's clerk, conferenced Kandi in, and scheduled a bail application for the following day. Wouldn't be fun. I was trying to conjure up something fun to do next—Gym? Shop? Lunch?—when I got an e-mail that at first seemed odd, but upon reflection was promising.

It was a video promoting a group called the Shkillas who were going to perform their Shcash dance in a schoolyard on East 95th Street; same yard I used to play stickball in. The video was homemade: lighting too dark, sound screechy. But what came through loud and clear was a ghetto dance and sound I hadn't heard before. Not that I'd heard many, but this stuff was good. Six or eight hooded bad boys Shcash dancing: giant steps, arms akimbo, waving big, automatic handguns. That part was a bad idea, no matter whether the guns were real or fake. All illegal handguns in the Apple meant a minimum three-year bit. And, real or not, waving a gun attracted bullets from both cops and robbers. The aggressive, dangerous parts aside, the Shkilla stuff was better than just good. It was great, at least to this old white man. A little refinement, and a commercial future loomed. I made a mental note to talk to a guy I knew, a mafioso who had a grubby finger in the music business.

The music stopped, and a camera light spotted a dancer's face that I'd recognize anywhere: sweat-sheened blue-black skin, big white teeth, see-all buggy eyes. I grinned. It was my old young pal, Billy Shkilla. He rapped, "I do the Shcash dance. Then I kill and cash ya, bitch. Just like I did the other one."

The screen went dark. So did I. I'm all for art, but not if it meant trouble. No question that the video already had been watched by a street-crime task force, guys who daily do battle with stacks of unsolved homicides. They'd be at the schoolyard, curious whether Billy Shkilla was an artist or actual murderer. Or both. I thought about calling Billy for a heart-to-heart, then decided it was a waste of time.

* * *

The next day when I entered Trieant's courtroom, Kandi was already at the government table, along with the case agent, Chaz Scally. Again, I sensed distance between them. The other agent, Nelson Cano, was slumped on a spectator bench. In jeans and high-tops, he looked more like a defendant than a fed.

The marshals escorted Bolivar in, and again I became aware of Kandi's reaction: like a little kid eyeballing a cone of cotton candy. To my annoyance, Bolivar smiled at her.

Judge Trieant twirled his waxed mustache and nodded.

"Kandice Kauffman for the government. Good morning, Your Honor."

"Benn Bluestone for Joaquin Bolivar."

"Proceed, Ms. Kauffman."

I was mildly surprised. I'd made the bail application, and the usual protocol was that I had the first opportunity to speak. But I let it pass. Trieant's intentional disregard—make that *disrespect*—allowed me to hear Kandi's argument first and adjust mine accordingly.

"The government calls Special Agent Charles Scally."

Kandi began with the usual qualifying questions as to Scally's law-enforcement background and familiarity with the case.

"Agent Scally, during the course of your investigation, did you learn anything relevant to these proceedings?"

"I did," Scally replied.

"Tell us what you learned."

"Mr. Bolivar is not a United States citizen."

"How do you know that, Agent?"

Scally produced a burgundy-colored passport. I'd seen enough similar passports to recognize what country issued it. "His passport is Colombian."

"No more questions," Kandi said.

Trieant scowled at me. "I assume you have no questions?"

I stood. "I do, Your Honor."

Trieant sighed. "Proceed."

"Agent, did you ascertain whether Mr. Bolivar has dual citizenship?"

"I have no information or evidence to support that."

"I have a question, Mr. Bluestone," Trieant said. "Do you have evidence that your client has dual citizenship, or are you fishing? If so, you're wasting my time."

"If Your Honor will adjourn the hearing, I believe I can obtain evidence."

Bolivar tugged my sleeve. His whispered, "Let it go. Set up a proffer."

A proffer? Now? I was astounded, but no way I'd let Kandi see my reaction. "Application withdrawn, Judge. Sorry for the inconvenience."

"Don't let it happen again," Trieant said, and left the bench.

I spoke to Kandi outside the courtroom. "My guy wants to proffer."

Kandi smiled. "You have a short memory. I told you that if he tried for bail, I wouldn't proffer him."

I knew she would proffer Bolivar but wanted to rub my face in it first. "Yes, you told me, but I didn't tell him. Don't punish him for my poor decision."

Kandi made a show of exasperation. "The mighty Bluestone admits a mistake. *Finally*. Maybe, if I have time next week, I *might* proffer your client. Don't call me. I'll call you. In the meantime? Don't make any more poor decisions."

Scally nudged Cano and spoke loud enough for me to hear. "*Told* you he'd flip."

That night I drove to Brooklyn. Billy's performance was over, but the schoolyard was still crowded. The vibes were sullen as the cops ringed the yard. Oh well. Billy would learn. Or not.

CHAPTER 39

The next day I got an e-mail from Kandi confirming an afternoon prof-fer for the following week. My desk suddenly clear, I decided it was time for some R and R. I flew to Miami and spent a couple of days working out, eating healthy, sleeping late. Then came an evening I decided to prowl for a woman. I needn't have bothered.

One found me.

When the doorman brought up my Bentley, a woman was seated in the passenger seat. Jilly. Her hair was swept above her tanned face. She wore oversize shades and a men's white tee knotted at the waist and a pair of cutoff Levis and scuffed white Keds. For a moment, I was too stunned to speak and then I figured best not to; clearly, I was there to listen. So I just got behind the wheel, and off we went.

"Mister Cool," she said. "No what, why, whatever. Not even a 'How are you?'"

"How are you?"

"Fine, thanks for asking. I have a question."

"Ask."

"Natty wants to know if you can arrange for a paralegal to visit Mr. Bolivar. He says he'll pay for the paralegal. He says all you have to do is write the jail a letter saying a person is your paralegal, and they'll be able to visit Mr. Bolivar whenever they want."

Incredible as it sounded, this was true. The fed jails are crawling with unqualified paralegals coddling well-heeled inmates while scouting new work for the lawyer who'd sponsored them. Every so often, one of these snakes gets caught in an unethical or illegal bind, and both they and their sponsoring lawyer are barred from the jail. One common violation was making a relative or friend of the defendant a paralegal, so they could visit as often as they liked.

"Does Natty have anyone in particular in mind?"

She hesitated a beat too long. "I don't know."

"Give your business associate a message."

"My business associate?"

"Tell him I won't do it."

"He'll ask me why."

"Tell him to ask me."

I'd been tooling along side streets in a nice part of the Gables. It was a perfect Florida evening. Soft breeze. Cicadas. Tang of salt air. In the rosy light, Jilly's hazel eyes were lime green, her lips cherry. There was a small shadow where her chin was dimpled. I hadn't noticed the dimple before. Maybe because she was smiling widely, and I'd never seen her smile that way before.

"Natty won't like that," she said.

"How'd you find me here?"

"Natty did. Through some kind of, what . . . title search?"

"Why'd he send you?"

"I guess he thought you'd be more willing to do it for me than for him."

"He's right. But the answer's still no. Long trip for nothing."

"Actually, I was coming here, anyway. And I thought it would be nice seeing you. The highway just ahead? Get on it, please."

"You just got here? You tan awful quickly."

"I was in France. Skiing the Alps."

I flashed on Kursk's chalet in Courchevel.

Jilly smiled. "The sun's murder on your skin, but who wants to live forever, right? Filly liked me tan. That Hollywood glow, she called it. She said I had what it took to be a star. To be what she always wanted for herself. She almost made it, too."

Jilly's eyes were bright with sincerity. Too bright. Maybe there was a chemical in her bloodstream. But then again, when it comes to talking about mothers, some people can turn on tears like a faucet.

"Filly was in a big film once, about ancient Egypt. She played the pharaoh's dancing girl in a scene with the leading man. Actually, they had a real-life relationship, sort of. Anyway, her speaking part, it wound up on the cutting-room floor, and afterward, well . . ."

There was a microsecond flash of green over the elevated highway, and when I turned, the sun was gone below the horizon. As if unaware of the abrupt sunset, Jilly continued speaking, her voice dreamy now.

"The leading man was this big English star named Hawkins. He told Filly she was prettier than the woman who played the Egyptian princess. Filly always remembered that. Said it was her dream someday to be buried in a pyramid, like in the film."

Funny, I thought. Just the other day I'd been reminiscing about a replicated Egyptian tomb, and now Jilly had mentioned Egyptian pyramids. Weird coincidence. As I so often think, true coincidences are an endangered species; here and now on Planet Earth, most things are preordained. But this was neither coincidence nor preordained.

This was karma.

I pulled to the curb. "Natty can wait," I said. "Come with me."

"Stop at my place so I can change. It's not far."

The sky was dark now, as if curtained.

End of act one, I thought.

CHAPTER 40

There are plenty of over-the-top pads in Miami, but Jilly's was out of this world. It was on a private island, an enormous glass cube on grounds sprinkled with the kind of art favored by billionaire collectors: so-called installations, the kind of phony nonsense that makes me want to scream that the emperor's naked.

Jilly picked up on my thoughts. "I know. My decorator calls it a 'garden of art.' Me, I like gardens with plain old trees and flowers. Maybe one of these days, I'll stop listening to other people and start doing what I want."

"Why not start today?"

"All right," she said, and kissed my mouth.

Exactly what I wanted, but I was stunned.

"Wait here." She went inside the house.

Leaving me in a garden of art marveling at the vagaries of the human condition. Jilly had morphed from an impossible dream to one about to come true. Crazy. But no crazier than my presence amid a pile of junk that was the pinnacle of creativity in the modern world; long gone and forgotten was the creativity of thousands of years ago, when civilizations erected majestic pyramids as monuments to . . .

Thinking of which, I searched my device for the actor she'd mentioned named Hawkins. Turned out he was the Jack Hawkins who'd commanded a Brit frigate in another of my favorite old war films, *The Cruel Sea*. *Land of the Pharaohs* was the in-living-Technicolor story of a pharaoh who wanted to take it all with him, and so he devised a scheme that would impregnably lock his remains and riches in a pyramid forever. Filly must have been a beauty if Hawkins preferred her over the king's lady, who was played by Joan Collins. Like mother, like daughter—

"Benn," Jilly called.

I looked up and saw her at a window. She crooked a finger, then disappeared.

I found her in a bedroom larger than my apartment. The only furniture was an enormous bed veiled by gauzy linen billowing in a breeze coming through the window. She sat cross-legged on the bed, naked except for a gold chain from which a heavy gold ankh hung between her perfect breasts.

"Why are you looking at me like that, Benn?"

"I'm wondering why this is happening."

"I'm attracted to you. Isn't that enough?"

"It would be . . . if it were true."

All at once, she looked about to cry. "I'm not much good at this, Benn. I don't know much about sex. I never did. The only man who understood me was my husband."

"Sholty Chennault the Third."

"You know about Sholty?"

I shrugged. "Do I?"

She sat up and pulled a length of linen from a bedpost, knotted it around her like a sarong, and sat on the side of the bed. She clenched the ankh in her fist as she spoke.

"Sholty was the only man I ever loved. The day he died was the worst day of my life." She wiped her eyes and sniffled, her stare growing distant. "I should have been with him, but I was shopping in town. For such a god-awful day, the weather was so beautiful. From town, you could look across the water and see our house."

She wiped her eyes again, then looked squarely at me.

"That day was the last time I felt happy. Afterward, his family piled on me, real bad. His mom and sister didn't like me from the start. They said I was responsible—a murderer. You can imagine what that did to me. A friend of mine hooked me up with Raphael Borg. Rafe came west and kicked the hell out of the Chennault lawyers. I know you don't like Rafe, but if it wasn't for him, I wouldn't have anything. I don't even know how much I'm worth, but Rafe says I'm a billionaire. But the money doesn't mean anything. All money can buy is toys. Like this."

She picked up a remote, and a wall became a 3-D screen, on it a TV broadcast of an awards show.

"Rafe surrounds me with toys. When I first saw the shit—pardon my French, the *art*—he set outside the house, I thought he was playing a joke on me. But Rafe said they were an investment, that they appreciate in value."

"Forget Rafe. Tell me about the man you were with in Panama."

"What man?"

"Evgeny Kursk."

She winced as if I'd struck her.

I sat next to her and cupped her chin. "We're friends, remember? Friends need to be honest with one another. Be honest with me."

She nodded. "I haven't even seen him since Panama."

I thought about Courchevel but said nothing.

"I pretended to be nice to Evgeny as a favor to Natty."

"Because Natty's your business associate, right?"

"Don't mock me, Benn. Sometimes things are hard to explain. Rafe got me involved in business with Natty. Maybe too involved. That's why I have to go along with things. But the truth is, I'm trying to break things off with Natty. Rafe knows he made a mistake: he wants me to end it, too."

Because Rafe's scared to death of the consequences. "Exactly what was this business?"

She didn't reply. She was looking at the wall screen, where a woman in a glitzy dress holding a statuette was making a speech.

"I knew her in acting school," Jilly said, nodding toward the screen. "Don't know why I bothered going, but looks like she made it to the top. Momma was wrong about me being an actress. Can you picture me, an actress?"

I nodded. "Actually, I can."

I meant it. She had the necessary ingredients. Not just the physical attributes, but the me-first attitude of ultranarcissists. I should know because I'm one of them. A closet *artiste*. Back when I was middling along, I'd even written a novel: *Drug Lawyer*. Got rejected up the kazoo.

"I wasn't much at acting," Jilly said. "I was too scared to let it out in front of people. Closest I ever got to it was the kind of film where the maids wear black-lace undies. Took a long time before I felt clean again after that."

I wanted to get out of there. Jilly needed taking care of, but not by me. That was Rafe's job. She no longer was the unattainable object of my desire. I'd wanted to know how she was connected to Natty and Kursk, but clearly, I wasn't going to get a straight answer out of her. She was either cleverer than I was or truly didn't know anything. Didn't matter. I'd find the answers elsewhere.

"Benn? Where're you going? Don't leave . . ."

I hustled downstairs. By the front door, Jilly's bag sat atop a side table. It was open. Folded documents protruded. The corner of one bore a familiar logo: BOP—Bureau of Prisons. I took it from the bag. It was as an application for a sponsored paralegal to visit federal inmates. The blanks were filled in.

I was named as the sponsoring attorney.

The paralegal was Jillian Sholty.

I ripped the application into pieces and threw them into the air. They were still falling as I left.

At four in the morning, Miami Beach was a dump. The A-listers were cooping up, and the streets belonged to working girls and dopers. When I got home, I couldn't sleep, so I sat on the terrace, considering the state of my life.

The year had started with the soaring promises of my trilogy of new cases, all of which had flattened out to the same old, same old. Rigo was shaping up to be a small score, maybe even a total beat. Bolivar was a million-dollar man, but after Foto's cut and taxes, the number would finance just a couple of years of my retirement. As for *Sombra*, he was all smoke and mirrors; most probably, he was playing me.

After all, everyone else was.

CHAPTER 41

Back in New York, I got a call from Paz: *Sombra* wanted to meet me again. Paz was ecstatic. I wasn't.

"You should be," he said. "He'll pay for your time. So, then, tomorrow?"

I told him we'd meet tomorrow and hung up. I was just leaving the office when I had an unexpected visitor. Sandra Milena, Rigo's wife. She looked as if she'd been having a bad time.

"All these people I don't know claim Rigo owes them money. They make threats."

Standard operating procedure in the drug world. Eat the weak. She asked me to arrange for her to visit Rigo. She didn't need me to do it, but I helped, anyway. She was a nice lady who'd been trapped in a bad marriage.

"My advice is to tell these people that Rigo refuses to tell you where his money is . . . What?"

She'd begun crying. She said she'd told the people exactly that—because it was true. So they had taken her son Omar as a hostage to force Rigo to pay. That was why she was visiting, to beg Rigo to save Omar's life.

"I feel terrible about you, too, Doctor. I know Mondragon stole your fee. I was able to borrow some . . . I know it's not much, but I'm trying to sell some cattle . . ."

She gave me a thin envelope. Seven thousand dollars. An insult. For a moment, I was about to return it; then I realized she wore no jewelry. Even her wedding ring was gone. Obviously, Rigo's family was on the run, selling their gold to survive.

"Thanks," I said. "Let me know when you do."

The next day, Paz picked me up at the airport in Bogotá. Since I was embarking on an unscheduled journey into the unknown—likely to another remote location with rough characters—I carried my passport and money in a belt beneath my shirt.

Our ride was an anonymous *amarillo*. Paz told the cabby to drop us at the base of Monserrate, the revered mountain below which the Spaniards had built the original settlement of Santa Fe de Bogotá. Now it was a tourist destination. I figured we were there to get lost in a crowd, shaking off any following parties before the next leg of our trip.

Wrong. At this hour on a weekday morning, no tourists were there. The red cable cars that carried visitors to the top of Monserrate disappeared into clouds halfway up the mountain. We stood beneath the overhang of the ticket booth while Paz sent a text. It began raining while we waited for a response.

Behind the ticket seller, an old black-and-white television was tuned to the news. I paid it little attention, but then the images caught my eye, and I stared at the screen, riveted.

A mustached military officer whose uniform breast was plastered with fruit salad was conducting a news conference. Beneath the visor of his oversize hat, flashbulbs reflected off his sunglasses, but I recognized his face. It was General Uvalde, relating the latest blow he had inflicted on *Los Hachos*.

His antidrug commandos had surrounded a *finca* in Envigado, and a firefight had ensued. The screen cut to corpses littering the ground alongside a corral. The bloody, battered faces of three *Los Hachos* who had been killed there appeared: Rigo's son Omar; father-in-law, Ochoa;

and wife, Sandra Milena, who had clearly returned to Colombia just ahead of me and been murdered for her effort.

The men I understood. They were players and accepted the rules. But poor Sandra Milena's only crime had been marriage to an ugly misogynist who'd gotten on General Uvalde's bad side.

"You okay?" Paz said. "You're pale."

"Something I ate. Be right back."

I went to a men's room, where I splashed water on my face. In the mirror, my face looked haunted. Hunted.

Would I be next on Uvalde's hit list?

Too late to worry about that now.

When I emerged, Paz was reading a reply to his text. He motioned for me to follow, and we boarded a cable car. There were no other passengers. The car started with a lurch and rose quickly, and soon entered fog thick as cotton candy. I couldn't stop thinking about Rigo's family. Without Rigo, they were harmless; yet they'd been killed. But not—as Sandra Milena had inferred—by other drug bosses. No, the killers were Uvalde's men. *Why?*

And again, I wondered:

Am I being set up?

The cable car stopped, and we stepped onto a platform. I could see no farther than my shoes. I followed Paz along a path. A few dozen yards ahead, a figure appeared from the mist, the Indian giant I'd dubbed Zapata but knew was *Sombra*. I sensed another person hidden in the fog as well.

Paz left us alone.

Magically, a small figure appeared. Holding an envelope in the web between his shortened fingers, he handed it to me. Another fifty-grand-size brick. "For your expenses," he said. "You will receive the remainder after you succeed in freeing Joaquin Bolivar."

Say what? I was amenable to installment plans, but *never* to not-enough money-downs. Then again, *if* Bolivar was *Sombra* after all—the

Colombians were expert at covert games—then I'd already gotten a hefty down payment, courtesy of Natty Grable's Murmansk-54 check for a mil. If—a big *if*—Zapata was *Sombra*, then his and the Russian's mutual interest in Bolivar's well-being was motivated by the fear he'd flip on them. If that was how things played out, I didn't even want to speculate on what Zapata and Natty might have in store for me. It was, as Pablo Escobar used to say, an endgame of either *plata o plomo*. Silver or lead.

A scream echoed from the mist.

I turned, but there was nothing to see. Stillness in the whiteness. When I turned back around, I was alone.

I went back to the cable car. No Paz. For a moment, I feared the scream had been his, that he'd slipped and fallen on the slick landing. But the area was protected by high railings. So I assumed the scream was a bird—a condor or something—and Paz had already returned to the base below.

I entered the cable car. When I closed the door, it began descending. Alone in a box in a white world, I was plenty spooked. Seconds seemed like hours, until the car finally emerged from the fog, and—

Stopped short, swaying.

A distant siren sounded from far below. At the base, bubble lights were turning; the tiny figures of cops were pointing. Not at the cable car but beneath it. I looked down and saw a small figure sprawled on the mountainside.

Paz.

He had to have been pushed. But by whom? *And why?* I'd been left—literally—dangling. Was I being set up as the prime suspect in Paz's death?

Come to that, how had the cops responded so quickly? And then it dawned on me. They hadn't come for me, but for Zapata . . . *Sombra*.

As if validating this deduction, a dark Lincoln with tinted windows and Colombian flags on the hood appeared below, and a uniformed figure got out.

General Uvalde.

CHAPTER 42

The forested mountainside where Paz lay was a hundred feet below the car. A ridge paralleled the cable route. Along the ridgetop was a stand of pines whose tips reached to within a few feet of the car. If I could jump from the car and grab a limb, and if it didn't snap, and if I managed to climb down, and if I found my way off the mountain, I could . . .

Too many *ifs* . . . but only one choice.

I tried the cable-car door, but it was locked. Probably it only opened when the car was docked. The hinged windows opened outward. I undid a slide bolt and pushed a window open as far as it would go.

That gained me a small opening: Enough to squeeze through?

I looked at the base: an army truck was depositing soldiers, some already climbing toward me.

I put one leg through the window, and then the other, and bent backward as I pulled my upper body through the opening. A final lurch, and I was out, but I nearly lost my balance—a stomach-churning moment with nothing but air below my feet—before I managed to grab the window frame.

My movement had started the car swaying, and I now hung at the most distant point in the arc from the treetops. At the opposite apogee, I reached for the limbs and let go of the car.

The limb I seized bent precariously, but just before it snapped, I wrapped my legs around the treetop's narrow trunk. Oblivious to scratches and scrapes, I worked my way down as the trunk grew thicker, falling the last few feet to earth, then rolling down a steep slope until coming to rest against an object. A fallen limb?

Gah!

I rested against Paz's torso.

I recoiled, staggered upright, and limped away. I hurt all over and couldn't move fast, but the ridge blocked me from the base below, and the soldiers would think I was still in the cable car. I hoped. I figured my only escape was by moving sideways along the face of the mountain, descending when well away from the cable-car area.

It wasn't easy going, but soon the sirens were barely audible. Now, the way was more arduous, along rocky ledges on the high ridge until I found myself on the edge of a precipice. I heard a sound behind and turned—

A big black dog sheathed in a police coat raced toward me. I moved back, but tripped and fell as the dog leaped. Instinctively, I raised my arms and gripped the dog's forelegs; aided by its momentum, I yanked it overhead, and the beast hurtled past into thin air. I heard it hit, far below. I looked and saw the dog lying on a beaten track that led to thick vegetation.

I slid down the cliff side.

The track was a forestry trail. I followed it until it ended at a paved road with traffic. After a while, a taxi appeared. I must have looked a mess because the cabby didn't seem as if he was going to stop, not until I took a fistful of American dollars from my money belt and flagged him down.

I told him to head to north Bogotá. I calmed myself and devised a plan: clean myself, change clothing, make as if nothing had happened.

The cabby's radio was tuned to Grupo Niche, an oldie but goodie salsa band, ironically promoted by my first Biggy . . . Nacho—

The music was interrupted by breaking news: *Sombra* and several associates had been spotted at Monserrate; at least one man was dead, and others were the subjects of a manhunt being personally directed by General Uvalde—

News flash: If Uvalde were hunting Zapata, then he had to be *Sombra*. Didn't he? But then again, in the Byzantine world of Colombian drugsters and their enablers, nothing was ever as it seemed.

We were back in north Bogotá now.

"Take me to El Retiro," I said.

I thought the driver was eyeing me in his rearview. No way I could trust him knowing where I was going. El Retiro was a mall in the crowded, upscale T Zone, a place from which I could take another taxi to a safe place. If there were such a thing.

I had to disappear before Uvalde disappeared me.

Passport!

In my money belt, thank God.

El Retiro had four entrances. I fast-walked through one, purchased clothing off the rack, washed in a men's room, changed into my new clothes, and left the old in a waste bin. Nothing I could do about the scratches. I left El Retiro via a different entrance than I'd entered. Another taxi took me to the airport.

My body ached in earnest now.

Army trucks were parked outside the international terminal.

"Take me to the domestic terminal," I said.

"You said international—"

"I misspoke. Domestic."

No troops at the domestic terminal. If Uvalde were watching international, that probably meant he knew who I was. My nerves felt electric as I purchased a seat—for cash, my credit card being a homing device—on the next flight to Cartagena.

The agent issued my ticket. So far my name wasn't on the no-fly list. But I knew it would be soon enough. I waited for the flight in a stall in the men's room.

I didn't come out until final boarding, averting my face as I went through the gate. My heart didn't slow until we were wheels-up.

Forget 1-A, too visible. I had a window seat in the last row. The plane was old, and the tail section vibrated. Just a few inches of aluminum composite separating me from a five-mile trip to eternity.

I was too hot to chance working, much less remaining, in Colombia. My glory days here were done. Maybe I'd revert to being just another criminal-defense lawyer, a scrounger in the state courts. If I were lucky.

For sure, Uvalde knew guys with guns who would travel—

Stop it, Bluestone. Slow down. Forget tomorrows. Take it one day at a time. Starting right now.

Cartagena: Find a quiet corner of the airport. Two minutes before the next US-flagged carrier heads stateside, buy a cash ticket and board at the last minute.

Which, tight asshole and all, is exactly what I did.

I thanked God as the flight lifted from Colombian soil.

After midnight, Miami International was slow enough for an immigration agent to give me a long look before scribbling on my entry form. Whatever he wrote prompted a customs agent to suggest I accompany him to a private room. When I did, he asked why I wasn't carrying luggage.

"It was stolen."

"What happened to your face?"

"Fighting the thieves."

"I need for you to take your jacket off."

I took my jacket off. He looked at my middle, and I realized my money belt showed. "Shirt, too," he said.

I took it off and undid the money belt. He took out the money and counted it. Three thousand American and a thousand in Colombian. Less than half the $10,000 maximum that could be brought into the country undeclared.

"You want, I'll get naked," I said.

"Yeah? Well, maybe I want."

"Okay . . ."

He smiled. "It's April Fool's Day. Now get out of here. And take a bath."

It wasn't until I was undressing to take the recommended bath when I realized the envelope containing $50,000 that *Enano* had given me was in my coat pocket. Forty thousand more than the undeclared limit. And here I'd been practically daring the agent to continue searching me. Had he done so, I'd have been busted.

He busted me on something, though.

I was truly an April fool.

CHAPTER 43

The next morning, I woke up angry. Functioning on a diet of lies was like doing brain surgery with one hand tied behind your back. My life had become hardwired to three cases chock-full of half-truths. Time to untangle the mess.

I drove to Jilly's island estate outside Miami. The front gate was locked. No one answered the bell. I looked up the driveway but saw no cars parked. I tried calling, but Jilly's phone rang unanswered. No voice mail. I tried calling Natty Grable. No answer. His voice-mail box was full. I tried calling Foto, but his phone went unanswered. I left a message for him to call me ASAP.

Was I paranoid? Was everyone connected to Joaquin Bolivar avoiding me? Well, not everyone. I got back into the Bentley and drove to the jail.

Fercho sat across from me with his hands in his lap. Ronald Relaxation.

"Fuck you," I said. "Tell me what's happening, or we're history."

"You're upset because of what happened to Rigo's family?"

"That and some other things you know about. Talk to me."

"Rigo's family weren't good people. Forget them."

"You knew it was going to happen."

"Some things are obvious—"

"Their murder was *obvious?*"

"I warned you. Mondragon. Uvalde. Same shit, different color."

That's all he had to say. I should've known confronting him wouldn't fly. Fercho would divulge what and when *he* wanted to.

"How's Rigo handling it?" he asked.

"Haven't seen him lately."

"Maybe you should."

I waited for Fercho to elaborate, but he didn't. In fact, I was dreading visiting Rigo. I felt bad about his family, but not so bad I wanted to hold his hand. I wished I could dump him as a client. Not a viable alternative. Abandoning a client like Rigo mid-case would spell the end of my rep as a stand-up guy.

"The scratches on your face," Fercho said. "From when you were running from Uvalde, after you met the man you hope to make your client."

Fuck Fercho. "There are many men I'd like to have as clients."

"I'm referring to number one on the hit parade."

"Fercho, you're too smart for your own good. You need me to get you out of your jam. Help your cause by making me happy. Be smart, and tell me who you work for."

"If I was smart, I wouldn't be in here."

I stood. "See you next time I'm around."

"You're going south again?"

I decided to throw Fercho a bone, hoping it would loosen his tongue. "I'll never go back to Colombia. Your thoughts on why?"

"Never say never, Benn."

CHAPTER 44

I returned to New York. Fercho wasn't the only one who could unlock my mysteries. Foto had been in the game from the beginning. I tried calling him, but a recorded message said he was not available. I realized he must have gotten my earlier voice mail but for some reason had chosen to ignore it.

Was Traum right about my not trusting him? I'd thought Foto was my friend. When my phone rang, I grabbed it immediately. "Where you been?"

"As if it's your business?" Kandi Kauffman said.

"Oh, ah . . . what about Bolivar's proffer?"

"Like, why I'm calling? Tomorrow."

I could tell Kandi was hot to trot, but I wanted to speak to Bolivar before he proffered. "Before the proffer, it would be helpful if I went over the discovery with him. When will you be sending it?"

"Um, like, a week ago?"

I glanced at the mail stacked atop my desk. Sure enough, there was an envelope whose return was EDNY US Attorney, with her name inked below. There was a teensy circle atop the *i* in *Kandi*.

"So you did," I said. "How about, say, three days?"

"How about, say, two days? Day after tomorrow?"

I agreed and got to work. There wasn't much in the discovery envelope. An intake sheet detailing the extradition of Joaquin Bolivar. A copy of a hand-drawn map signed by Special Agent Charles Scally: a wavy line indicating a shoreline; an *x* marked *House*; an *x* marked *Sailboat*.

There were also several photographs:

A shot of a black sailboat at anchor. Bolivar's *Swan*, I assumed.

Bales of weed stacked in a hold.

A cabin with a bed, sheets askew. On a table a candle burned alongside two empty wineglasses, on one rim a smear of lipstick. An apple someone had taken a bite out of.

The envelope also included a CD and an accompanying transcript of four recorded conversations that were exactly as I'd expected: four UMs—unidentified males—each phoning another and drawing them into agreeing to accept payment of an old debt, for monies advanced in "the venture we tried up there six years ago." The final call was to Bolivar.

That was it.

What wasn't there verified what I'd already thought: that, apart from the seized weed, the sole evidence against Bolivar was testimonial. The only question was whether the cooperating crew members were believable. Since they'd be telling the truth, they'd be difficult to shake, but I'd done so before, and blessed with a little luck, I might work my old blue magic again—

My phone rang.

Again I grabbed it, hoping it was Foto. Again I was disappointed. The caller was Natty Grable's sidekick, Andrey. "Is our friend going to court soon?"

Andrey was close to the people—Jilly and Natty—facilitating Bolivar's fee, but that didn't give them dibs on knowing about the case. Especially since Bolivar's next trip from jail wasn't to court but to proffer, which meant he was cooperating. But refusing to answer Andrey would raise suspicion. Best to keep things vague.

"Day after tomorrow," I said.

"What time?"

I hesitated. They might, as they'd pretended to do with Jilly, send someone to observe the proceedings. Okay: Kandi's habit was to meet cooperators early. Therefore: Bolivar would proffer until early afternoon.

"Probably late afternoon," I said.

"We appreciate your assistance."

I wondered: *What assistance?*

CHAPTER 45

The next morning, I went to MDC Brooklyn. I offered my right hand to be stamped.

"Left hand today," Bonesy said.

I got stamped and went through the metal detector and put my left hand beneath CONTROL'S black light. The daily password was a fluorescent green smear; illegible, but apparently the jail didn't give a shit. Neither did I.

"Enter."

While waiting for Bolivar, I hit the vending machine for an espresso. Not bad, considering. And the coffee smell killed the disinfectant stink permeating the visit room.

While sipping, I noticed the last visit room, the big one, was now completely filled with cartons, rows of them, stacked floor to ceiling. Between the rows a couple of inmates and some flunky lawyers associated with Morty Plitkin were gabbing.

Bolivar showed up in the visit room looking as if he'd dropped a few pounds, and his hair was longer since I'd seen him last. We went into a room, sat facing each other.

"What's the word, Benn?"

"You proffer tomorrow."

"I'm ready for Freddie."

"Lose the jailhouse banter. You're not ready. I've changed my mind about our approach. The prosecutor's too eager to proffer you. My guess is, she knows the weed was a prelude to bigger things. She's going to expect you to tell her who else was involved on the cocaine end."

"Let's stick with Plan A," he said. "It was in my mind only."

"I don't think she'll buy it."

"Why not?"

A question I preferred not answering. Although certain Bolivar would prevaricate, I'd arranged the proffer hoping it would be a meet and greet; Kandi would admonish and threaten Bolivar with trial and its consequences if he didn't truthfully cooperate, after which he would do so. Maybe. In truth, I half hoped we'd go to trial.

"She just won't," I said.

"So, I'll tell her what I was really up to."

"Not enough. Successful cooperation doesn't mean giving yourself up. It means giving other people up."

"Let's see how it goes tomorrow."

"Don't nonchalant this, Joaquin."

"I have faith. You're an ace."

I was sure he'd flunk the proffer. Then again, Kandi would probably allow him a second try for the gold ring. Actually, it wasn't a bad strategy: even a failed proffer might result in the government tipping its hand.

"A woman scratched you? I hope she was worth it."

"I don't scratch and tell," I said.

CHAPTER 46

Kandi arrived with her usual pomp and circumstance: carrying a tin of home-baked cookies, wearing a tight-fitting blouse and skirt, streaked hair blow-dried just so, lips perfectly glossed. Her face was smooth and plump, but her neck resembled snakeskin.

She offered Bolivar the cookie tin. He chose a chocolate chip, shyly murmured thanks.

Kandi smiled. "May I call you Joaquin?"

"Yes, of course."

"Joaquin, your lawyer has explained the proffer rules?"

"He has."

"Excellent. Why don't you start by telling us about the marijuana you attempted to bring into the United States?"

Bolivar immediately went into the narrative. He said that six years ago, he'd assembled a crew. Four Americans. They'd anchored a sailboat off Colombia's Guajira Peninsula, where they loaded their vessel with three tons of weed purchased from growers in the Sierra Nevada coastal range.

Scally asked, "Indians?"

Bolivar nodded. "Everything went smoothly. We took our time sailing northward and dropped anchor off Long Island. It was an area of vacation homes, so we thought there'd be no Coast Guard patrols. We made sure to arrive two days before the guys who'd be buying the weed so we could scope the scene. The first night I took the Zodiac ashore. The area was very posh, big mansions far apart. On the beach in front of one, there was a party going on. I wandered into it and met this girl. We smoked a J and took a walk. All of a sudden, fireworks went off—I didn't realize until then it was July Fourth—and in their light, she saw the sailboat. When I told her it was mine, she wanted to go out to it. I wanted to go, too, away from where the guy who owned the mansion might find us."

"Understandable," Scally said.

Joaquin smiled boyishly. "The guy who owned the mansion, some ancient playboy, thought he was her boyfriend. So when she went missing, someone told him about me and her smoking a J and taking off in the Zodiac. He went ballistic. Called the local cops. They didn't think it was so important, but he was a big shot, so they sent an off-duty cop who lived in the next town—Hampton Bays, as I recall—to find us and roust me."

Kandi and Scally exchanged glances. "Please continue," she said.

"The cop wasn't happy about holiday duty and took his own sweet time getting there. For company, he took his dog along. Didn't take long for him to follow our footprints in the sand, to where the Zodiac had been ashore. Naturally, they spotted the sailboat, and the mansion guy offered his speedboat for the cop to go there. The cop was reluctant, but the rich guy was making noise that the girl had been kidnapped, so the cop and his dog went out to the sailboat. Turned out the dog was a K-9, or whatever they call it, and when they neared the sailboat, the dog started sniffing and went nuts."

Scally looked about to speak, but Kandi raised a palm. "Please continue," she said.

"The cop realized he was onto something big and went back ashore and notified his boss. They were just village police, and this was a potentially armed target, but because it was a holiday, no state cops were available in the vicinity. But it turned out some federal agents were on duty in Hampton Bays, and a couple hours later, they showed up—"

"Stop," Kandi said. She nodded at Scally.

"Everything you say is true," Scally said. "What's bothering us is how you know what happened before me and my partner went out to the sailboat."

"Afterward, I hired a lawyer, a local guy, to find out."

"How'd a lawyer know about private police communications?"

Bolivar shrugged. "I had the impression he was friendly with the local cops."

"What's the lawyer's name?" Kandi said.

"I honestly don't recall," Bolivar said. "Anyway, we never saw the cop in the first boat. But it was getting light when the feds came out. My crew spotted them first and took off in the Zodiac. Last I saw, they were going like a bat out of hell, heading who knows where. Me, I was belowdecks with the girl, but when I heard the commotion, I split. Jumped, swam ashore, and made tracks."

"Who was the woman?" Kandi said.

"Don't recall her name, either."

From a file, Scally took a mug shot. "Recognize this guy?"

"Looks like my first mate, Rocky. Hard to tell. He got old."

"You recognized his voice pretty good, though."

Bolivar nodded ruefully, and I guessed Rocky was the UM whose recorded call had revived the conspiracy. Rocky wasn't the only crew member prepared to testify against Bolivar. Scally showed Bolivar three more mug shots, which he identified as Fuji, Teddy, and JD.

Scally said, "Forget about the weed. What else you want to tell us?"

Bolivar seemed puzzled. If I didn't know otherwise, I'd have bought it.

"Joaquin, we know certain other *things* about you?" Kandi said.

Scally set down two more photographs: one of the sailboat and one of its cabin, both of which had been in the discovery. His index finger tapped the sailboat. "You don't make money running small loads of weed. Who was your partner for the cocaine run you had planned after the weed route was secure?"

Bolivar looked at the photograph. "The *Swan* . . . if that boat was a woman, I'd have married her . . ."

The same line he'd fed me. I remembered an adage an old-time trial lawyer told me when I was starting out: *When a story is word-for-word pat, there's a plan behind it.* I wondered what Bolivar was plotting.

Kandi tapped her red nails on the tabletop, waiting.

"No cocaine run was planned," said Bolivar.

I drew a breath. Goddamn, it was really happening: I was going to trial against Kandi.

Scally's finger moved to the second photograph, pointing at the wineglass whose rim bore lipstick. "Again, who was the girl?"

"Remember the body, not the name," Bolivar said, wistfully.

"Remembering when your life was good?" Scally snarled. "Too bad you ain't going back to it. Because you're full of shit."

"Joaquin," Kandi said gently, "you must be truthful about *all* your criminal activities, okay? We want to know about your partner, and what was planned after the marijuana import."

Scally said, "Also about the woman whose lipstick is on the glass."

"I don't know any of these things," Bolivar said.

"We're going to take a break," Kandi said. "During it, confer with your lawyer."

Kandi and Scally left the room. Nelson Cano took a cookie; then he, too, left. The door shut, leaving us alone.

"So now decide," I said. "Give her what she wants, or the proffer's over."

"Tell them I need to think about it. Tell them I need an hour, whatever. In the meantime, it would be good if someone could get me lunch from the cafeteria."

Kandi and her cops and marshals were in the corridor. She was talking and texting. She paused and looked at me.

"He wants to think about it a couple minutes, have some lunch," I said. "Then I think he'll be ready to talk truth."

Scally snorted. "This fucking guy doesn't set our timetable."

Kandi shrugged. "We'll give him time. Like, two days?"

I went back inside and told Bolivar.

He frowned. "What time is it?"

"Eleven thirty."

"Tell them I'll talk now."

I went back out, but Kandi was gone. Scally and Cano went into the room and cuffed Bolivar. As I walked off, I heard Bolivar asking Scally to call Kandi and say he was ready to tell the truth. Scally demurred. All of which left me doubly troubled:

What was behind Bolivar's sudden turnaround?

And why was Scally so interested in the woman?

CHAPTER 47

When I got into the Flex, it smelled of home cooking. Val was about to dig into a dish Sonia had prepared. "Sorry, Mr. Benn. I thought you'd be gone longer. Where to now?"

Good question. I had no idea. It was a sunny day in big-sky Brooklyn, and I didn't feel like heading back into shadowed Manhattan. I looked at the lawn of Cadman Plaza Park, the trees on the verge of full bloom.

Val picked up on my mood. "My Sonia, she gives me food for *two* people. Why we should go back to city? Why not we have a picnic?"

Why not, indeed? I nodded, and we drove off.

"I know nice place not far," Val said.

We drove through brownstone Brooklyn. Boerum Hill and Carroll Gardens and Park Slope. I figured we were headed into Prospect Park and perked up at the thought of visiting the greens where I'd played away my boyhood. But the Flex passed the park and entered the Windsor Terrace neighborhood, then slowed as it neared the grandly Gothic entrance of Green-Wood Cemetery.

"Val—"

"Trust Valery, Mr. Benn. Gonna show you very nice place for picnic. Relax and enjoy view while we go to top of hill. Meanwhile, tell me, what song is this?" Val hummed a vaguely familiar tune.

"I don't know. What?"

"'Whatever Lola Wants.'"

"Right. Lola gets."

"The Lola of the song? Lola Montez, she buried over there."

"Really?" I looked around, slightly stunned at what a lovely place this cemetery was: attended greenery and grand old trees, studded with lavish vaults and mausoleums, all on a cone-shaped hill in the middle of flat Brooklyn. I must've driven past Green-Wood a thousand times but never imagined what it was like.

"Over there," said Val like a bona fide tour guide, "is grave of Governor DeWitt Clinton, who builds Erie Canal. Over there is newspaperman Horace Greely, who tells young men go west. History of America, this place. Top is called Battle Hill, where English killed four hundred Maryland soldiers, but delay allowed General Washington to save rest of army, and eventually US of A is born, thank you, God."

The Flex rounded a curve and stopped. Val got out and set Sonia's lunch down on a stone bench. We ate in silence. It was a clear day with a forever view. Birds chirped, and insects hummed amid the young flower beds. Incredible that such a place existed in the middle of the big city.

I looked at Val, chewing contentedly. "You come here a lot?"

"I like here very much. I come here while waiting for you in MCC. That mausoleum there?"

I followed his gaze to a white-marble vault shaped like a pyramid. I supposed it was intended to be a grandly magificent structure, but it resembled a Hollywood set. Maybe because it looked new. On the lintel above its sealed door were gilded rudimentary images resembling Egyptian hieroglyphics. Birds. Soldiers. Maidservants. A reposing queen. And a name.

I squinted to make it out but couldn't in the glare of day.

"I went there," Val said. "It say letters. F-I-L-L-Y."

I felt as if an unmarked box were being opened.

"Last time I here?" Val said. "Car I know parks in front of it. Big gray stretch with front like dog. Same stretch that bring Jilly lady to court. Remember, when she pretends she meets you by accident?"

I remembered.

CHAPTER 48

When I got home that evening, Traum called.

"Turn on the news."

When I did, an on-the-scene reporter was breathlessly relating a story about a violent encounter. Even before I comprehended the subject matter, I recognized the crime scene behind the reporter: in the foreground, a dreary cobblestone street where police vehicles were haphazardly parked around a bullet-riddled white van, seagulls wheeling above piers, and green harbor water. In the distance was a large building whose unadorned facade was lined with slit windows.

MCC Brooklyn.

The reporter said, "Federal authorities are not disclosing any details about the incident, which apparently was an attempt to liberate one or more inmates on the late-afternoon bus carrying them from court back to the jail where they were incarcerated—"

"You watching?" Traum growled in my ear.

"Yes."

My voice sounded far away, or maybe my heart was pounding so hard, I could hardly hear it. But the reporter's voice was loud and clear enough. *Too* loud and clear:

"The Bureau of Prisons has not yet stated whether any of the inmates escaped. All that is certain is that the two correctional officers on the bus are dead, as is one of the attackers."

The screen cut back to the studio.

"See you soon." Traum hung up.

I hardly recalled walking to the office; that's how totally distracted I was. Now I understood why Joaquin Bolivar had pressed for an unwinnable bail attempt, then abruptly decided to cooperate, then deliberately stalled. Every move was designed to generate extra trips from the MCC to the courthouse and back. Each round trip confirmed the route and procedure. They were *rehearsals*, just as the *Swan*'s weed run had been a rehearsal for a cocaine run. The cocaine route had not worked out, but had Bolivar been successful this time?

And would it affect me?

Unquestionably, the government would think so. But could they prove it? I replayed things in my mind's eye.

The multiple trips to court Bolivar had orchestrated were part of the normal process, perhaps a bit unusual, not at all incriminating.

Bolivar had asked me if the vans were escorted, and I'd replied that escorting was random. That conversation was private, so no problem there.

Then there was Bolivar's sudden insistence on continuing today's proffer, in reality an attempt to prolong his stay at the courthouse, to be on the late bus back, the one that had been targeted. Both Scally and Cano could testify that I'd tried to assist him, but that just meant I'd done what my client had asked, so no real problem there, either.

Most frightening of all was Andrey asking me when Bolivar would be in court, and my reply that it would be late afternoon, which could be construed as assisting the escape conspiracy. Still, no problem there; even if Andrey flipped, it was his word against mine.

I paced my office, waiting for Traum.

An hour passed, then two. I kept checking my device for a news story update, but the details remained unchanged. I tried calling Traum but got a recorded message saying he was unavailable.

Another hour passed. Another. He showed up just before midnight, chewing on a toothpick and reeking of Chinese food.

"For Chrissake," I said. "You keep me waiting while you stuff your gut?"

"Relax, Benno. I was waiting for the real dope. I'm not allowed to eat?"

"Whatever. Just tell me what happened."

"Rush hour," he said. "Traffic on the BQE and the Gowanus dead still, like a parking lot. When the jail van finally reaches Sunset Park, it's getting dark. It takes its regular route on Second Avenue along the waterfront. No people, no cars. All of a sudden, a pickup tears ass through a light and blocks the van from going forward. Another pickup comes from out of nowhere and blocks the back of the van. Trapped. No escorts for the van this trip. Before it can radio for help, its windshield is blown out. The driver buys it right away; the shotgun's hit bad."

Traum paused. I wanted to ask him what, if anything, had happened to Bolivar, but I didn't. We both knew that was all that mattered, but I didn't want to acknowledge it.

"The prisoners behind the cage were freaking. Some guys shitting bricks, thinking it's a hit on them. Others thinking they're Vin Diesel, busting out. They all shut the fuck up when half a dozen commando types in ski masks start opening the van with auto shears. Professionals, right?"

I shrugged.

Traum smiled. His teeth were gapped, and when he smiled, he reminded me of Ernest Borgnine, not Ernie the good guy, but the Ernie that nearly killed Sinatra in *From Here to Eternity*.

"Stop playing with my head, Traum. What else?"

"Bolivar wasn't on the late van. He was on the morning van."

I was still worried. I didn't care who Traum's sources were, but if he'd asked them about Bolivar's whereabouts, it potentially led back to my involvement.

He grasped my concern. "Relax, Benno. The friend of mine who tells me things let me have a look at the inmate court list for the day was all. He didn't have a clue as to who I was looking for. Besides, none of the inmates got away."

Without realizing it, I'd been holding my breath. Now I exhaled.

"The shotgun guard got off a shot before he croaked. Killed one of the attackers. My source in the medical examiner's office said the dead guy had jailhouse ink from some gulag camp. A hammer-and-sickle inside a barbed-wire star. I checked the tat out. Was all the rage in a camp called Murmansk-54. Want to know the dead guy's name?"

I kept my face still, my eyes heavy-lidded.

"Rodchenko. First name, Andrey."

I shrugged.

"This Andrey guy had the same tattoo as Natty Grable. And Evgeny Kursk. Kursk's come a long way since his jailbird days. Became one of them oligarchs. Mining, timber, a fleet of fishing boats that operate in the north Pacific, the import-export company name of Murmansk-54. Same name as the camp. Same outfit that paid you for Bolivar."

I hadn't mentioned my fee source to Traum. He waited for me to say something. When I didn't, he said, "Natty's gasoline-scam case? The one your pal Plitkin is his lawyer for?"

"Not my pal."

"The case against Natty's falling apart. Witnesses disappearing, that kind of stuff. The government's practically giving the case away. Time served, straight probation. But Natty and two illegal Russkies who couldn't make bail are going to trial. Weird, no? Weak case or not, who knows what a jury might do? Natty and his boys are risking a twenty-year downside, just to demonstrate that they're honest. Why?"

"Maybe Plitkin's stretching things out to make a few more bucks. None of my business. Or yours."

"Maybe. You never know. Mind if I smoke?"

"Yes. Even unlit, your stogie stinks."

"You're hurting my feelings. Here's another maybe-coincidence. Murmansk. During World War Two, icebreakers worked around the clock to keep the city open because it was the principal import point for supply convoys from the States. The route was called the Murmansk Run. A tough go. The U-boats made sure a lot of sailors never made it to Murmansk."

"That was then. What's it have to do with now?"

"Seems the principal *export* port to Murmansk was the Busch Army Terminal. In the middle of which is—"

"The MDC. I don't see any connection."

"Me neither. See, coincidences exist."

"Where you going with this?"

"Coincidences. You made a big score from these people. I want to do the same."

"My business is none of yours."

"I want to protect you, Benno."

"I don't need protection."

"Wrong. You may have a problem in your future. Guess which AUSA got tasked with the escape investigation?"

I didn't bother guessing. From Traum's demeanor, I knew it was Kandi. He took out a Zippo and lit the cigar.

"Put it out," I said.

"I don't think so," he said, blowing smoke. "Listen up, now. Scally's also working the escape. He's crazy, comes to Bolivar. Not because the case is unfinished business. He don't give a rat about that. Something else. That night, six years ago, when Scally made the seizure out on Long Island?"

"What about it?"

223

"Scally's partner at the time was a guy name of Mongello. The two of them were working with a joint task force based on Long Island. They were waiting on an informant for a coke bust, but word came that it wasn't going to happen until after the Fourth. So the local guys went home to be with their families, but Scally and Mongello weren't family types. They were more into drinking brewskies, and maybe getting lucky with a waitress. That's what they were doing when DEA told 'em to assist the local cop who stumbled over the weed. Which they did. They seized a boatload of weed, but the bad guys got away. Mongello heads back to the motel while Scally secures the load. When Scally gets back to the motel, Mongello's brains are splattered all over the wall."

"Who killed him?"

"Coroner's report found nothing suspicious about the circumstances, concluded suicide as the cause of death."

"Fed offs himself, that's big news. How come I never heard about it?"

"Blue wall of silence. DEA don't like showing its dirty laundry."

"All this is interesting, but it's not switching on any light."

"Not yet. That's what you're going to need me for. To switch on the light because, trust me, you don't want to be in the dark, not with what's maybe coming down the pike. So, be a smart guy. Give me ten grand against my hourlies."

Traum's fee was $150 an hour, plus expenses. When I'd first put him on the research into Murmansk-54, I'd written him a check for $5,000. "No way you've even billed out what I already paid you."

"Sure I have. See, a situation like this, I don't bill for quantity. I get paid for quality. Know what I mean?"

"No, I don't. And I'm not paying you another dime."

Traum shrugged, gave me another gap-toothed smile as he leaned over my desk, and ground out his cigar atop my lucky horseshoe.

"Hey," I said.

"Next time I'm here, have an ashtray. And I will be here. And you will pay me. And you'll thank me to boot."

"Get out."

"Good seeing you, too." He stood, stumbled, looked down. "Nice bag. Must've cost a fortune. Then again, you can afford a fortune."

I was fuming. *Fortune?* My briefcase was quality, but old and battered. Traum's remark sounded like the opening gambit in a game of extortion.

He paused on his way out the door. "Have a nice day. While you can."

"You threatening me?"

"Just telling you like it is. We're friends. Who knows? We may even turn out to be partners."

CHAPTER 49

Traum left me in a funk. The fact that he'd so easily figured Bolivar as the object of the prison-break attempt meant others would, too. In my business, image is everything, so I was automatically on a hot seat. Especially with Kandi running the investigation. Add to that Scally taking this personally because of his partner's death . . .

I wondered how Traum found out about that. Had to have been through someone close to Scally.

Such as DEA Special Agent Nelson Cano.

And how did Traum know the source of my fee? Did Cano have a contact in my bank? Or, more likely, a way to access my banking records? Maybe Traum had another person for that.

No matter which, it was troubling.

I flushed Traum's cigar butt and washed my horseshoe. Stood to leave—and tripped, then regained my balance, mouthing a curse at my briefcase, the one Traum had mockingly admired.

Only he hadn't been mocking it at all.

Because it wasn't my old briefcase.

This bag really did cost a fortune: green crocodile with heavy brass hardware. I opened the case. On the inside flap, a gold-leaf inscription read: *Raphael Borg, Esq.*

I remembered Borg fleeing my office, but not him leaving behind his bag. Set the way it was—leaning against the other side of my desk, partially obscured by a chair—I hadn't noticed it. Now I wondered why he hadn't called to ask for it. Had he thought he'd lost it somewhere else? Either way, I figured I'd call him and say I had the bag, and while I was at it, ask a few indiscreet questions about Jilly.

I found Borg's card and picked up my phone but paused, remembering to do unto others as they would do unto me. If the case were locked, I'd call Borg. If not, I'd have a look inside, maybe learn a little more about Jilly's world—and by extension, that of Bolivar, the Russians, and *Sombra*.

The case was unlocked.

Inside it, a file and a sheet of Borg's stationery. Nice paper, heavy stock, cream colored. Handwritten on it was a single line:

One million shares at $850 per share = $850,000,000.

Inside the file were copies of stock certificates from a company: Murmansk-54 Imports, Inc. The shareholder owning one million shares was Jillian Chennault.

Copies of two other documents were in the file. One was a bill of sale from a precious-metals company confirming the transfer of five tons of gold to Jillian Chennault. The second was an invoice from a company called Metalworks.

I looked up the price of gold and ran some numbers. Five tons of gold was worth approximately $150 million. An investment advised by Borg? That transaction plus the $850 million in stock totaled $1 billion—

Ping!

I had an e-mail from Traum. No message, just an attachment. I opened it and saw a headline:

CELEBRITY LAWYER FOUND DEAD

The circumstances were mysterious. The death had occurred some time ago, but the body wasn't discovered until the neighbors complained about the odor coming from the lawyer's luxurious downtown apartment. The police refused comment, but unnamed sources confirmed the cause of death was a gunshot wound "inconsistent" with suicide.

The lawyer was Raphael Borg.

CHAPTER 50

I had no doubt the unnamed source was correct: that Borg's death was not suicide but homicide. Poor Borg. Despite his drug-fueled paranoia, he had been right: people wanted to kill him. Colombians and Russians.

The sum of the parts was obvious: the killers were Bolivar's people, or Natty's crew, or both. But no matter which, they were mere cats' paws. The power wielding them had ordered the hit on Borg.

Sombra or Kursk.

Why? I had no idea but was certain of one thing: somehow Jilly had a part in the big picture.

Big, as in $1 billion.

And here I was, holding the bag that proved it.

Whoever killed Borg would not be pleased that I had it. But my giving the file to the police would serve no purpose other than entangling me in the circumstances.

I put the papers back in Borg's briefcase. From my armoire, I took a knapsack left by some forgotten Mr. Green. I wiped my prints from the briefcase, then put it inside the knapsack. I rummaged in the armoire and found a pair of five-pound weights I'd often vowed to exercise with but never had. I dropped them into the knapsack and buckled it shut. Then I slung it over my shoulder and left.

I walked a few blocks and found a phone shop, where I purchased a throwaway and some airtime. Then I called the precious-metals firm that had sold Jilly the gold. I told the receptionist I was interested in purchasing a large quantity of gold. She connected me to a man who asked what I meant by large.

"Upward of ten million dollars."

"We can accommodate you. Ingots or coins?"

"Um, a bit of each."

"Come in, and we'll discuss it," he said, and told me the address.

I told him I was on my way, although I had no intention of going there. No way I'd risk revealing myself, but at least I had verified the invoice as real. That left unanswered whether Jilly had purchased coins or ingots. And why.

I looked up Metalworks, which seemed to be some sort of specialty fabrication firm. I called and asked for a salesperson. When one came on the line, I said, "I'm interested in a special job. A *large* job. Do you folks have experience working with gold?"

"We do. In fact, we recently did a *very* large job, customizing gold for a customer."

"Would it be possible to see the finished product?"

"Sorry, sir, but at the customer's request, that information is confidential. But if you'd like to come to our factory showroom, we can show you photographs of other jobs."

"I'd like that, but I'm kind of busy just now. I'll call you back."

I went to my garage, got the Mini, drove to Brooklyn.

It's not easy disposing of something in the city. Too many people, too many cameras. Too few places where disposal is permanent. But I knew of one. I navigated the nearly deserted streets of the old Busch Army Terminal, my route a crazy quilt of squared blocks. I didn't think anyone was following me, but I was on a mission that inspired elevated security.

Finally, I turned a corner, and the MCC appeared ahead. I might be recognized here, but my presence in the area was perfectly normal. Lawyers and jails go together like a horse and carriage. It was 4:00 p.m. The jail count was on, and no visitors would be allowed to enter. Perfect.

I turned into the MCC's dead-end street but drove past the jail, continuing on for a few hundred yards, parking on the end of the pier jutting into the lower harbor.

I sat there like any lawyer with time to kill.

But my eyes were on the rearview mirror. When I was sure no one was remotely near the pier, I opened the door and got out, stood there with one arm propped on top of the car, looking at Miss Liberty. The knapsack dangled from my other arm.

I gave a casual look around and satisfied myself that the Mini blocked me from curious eyes or cameras. Then I swung the knapsack and released it. It hit the oily, green water, dipped for a moment, resurfaced, then slowly sank.

I drove back to MCC and entered the lobby.

"Count's still on, Counselor."

"Jeez, Bonesy, I forgot. And I got another appointment. I can't stick around until the count clears. Oh well, my client can wait."

"They're good at waiting, Counselor."

"Some business we're in, huh?"

I drove back to the city, feeling better. *Lighter*. It wasn't the loss of ten pounds of weight, rather the realization that Traum's veiled threat was controllable. Even if Traum had seen Borg's bag and realized what it was, there was no way he could prove anything. A question of "he says" versus what I say.

Dumping it had inspired my little ploy of trying but failing to see Bolivar, which had another benefit: Bonesy would remember the joking manner in which I had left, which suggested that I was not concerned about immediately speaking to Bolivar so as to concoct a story distancing ourselves from the escape attempt.

And if, unlikely as it seemed, Bolivar had not conspired to attempt his own escape, then I had no reason to speak to him now, either. The opposite. Given the failed proffer, best to let him stew in his own juices before opting for the next step, which I was reasonably sure would be another proffer that would hopefully lead to successful cooperation.

That night I slept soundly.

CHAPTER 51

The next day, the pendulum swung once again. When I got to the office, a man was standing outside. Nelson Cano.

Immediately, I recalled the idea of Cano being Traum's source of information concerning Scally. Even as Cano opened his mouth to speak, I wagged a finger in his face.

"Fuck Traum," I said. "And fuck you."

Cano arched a brow. "Take it easy, Counselor. Nothing personal. Just doing my job is all."

"Tell Traum he's not going to blackmail me."

"I don't know anyone named Traum. It might jog my memory if you tell me who he is."

I like to think I can read faces. God knows I'm often wrong, but I could have sworn by Cano's guileless expression that he was telling the truth.

"Never mind," I said. "Sorry."

"This is for you," Cano said, thrusting an envelope in the hand I'd just been pointing in his face. "Consider yourself served."

He left me there, holding the envelope.

I took the steps instead of the elevator. The four flights take a toll on my bum hip, but I didn't want to be in the cage elevator. Too jail-like, given my situation. I double-locked my office door, sat behind my desk, opened the envelope. Three documents were inside.

One was what lawyers call a target letter, informing me that I was being investigated for criminal conduct. It went on to say that as a consequence of the investigation, my presence was required at a Curcio hearing in the case of *United States of America v. Joaquin Bolivar*. More on Curcio-hearing particulars later: for now, suffice it to say they suck.

The second was a subpoena demanding that I appear to testify before a grand jury in the Eastern District of New York.

The third was another subpoena demanding that I turn over all my financial books and records between December of last year and the present. It took about a nanosecond to spark the realization that the dates corresponded to my receiving monies to represent Bolivar, Rigo, and *Sombra*.

I needed help.

Back in the days when I had been the head of a sizable firm instead of a one-man show, a lawyer named Joshua Waldman worked for me. Josh was what we in the business call a paper man. Hustlers like me are too busy or lazy to do legal research; instead, we hire legal brains like him to churn out motions and memoranda. Josh was the best paper man I ever knew. He had the rare gift of being able to analyze a broad situation, then clearly focus on the heart of the matter.

I phoned him and made an appointment.

The following morning I went to Josh's office. I hadn't been there before. It was way downtown on Fulton Street, a deco building with brass-trimmed elevators that whisked me up to a high floor with long corridors ending at windows offering bird's-eye views of New York Harbor. Nice. I'd expected Josh's office to be modest, because paper men don't make big bucks, but I was pleasantly surprised to find it a well-appointed suite.

Josh and I hadn't met in person in years. I'd heard he was building a white-collar practice. I don't even own a white collar, but he was the straight man I wanted between me and the law.

Josh didn't look the way I remembered him. The rumpled troll who used to slave at a keyboard was now a well-suited smoothie whose corner office had a curved-earth ocean view. When I entered, he greeted me with the same cheerful smile I recalled, but by the time I sat and we got down to business, he was no longer smiling.

"After you called, I had a conversation with Kandi Kauffman," he said.

"Fuck her. She loves this, putting me through the wringer."

"Yes, I did sense she was enjoying this matter. Have to keep an eye on that aspect. Moving on. I told her no point in your appearing before the grand jury, because you'd be taking the Fifth—"

"Fifty times, right in her face."

"Not necessary. She agreed. She was quite reasonable. The investigation, as you may have guessed, is centered on the escape attempt."

"Centered?"

"Her word, not mine. Centered, which I took to mean that there are collateral matters the government is interested in. We shall see. For now, we need to deal with what's on the table. Far as the subpoena for your books and records, we could move to quash, but in my opinion, Judge Trieant will uphold it. It being a given that we'll lose; no point in irritating the old gentleman."

"He is not a gentleman and never was."

"Possibly true, but irrelevant. Despite his progovernment proclivities on drug cases, when it comes to citizen's rights, Judge Trieant is surprisingly libertarian."

"Unfortunately, this is a drug case."

"A stretch of Ms. Kauffman's imagination, I think. Despite the nature of his clients, my client does not participate in their business affairs. Am I correct?"

"Absolutely, I do not," I said emphatically.

Did Josh buy it? Didn't matter. He was so straight, he refused to use office postal stamps to mail a personal bill. So straight, his ethics dictated that he not hear clients confess their sins, for if they ever were to testify, he would not assist them in being untruthful.

"Good," he said. "Ms. Kauffman sent over something by way of discovery in support of her motion for a Curcio hearing." He slid a sheet of paper across the desk. "It's the transcript of a conversation in which you allegedly participated."

I read it and nearly wept.

> ANDREY LNU: *Is our friend going to court soon?*
> B. BLUESTONE: *Tomorrow.*
> ANDREY LNU: *What time?*
> B. BLUESTONE: *Probably late afternoon.*
> ANDREY LNU: *We appreciate your assistance.*

When I looked up, Josh was looking at me.

"It's not what it seems," I said.

"No need to discuss that just yet."

"They're listening to my phone?"

"To the phone belonging to the gentleman who called you. For the moment, our focus should be on your books and records. Send them over. I'll Bates stamp them, then deliver them to the government. I assume you've prepared your client for the Curcio?"

"Not yet."

"Do so."

I nodded glumly. I dreaded the Curcio process, which had to do with conflicts. In this variation, the theory was that the investigation into me personally might so distract me that I would not pay attention to Bolivar's case; or in an even worse alternative, I might try to curry favor with the government by not representing Bolivar vigorously.

Josh stood. The meeting was over.

Josh was one of the rare lawyers who didn't like being paid in cash. I took my checkbook out, but he waved dismissively. "Don't pay me, not until I can get a grip on what this is all about."

"When you do, tell me."

"I will. I'm not shy."

As I left, Josh was already engrossed in another case file, one of many neatly arranged atop his large, elegant desk. It occurred to me that my old paper man most probably was making the kind of bucks I aspired to, and sleeping well to boot. Our paths had crossed, and his had climbed while mine had descended to a lowland trail through an unmarked minefield.

I was glad Josh was on my side. My problem remained unchanged, but my relief felt palpable. Josh had my back. I could set my cares and woes aside. Not only was Josh a professional; he truly cared about me.

I was confident he'd win one for the home team.

CHAPTER 52

As I entered my office lobby, my neighbor, Gracie Loeb, was leaving. When Gracie saw me, she quickly looked away. I became aware of another presence, turned, and saw my neighbor, Sol Sonnenberg. He was smiling.

"Forget about Gracie, Benn. Some people, you just can't count on. Don't worry about it. Gracie might run off at the mouth, but there's nothing she could say that hurts you, right?"

I had no idea of what he was talking about.

"They were here this morning," he said.

"They?"

"Two DEA agents. Tall, older guy with acne scars. Short, young Spanish guy."

I felt the earth move under my feet, as if a sinkhole were opening, about to swallow me. Scally and Cano. Poking into my doings, laying a foundation for a case. I shouldn't have been surprised. It was the kind of thing I'd seen happen to hundreds of clients . . . but to *me?*

"You okay?"

"Why shouldn't I be?"

"I mean, this is what you do, right? The cops-and-robbers game, right?"

"Right. Ah, Sol . . . I mean, Solomon—"

"Nah. Call me Sol."

"Sol. Did they speak to you?"

"Of course. But not to worry. Like they say in your business, I don't know nothing from nothing. That is what they say, isn't it?"

"Right. What did they ask?"

"Whether I knew anything about your clients, or your finances."

I winced. Undoubtedly, they'd asked Gracie the same questions . . . Gracie, who'd seen me on my hands and knees amid a scattered pile of money. "Uh-huh. What did you say?"

"Like I said, nothing. I just told them, all I know is that you get visits from beautiful women. They asked if I knew their names. I said no, but the tall guy wouldn't let it go, kind of like a dog with a bone in his mouth." Sol shivered a little. "That one's trouble. I could see it in his eyes when I told him."

"Told him what?"

"He asked if I could describe any of the women, and when I described that gorgeous blonde, he started, like, well, almost drooling. Got that hungry look in his eyes and kept asking if I was *sure* I didn't know where to find her. I said, how should I know? Just between us, Benn, *do* you know where she is? I mean, if you and her are quits, I'd like to give her a whirl."

"Prince Boris," I said, referring to our mutual neighbor. "They spoke to him, too?"

"They wanted to, but he's in Europe. Benn, you don't have a problem, do you?"

"No, no problem."

"That's what I figured. So. The blonde. Where can I find her?"

"I wish I knew."

CHAPTER 53

I had to wait a long time for Bolivar to come down, and when he finally appeared, the reason was obvious: he wore the bright-orange jumpsuit of a SHU inmate. His hair was lank, his face drawn, and he needed a shave, not surprisingly. The SHU allowed showers only once a week among its other deprivations, including cold, meager food.

"They tell you why you're in the SHU?" I asked.

He shrugged. "An investigation for something."

I led him to a vacant visit room, which by chance was the one next to the last, biggest room. Inside that last room, among the rows of discovery cartons, I glimpsed Plitkin's cronies conferring with Natty Grable's codefendants. Despite the mass of boxed documents, no documents were on the table, and the conversation appeared relaxed. I thought that was a waste of billable hours, but then again, many lawyers prefer bullshitting to laboring.

For a moment, I looked at them, recalling what Traum had said about Natty and his two remaining codefendants' refusal to accept sweetheart, non-jail-time deals. Even as I thought this, I realized Bolivar was making a conscious effort not to look at the other room. I wondered if it had to do with Natty, but that was another topic I didn't want to discuss.

I set the transcript of my conversation with Andrey between us. He scanned it and looked up, his expression blank. "So?"

"So? You dumb motherfucker," I said. "You put me right in the middle of your miserable life. This is the transcript of a conversation intercepted on a wiretap, a conversation between myself and a man named Andrey."

"I put you in the middle of nothing. Are you finished?"

"Not quite. That call is the basis of a government investigation as to whether I was involved in your harebrained escape attempt."

"Why would they tap your phone?"

"They were tapping Andrey's phone. The point is, the transcript motivated them to investigate me, creating a possible conflict with my continuing to represent you."

"Explain, please."

I did, laying out the underpinnings of the Curcio hearing and how it applied to me.

Bolivar laughed. "*You,* currying favor with the government?"

"At the hearing, you'll be given an opportunity to confer with independent counsel and, if you choose, to retain another lawyer in my place."

"I won't do either. Tell them there's no need for a hearing."

"I'm afraid we have no choice. Another thing. If you're still considering cooperation? For certain, they'll expect you to own up to prior knowledge of the escape attempt, which means giving up everyone involved."

"Can't own up to what's not true, can I?"

"If you don't cooperate, that means either you plead to a mandatory minimum ten for the case, or you go to trial."

"The trial date is set for the Fourth of July, am I right?"

"Almost. Jury selection's July second. Trial starts Monday, the sixth."

"I like the timing," he said, a hint of his old swagger returning. "Independence Day."

CHAPTER 54

The Curcio hearing had been scheduled for two in the afternoon. The courtroom was crowded, as a dozen other matters were on the calendar. By accident or—as I suspected—design, mine was called first, so I suffered other members of the bar observing my integrity being questioned. In my paranoia, I even worried that I might be arrested then and there.

Kandi must have known the order of things, because she preened into the courtroom just as the case was called. My immediate reaction was that Kandi would play to the big stage, have me cuffed as I stood.

But nothing like that happened, and the Curcio began as scheduled.

Judge Trieant took his time, somberly intoning the pitfalls Bolivar might face if he kept me as his lawyer, pausing between each possible dire consequence to ask Bolivar if he was *sure* he wished to continue with me. I sat through it quietly, but when Trieant started repeating himself, I stood.

"Your Honor, with all respect, I object to the court's repetitious—"

"Sit down, sir. If you interrupt me again, I will hold you in contempt."

Fighting back an urge to say I found the court contemptible, I sat.

Finally, Trieant asked if the government had anything to add.

"Your Honor has covered everything," Kandi said brightly.

"Very well. Mr. Bolivar, be aware that *if* you continue with Mr. Bluestone, you are waiving any future claim that he was conflicted. Understood?"

"Yes."

"Do you wish to continue with Mr. Bluestone?"

"Yes."

"You're absolutely sure?"

"Yes."

Trieant banged his gavel.

"All rise."

Kandi was smirking. She knew the target letter had gotten under my skin. Now she wanted me to be worried to the point of distraction instead of properly preparing for trial. But fuck her and her agents. I might lose the trial, but they'd suffer the slings and arrows of having been in an outrageous, anything-goes war. There will be blood, I swore silently.

I walked from the courtroom and kept on walking right out of the courthouse, then across Cadman Plaza Park, unaware of a man nearby until he spoke.

"Here's a piece of advice, Counselor," he said.

I turned and, to my surprise, saw it was Scally. Surprising, because once a case reached court, agents were not supposed to converse with attorneys, not unless the prosecutor was present.

"When you're up to your chin in a sea of shit," he said, "don't make waves."

"Piss off."

"Touchy, are we? Rethink things. Feel free to reach out to me anytime."

Scally sauntered toward the street. An unmarked car was parked there, Nelson Cano leaning against it. Scally got in, and Cano got behind the wheel, and the car pulled away. I watched it go, trying to make sense of what lay beneath Scally's banter. Rethink *what* things?

But I couldn't even scratch the surface. I had a feeling Scally was talking about something other than Bolivar's case. But I had no idea what it was.

We headed back to the city. Across the Brooklyn Bridge, the downtown skyline glittered in the sun, and I could see the golden statue of the woman atop the Municipal Building, and from there my thoughts segued to Jilly—

"Everything okay, Mr. Benn?"

"Everything's fine, Val."

But it wasn't.

CHAPTER 55

A few days later, Traum appeared at my office. I blocked the doorway, said, "I'm not shelling out a dime."

"Easy, Benno. I'm not asking for a fee. Not yet, at least. I just want you to reimburse my traveling expenses."

"I don't know what you're talking about."

"Trying to tell you, kid. I took it upon myself to fly out to the state of Washington. Rented a car in Seattle, drove out to the Olympic Peninsula. Beautiful country, if you like pine trees and rain."

"I'm busy."

I went to close the door, but he interposed a foot. "Too busy to hear the skinny on the late Sholty Chennault the third, eminent trustafarian and husband of a certain blonde?"

I let go of the door.

"Not that busy, huh?" he said. "I can continue talking out here, but I bet you don't want your neighbors knowing any more of your business than they already do. Am I right?"

I took that as a reference to Scally's rousting my neighbors. No way Traum should know about it, although it was standard operating procedure. I moved aside, and he entered.

He sat on the couch, splayed his legs as if he owned the room, and stuck an unlit cigar in his mouth. He took a memo pad from a breast pocket, flipped through pages, read aloud.

"Sholty Chennault the third. Only son of the Ozelle County Chennaults. Ozelle County High School yearbook separated-at-birth joke was Sholty and Mr. Peepers. Twenty-five years later, people stopped laughing at him. No laughing at a billionaire married to a beautiful woman name of Jilly, not while you're busting your ass and losing fingers in a sawmill and your wife wears varicose socks."

He laughed. I didn't. He shrugged and went on.

"Had a cup of coffee with the Ozelle chief of police. Nice old dude. Told me he couldn't discuss the case. Officially. But cop-to-cop in his private opinion, Jilly was innocent. A dozen witnesses could testify she was in town at the time of the crime. Trouble is, in Ozelle when the Chennaults speak, people listen, and the family was talking plenty loud. Saying the day before the murder, Jilly was screwing an itinerant whose sailboat was docked at the town pier. Saying just days after the murder, she was in bed with her New York lawyer."

Sailboat. The word resonated, but I kept a straight face. Same as to Jilly sleeping with Borg, though that *really* bothered me.

"I drove out to the house Jilly and Sholty lived in. Big place between the mountains and the ocean. One way in, one way out . . . by land. From the restaurant where Jilly was eating lunch at the time of the crime, you can see the house and dock across the bay, maybe two miles away."

I remembered Jilly talking about the view. "You ask the sheriff about the weather on the day of the murder?"

"Foggy. Pea-soup foggy."

No way she could have seen her house across the water, then. A small lie, which meant there'd been larger ones. "The sailboat?"

"It docked in Ozelle the day before the murder and left the day after. Despite what the family claimed, no one actually recalled seeing the sailor with Jilly. A sailboat and a sailor on a foggy day. Heh-heh . . ."

I was thinking the same dirty thought as Traum: on the day Jilly's husband had been murdered, she was belowdecks with the sailor. Who, for whatever reason he was sailing the northwest Pacific, was Joaquin Bolivar. Now I understood why she'd shelled out a million to defend him. The same reason why she'd offered to spread her legs for me: to ensnare me into making her a paralegal so she could visit him.

"My expenses were five grand," Traum said. "I flew first class."

I didn't want Traum bulling around my life. "I didn't ask you to go," I said. "I'll write you a check, but that's it."

I wrote the check and handed it to him. He lit the cigar, blew smoke. Crossed to the door, paused. "The sailboat had a smaller boat in tow. One of them rubber Zodiacs with an outboard, fast like nobody's business."

He winked as he closed the door behind him. I sat there, thinking.

Fast enough to cross the harbor unseen in the fog. Fast enough for the sailor to kill Sholty. Fast enough to do it and return in half an hour. Fast like nobody's business . . .

Ah, Jilly. A true beauty destined to become entwined with big money and crime. Were you also the beautiful beach girl who ditched a septuagenarian billionaire for the company of the dashing sailor Joaquin Bolivar? Didn't matter, although if not you, another girl much like you. Normally, I'd shake my head and say it was none of my damn business.

But it was my business now.

CHAPTER 56

I was pondering Jilly's role—or lack thereof—in her husband's murder when AUSA Barnett Robinson called. His tone was serious. "Benn, Rigo has been diagnosed with a serious ailment. All I know is that he's been moved to FMC Prattsville."

"Where's that?"

"West Virginia. Federal medical centers are weird about visits, even from lawyers. I took the liberty of cutting red tape, and you're cleared to see him."

On a human level, I couldn't care less about Rigo's health. As an attorney, I had no need to see him at this time. "Don't think I can fit a visit into my schedule, Barnett."

"I'm told his condition is critical."

I realized my speaking to Rigo was a major part of Robinson's agenda. Too bad. I was done wasting time on a deadbeat.

"Speak to him while he's still cogent, Benn."

"Barnett? Please take no for an answer."

"I can't do that, Benn. I'm not free to explain anything. Just know that a lot of people need for you to speak to Rigo. Get a written statement."

"Which people?"

"Rigo. The government. You."

"Me? I don't think so."

"Benn, please—"

"There's no reason for me to go."

His voice lowered as if he didn't want to be overheard. "It has nothing to do with your investigation in the Eastern District."

Whoa. I hadn't seen that coming. Of course my seeing Rigo had nothing to do with my investigation, so why would he say . . .

Then I got it: Robinson was insinuating he could make Kandi's investigation go away. He'd deny any quid quo pro to the heavens, but it was pure and simple blackmail. It seemed incredible he could reach across districts, not unless it was sanctioned by Main Justice in DC.

"I'll move some things around," I said.

"Tell me soon as," Robinson said.

I rummaged through a drawer until I found a certain special pen. I slipped it into my breast pocket. Then I went on the BOP website and found FMC—Federal Medical Center—Prattsville. It was in West Virginia. As the crow flies, three or four hundred miles from New York. No air or train connections, so the trip would be by car. No fun but no choice. The upside was that I needed to clear my head.

Early the next morning, the Mini growled out from the Lincoln Tunnel. The city skyline soon faded in the rearview mirror, and ahead the Jersey Turnpike unspooled into a countryside I knew only by flying over.

I drove southwest, past smokestack industries and suburban sprawl. I passed three cop stops on the northbound lane. Black and Hispanic faces with hands in plain sight atop steering wheels, burly troopers wearing visor caps and tall lace-ups. An agent once told me that one in six turnpike stops comes up positive for drugs.

The stops were outrageously blatant racial profiling, but I was all for them. Not because I'm a bigot or fire-breathing law-and-order person. My opinion boils down to three words. Fuck them all. The scumbag criminals whose rights were violated and the scumbag cops who did the violating. My approval of the turnpike stops was fact based: the more drug arrests, the more rats whose tongues loosen, ultimately threatening the guys at the very top, aka my kinds of clients.

Life was ugly.

As the Philly exits fell behind, I stopped thinking about work, turned on the radar detector, got off the interstate and onto a state road, and stepped on the gas. I felt the stress drain from me as my senses opened to another world.

I'm loaded with opinions about the state of the nation, but in truth, all I know is hearsay filtered by media distortions. But now that I was out in the countryside, navigating a two-lane blacktop that wound between hills and skirted small towns, my preconceptions were whittled down to a one-word feeling:

Freedom.

From my side of the windshield, this was Norman Rockwell's America of hills and dales and modest homes, inhabited by decent, hardworking folks.

Or so it seemed.

Eventually, the roadway narrowed as it crossed a steel span above a rushing stream, and on the other side was a main street veined by lanes meandering up the hillsides. There was one traffic light, and while waiting for it to turn green, I verified through GPS that this indeed was Prattsville, West Virginia, although there was neither sign nor sight of the FMC.

There was a gas station where I stopped to ask for directions. Outside the neighboring diner, many of the parked vehicles had federal plates and BOP markings. The station and diner appeared to be Prattsville's downtown. People were about. Most all wore FBOP parkas or caps, and most all were grossly overweight. I caught a particularly fat guy's eye and asked which way to the FMC.

He took in my city-slicker suit, eyed my cute toy car with New York plates, emitted a phlegmy laugh of the type that requires a weekly carton of nonfiltered Camels to maintain, and said, "Checking in, are you?"

His pals grinned. One popped a can of Bud in a brown bag.

I keep a Maglite in the glove compartment. I felt like using it to bash the guy's head in. But instead I just said, "Checking in to work. I'm from the surgeon general's office."

The grins faded, and the Bud disappeared. Federal employees have a healthy fear of those above their pay grade. Like government doctors.

"That'd be the next right, sir," said the fat guy, pointing.

I followed his pudgy finger to a ridge, where a ring of barbed wire glinted in the sun. I allowed a small nod, got back in the Mini, and took the next right up a road that made me think of Dylan's Highway 61, the road of contradictions.

Where have all the good people gone?

The view was good, though. Judging from the cleared hilltops, Prattsville must once have been a farming burg. Now it was a company town and the company was BOP, and the company store was now a Walmart. Sad. Despite my earlier sense of America the ever-beautiful, an unconscionable number of small communities have changed for the worse, becoming correctional-institution towns. Jail burgs. Another way the war against drugs has dumbed down the populace. At one time, Prattsville probably had its own newspaper and movie theater, but now all the news that fit was Fox on the boob tube, and entertainment meant reality TV shows. During the Civil War, when citizens fought and died for their beliefs, West Virginia split from Old Virginny and opted to stay in the Union rather than sing along with Dixie. But now our armies were bought body and soul, and West Virginia was red, fat, and ignorant.

I had a thought that made me laugh out loud.

Rigo, Colombian drug kingpin, here.

CHAPTER 57

FMC Prattsville was pristine. White-coated doctors, green-smocked nurses. Immaculate corridors lined with CT-scan rooms, labs, ICUs. The cost of building and running such an institution was mind boggling. Crazy. Law-abiding citizens were arguing the virtues of health-care reform while fortunes were being spent caring for prisoners, the majority of which were drugsters like Rigo.

There were two signs on the door to his private room: one a warning that visits must not exceed fifteen minutes; the second, a yellow-and-black logo similar to those seen in radiology units.

Once inside, I realized Rigo was extremely ill. Tethered to an IV, wired to a monitor, leashed to a bed rail by steel cuffs, his free hand heavily bandaged. A blue vein pulsed in his paper-white temple. His dark eyes were rheumy; the only light in them reflected fluorescence.

What can you say to a guy who looks as if he's circling the drain? Nothing. I sat down and waited for him to speak. A tear leaked from the corner of his eye and ran down his cheek. He swallowed hard, wet his lips, whispered: "*Puta* . . . killed my family . . . killed Estefania . . ."

"Who are you taking about? What *puta?*"

"*Sombra.*"

I'd feared Rigo's cooperation would create a conflict precluding my representing *Sombra*. Now I realized there would be no conflict because *Sombra* would be the only man left standing.

"The video," he rasped. "You gave the prosecutor the video of the bribe?"

"Yes."

"You told him that it's *Sombra* there with me?"

"You and Uvalde were on the video—"

"Understand, the video was six years ago. *Sombra's* organization was just starting. Personal attendance was necessary. You must make the prosecutor believe this."

"I'll try." I had zero sympathy for this murdering thief.

His eyes brimmed with tears. "How stupid I've been."

One of your many poor traits, I thought.

A monitor began beeping. He tried to sit up, only to be jerked back by his cuff. The monitor began beeping faster. "Mondragon . . . killed me."

A nurse appeared. "Sir, you need to leave. Now."

Rigo was running on fumes, but he seemed desperate to speak to me. "Mondragon, he shook my hand. After, it felt like an insect bit me."

Another nurse appeared and elbowed me aside. I left the room.

In the corridor, I stopped at the desk. The young nurse behind it was plump and pretty. I put on my best smile. "Hello."

"Hello," she said.

"I was just visiting my client."

"Yes, I know."

"I was wondering what his illness is."

"Sir, we can't divulge medical information without a formal request. If you go on the BOP website, you'll find the appropriate form."

"Thank you so much for telling me."

"You're very welcome."

"I'm going to go on the website, but I'm from New York, and by the time I get home . . . what I'm trying to say? His family is very concerned."

"Oh, I can understand."

"They're waiting to hear from me. I feel as if I need to tell them something now. Nothing major, I respect the BOP rules. Just something. Like, I noticed his hand was all bandaged. I'm sure that's not his major problem, but I was wondering why it's bandaged?"

She glanced around. Leaned toward me, spoke quietly. "I'm not supposed to . . . actually, his hand *is* the problem. It's very infected, so much so that the infection has spread to his body."

"Infected? How?"

"That's the problem. The doctors don't really understand how, or by what. They said it was almost if he'd been bitten."

"Bitten?"

"Like by an insect, but not—"

"Sir, leave *now*," a male attendant said, taking my elbow.

I turned on him. "Don't put your hands on me."

Out of nowhere, two more attendants appeared. Big guys.

I stepped out of their way and out the door of the unit.

I left the facility thinking I'd solved one puzzle.

Problem was, there were others.

CHAPTER 58

Once in the Mini, I took out the pen tucked in my pocket and clicked the cap. The pen emitted a whirring sound, then played my conversation with Rigo. Why had I recorded it? On a hunch that it might prove useful. I doubted it now. Rigo's words were the demented ravings of a dying man. A wasted trip.

I sped toward home on autopilot, my thoughts racing faster . . .

Supposing *Sombra* had been present at the bribe? Even before Rigo was sick, he'd said the same thing . . . and both Robinson and Agent Gus Romero seemed to think so, too, for they had hammered Rigo about who else had been present when he'd bribed Uvalde. And Fercho had pointedly asked if I was sure no one else was in the video.

Only Uvalde and Rigo were there. I'd seen them . . .

But had I *understood* what I'd seen? What *if* . . . General Uvalde was *Sombra*? Come to think of it, how perfect a scam would that be? No one would ever—

Stop! Stop thinking, and follow your nose.

Rigo had referred to an insect bite, although I suspected something deadlier. The sign outside his room door was a yellow-and-black trefoil, the universal warning of hazardous radioactivity.

That explained why at the top of the case Mondragon had visited Rigo so often: to accomplish the assassination that had failed at the cathedral. Mondragon's delivery device could have been quite simple—a pin, probably plastic to evade the metal detectors, bearing polonium or whatever deadly isotope was in fashion among assassins these days. Cupped in his palm when shaking Rigo's hand, it would have delivered a tiny dose that eventually poisoned Rigo fatally.

Confirming still again that Mondragon was either working for *Sombra*, or working for someone who shared the same goals as *Sombra*.

Rigo had known this all along. He'd appeared at the cathedral without Mondragon to make sure he was still alive when the agents got there.

Just past the West Virginia–Maryland state line, I pulled into a rest stop. I hit the men's room, splashed water on my face, drank black coffee. Over a second cup, I opened my device and viewed the video Mondragon had given me to forward to Robinson.

It was as I'd remembered: just Uvalde and Rigo. I zoomed in on the image and thought I saw a shadow in the corner of the room. Another man? Maybe.

I continued toward home with the radio on, a twenty-four-hour news station blathering bad news: the Middle East was aflame, the Far East was simmering, the north and south poles were melting, climate change, doom . . .

I shut the radio and made a phone call.

Raul Rincon picked up on the first ring. Figured. He saw my number and deduced I'd be calling about money. Colombian criminal lawyers were a hungry lot, and Raul was the hungriest one I knew.

"What can I do for you, my dear friend Benn?"

"I'm angling for a client. A very big client, whose fee can make us both happy. Problem is, a Colombian lawyer is trying to steal the client. Felipe Mondragon."

"A greedy bastard."

"It's not just Mondragon I'm fighting. It's someone with him who influences the client. If I knew who the person was, I'd be able to make the client understand why I'm his man. There'd be something for you, of course."

"Mmm. Trouble is, Mondragon knows everyone. But there is one man Mondragon is close to. A lawyer. I've heard they work together."

"The lawyer's name?"

"From what I understand, the lawyer is obsessive about maintaining his privacy. His practice is limited to a few special clients, if you know what I mean."

"Yes. The name?"

"Just between us?"

"You have my word."

"Actually, I don't know his first name. Just his last. If in fact it's his real last name, you know how it is—"

"Jesus, Rincon. The *name*?"

"Paz."

CHAPTER 59

Paz. Except Paz was dead, and I felt as if I were on my last legs as well. Traffic had thickened, and it was raining as I neared New York. Four hours working my brain in my little steel cocoon had left me tired and confused.

I garaged the Mini and walked toward home, dreaming of a Bison Grass and a long, hot shower and a couple of blue Valiums and a deep sleep. With that in mind, I began to relax. The rain had dwindled to a fine mist, and in the side streets off Madison, candles flickered beneath bistro awnings. There were women there. I spotted a pair of crossed legs to die for . . .

Which got me thinking that I hadn't been with a woman for a long time. Too long a time. Not good. I was, literally, bottled up. Maybe instead of calling it a night, I should phone—

My own phone rang. Unknown caller. I answered.

"Benn, Barnett. You saw Rigo?"

"I did. He's not in good shape."

"But you did speak?

"Barnett, I'm wondering . . . Rigo arrived here healthy as a pig, and all of a sudden, he's in extremis. What kind of infection does that?"

"Actually, I really don't know the details."

"But you do know he was irradiated?"

"We're trying to figure . . . fuck you, Benn. What did Rigo say?"

"That Felipe Mondragon was involved in the murders of his girlfriend and family."

"That's all he said?"

"That Mondragon poisoned him, too."

"You got a written statement?"

"No time. They tossed me out."

I didn't mention the recorded statement because it included a reference to *Sombra*. No way was I going to throw that into the mix and conflict myself out of whatever chance remained of my representing *Sombra*. Nor was it my job to snoop for the feds. As far as I was concerned, justice had been served to Rigo. I had no illusions.

Sombra killed those who ventured too close to him, but if I wanted my fortune, I'd be bound for either glory or hell. *Fuck it*. In for a dime, in for twenty mil. Roll the dice and hope they come up sevens.

"It was a brief conversation, Barnett."

"I see." Robinson sounded tired.

"Maybe he'll come around."

"No, he won't. I just got a call from Prattsville. Rigo died an hour ago."

I didn't reply. Now Rigo belonged to the ages, and along with him had vanished any possibility of Barnett Robinson getting me out my Eastern District jam. I let it go at that. The Southern District played hardball. Tit for tat, this for that. Nothing for nothing. I hadn't given them anything, and they wouldn't give me anything.

"Good night," Robinson said, and hung up.

In retrospect, Rigo's course of action made sense. He had felt so threatened by *Sombra* that he feared staying in Colombia. He knew Mondragon was working for *Sombra* but wanted to keep his enemy close—almost too close, letting Mondragon surrender him in Antigua nearly being a fatal mistake. Wanting to protect his family, he'd kept Mondragon on the case, living proof that he wasn't flipping on *Sombra*. Mondragon hadn't bought it.

Which raised a question: Why was the video such a hot topic if it only implicated Uvalde and Rigo?

Which spawned an answer: because another person really was on the video. Only Rigo, in keeping with his game plan of releasing information in small parts, had cut out the part of the video showing *Sombra*.

Which raised another question: Where was the missing clip?

I was out of answers. I was weary of the whole business. Too many twists, turns, and betrayals. I needed to distance myself. I needed some loving. I *really* needed to be with a woman. As soon as I got home, I'd go through my book, start making calls until I got the answer I wanted.

I turned the corner to my tree-shadowed street. Quiet and peaceful. The mansions of both my billionaire neighbors were dark. I neared my building and became aware of someone moving quickly behind me. I turned—

Into a white, powdery cloud that enveloped my face.

CHAPTER 60

Coke, I thought in the following millisecond, then realized, no, not a chemically processed product; something organic, plantlike. But whatever it was blanketed my senses immediately. Stung my eyes shut, filled my nostrils, numbed my mind; I tumbled into another dimension, a there that wasn't there . . .

I became dimly aware of an arm slipping through mine. Of a person pressed against me as I entered my building's lobby. Of Viktor's weirdly echoed voice saying, "Good evening, Mr. Bluestone."

Then, somehow, I—we—were in the elevator, and I felt a jumble of feelings, sensations, a chaotic wonderment signifying nothing. The one and only constant in the maelstrom was a dank, plantlike smell, and another, fainter smell, a familiar scent I couldn't quite recall . . .

My apartment now.

The light was dim.

I heard my voice.

I was going . . .

Over.

And.

Out.

CHAPTER 61

Someone slapped my cheek. Hard.

"He's waking up," a woman said.

My lids creaked open. Light like needles pierced my eyes. An instant category-five migraine made me gasp.

"Drink," the woman said.

A glass touched my lips. I parted them and sipped water that felt like acid on my esophagus. Behind the glass, a plump woman with rosy cheeks smiled. I'd never seen her in my life. Was she an angel? Was I dead?

"Valery, help him up."

Val?

Consciousness returned and, with it, clarity. I lay on the floor of my apartment with Val kneeling at my side. The woman must be his wife, Sonia, whom I'd never met.

"I'm making a bad first impression," I said.

"No talk," Val said. "Take hot shower."

"*Cold!* You want kill him, Val?"

"Pliz, Sonia. For a man, *hot*."

Val guided me into the bathroom. Stripped me naked and sat me in the steam shower and closed the door. Why was I so compliant? Much like I had been last night, with . . . with . . . a person I hadn't caught sight of. I couldn't remember much . . . except for a fleeting recollection: familiar olfactory memories, a tropical fragrance, the smell of sex . . . had I unconsciously copulated while too stoned to be aware? Wouldn't have been the first time that happened to me, but in the past I'd remembered afterward, usually regretting that it happened.

Raped. That was food for thought. But I didn't feel the discomfort of violation, so maybe not. Or maybe I was the violator?

Water drummed against my head; memories and thoughts washed away.

I sat there for a very long time. Or thought I did.

Val leaned inside. "Long night, huh? You okay now, boss?"

"Yeah. What time is it?"

"Afternoon. Sonia call me when she find you. You go to sleep. We go now. Sonia clean another day, yes?"

"Yes." My voice sounded far away.

I stood beneath the water, and gradually coherence returned. I shut the water and stepped from the shower, feeling better, but—*Jeez!*

In red lipstick, two words were scrawled on the vanity mirror:

Drug Lawyer

The title of the unpublished novel I'd written. The failure that had ended my dream of being a writer—

My God. Had I told the woman about—

It hit me. It was a *woman.*

Had I revealed other secrets?

Get a grip, Benn. Think!

Blankness. I needed help.

I got dressed and left.

I called Doc Concierge in Miami. He sent me to a New York doctor and remained on the speakerphone as his colleague drew blood and checked my vitals.

"Tell me about it," Doc said over the phone.

"I, ah, inhaled an unknown substance." Doc knew my addictive history, and I figured he was thinking relapse. I said, "I didn't get high. Well, not intentionally. It was against my will. So to speak."

"Like date rape."

"Something like that. Some sort of powder. Airborne."

"Airborne."

"Okay, it doesn't make sense. The point is, there's a hole in my memory . . . a number of hours I can't remember."

He told his colleague to write me a script. Until then the guy hadn't said word one. But as I left, he said, "A psychiatrist might help."

I filled the prescription. Then went home, took one more pill than directed, and immediately passed out.

CHAPTER 62

I awoke well along the return trip to myself. Except for the blank spots in my memory. I knew there was a woman to whom I'd babbled like a meth freak, but that was all. I called Doc Concierge again, but my blood work wasn't back yet. It occurred to me to speak with the other concierge in my life.

"Viktor, you were on the other night?"

He smiled. "You were bombed."

"The woman I was with?"

"A real good looker."

"Describe her."

"I wasn't working that night. My cousin Viktor was. He told me."

"What time does he come on?"

"He left on vacation. In Serbia."

"Can you call him?"

"He's hiking in the mountains. No cell service."

I slipped Viktor a Franklin. "Get me a copy of the security-camera videos of that night."

"You got it, chief."

The next day Viktor gave me a thumb drive. I inserted it in my device, took a deep breath, thought, *Let's go to the videotape*, then pressed "Play."

The lobby video counter said 9:45 p.m. The view was of the lobby. The other Viktor was behind the desk, reading a newspaper. He looked up as people entered:

Me, looking reasonably okay, perhaps a little wobbly, but par for my course. I walked close against a woman shielded by a floppy hat. An Unknown Female—UF—*fucking acronyms* . . .

The elevator video showed my face: white as the Joker's, an idiot smile. The woman's face remained hidden by her hat. Her hand went in my pocket. Keys flashed; she fit a key to my apartment door. It opened, and we went in.

The video ended . . . a second later, it started again.

Now the time counter said 2:45 a.m. The woman reentered the elevator, still hidden inside her coat and beneath her hat. Cut to the lobby camera. She walked through the lobby. The video ended again.

And again resumed at 4:10 a.m., when the woman returned. She went back to my apartment . . . another break until . . . 5:00 a.m. She left, carrying an overnighter. Mine. Inside it was . . . *what*?

Doc Concierge called: my blood work was fine. No controlled chemical substances in my bloodstream. But I'd been drugged with *something*. I closed my eyes and tried to re-create sensory impressions. Nothing. The powder had been so powerful, I'd gone right out. Yet I'd still functioned.

What kind of a substance does that?

A suggestive. I remembered a case:

A jeweler had thrown a bash for his new line. Woke up the next morning to find his multimillion-dollar collection gone. He didn't remember a thing, and his blood test showed nothing amiss. But an insurance investigator found a residue in the punch bowl. A lab ran extraordinary tests. A result came up with a trace of scopolamine, a plant-based derivative used by the Nazis and the CIA as truth serum. Puts the victim in a compliant, zombielike state, although afterward they remember little. The investigator discovered one of the guests had done time as a jewel thief.

My client wasn't the jeweler. He was the jewel thief.

Talkative guy. Told me scopolamine grows in the wild all over Colombia, where it's known by other names—devil dust, *burundanga*—and ground to a white powder by thieves, who blow it in an unsuspecting victim's face, after which the victim is compliant, talkative, unreserved—

Oh no.

My gut sinking, I punched numbers on my microwave, and a panel opened to the safe where I kept $25,000 in emergency money. It was empty.

I went in the living room. I moved the sofa, exposing the floorboards. Between the seams were hinges to a safe embedded beneath where I kept a stash. I punched in the complicated sequence that opened it—

Gone.

I ran the few blocks—fuck my aching back—to the office. The door was unlocked. The safe hidden in a faux column yawned open. The money that had been in it was gone. My hidden-in-plain-sight money in the armoire:

Gone.

I slid down the wall to the floor and sat there for a long while. Nothing moved except the second hand of my watch. It swept past the date . . . May 1.

Mayday.

I was wiped out. Picked clean. Violated. All I had were memories . . . I gave a little start—

Memories!

I sat at my computer and entered the code to PARANOID.FLOYD, in which I kept my double-bookkeeping system listing cash transactions in case I was audited and needed to re-create records. PARANOID. FLOYD was encrypted to list prior entries.

The screen blinked the previous access: April 28, 3:30 a.m.

She—whoever she was—had gotten in.

Was I going to be blackmailed? Pay, or be whistle-blown as a tax cheat and sent to federal prison? What did she—they—want of me?

But then my despair segued into cold anger.

Mayday. Yes. But it wasn't me in distress.

She—they—were in for payback.

CHAPTER 63

I was still stewing in unrequited anger when I got a jail call, an operator asking if I would accept charges. I did. It was Billy Shkilla. He and the other Shkillas had been arrested on drug and murder conspiracies. He was in state court, 100 Centre Street, awaiting arraignment. "You got to hurry, man. They're gonna call my case soon."

I sighed silently. Here I was, surrounded by the broken remnants of my life, my future hidden by black clouds, and now another demand was being foisted on my diminishing resources. I hadn't been to state court in years . . . so many memories, many good, but too many tawdry, draining. I probably would have gotten out of the defense business had I not escalated to a federal practice. What could I possibly do for Billy that any state lawyer might not do better? No matter the lawyer; bail on a murder case would be astronomical. As for a fee, I wasn't about to take Billy's few bucks. I sighed again.

"On my way."

Traffic was heavy. My mind was still muddled, so I lowered the window. The wind was ice cold. Clouds of steam pouring from manholes; bus exhaust and distant sirens. Plainclothes cops working doubles needing a shave. Relatives. Girlfriends and wives giving one another the stink-eye.

But strangely, the closer I got to 100 Centre, the higher I felt. When I was a young public defender, pot was an exotic smoked only by the cool. Mady and I spent long weekends in bed, smoking and murmuring, "Oh wow." I felt that kind of high now, aware, anticipatory. All was well. Oh wow.

Billy's predicament brought me back to earth. I had to find the kid a way out.

I went into the clerk's office and asked for a copy of Billy's complaint. Waiting behind the wire-glass window, leaning on the scarred countertop, I felt as if I'd never left. My American life did have a second act: a repetition. I was stoned in the state courthouse again.

I entered the courtroom just as the arraignment concluded. The judge had gotten tired of waiting and assigned Billy a public defender. Bail for all defendants was $1 million. Billy's head was down, but he lit up when he saw me.

"Call me," I said as they led him away.

Not that I'd have anything of substance to tell him. One of the worst aspects of state cases is that they move slowly, and invariably the prosecutors play discovery games so defendants don't know all they're up against until just before trial, when they're offered a take-it-or-leave-it-right-now deal. The way it was, but hardheaded me would butt the system every step of the way.

The next day, another unknown caller reached out to me: a man who said he was calling on behalf of Josh Waldman. His voice was unfamiliar. He seemed edgy. I was wary.

"Sorry, but I didn't catch your name," I said.

"Meet Mr. Waldman. The Oyster Bar, noon."

With that, he hung up, leaving me still another puzzlement. I recalled Josh as a brown bagger, not at all the type who did lunch. Then again, he'd changed from the young lawyer who'd been my paper man. But why not call me himself? Why interpose someone between us, calling from an unknown number, no less?

No matter. I needed to *hear* Josh speak. To *see* through his eyes.

The Oyster Bar was in Grand Central Terminal. When I arrived, I didn't see Josh. I took a seat at the bar and ordered water with a slice of lemon; that's how clear I wanted to be. A young guy in a good suit sat next to me. Looking straight ahead, he spoke out of the corner of his mouth.

"Mr. Waldman is waiting for you on the shuttle platform," he said, then got up and disappeared into the crowd.

I guessed Josh wanted to discuss my problem while traveling elsewhere. Two birds with one stone, so to speak. But even as I descended into the bowels of Grand Central, leaving the suburban commuter tracks and entering the NYC subway system, I disabused myself of that notion. I was kidding myself, because it was obvious why Josh wanted to meet me elsewhere.

He didn't want to be seen with me.

My anger refocused on Josh. For Chrissake, he was my lawyer! What in hell was he worried about?

When I got to the shuttle platform, Josh was nowhere in sight.

After a minute, a train pulled in. As its doors slid open, Josh stepped from behind a steel pillar. He paused long enough to catch my attention, then boarded. I did, too.

Josh sat without looking at me. I sat across from him. The shuttle ride was short, from Grand Central to Times Square, from Midtown east to Midtown west. When the shuttle stopped at Times Square, Josh got off. I did, too.

He remained on the platform. I did, too.

When the conductor announced the shuttle was about to leave for Grand Central, he got back on. I did, too.

Just before the door closed, he got out. I did, too.

He left the station. I did, too.

Times Square and 42nd Street are smack-dab in the middle of Manhattan, but it looked like Disneyland. Not for the first time, I reflected on how the Square and the Deuce had been nothing but porn, pimps, and prostitutes when I was growing up. Nothing remains the same in the Apple. Josh was a living example.

What was he so afraid of?

He walked west, and I followed. Past the theater district, down tree-lined residential streets, relatively quiet at this hour. Josh stopped and put a foot atop a fire hydrant, pretending to fuss with his shoelace. When I paused a few feet away, he spoke, without looking at me. His voice was tight, clipped.

"I won't risk the slightest chance of being seen together," he said. "Just so you understand, since I left your office, I don't do drug work. Too dirty. And in this particular instance, the kind of dirt that rubs off. I've worked too hard for too long to build a practice with clients who can't afford to be associated with you and your problem."

"Because we share the same lawyer? I can't believe I'm hearing this."

"Believe it. Far as I'm concerned? You spoke, and I listened. Afterward, I communicated with the government, and then informed you I will not represent you."

"You won't?"

"End of story. Got it?"

"No. At least spell it out."

He sighed. Glanced around. Sighed again. Nodded. "What I'm about to say violates professional ethics and could get me disbarred. So for once in your life, shut up and listen, and consider yourself lucky that, despite the fact that you were a prick to work with, for no good reason, I loved you like a brother. An abusive brother, but . . ."

He glanced around again, continued.

"I'm retained in a case in which I'm privy to proffered information about Evgeny Kursk. Billions of dollars are in play, a lot of it earmarked as legal fees. Kursk is the subject of a joint DEA-FBI investigation. Other agencies are involved, too, but all you need to know is that the case is heavy, with international implications. As in, his country and ours. Bottom line? Kursk's red hot. And anyone near him risks getting burned. Get the picture?"

I nodded. Thinking that my only contact with Kursk was in a steam bath designed to thwart spying eyes and ears . . . actually, twice, counting the time I'd seen him with Jilly, in Foto's place in PC.

"Another thing," he said. "I want your word that, no matter what, you won't reveal that we had this second conversation. Do I have it?"

It took a moment before I could bring myself to reply. Josh's reticence wasn't prudent; it was fucking cowardly. Lawyers were supposed to stand tall for even the lowest of dirtbag clients. But I wanted to know what Josh knew. So I nodded.

"I've seen you do things that left me shaking my head, but going back on your word isn't one of them. So at the risk of ruining my life, and my family's lives, here it is . . ."

He drew a breath, as if steeling himself. I did, too.

"Kandi *really* wants to nail you," he said.

All things considered, I was relieved. Kandi's ambition wasn't exactly a news flash. "That's it?"

"Don't blow this off. Kandi's investigation goes much deeper than you think. Beyond the escape attempt into some very heavy things. *Very*."

"What things?"

"That's all. You don't owe me a dime. One more thing. A word to the wise. It's all connected."

"What is?" I asked.

"Everything."

CHAPTER 64

Val was elsewhere, and I couldn't find a cab and was in no mood to take the subway, so I decided to walk back to the office. I'd just begun when Billy called me. In the background, the usual cacophony of jail: cries and shouts and metal clanging.

"When you coming to see me, Benn?"

Oh jeez. Going to state court was bad enough, but a trip to Rikers was hellish. I recalled Billy's fear on the phone, and in person when I saw him after the arraignment. Rikers was a horror show. Homicide cases could take years, during which defendants themselves were sometimes murdered. I recalled the kindnesses Billy had done for Bea. I wasn't a cold fish like Josh Waldman, who repped the rich and famous and their corporations. I owed Billy a face-to-face.

"Don't worry, Billy. I'll be there. Give me a couple days. Meantime, get your public defender to call me."

"I *knew* I could count on you."

I kept on walking through the concrete jungle. The city looked particularly grim today. White sky. Grimy wind. Too much traffic. Too many people. Thirty-plus blocks uptown, then six long avenue blocks east. The pavement was hell on my knee, and after a while my hip acted up, and soon my back joined the act.

In a strange way, I welcomed the pain, each stab a reminder to keep on keeping on until I found a way to turn off the people bent on hurting me. I thought and rethought things from every angle, but by the time I reached my office, I was still lost at sea.

What kept me afloat was my anger. As if my blood were bubbling oil, ready to be poured upon my enemies. I wasn't even sure who they were, except for one: AUSA Kandi Kauffman. A prevaricator who wielded the power of the government, a monster who planned on crushing me at trial, then scattering my pieces.

As I was about to get on the elevator, a neighbor exited. Took me a moment to recognize him, because I'd only seen him a few times. Like me, he traveled more often than not. Difference was, Prince Boris de la Bourdaine was dealing with the legitimate world, while I consorted with the underbelly of society.

"Ah, there you are," he said. "I was just knocking at your door."

Thinking he was about to relate his experience with Agents Scally and Cano, I put on my best who-cares smile, which probably came out closer to a fragile, shit-eating grin.

"I was away," Boris said. "When I returned, I found this."

This was an envelope he handed me: folded, slightly scuffed, with a name scrawled on it. A large *B*, followed by illegible lettering.

"Apparently, it was left at the front desk," he said. "Seems our mailman is unable to differentiate between B. Bluestone and B. Bourdaine."

"Thank you."

"Of course."

Up in my office, when I opened the envelope, a thumb drive fell out. Same brand as the thumb with the video of Rigo bribing General Uvalde, the video Rigo claimed *Sombra* was on.

I sat at my computer and watched it.

The same scene as the first video came on: an obviously hidden camera shooting in black and white, Rigo bribing General Uvalde. It played for several minutes, then the screen went black. End of scene.

It was a duplicate of Mondragon's video.

A waste of time . . . or was it?

Josh said Kursk was the subject of a joint DEA and FBI investigation. A rarity because the two agencies were highly competitive. Fart, Barf, and Itch disdained the Drunk Every Afternoons, and vice versa. Other unnamed agencies were also interested, Josh had said, which I took to mean CIA types.

Josh said there were serious international repercussions.

But what were they? Then I heard another voice.

Where do you keep your private files, Benn?

A woman's voice. The UF who'd doped me.

I'd told her where: in PARANOID.FLOYD.

What about the video of Rigo and Uvalde?

I'd told her it was in my computer.

That's all there is?

I'd told her it was copied from the thumb Mondragon had given me. I recall her being disappointed. Asking me if I was sure. I'd said I was sure . . .

But this new thumb had come from Prince Boris, who'd mistakenly received it while he was away—during which time Stefania had been murdered . . . Suddenly, it fell into place: the new thumb drive had come from *Stefania*—who had not been on her way *to* my office when she was murdered; she had been on her way *from* my office, *after* delivering the thumb to Prince Boris's office *before* being murdered.

I replayed the new video. Rigo and Uvalde came on, two turds doing business in a cesspool. The same shadowed hint of another presence.

The video ended; the screen went to black.

Only this time I went on watching.

The screen flickered, and an image appeared . . . the same room, but as seen from another camera at a different angle, the shot now including another person:

My first instinct was right after all:

Joaquin Bolivar *was Sombra*!

The screen flickered again . . . still another camera from another angle . . . including a fourth person in the room:

Laura Astorquiza.

CHAPTER 65

That night I didn't leave the office. I sat at my computer, replaying the video over and over, as if trying to see something new in it. But I saw nothing that changed the naked facts.

Rigo, for all his duplicity, had been telling the truth: Bolivar was *Sombra*. Not important how he knew, only that he did. It explained why Rigo had been marked for death—to stop him from sitting on *Sombra* . . . and why Kandi was so fixated on pressuring Bolivar to cooperate:

So the indomitable AUSA Kauffman became the prosecutor who took down the legendary *Sombra*. Her screen test for stardom after years of bit parts of run-of-the-mill criminality. Probably she'd busted some Russian who'd cooperated up to Natty Grable and then Evgeny Kursk, and then the ultimate prize: *Sombra*.

And why Barnett Robinson wanted the case in the Southern District of New York, the jurisdiction that prosecuted the worst big, bad guys. Probably Robinson's initial information came down from Main Justice, via a deep-cover informant.

It also exposed Laura Astorquiza, antidrug crusader, as a fraud. A narco-trafficker. Perhaps a partner of Bolivar, perhaps his lover, perhaps both. Laura. She sure had fooled me.

My phone rang, startling me. The caller was a woman who introduced herself as Billy's court-appointed public defender. "Billy mentioned you'd be coming in for me, so I wanted to fill you in on some things."

"Sure. I'm all ears."

Public defenders too frequently buy into their clients' stories. This woman was no exception. According to her, the real scenario was that a guy named Haunty had murdered his girlfriend. Foolishly, Billy and his Shkillas had incorporated that deed into their act. That, together with the gun-waving and mocking the cops—and Haunty's "confession," in which he made Billy as the shooter—had convinced the cops that Billy was their man.

"Why are they holding the others?"

"Same old story. Pressuring them to crack and back up Haunty's story."

"Will they?"

"What do you think?"

"Thanks for letting me know."

Sometime during the night, I fell asleep. I awoke at first light still at my desk, grainy-eyed and stiff. My screen was blinking; I had a CORRLINKS message:

Fercho had been transferred from Miami to MDC, the Manhattan federal lockup. I wasn't surprised because he was due to meet with SDNY prosecutors regarding his cooperation in his New York federal indictment. I showered and changed, then headed downtown to the MDC.

Fercho greeted me with his sphinxlike smile. "What's happening, Benn?"

"You tell me. You're the fucking answer man."

"You're limping. You limp when you're stressed."

"No more games. If you don't start talking straight, you're on your own."

Fercho turned his face from the glass wall of the visit room so no one outside might read his lips, and spoke in a whisper.

"Forget my cooperating against General Uvalde. Far as DEA is concerned, he's no longer a person of interest."

I opened my mouth to speak, but he raised a finger.

"Just listen," he said. "You're afraid to return to Colombia because you think General Uvalde killed Paz and he'll kill you if you return. But the general doesn't care about you, just as he didn't care about Paz. He didn't kill Paz. *Sombra* did."

Fercho paused. I sat still, waiting.

"Paz was killed because he knew who *Sombra* was. Paz wasn't the first and won't be the last. I'm telling you because I don't want the same fate for you."

"What about you? If you know all this, you must know *Sombra*."

He chuckled. "Never did, and never will. Don't worry about me. It's you who must be careful. *Sombra* can make you rich beyond your wildest dreams. But that's when things get really dangerous. They say the Indians *Sombra* lives with kill anyone who photographs them because they believe photographs steal their souls. *Sombra* takes it a step further. Just to *see* him is to die. Clear?"

"Clear."

"What about you, Benn?"

"What about me?"

"Do you know who *Sombra* is?"

I nodded. "Sure. You."

Fercho laughed long and hard. "From what I understand, you suddenly find yourself in need of cash, yes?"

Again, I was amazed by his knowledge of my privacies. I nodded.

"Then go see Helmer again. After I proffer tomorrow, go."

Despite Fercho's unwillingness to answer a straight question, I'd learned something of importance: *Sombra*'s proclivity for silencing those who knew him.

Problem was, I knew him. Thankfully, Bolivar didn't know I had the complete video incriminating him. I couldn't give it to the government because it would incriminate my client. Nor could I allow anyone to know I possessed it, as it was a guaranteed ticket to the boneyard.

It had to be destroyed.

When I got to the office, I locked the door. Then set the thumb drive atop my acrylic-covered golden horseshoe and ground it to bits beneath my heel. I took the fragments to the restroom and watched them swirl down the toilet.

I'd had it with everything and everyone, on both sides of the law.

Kandi was evil. Bolivar was a serial killer. Josh Waldman was a fair-weather friend. Fercho, for whom I'd walked the line, was just a two-faced criminal after all. And Laura was a liar. The only person I trusted was Mady, but she wanted no part of me—

Bzzzz!

I was startled. Pleasantly, for it was a familiar Mr. Green. Fercho's nephew. He handed me money for my trip to visit Helmer and left without a word. Turned out the number was one hundred large, rather than the usual seventy-five Fercho paid, which got me to thinking he expected something more of me than the usual. Scary thought . . .

I felt like the character in *Li'l Abner* who walks around with a perpetual rain cloud over his head. Now that my old hidey-holes had been discovered, I needed to find places to stash the money until I returned from Helmer. I stretched behind my armoire—

And twisted my bum knee. Just a twinge, but soon enough my knee and then my hip and back would . . . An old tune came to mind: the one about the leg bone being connected to the thigh bone—and, just like that, I saw things clearly.

Josh Waldman had it right: *everything was connected.* All I needed to do was find a string, pull, and watch the Gordian knot unravel.

* * *

The following day, Fercho proffered.

I walked into the debriefing room, expecting to see a couple of agents and the INB chief, but another person was also present. A rangy guy, outdoorsy face, late thirties, slightly rumpled suit. I made him as an agent, but the INB chief introduced him by another title.

"Richard's an analyst," the chief said.

Most so-called analysts are really just shorthand transcribers, as opposed to those few who stare at charts until dots connect and they yell, "Eureka!" Agents refer to these latter as "Brains," although they're the same pay grade as shorthand transcribers. Neither had any power, and I paid the analyst no mind.

The INB chief led off grilling Fercho.

"You've successfully accomplished quite a bit of cooperation, sir. We may have some questions as to how you did so from a cell in the SHU, but that is not our concern at the moment. Right now, we are interested in another topic. You are aware that your attorney represented a man commonly known as Don Rigo?"

"It's known in the jail."

"You are aware Rigo was attempting to cooperate against General Uvalde?"

"I heard a rumor."

"Where?"

"In jail."

"What about you? Are you intending to cooperate against General Uvalde?"

"I have my suspicions, yes. I'm working on obtaining real proof."

The chief paused a beat. "Who's *Sombra*?"

Fercho shrugged. "How would I know?"

Fercho's initial reticence wouldn't be held against him; it was the norm for guys in his seat to reluctantly advance to truthfulness. That the SDNY target was *Sombra* confirmed what I'd thought about Barnett Robinson's interest. Big players often are indicted in several districts before they're extradited. After the defendant is extradited, the districts hash out who has the honor to prosecute. This SDNY interest seemed odd, given that the Southern and Eastern districts try not to step on each other's toes.

For a moment, no one spoke.

Then Richard said, "Let's get down to it, Fercho. Give us *Sombra*, and you walk."

I'd been wrong. The analyst was a heavyweight. Line prosecutors don't have the authority to promise specific sentence reductions. But obviously Richard did. "Think about it," he said. "When you're ready, tell your lawyer."

The INB chief stood. "End of meeting."

CHAPTER 66

For the second time in six months, Fercho was paying me for an errand in Panama during which I could attend to other business. And, like the first time, I suspected Fercho knew my other business. Worrisome. Even if Fercho was merely a messenger, I knew the messages originated with *Sombra*.

Despite having the same destination, this trip felt completely different from my prior run to Panama City. The first time I'd been flush, horny, and aggressive. This time I was flat broke, chaste, and chastened.

Once past customs, I texted Helmer Quezada.

Immediately he replied:

WAIT.

Good. I needed some time to accomplish my other business. Instead of checking in to my regular posh suite, I took an economy room in a ubiquitous hotel. The better to see and not be seen.

Then I set about finding Foto.

I called him but got no answer. I texted and e-mailed him. Nothing. After dark I went to Foto's building. His penthouse appeared unlit. I pressed the street buzzer. No answer.

I took a taxi to a corner below *El Tornillo*, The Screw. The sidewalk was crowded. Money people with bodyguards, South American vacationers, hustlers, pimps.

I left the boulevard and went down a leafy side street. Hushed here, where private homes were set behind gates.

I walked on the other side of the street from the house I was looking for.

In a second-floor room, a television flickered dimly. I'd been in that room before. It was a bedroom with a big bed atop which, one long day into night, Foto and I had smoked weed and drunk beer while counting the equivalent of $2 million in Colombian pesos. To make matters worse, the AC had been out, and even with the windows open, we were sweltering. He had started to say, "An ugly job—"

"But somebody has to do it," I'd finished.

He'd giggled. When we were done, Foto wanted to go party. "But not here. This is my safe house, bro. You're the only one who knows about it. Good weed, huh?"

Foto had been so stoned, I doubted he'd remember my having been there. In truth, it seemed long ago. Back when we were friends.

The street was quiet. Empty. Above the entrance to Foto's house, a tiny red light shone. A security camera. I kept walking. The neighboring house was dark. No camera. I vaulted a low fence and went behind the neighboring house. The rear of Foto's place was dark. A trellis thick with night flowers was fixed to that wall. I remembered because we'd had the window open that night.

I climbed the trellis to a rear window.

Paused, listening. Nothing but cicadas and the low *whirr* of an air conditioner and, faintly from within, a soccer match on television. The announcer spoke Colombian Spanish. I smiled. Foto was there.

I took hold of the window, tensed. For sure, it would be locked, but I intended to smash it open and be inside before Foto could react.

I hoped. Maybe he had a gun. Maybe he'd use it before I could get to him. Maybe I was too old to even think of trying such a move—

Fuck old. Fuck maybe.

I gripped the window tightly, was about to put my shoulder to the glass . . . but it wasn't locked. It opened smoothly. A typical Foto stoner lapse. It was a "safe house," after all; why check the windows?

I crawled through the window.

Found myself in a small bedroom. Barbells on the floor. A rack of expensive suits. A door opened just a crack but enough to see the television in the master bedroom.

I inched the door wider.

Foto lay in bed with a beer bottle propped on his stomach. He was naked except for shorts. He was unshaven. He looked drunk. I counted to three . . .

Then burst through the door.

Drunk or not, Foto reacted quickly, reaching toward the nightstand. My hand was in my jacket pocket as if I held a gun. "Move, and I'll kill you."

He froze. Blinked. "Benn?"

I crossed to the nightstand, opened the top drawer, took a small automatic from it.

"Why are you here, Benn?"

I whipped the gun across his face. "I'm asking the questions. Why are *you* here?"

"No reason. Come on, Benn, we—"

I hit the other side of his face.

"When I was in PC before the holidays?" I said. "You already knew I was on my way to Guatemala."

He began shaking his head but stopped when I raised the gun to his face.

"I don't recall. What's the fucking diff? I was referring you a case."

"Who was your source? Mondragon? Kursk? *Sombra?*"

He swallowed hard. His silence was a tell that spoke volumes. I smashed him again. I saw blood flying and didn't care. "First, I'm going to take your face—"

"Benn, I meant you no harm—"

"Then I'll take your balls."

"Okay. I'll tell you—"

He lunged for the gun.

It flew from my grip and skittered across the floor. We both went after it. I grabbed it first and leveled it at him, and he stopped short. For a moment, I thought he was considering taking a bullet, but then his lips quivered.

"All right, all right. I'll tell you—"

His expression froze. A red rose bloomed on his shirt front. He tottered and fell onto the bed.

I turned and saw, framed by the same window I'd entered, a small man holding a large pistol with a long silencer pointed at me.

Enano.

A phone was pressed to his ear. He listened, nodded, hung up. Then lowered the gun and climbed back through the window and was gone.

I left by the front door.

My shirt was splattered with blood. I buttoned my jacket, turned the collar up. Forced myself to walk slowly for several blocks, then caught a cab to my hotel.

One thing was clear: I hadn't been dispatched to Panama City to meet Helmer Quezada. No, I'd been sent because I could be followed to Foto, so he could be located and silenced. Like Paz, he knew Bolivar was *Sombra*—

My phone rang, startling me.

I put it to my ear, grunted.

It was Helmer Quezada.

He said, "Caracas."

CHAPTER 67

Returning to New York was the safe, smart thing to do. But if *Sombra* had marked me for death, I'd have already been lying alongside Foto. Besides, New York wasn't safe, either: Stefania was proof of that. So, in for a dime, in for a dollar.

The next day, I flew to Venezuela.

I hadn't been to Caracas in years. I remembered it as a bustling city throbbing with rumba. But that was when Venezuela was just dipping its toe into vast pools of oil, the start of what promised to be a long swim in a sea of wealth. But the price of oil had plummeted, and the country had gotten sidetracked by the false promise of *Chavismo* and descended into a full-fledged narco-state, much as Colombia had during the late twentieth century. Still, Colombia had fought its way through, and although drugs still accounted for too much of its econ, its society was relatively free and decidedly upwardly mobile. Venezuela, however, remained the domain of drugsters and military strongmen, its economy depressed and in ruins.

I felt the vibes as soon as I walked off my flight. Eleven in the evening, and the international terminal was nearly empty. Just a few lonesome travelers with eyes averted from men loitering in darkened boarding gates. Plainclothes cops. They eyeballed me, but I passed unhindered through customs and immigration.

Helmer Quezada had given me a number to call, and during the cab ride to Caracas proper, I dialed it, but it didn't ring. Bad connectivity, or old-pro Quezada being cautious? Whichever, he'd call when he wanted, and not a moment before. So I sat back and enjoyed the ride.

Or tried to.

A half mile out from the airport, the roadside was dark. Desolate. Just our headlights, eating up highway totally bereft of other traffic. The sad legacy of Hugo the Munificent.

My cab sped along for forty-five minutes: no lights, no signs, nothing.

Caracas was barely lit, its downtown deserted. I went into a large hotel that looked transplanted from 1960s Miami. The lobby was empty. I told the desk clerk I wanted an inexpensive room. He replied there was a promotion going on; he would upgrade me.

The promo turned out to be a presidential-size suite. Made me wonder if Quezada, acting on Fercho's wishes, was making nice. Whatever. It was a welcome nest for this weary traveler. I placed an order for room service, then showered. I was toweling off when room service arrived. I dressed while the white-jacketed waiter set up my meal.

When I came from the bedroom, he stood with his face turned away, as if embarrassed to be waiting for remuneration. I put ten American on the table. He murmured thanks and lifted the cover off my steak plate.

Only there wasn't a steak on my plate.

It was a stack of crisp new Franklins.

The waiter laughed. I blinked.

The waiter was my longtime client PF, the permanent fugitive, now far from Honduras. Raising a hand for silence, he picked up a remote and switched on the television, then ran through stations before stopping at a news commentary. He increased the volume to a roar and leaned closer.

"To understand the present, understand the past," he said. My obvious confusion made PF smile. "Remember years ago, when all of a sudden you began getting major Colombian clients?"

I nodded. I remembered all too well.

"Then you met a certain man and learned your clients were his people."

I wondered why PF was talking about Nacho Barrera but didn't want to be drawn in to the conversation. Assume everyone—even a longtime client—is wired, and you have one less thing to worry about. There's a huge difference between representing a criminal and being house counsel to a criminal organization. The former is criminal-defense business as usual; the latter criminal monkey business. No way I was going to own up to anything resembling that, so I simply nodded.

"Weren't you curious that, even after Nacho was dead, you continued representing big players known as . . . what do the federals call them?"

"Consolidated Priority Operational Targets. CPOTs."

"Ah, yes, CPOTs. Like Fercho. Like me. Like a dozen others since Nacho's death. All of whom know of, or actually know, one another. Why do you think we all retained you?"

"Because I'm good at what I do."

"Nacho was a private man. Few people knew he was survived by a son. Many lawyers are good at what you do, but you proved yourself to be loyal to the family and the survivors of Nacho's organization."

"Which survivors?"

PF grinned. "There's me, and . . . I'm sure you'll discover who else on your own. We're not an organization. We have no name. We're just a group with a shared history of loving Nacho. We only deal with one another and are sworn to never reveal our ties. Still, given the nature of our business, sometimes we must deal with an outsider . . . and sometimes that outsider breaks our code of silence. I am referring to a particular client of yours, or perhaps I should say, a *recent* client. You know who?"

I nodded. "My only *recent* client was Rigo."

"Yes, him. You knew what Rigo planned?"

I nodded. "Why are you telling me this?"

PF regarded the television. The commentary was over; now a beauty contest was on. He sighed. "Women. I'm tired of one-night *putas*. I want to settle down with one woman. Just like you, Benn. I remember Nacho was impressed with your wife. Brains and beauty, he said. A *Puertorriqueña*, if I recall. How is she?"

No way was I going to discuss Mady with these people. "I wouldn't know," I said. "We divorced long ago."

"I'm sorry to hear that, but not surprised. Difficult maintaining a home life in the business we're in."

I wanted to say I wasn't in his business, but PF was right. I was right in the middle of it. I was the missing link among those in jail and their brethren outside. Drug money paid my bills.

"You asked why I am telling you this, Benn. It's because we need your services again. One last time. Accomplish the task, and you'll be rich beyond your dreams."

"I've heard that line before."

"Your answer is yes?"

"Do I have any choice?"

"No. Tomorrow we begin."

When he was gone, I counted the money. One hundred thousand, exactly what Fercho had paid. *Sombra's* organization was paying me twice for the same trip. Dangling two juicy carrots before one hungry horse.

Putting me in double trouble.

CHAPTER 68

When the phone rang, I bolted awake. Still dark out. I answered. "Your car is here, sir."

What car? I squinted at my watch: 3:00 a.m. Right. It was tomorrow.

Fifteen minutes later, I checked out. My car was an old taxi, its driver unremarkable.

Last time I'd been in Caracas, the clubs were just getting going at this hour, but now we drove through dark, deserted streets. We went down a boulevard that petered out at a dirt field. Apparently, the driver had been paid to go this far but no farther because he stopped, reached back, and opened my door.

I didn't like the idea of being left alone in the middle of nowhere, but it had been preordained. As soon as I got out, the taxi pulled away. Dead quiet and pitch dark—

Suddenly, bright lights came on. Behind their glare, an insectlike contraption was perched in the field. A small helicopter. Its blades began turning as its cockpit door swung open and a man leaned out, motioning me toward him.

As I approached, a second man appeared. He wore flight coveralls and a handgun in a shoulder holster. The first man was also armed. He spoke into a radio. His accent was Colombian. Not surprising. Venezuela was loaded with *colombianos* doing business protected by the corrupt military. I supposed whomever I was about to meet operated somewhere in western Venezuela, in a mountain redoubt hard by the Colombian border.

The second man indicated for me to board.

I climbed into the cockpit and sat behind the pilot. I was given a headset and told to buckle up. The motor coughed to life, the rotors picked up speed, and we lifted off.

There was a quarter moon, and in its pale light the downtown buildings looked like tombstones. There was no traffic on the streets. No signs of life. We tilted upward and gained speed.

For an hour, we droned through darkness. Then a few tiny, flickering flames appeared. As we neared, they grew numerous, so many it looked like a firefly convention. Their illuminated reflection was on water, and I realized the lights were the gas flares of oil rigs on Lake Maracaibo. Meaning we were headed due west. The flares receded behind us. The eastern sky was lightening—

All at once, the sun rose above the earth's rim, and ahead in the far distance were mountains topped by snowcapped alps. I'd seen the peaks often from jetliners and recognized them as the Sierra Nevada de Santa Marta—

In Colombia.

The altimeter read six thousand feet, but that wasn't why my heart was pounding. Never mind that Fercho claimed General Uvalde hadn't killed Paz and didn't care about me: the fact remained that people knew I'd possessed a video incriminating Uvalde. And now, I was entering Uvalde's domain, bereft of either a passport stamp or customs declaration.

Below in the predawn lay a white-sand coastline I knew to be the Guajira Peninsula, where six years ago Joaquin Bolivar had loaded a sailboat with weed brought down from the high Sierra, weed harvested by the Logui Indians.

Now the jungled coastline gave way to fields and buildings, and beyond them was the grid of a seaside city. Santa Marta.

We corkscrewed lower. At the edge of a field, headlights flashed on and off three times. The helicopter landed in a cloud of dust. Its rotors slowed and stopped, and when the dust had cleared, an automobile became visible. It was a dark Escalade like the one Castri drove me in.

I felt a twinge of unease: the pilots' body language was wary, as if the scenario were not what they'd expected. They had their hands on their guns. The Escalade's rear door opened, and a man got out.

Felipe Mondragon.

"A small change of plans, guys," he said. "It was thought that Indians might be noticed, so they asked me to escort the doctor instead."

"No one told us," the pilot said. "I don't like it."

"Understandable. One can't be too careful. As proof, they asked the doctor's man to vouch for me." Mondragon gestured, and the Escalade driver got out.

To my astonishment, it was my driver, Castri.

The pilot looked at me. "You know this man?"

I nodded. The pilots holstered their weapons.

"Come, Doctor," Mondragon said to me.

Even as I started toward the Escalade, two men brandishing automatic weapons emerged from its rear. Their guns chattered, and the pilots crumpled.

I stood still, stunned.

"I had no choice, Doctor," Mondragon said. "People who know *Sombra* have a troubling manner of disappearing. The list, unfortunately, includes me."

I was on the list, too, but said nothing.

"Oh, I intend to disappear from sight, but very much alive and very wealthy. You see, all you have is now mine. This vehicle, and the twenty-million-dollar fee you received for representing Bolivar."

Received? Mondragon was an even bigger fool than I. I hoped to be paid. He thought I had been.

He smiled wolfishly. "Pretending you don't understand? A poor act, Doctor. We will arrange for you to wire the money from your account to mine. Get in the car."

Castri held the door for me. Whatever small hope I had that he was still with me was extinguished when our gazes met. His looked defiant. He said, "You didn't think I'd be a driver for the rest of my life—"

The side of Castri's head imploded—a flashback to my near-death experience in Antigua. Before I fully comprehended what was happening, I had instinctively thrown myself to the sandy soil, processing the fact of an ambush while pressing myself against terra firma. Above me flew a deafening exchange of incoming rounds and outgoing responses, which slowly lessened and finally ceased.

Tentatively, I got up.

Castri, Mondragon, and the two *sicarios* from the Escalade lay in their own pooled blood, eyes vacantly staring at the rifle-toting new arrivals above them, two Indians and a short man with truncated fingers I recognized:

Enano.

CHAPTER 69

Again, *Enano* chose to let me live. Which did little to calm my fears. I didn't feel as if I'd been pardoned, rather granted a temporary stay of execution.

I was put into the back seat of the Escalade. We drove along the beach, headed east, into the low-rising sun. I didn't know if I was a prisoner or a guest, or where we were going or why.

Enano sat up front with the Indian driver; the two Indian gunmen sat beside me. The Escalade's big V-8 was soundless; the air conditioning blew softly. I could smell *Enano*'s brilliantine in his matted hair. The Indians' bronze skin had an herbal aroma. They looked alike except for their sizes: large and extralarge. They were lean in loose cotton pants and shirts. Their aura was calming: be here now; be patient, relax.

An hour out of Santa Marta, the paved road became a packed-earth track. There was no other traffic. To the right was impenetrable green jungle; to the left, white sand and pale sea. The Guajira. We passed rusting wreckage sunk in the sand. Dope planes that had never made it. A lot of people had struck it rich in the Guajira, and a lot had died here miserably. Which was my future?

The Escalade glided along.

An hour passed. The sun was full up, the day blindingly bright. Ahead, dark against the sand, tiny objects wobbled in the heat waves. As we neared, the objects became distinguishable. Indians and horses.

We stopped alongside them. Left the Escalade for dense heat. Immediately, I began perspiring. The driver said something to *Enano*. The little man laughed.

"They say you smell bad," he said to me. "Go for a swim."

The Indians were grinning. I shed my clothes and dived in. The sea was cool. On the beach, the Indians were forcing *Enano* into the water. He protested until stepping off a sand shelf so his head dropped below the surface. He came up sputtering. Funny. I laughed along with the Indians.

They gave me cotton clothing and a canteen. Rubbed leaves between their palms until they became pasty, then smeared their bodies and wiped their faces. They motioned for me to do the same. I did. The stuff felt medicinal in a minty way. When I lowered my hands, colors seemed brighter. *Enano* asked for leaves, but there were no more. The Indians thought that funny, too. *Enano* got angry. He cursed and put his hand atop his gun—

Faster than I comprehended, the smaller Indian twisted *Enano*'s grip and took the gun away. An automatic. He jacked a round from the chamber and removed the clip, then threw the weapon into the jungle.

We mounted horses, and the bigger Indian led us into the jungle. Him, me, *Enano*, the other Indian. The path was narrow. My horse knew the way, plodding behind the horse ahead. Beneath the treetop canopy, the air was cool.

We rode for several hours, always on an incline, higher into the Sierra.

My butt was rubbed raw. I lost my sense of direction. I had no idea of how far we had come or how much farther it was or why the fuck we were going there. All I knew was that it was not to see *Sombra*, who was called Bolivar and sat in an SHU cell of MCC Brooklyn four thousand miles away . . .

Around noon, we entered a clearing. Long miles away and below I glimpsed the sparkling Caribbean. Longer miles above us were snowcapped peaks. The mountainsides were cleft by streams and water-falls. Spread miles apart along the top of a semicircular ridgeline were clustered villages, smoke rising from their cooking fires.

We rode on.

Gradually, late afternoon gave way to early evening. The jungle cooled and darkened—

Ahead, a light flickered.

We'd come to the edge of the jungle where the tree line gave way to the *páramo*, the Andean plateaus below the peaks. Above was a star-filled sky. A patrol of men on horseback cantered past. Further on we passed a sandbagged trench where I glimpsed a shoulder-carried antiaircraft missile. I realized this was the village of the Logui, the lost tribe of the Nevadas.

Their village had an air of permanence: a grid of immaculately thatched houses, the streets hard packed. There were people about: men, women, and children, none of whom paid us the least attention.

I slid from my mount. I was led to a stone hut. Large, circular, covered with moss. When I entered, the door shut heavily behind me. A bolt was thrown.

I was alone.

Next to one wall stood a waxen mountain of candle drippings atop which a single candle burned. In the center of the space was a plank table and brightly woven seating below a domelike roof. A cooking fire whose smoke ventilated through an oculus. Food and drink were laid out. Fish, grains, vegetables. I ate voraciously.

Sated, I lay staring at the oculus, the smoke dissipating, changing form.

I wondered: *What now? The beginning? Or the beginning of the end?*

A memory tugged at me. A sensory recollection.

An herbal scent that became tangible—

CHAPTER 70

"Hello, Benn," Laura Astorquiza said. It was her aroma—herbal. Both delicate and earthy—that alerted me to her presence. She wore white cotton and her hair loose. Her expression was placid, as if her presence was perfectly natural. I had no idea how she'd entered the hut. Had she been inside all along, observing me?

"Benn has so many questions, he's not sure where to begin."

"No need for me to ask. You're going to tell me."

She laughed. "You know me so well."

We'd met but once, briefly at Foto's party, and yet it was true. I felt as if I knew her well, as if we had a shared history. Again, I inhaled her scent, and suddenly another gap in my memory filled; a recollection of another time and place so astounding I had to will myself not to blurt it out. Not yet.

"I'm here because I believe in *Sombra*," she said. "You're surprised?"

I nodded. "Mildly. Like learning Joan of Arc was English."

"Then and now, there's only one crusade. Defending the defenseless. Were it not for *Sombra*, the Logui and the other tribes would have been eradicated. If there were no *Sombra*, there'd still be drugs. But instead of the profits buying cheap women and vulgar mansions, they are used to ensure that an ancient civilization survives. Choosing *Sombra* is choosing the greater good."

Or the lesser evil, I thought. There was nothing good about drugs, nor about those who sold them. *Sombra* was not the first drug lord to cloak himself in populism; witness the political ploys of Nacho's arch-enemy, Pablo Escobar.

"Did you expect *Sombra* to be here?" she asked.

I locked my baby blues with Laura's big browns for a long moment before I replied. "Just between us, I'm relieved he's not. *Sombra* kills those who can identify him."

"How do you know that?"

"I had a client named Rigo. He was murdered because he was going to identify *Sombra*."

Laura nodded thoughtfully. "Did Rigo share that information with you?"

"He didn't trust me. He was going to use it to negotiate his release."

"How do you know that?"

"I was told so by a lawyer who himself was killed because he knew who *Sombra* was. His name was Paz. He didn't share the information with me, either."

"So, you've no idea of *Sombra*'s identity?"

I knew I was walking a razor's edge. Shaking my head might cost me my balance. I needed to stabilize. "I'm not sure. At first, I thought it was someone the lawyer Paz introduced me to."

"At first? But no longer?"

"No. Then I thought *Sombra* was a Russian named Kursk."

"A Russian? What made you think that?"

"Kursk approached me to discuss a client of mine. A man named Bolivar. A Colombian. I had the impression Kursk feared Bolivar would identify him—Kursk—as *Sombra*."

Laura nodded to herself, as if confirming a thought. "Has it occurred to you that *Sombra* is not a man, but a myth?"

I shrugged. "Perhaps. I don't want to know. Neither should you, Laura. It's too dangerous."

She drew a breath as if composing herself. "This man Bolivar also knows *Sombra*. I wanted you here so you could look in my eyes and promise you'll do whatever it takes to gain Bolivar's release. Will you?"

"I already told Kursk I would."

"I want to hear it myself. And it's not just Bolivar. There's a woman close to Kursk who knows. The wealthy widow. Stand aside from her, and whatever happens, happens." She waited a moment to make sure I was registering what she said. "We're clear then, Benn?"

"Not yet. Why did you drug me?"

To my surprise, Laura laughed. "I was wondering when you'd realize it was me. It was for insurance. Without money, you'd be desperate to earn more. If your records were given to the government, you'd be ruined. I needed to be certain you'd do whatever was necessary to free Bolivar."

"Why bring me here?"

Her eyes grew soft, and she leaned closer across the table and traced her hand along my cheek. This close, her scent was engulfing, my thoughts replaced by desire. I feared her yet wanted her.

"So you could hear it from me that your records will be returned and your money a thousandfold. Just carry out your part of the bargain."

I nodded. Our lips were close . . .

But then she hesitated; her eyes no longer focused on me, but past me. In that instant, I felt a sense of loss: I knew our moment had passed, and why. The worlds in which we dwelled were too far apart. Despite all the justifications, she reveled in being a drug dealer . . .

And yet I'd been ready to take part in an affair that surely would end badly. And now I suffered the inevitable loss of a man watching the last vestige of his younger self disappear. I knew Laura Astorquiza was the last young woman who'd been, however briefly, attracted to me for myself alone. *There goes my baby . . .*

She stood. "Good night, Benn."

She left the hut. A single flame still flickered atop the waxen shrine. It was what she had been looking at. Above the melted wax was a faded photograph of a man. I was curious because the Indians did not allow their photographs to be taken. I looked closer.

The man in the photograph stood atop a pyramid of crates filled with weapons: small arms, ammunition, mobile missiles. His face was familiar. Bespectacled, calm.

Nacho Barrera.

CHAPTER 71

A single rider guided me down the mountain. Wearing crossed bandoliers and a slung rifle, he reminded me of a Plains Indian warrior. We rode through the night without exchanging a word. A rusted pickup waited on the beach. By early afternoon, he delivered me to Cartagena's Núñez International Airport. Not long ago, I'd been there as a fugitive. Now I was a frequent-flying gringo dumb-lucky enough to keep his passport in a money belt. I caught the next flight to Miami, and as soon as we were wheels up closed my eyes.

I awoke to the announcement that we were about to land in Miami. My head was clogged with a morass of thoughts, but I was fixed on only one. *Jilly*. Laura's comment confirmed Jilly was *Sombra*'s next target. I had no idea why, but my obligation was clear. To hell with what I'd promised Laura, I had to warn Jilly that she was in the crosshairs.

The gates to Jilly's estate were open. I drove through. At the end of the shell driveway, men driving forklifts were loading Jilly's garden of art into trucks. I got out and approached them.

"Junkyard, here we come," I said to the foreman.

He laughed. "What crap. Nicely welded, though. He'p you?"

"I hope so. I'm looking for Mrs. Chennault."

"Afraid I don't know the lady."

A fork driver said, "The blonde."

"Oh, *her*. Some guys have all the luck."

Guys like talking about gals. I got right into it. "You said it," I said. "Babes like her don't come around often. Not to mention that she's rich. All this stuff, it's worth millions, they say."

"Tens of millions, I heard," the boss said.

"Why don't we sell it?" the driver said.

"Because we ain't got the right pedigree for the people who buy it. Coming from us, it's scrap. Coming from the rich lady, it's priceless."

"She's selling it?" I said.

"Sold already, I think. This Russian who's supposed to have more money than God bought it for his pad in New York. Must be some kind of big place if he can fit this shit in."

I got back into my hired car and headed to the airport. Apart from conveying a warning, I'd wanted to see Jilly. I wasn't sure why. I just wanted to see her. The thought made me smile. I'd failed to capture a beautiful raptor; now I was ready to settle for a wounded dove.

But I was destined to fly solo. About to enter uncharted territory, the consequences of which were extreme. Joaquin Bolivar's trial would be loaded with twists and turns. Kandi would be waiting to pounce.

At the end, I might be rich and free.

Or poor and jailed. Or dead.

And yet, I felt like singing.

Ever since I'd started cooperating clients, I'd missed trial work and all its uncertainties. The need to think on my feet. The joy of victory and agony of defeat. Be careful what you wish for. Now I had myself a trial, and not only my ego but my personal and professional life was on the line. More important, I was up against an opponent I dearly wanted to crush. The mere thought of Kandi Kauffman riled me.

It was time to hone my anger.

Time to begin training.

Which meant no more Bison Grass or little blue pills for the duration because, contrary to popular belief, trials are not won in the courtroom but during preparation.

I'd be ready.

Oh yes.

CHAPTER 72

Bonesy said, "Don't you ever take a day off?"

It was Memorial Day, and I was wearing my civvies: jeans, loafers, blazer, and shirt unbuttoned at the collar. For once, the MCC lobby was empty. While signing in to the legal-visit entry book, I spotted the signatures of previous visitors that took me aback.

I passed through the metal detector and got my hand stamped—another illegible fluorescent smear beneath CONTROL's black light—and went through the final air lock that opened into the visit room.

It, too, was empty. I was the only desperado working on the holiday.

I walked to the far end and fortified myself with machine-made coffee. Black, two sugars. I took a gulp that burned my tongue. I blew on the cup and cautiously sipped.

Over its rim, I saw the big visit room at the end. Unlit now, jam-packed with Natty Grable's case discovery cartons: stacks and stacks of them, a maze. I knew Plitkin hadn't read page one. No need to. When satisfied he'd squeezed every dollar from Natty, he'd make the same deal as the codefendants who'd already pled.

It was Natty Grable's signature in the visit book that had disturbed me, along with, immediately below it, the signature of another visitor I knew.

Bolivar appeared in an overlarge orange SHU jumpsuit draping his frame. He'd changed for the worse. Lost a lot of weight, tan faded to a wan complexion, hair longer and even lanker than before. He'd morphed from Latin Lover to Billy Trash. Nothing like the man I'd met less than six months ago in *La Picota*. I tossed the coffee aside and offered my hand—

He recoiled as if I were a leper. Close up, his eyes were sunken. "Nothing personal. I had the flu, and with trial coming up, I don't want you catching it."

We went into a glass-walled visit room.

"Trial still on July sixth?" he asked.

"You have another appointment?"

"Guys in here talk shit. That trial dates always change, how one month can be one year."

I thought about how Bolivar had been anxious about the specific date of the escape attempt. The US Marshals would make sure that wouldn't happen again. "Trials get delayed. But yours won't. First day is Monday, the sixth of July, right after the July Fourth weekend."

"When we getting the thirty-five hundred material?" he asked.

Section 3500 of Title 18 of the US Code mandated that prosecutors give the defense all previous statements made by witnesses—crucial in Bolivar's case, since the evidence against him was solely testimonial.

"At the final status conference," I said.

He nodded to himself as if checking off a mental list of questions. His movements were jittery. I supposed the reality of a trial that would determine the rest of his life was sinking in. I was reasonably sure he would cut a deal. Fine with me. I wouldn't get my duel with Kandi, but it made my fee much more probable. I had no illusions about Paz's $20 million fee babble; that was just chumming the waters, a promise that wouldn't be kept. Right there and then, I'd have settled for a plea, another million in my pocket, and a long vacation.

"You know a woman named Jilly, right?" I asked.

"How many times are you going to ask?"

"Until you and your people leave her alone."

"I have no beef with a woman named Jilly."

I took out the discovery material. Set down the DEA photographs of the *Swan*. Bolivar shrugged. He did the same when seeing photographs of the master cabin; its bed with unmade sheets, table with candle, wine bottle and glass, bitten apple.

"Anything about any of this I need to know?" I said.

"You tell me. The truth and nothing but, clear?"

He gave me a mean look. I knew I was coming down hard but didn't care if it rankled him. If he flipped, I'd be privy to his deepest dark secrets he didn't want known, and he'd be making nice all the way to my bank. If he surprised me by actually going to trial, our slim chance of winning depended on me running the show. Either way, he needed me.

"If we were a country," I said, "you'd be its president, but I'd be chairman of the joint chiefs of staff. You run the show in peacetime, but come to war, you listen to me. Trial is a time of war. You speak only when necessary; otherwise, shut the fuck up."

For a moment, he was silent. Then, as if swallowing his anger, his Adam's apple bobbed, and he nodded. "Okay, General, what's next?"

"The thirty-five hundred discovery."

We stood to leave. Again, I offered my hand, but he pretended not to see it. That provoked me to thinking that Bolivar wasn't worried about my catching his flu—no, he feared being poisoned, the way Mondragon had killed Rigo Ordoñez. At Bolivar's orders, of course.

Which raised a very interesting question: Did he think his people wanted him dead? I took that as evidence that he was planning to flip on them. But did they know? Did Laura know? The thought of her aging in a federal cage was depressing.

"Look me in the eye," Bolivar said. "Say you're going to get me out of here."

I looked him in the eye. "I'm going to do what I can to make that happen."

"For your sake," he said, holding my gaze, "you better come through."

ALUNE

Like all people, I am composed of dual natures. Opposing thoughts. I am wildly sexual yet so selective in my choice of partners that I am nearly abstinent. I am possessed of my ancestors' civilized genius and native intelligence. I have opposing visions of my future: of living a private life, or as a public servant. My schooling came in a combination of two disparate environments: my Spanish heritage, and my English-language education. I enjoy the best of both worlds. I can read the literary greats in their native tongues. Shakespeare in English. Cervantes in Spanish.

At times, I must choose between their differing wisdoms.

Shakespeare: "The first thing, let's kill all the lawyers."

Cervantes: "The lawyer is as transparent as glass."

So now, it comes down to the final choice:

Which truth shall I act upon?

It is a very difficult choice.

I must consult my brothers.

CHAPTER 73

I had just gone through the Battery Tunnel tolls and was zooming toward the tube entrance when my phone rang. When I answered there was the electronic sound of call rerouting, then a woman's accented voice said, "Mr. Bluestone?"

"That's me," I said. "Who're you?"

"Hard hearing you, sir."

"I'm on Bluetooth."

"Blue . . . stone?"

But inside the tunnel, the call was totally lost. The calling number was indecipherably coded. By the time I emerged from the tunnel, I'd forgotten the call.

Then my phone rang again.

"Benn? Me, Billy."

Ach. I'd totally forgotten I owed Billy a visit. "Actually," I said, "I'm on my way to see you now."

I got onto the FDR northbound, took the Triborough over to Queens, and got a temporary pass to cross the oversea highway to Rikers. The island houses more than a half dozen separate jails whose population hovers around ten thousand. There are no grimmer vibes than that of Rikers. I parked, then rode a Corrections bus to the OBCC facility, and ten minutes later was locked in a small room with Billy. The kid had always been thin, but now I could see the skull beneath his face.

"I'm praying to my momma and Bea and everyone else I knew that you're as good as they say you are," Billy said. "Cause I need help, big time. Haunty and the others, they're putting the murder on me."

What to say? The same story from a federal client with a quarter million in loose change bought my services to the bitter end. But Billy was a state-court defendant without a pot to piss in. I drew a deep breath. Held it. Said, "Here's the plan. Stick with the public defender for now. You can trust her. Nothing is going to happen until trial—"

"It's in July."

"I know," I said, although I didn't. "Come July, I'm your lawyer."

A tear ran down Billy's cheek. To my annoyance, I gave a little sniffle, too. Poor kid. Never caught a break, and now this. All right. Soon as Bolivar's trial was over, I'd shift gears to Billy's trial. Rip Haunty and the other liars to mincemeat.

On the drive home, the woman with the accent called again.

"This is Mr. Bluestone?"

"That's me, again."

"Bennjamin Bluestone?"

A sales pitch, I thought, but her accent seemed northern European. Not the type who made cold calls.

"Yes," I answered.

"Middle initial *T*? The Bennjamin with two *n*'s, middle initial *T*. Bluestone who maintains an account at MetroBank?"

"If you want to sell whatever you're selling, you need to brush up on the natives. Today's a big holiday in the USA. Memorial Day. Our banks are closed. So take the day off, too, wherever you are."

"Sir, it's not a banking holiday in Switzerland. My name is Ana Grundig, and I am calling on behalf of my client before transferring funds from their account to yours."

"You're persistent, I'll give you that. I suppose now you want my routing and account numbers: That's how phishing works, right?"

"No, sir. We already have that information. This call is for security purposes to verify that this calling number is that of the same B. T. Bluestone who is the referenced MetroBank account holder."

"Since you already know, sure. That's me."

"Thank you, sir. The transfer is approved."

"Nice. How much is it for, again?"

But Ms. Grundig had hung up.

I got off the FDR and parked on East 114th, across from Rao's, an old red-sauce Italian joint favored by cops and politicians. This part of Spanish Harlem was as safe as the White House. I opened my banking app, thinking *Sombra* had made an installment.

But my balance was unchanged—

Then the screen flashed. When updated, my balance had changed. Increased. Tremendously. By $20 million fucking dollars.

It had happened. My Biggy had landed.

First thoughts: I dared not touch the money. Not yet. First, let it lie undisturbed by a forfeiture complaint. By not participating, I was insulating myself with the lack of knowledge required for a conspirator. One alternative was to withdraw it all and run, but there was no place I might hide. If the feds didn't get me, the Colombians would.

There was another alternative that was more disturbing. If I failed to accomplish my part of the bargain—whatever that was—my benefactors would demand a refund. Returning drug money could be construed as money laundering by an opportunistic prosecutor like Kandi. I gave an involuntary shiver.

Damned if I did and damned if I did not.

Extradite yourself from this, Bluestone.

CHAPTER 74

June 1 dawned with blast-furnace heat. I let Val do the driving while I sat in the back, plotting. We worked our way downtown. The first stop was a class B office building on Park Avenue South, a once-grand deco edifice that had long ago lost its way.

Same as its tenants.

The suite I entered needed carpeting. The receptionist was a Dominican woman named Carmen whose ass was the size of a bodega. Unfortunately, her butt was a too-familiar sight in attorney-visit rooms, where she was a paralegal hustling cases for the lawyer she fronted. On several occasions, I'd told her to stay the fuck away from my clients. She pretended not to know who I was, asked if I had an appointment.

"Tell Morty Benn Bluestone's here about a matter."

"The name of the matter?"

I spelled: "M-O-N-E-Y."

Plitkin greeted me with a clap on the back. "Good to see you, Benn. Carmen says her intuition is you want to talk about a new case?"

"Carmen's quick."

"Why I use her. Ah, Benn. You know how many years I been asking myself how come we don't give each other work?"

"How many?"

"Tell you the truth? I always wanted us to, but you're always, like, what's the expression? A lone wolf."

"That makes you Little Red Riding Hood."

Morty flashed his Chiclets. "Funny."

"Morty," I said.

"Yes, Benn?"

"You're a lying thief."

"Benn—"

"You never recommended me for the Bolivar case."

"I mentioned your name. Favorably. I didn't ask for a commission, remember?"

Morty's a big lug: two inches taller than me, a fifty-pound paunch wider, but I got in his space and put a finger in his face. "Why didn't you make the score yourself?"

"Believe me, I tried. But they wanted you."

"Who did? Kursk? Jilly?"

"I don't know them—"

I grabbed his tie and yanked his face down. He smelled of a half century's worth of cigars. "I'm out of control, Morty. I got nothing left to lose. Fuck with me, and I'll take you down with me. *Who?*"

"Okay, okay. Kursk, I met. We didn't say word one. The one who wanted you was Kursk's arm candy. Jilly, whatever's her name. Leggo my tie."

"Sorry." I let him go. "Still friends?"

I held out my hand, and we shook. But I held tight to his hand and with my free hand gripped my right thumb and ground my knuckles against the back of his hand. It's a not-so-tender touch that never fails. Plitkin gasped with pain.

"The blonde arm candy," I said. "You got her a paralegal card."

I ground harder, and he went to his knees. "Benn, *please*—"

"And then you sent her to visit *my* client, yes?"

"*Ow!* No. She isn't visiting your guy."

"No? So, *who* is she visiting?"

"Natty Grable's codefendants. Natty gets off on the way all the guys in jail look at her, like he's a big ladies' man."

"Bolivar and Natty. What's their connection?"

"I don't know. Benn, my hand—"

"Tell me about Kursk."

"Natty works for him."

"Why's Natty going to trial if he can get probation?"

"The guy's crazy. Benn, you're really hurting me."

I knew I was. It felt good. Hurting Plitkin was like hurting everything I hated about the business.

"How do I find Jilly?"

Tears of pain, or maybe of humiliation, streaked Plitkin's porcine face. He said, "I don't know. One time when I went to jail with Natty, we picked her up at some hotel downtown. In the Village somewhere."

"Listen up good, fat boy. If anything happens to Jilly, I've got ways and means of putting you into the thick of it. Understand?"

"Understand. Benn, my hand, please . . ."

As I released Morty's hand, I twisted off his pinky ring. I dislike pinky rings and the type of men who wear them. This one was a star sapphire set in white gold. I turned a metal wastebasket upside down, put the ring atop the bottom, and crushed it beneath my heel.

"Tell Carmen her intuition sucks," I said as I left.

I hit the street feeling wild. Plitkin had read me right. I was a lone wolf. And right now, I was howling like crazy. I got into the back of the Flex.

"Someone follows us," Val said.

"What are you talking about?"

"A big, black Mercedes."

"There's a ton of them."

"We drive; they drive. We park; they park."

"Show me."

Val looked in the rearview. Frowned. Twisted in his seat and looked behind. Frowned again. "He gone now."

"Keep going downtown," I said.

CHAPTER 75

I'd avoided Fercho since returning from Colombia. Talking to him was, however indirectly, talking to *Sombra*. Yet just now I preferred a failure to communicate. Reason being—as I'd already made clear to Bolivar—I neither could nor would tolerate an iota of interference. I was going to live, breathe, and dream one singularity: Bolivar's trial. But now, despite that, I visited Fercho.

The reason why gnawed at my gut.

Val dropped me outside the no-go perimeter on Mosco Alley, an alley descending from Mott Street in old Chinatown that opened on Columbus Park. Above the treetops was the dull bulk of the New York State criminal courthouse and the traditional granite tower of the Southern District at 500 Pearl. The park was crowded with old Chinese men watching matches of Go, a game vastly more complex than chess that dated to before the dawn of Western civilization. I wondered how many times I had gone up Mosco to scarf Chinese food, then hustled back to lawyering . . . in 100 Centre.

Ah, Billy. What am I gonna do for you?

The day was steaming hot. One minute out of the cooled Flex, and my shirt was plastered to my back. I walked in sunlight behind the State Supreme Court building. The MDC loomed ahead, and I quickened my pace, for once anxious to enter the cooler.

But the count was still on.

And Val was long blocks away. Which made me a mad dog in the noonday sun. I went over to Police Plaza and the only building that had nothing to do with what I did for a living.

St. Andrew's Church was dim, cool, and empty. Nice. I hadn't been in a church since the fateful day Rigo surrendered. I sat in a rear pew and felt the tension drain from my aching back. Above the altar, outlined against sun-illuminated stained glass, was a huge cross from which a sad-eyed Jesus regarded me. An unfamiliar emotion rose within me, one I didn't know I had:

I'm sorry, Mady. Forgive me.

I felt as insignificant as the billions of dust motes hanging in the shafted light . . . but then they moved, as if the air were disturbed, and I turned and saw a man seated behind me, his thin lips parted in a smile.

"You, religious?" Evgeny Kursk said.

"Why have you been following me?"

"We need to have a talk."

"You don't own a phone?"

"Phones dangerous in this country. Many listeners."

"And not in Russia?"

"There, too." He chuckled. "But in Russia, I am friends with the listeners."

I was uncomfortable with the circumstances. The US Attorney's office was a stone's throw away, and Kursk was connected to Bolivar, a circuit already dangerously overloaded. Another man stood at the church entrance. Kursk's underling, Kyril.

"We have nothing to talk about," I said.

He held a hand up so I could see the tattoo on the inside of his wrist. Crude jailhouse ink, faded but still legible: a red star with barbed-wire borders, within it a hammer and sickle. Murmansk-54.

"You received our bank wire?" he said.

That reinforced my fears. Murmansk-54 was now permanently networked deep in my life. Not that the transfer was illegal on its face, but if the case went south, my fee might well become forfeitable.

"Natty and Kyril and Andrey—may he rest in peace—we are brothers. We die for one another. Kill for one another. Understand?"

"Natty already told me. Shove your threats. We're not in Moscow."

"A bullheaded man with no fear. I admire that."

"Another thing," I said. "If you want my help, make sure nothing happens to the girl."

"What girl is that?"

"Mrs. Sholty."

"Ah, *her*. We have no problem with her, but if you must hear it—"

"I must."

"Nothing will happen to her. Now that we're clear, continue your trial preparation. If some other opportunity arises, be prepared to grab hold of it."

"What kind of other opportunity?"

"A figure of speech. Free Bolivar, and you will be richer than you ever dreamed. We are like Henry Ford at the threshold of a new era. We have the opportunity to control emerging markets."

I didn't reply. Unless I was a total sucker—a distinct possibility—he really didn't care about Jilly. He stood and left. After a few minutes, I did, too.

The count had cleared. For the second time in recent days while signing in the legal-visit book, I spotted a disconcerting entry. A disappointment I tucked away for future reference.

Fercho was in a good mood. "Good morning, Benn."

I hit him hard and fast. "Lose the shit-eating grin. You've got yourself a big problem. I just returned from Colombia. Word is, you're going to give up *Sombra*."

His eyes widened. "No one would think that."

"They asked my opinion," I said, cold eyed.

"You told them it wasn't possible, yes?"

Fercho had gone as pallid as cheap copy paper. Tough on him. I was tired of him yanking my chain. Manipulating me. My turn now. The only way to get anything out of him was by squeezing.

"I told them it *was* possible. I'd let them know."

"You must tell them it's not true."

"The endgame. What is it?"

"You already know."

"Tell me again."

"Bolivar walks."

"And the girl?"

"What girl?"

I stood to go, but Fercho gripped my arm. There was something in his expression I hadn't seen before. Desperation.

"Benn, please. What girl?"

It occurred to me that he didn't know Jilly and probably knew nothing about her. *Sombra* compartmentalized his DTO, so no single person knew anything meaningful. I thought of the same name I'd seen in the Manhattan MDC legal-visit book.

"You're a snake, Fercho. For five years, I've been busting my ass trying to save yours. And you go behind my back and talk to Dreidel."

"I . . . How did you know?"

"The question is, *why?*"

"You're under a lot of pressure. Your investigation, the trial—"

"Your point being?"

"If things don't go well for you, I'll need another lawyer. I wish you the best, Benn. But if I'm going to need another lawyer, I need to put the process in motion now."

"You've hired Dreidel?"

"No. But if I have to, I will. I know Dreidel's a thief. But he worked for the feds a long time; he knows how the system works. For money, he'll do anything. Just like you."

Again, I stood, gathered myself to leave.

"Benn, straighten them out about me."

I didn't respond as I walked out. Fercho thinking he was a dead man walking provided perverse satisfaction. But nothing else. He was of no use in helping Jilly, and he'd only confirmed what I already knew was the hard work cut out for me:

I had to walk Bolivar.

And, somehow, Billy.

CHAPTER 76

I was concentrating on Bolivar's file when Traum unexpectedly showed at my office. I tried turning him away at the door.

"We need to talk, Benno,"

He brushed past me, stuck an unlit stogie in his mouth, and sat. The heat wave was continuing, and he was carrying his jacket. His belly strained against his short-sleeved white shirt, and although I couldn't see the telltale bulge of a recorder, he could have been wired a dozen other ways.

"I've got nothing to say," I said. "Say your piece, and scram."

"No problem, kid. I can guarantee you win the Bolivar trial."

I kept mum. There was no legitimate way anyone could guarantee a verdict . . . the key word being *legitimate*, which was why I dared not respond aloud.

He fired up the stogie.

I held my tongue.

"Naturally, it's gonna cost you. But you can afford it, the kind of bucks these people been paying you. See, I *know* about your wire transfer."

I pressed my lips together, but my leg was shaking. It seemed impossible that Traum could get into the Swiss banking system, but then again, he probably knew people who could. Like Nelson Cano.

"I'm a realistic guy, Benno. I don't expect you to pay for something until it happens. So here's the deal. *After* you win the trial, you pay me half your score." He held up both hands, spread all ten fingers, and mouthed, *Ten million.*

That *really* freaked me. Not only that he knew the exact number, but that he wanted half of what I'd put my life on the line to get.

"Another thing our deal buys? You get out from under Kandi Kauffman's investigation."

This was pure fantasy. I didn't respond.

"And maybe even take her down."

"How?"

He grinned. "You like that part, huh? It works like so . . . you know about Kandi's previous discovery problems?"

I knew, all right. Everyone knew. The government had been fined and Kandi personally sanctioned for several relatively recent, deliberate failures to provide discovery. At one point, it was rumored she was being fired, but apparently, the powers that be decided chastisement was punishment enough.

"The night of Bolivar's weed seizure?" he said. "A local cop name of Pimms called the feds in. Pimms's version of events is *very* different from what Kandi's case is going to be."

I was growing interested.

"Pimms didn't file an incident report because all he did was notify the feds, plus the thing went down on the Fourth of July, and he wanted to go home and enjoy the rest of the holiday."

"No report? You spoke to Pimms?"

"Nah. Pimms is worm food."

"When? How'd he die?"

"Seeing conspiracies, are you? There's plenty of them but not including Pimms. Guy dropped dead three years ago. Heart attack."

"If he's dead and there's no paper, what's the use?"

Traum smiled. "Being an old-timer, Pimms made notes in a flip pad. Kandi's got the pad, only she ain't going to give it to you. Reason being, there's things in it that blows her case out of the water. Trieant's a law-and-order judge, but if there's anything he hates more than bad lawyers, it's bent prosecutors. He finds out Kandi violated discovery rules, he'll go after her."

"And declare a mistrial, putting the case back to square one."

"Wrong. Because you don't rat Kandi out until *after* the verdict's in. Which is going to be an acquittal—"

"What are you talking?"

"Because you're going to destroy Scally when you cross him. He's going to admit lying. Trust me on that."

I didn't trust Traum on anything. It sounded too wacky to be true. But if it weren't true, he wouldn't be paid. "Just how do I destroy Scally on cross?"

He fired the cigar, blew smoke. "The fix is in."

"I don't believe you."

"Didn't expect you to. But it's true. Hit him hard about his pressuring Bolivar's old crewmates to tailor the same story, and he'll cave right in."

"How do you know that?"

"I just know."

"From Scally?"

"Next question."

I hated this conversation, but I was hooked. If Scally tanked and I could prove Kandi concealed discovery, then both their careers were history. Kandi wouldn't know until after it happened, but why would Scally self-destruct in advance?

As always, Traum knew my thoughts. He rubbed his fingers together: *Money.*

It figured. Scally was near retirement age. Maybe he no longer cared about his image—not if it meant getting a part of the cut. And maybe he liked the idea of fucking up Kandi. I recalled the way she'd disparaged him.

"How do you know Kandi will withhold Pimms's memo pad?"

"You know she's hardwired to do whatever it takes to win. Especially when it comes to you. Besides, she and Scally are simpatico on it. They agreed. Only his fingers were crossed. So their agreement ain't shit if our agreement is on. I'm gonna go easy on you. Pay Scally out of my share. You and me, we're still fifty-fifty. You don't even have to speak to him until you cross him."

I wasn't going verbal on this. Traum caught my drift. He took off his coat, unbuttoned his shirt, dropped his pants. Taped to his thigh was a small device I recognized as a voice scrambler that would render our conversation inaudible.

"Agreed, Benn?"

I nodded but wasn't agreeing to anything. No way I'd split the score down the middle. If things happened as promised, I'd be in the catbird seat come to parceling money.

"And now the big question, Benno. What's with the gold?"

"I don't know what you're talking about." But I was surprised that Traum had a line on Jilly's massive gold purchase. Had Borg spit it out along with his broken teeth?

Traum gave me a long, hard look. "The girl who bought the gold. Where is she?"

I told him I had no idea. He glowered, chomped on the stogie, and left.

I stood at the window, wanting to see if anyone was waiting for Traum. No way he'd gotten so educated by his lonesome. He had to have a partner, a worker, someone.

As he emerged from my building and walked toward Madison, a man stepped from beneath the awning of the café across the street. He looked up at my window, hesitated, then followed Traum. The man seemed familiar—olive skin, stocky, jeans and sneakers—and then I recognized him.

Scally's partner, DEA Special Agent Nelson Cano.

CHAPTER 77

That night I couldn't sleep. My volcano nightmare had returned with a vengeance I felt when I closed my eyes: a molten, roiling monster, and me crying, *Run, run, run* . . .

Instead of sleeping, I watched my bedside clock blink toward midnight. Toward another day. Another day closer to the trials . . . Bolivar's and my own.

As unlikely as it had first seemed—given all the givens—Traum's offer was plausible, even if a long shot. Traum must have a source. A hidden partner. Scally was the obvious choice. In fact, Traum's credibility cratered if he wasn't in cahoots with Scally. Which was most probably the sad truth because Traum being hooked up with Scally didn't compute. If they'd bonded, then Scally would give Traum a wide berth.

But Traum was being tailed by Scally's sidekick, Cano.

Possible Traum's information came from someone else?

Ping!

An e-mail at midnight? A problem; had to be. But the mail was generated from a familiar site. *Radio Free Bogotá*:

> Fellow citizens, the moment is critical. The drug
> lord known as *Sombra* is negotiating his surrender
> with the United States. Should this happen, his

cooperation will not only implicate drug kingpins but also the corrupt Colombian government officials and military and police who are their partners. If this happens, our nation will be transformed. *Sombra's* choice determines his own future. If he does not surrender, his earthly days are numbered. If he cooperates, the implications are enormous. Powerful people will fall. The blood of those involved will be spilled, but perhaps our society will be saved. Citizens, pray that *Sombra* chooses life, not death. Viva Colombia!

Trust Laura to do the unexpected. She and *Sombra's* DTO and the Russians, jointly, were making it crystal clear that if *Sombra* cooperated, those associated with him would be potential victims of violence. In a rare weak moment, Bolivar had told me that would happen if he lost the case, but I hadn't told anyone. So why, and to what purpose, was Laura messaging the possibility?

Unless it was not a message, but a signal. To me. Win and live.

My clock blinked: 12:01 a.m.

June 10, another day closer.

CHAPTER 78

The first day of summer was rainy and cool. Because Kandi had my personal investigation on hold until after Bolivar's case was over, I'd put it out of mind. But as Bolivar's trial neared and he considered the possibility it could be lost, I feared he'd be so desperate to cooperate that he'd implicate me in the escape attempt, a scenario Kandi would happily accept.

Never had I been more conscious of time. How slowly each moment passed; how fleetingly it was gone. I was torn between equally horrible opposing thoughts: the waiting so excruciating I wished the trial were tomorrow; the possible trial outcomes so ominous I wished it could be postponed forever.

Billy called. "You was right, Benn. The public-defender lady is good. The only evidence they got is Haunty and the other lying bitches. There's nothing gonna happen until the trial. I can hardly wait."

"That's the spirit," I said. "I'll be there for you. Hang in there, buddy."

Barnett Robinson called.

"Benn, we need to talk."

Since Rigo was dead, I couldn't imagine what Robinson wanted to discuss. Whatever it was, he was a serious man, and I sensed something substantive lurking.

"Sure," I said. "Say when."

"Two this afternoon."

Turned out the meeting was in the International Narcotics Bureau conference room, and in addition to Robinson, four others were present:

One was Robinson's boss, the INB chief with whom I'd negotiated a deal for Fercho—which got me wondering if the meeting presaged another attempt to probe Fercho's knowledge of General Uvalde's corrupt activities.

The three other men were not introduced by name but by title:

A DEA agent with the Special Operations Division—SOD—an acronym indicating that the meeting was heavy . . .

An attaché with the Russian UN mission—which I took to mean he was a spy, which in turn made me wonder if his presence concerned Kursk, meaning the meeting was even heavier . . .

The fourth man I had met before. Richard, the "analyst" who'd attended Fercho's proffer. His continuing presence reminded me of Josh Waldman's warning about other agencies being involved in my investigation. I reassessed Richard as CIA or some other intelligence outfit so deep cover, it was nameless.

The silence was pregnant. I said, "Five against humanity."

"What the fuck?" the INB chief said.

"Benn's sense of humor," Robinson said. "It comes out when he's curious."

"You're so right, Barnett," I said. "Say, did you hear the one about the agent who goes into this bar and asks the bartender . . . ah, fuck it. So. What's going on?"

Robinson said, "As you previously opined, we have in fact concluded that Rigo was murdered—poisoned—by his Colombian attorney, Felipe Mondragon."

It wasn't exactly a news flash. I allowed a nod.

The SOD agent said, "You're not upset?"

"Rigo was my client. Not my friend."

The INB chief said, "That's all you've got to say?"

I didn't like the vibe. I was being viewed as either a witness to, or as a member of, a conspiracy.

The SOD agent said, "When's the last time you saw Mondragon?"

I wasn't about to admit I'd been present when Mondragon was killed, nor would I lie to a federal agent, which is a felony. Now was a good time to say I didn't want to answer any more questions. But doing so would confirm I had secrets that would define me as a person of interest in their investigation. I consulted with the best lawyer I knew—me—then, said, "In Colombia, possibly."

"*Possibly?*" the chief snorted. "What did you speak about?"

I shrugged. "Gossip in the biz. The weather. Sports."

The SOD agent said, "Just two guys talking shit."

"I guess that's one way of putting it," I said.

Robinson stood. "Benn? A moment alone?"

I followed Robinson from the conference room to his office overlooking Police Plaza, its walls lined with the requisite ball caps—DEA, FBI, ICE, ATF—gifted by agents in the wake of successful prosecutions. He sat behind his desk.

"I'm going to speak frankly. Please don't respond as I don't want to complicate things. The government is aware you recently received a large fee by way of bank wire. Nothing illegal about it on its face, but we are very interested in the entity that sent it. To be clear, we're not targeting you, but we do expect you to be helpful."

Helpful? To whom? I didn't want to be truthful or kiss ass, nor did I want to lie, or refuse to answer. Instead, my response was the ever-useful non sequitur, "I see."

"Help us in regard to the principals who paid you."

"In which event I get to keep the money?"

"We're aware your fee was on behalf of a client over in the Eastern District, and we understand that any help you give us cannot compromise his circumstances."

"I keep the money?"

"Should your Eastern District client cooperate in our investigation, we would communicate to our colleagues in the Eastern District that they be generous at the time of his sentencing."

"My money?"

"I'm sure there's a solution all sides can agree on. That's if you stop stonewalling."

"I'm not stonewalling. Fortifying myself against the bullshit. You mentioned this once before: SDNY dismissing an EDNY investigation if my client does the right thing."

"Rigo died before—"

"Now it can happen if *I* do right? AUSA Kauffman won't be a happy camper."

"Washington tells the districts what to do. This investigation comes out of Main Justice, as I'm sure you've noticed by the presence of the SOD agent."

"Him, and your *analyst*. And the Russian."

Robinson didn't reply, and I knew I was right: the analyst was CIA; the Russian, his counterpart. But why? I flashed on Murmansk-54.

"Spell out the cooperation you expect from my client," I said.

"No need. He knows what we expect. *Everything.*"

They know Bolivar is Sombra. I needed to reassess the possibilities. "I'll have to have a heart-to-heart with my client. I'm assuming this is a big deal, right?"

"You assume correctly, Benn."

"Then it can't be decided quickly. Too many unintended consequences may come into play. I'll need to discuss this at length. Difficult under the circumstances. His trial is a distraction."

"We'll give him until trial to respond."

"A lot to consider in just fifteen days."

"The world was made in six."

"Good point, Barnett," I said.

That night I paced the corners of my office, circling the scant Bolivar discovery material spread atop my desk. Fifteen paces this way, fifteen that way, fifteen that way, fifteen back to where I started. I felt as if boxed in a cell in the SHU. The rain had passed, and the city had become heated—bad news because the air conditioning was wheezing ominously. To drown the sound, I clicked on the news on my desktop, half listening as I circled.

"Civil war raging . . . corrupt politician arrested . . . stock market falling . . . crime rates rising . . . new deadly virus emerging . . ."

I sighed. The world was in even worse shape than I.

"Tornado . . . flood . . . heat wave . . . climate change . . ."

I stopped pacing. At the beginning of the Bolivar case, when I'd checked out Murmansk, I'd downloaded and printed a map. I dug it out of a drawer and looked at it now. Saw Murmansk as a small dot on the coast of the Russian Arctic: a speck between brown land and white sea ice that seasonably choked the port . . .

Climate change.

I remembered the news story about climate change I'd been half listening to on the long trip back from visiting Rigo in Prattsville. I swiveled to my computer and searched "climate change in the Arctic," and there was the story:

The polar ice was receding, and Arctic sea routes were now open year-round.

I searched some more, found a map of future climatic projections. On it, the north Russian port of Murmansk faced blue water 365 days per year . . .

Which meant it could receive cargo—legal and illegal—year-round, which in turn explained the presence of the Russian spy.

The maps were flat, distorted Mercator projections. I needed a sense of dimension to better understand. I took an old globe from my cluttered bookshelf and placed it on my desk. The colored sphere gleamed beneath the desk lamp. I put my finger on Colombia's Pacific coast, in the Chocó, from which Helmer Quezada had said parasitic-torpedo coke shipments departed.

I moved my finger north in the Pacific along the west coast of the Americas, stopping at Washington's Olympic Peninsula. Where Bolivar and Jilly had rendezvoused on the same day Sholty Chennault was murdered. I wondered if Bolivar had stopped in Ozelle on his way north to scout the Arctic coke route. If so, I didn't think his meeting Jilly was by chance. No, they'd been in touch all along.

My finger kept moving northward as I recalled what Traum had said about Kursk's acquiring fishing fleets that plied the north Pacific. My finger moved across the expanse of north Pacific called the Bering Sea.

I recalled my mountaintop meeting with Zapata, Paz's question about the United States' interdiction capabilities in the north Pacific. My reply that it was between none and minimal, and that no other countries patrolled there at all.

I moved my finger farther north to where the Bering Sea flowed into the Chukchi Sea, then west along Siberia's northern coast to Murmansk. I recalled Kursk's boastfully offhanded statement:

We have the opportunity to control emerging markets.

South out of Murmansk, a spider's web of railways and highways extended to the Baltics and Scandinavia, into the Russian heartland and Eastern Europe, a vast pipelinelike system leading to hundreds of millions of people who only now were Westernizing, consuming, craving . . .

Colombian cocaine.

CHAPTER 79

Sleep provided no escape. I was in the thrall of the volcanoes now. When my head nodded, I jerked awake, consumed with an insidious sense of dread.

Something bad was my way coming.

In my mind's eye, I replayed the first fateful days of the year: the portents I had blithely ignored on my way to meet the INB chief, my excellent night indulging with the flight attendant, the three new cases that arrived like holiday gifts on a Christmas morning. But the gifts were not what they had seemed. They had become worn and distorted. Unstable, dangerous. I no longer recognized them. All that was clear were my options:

Win and survive.

Lose and die.

This was my state of mind when I went to Bolivar's final pretrial conference. Val kept the music off. No small talk. In the back of the Flex, I war-gamed plots and consequences.

Cadman Plaza Park was broiling, its turf warm beneath my shoes. Distant traffic hummed, flitting birds sang, children called one another. I felt about to explode.

But then the world changed.

A door revolved, and the world chilled, and I became focused. I was in a courthouse doing what I knew. Detector. Elevator. Marbled corridor. Hushed courtroom—

Autopilot went off.

I shifted to manual.

Bolivar was brought out. He smelled dank. He was gaunt, unshaven, hollow eyed. He didn't greet me.

Kandi appeared, perky as ever.

"The thirty-five hundred material?" I asked.

Her reply was a forced smile that, through bitter experience, I've learned is a tell of cruelties to come. She handed me a thin envelope. On its flap was written *Bolivar 3500 material*. I opened it, took out a dozen-odd pages, scanned them quickly.

She watched me read, arms crossed, smiling.

The pages were copies of DEA-6 forms recounting statements made by Bolivar's crew that detailed their participation in the failed run six years ago. Four sixes from four typical weed-runner types—Teddy, Rocky, Fuji, JD—knock-around, white-trash, stoner surfers whose statements were memorialized in a six signed by SA Charles Scally.

"That's all?" I said.

"All," she said.

I kept my face blank. Traum had been right. Kandi hadn't turned over Pimms's notes. But did they really exist?

"All rise!"

Judge Trieant took the bench. The clerk put our appearances on record. Trieant growled: "Jury selection July 1. Trial commences July 6."

The first was the Wednesday before the holiday weekend. The sixth was the following Monday. In the past, I'd have been going away for the holiday and would have requested an adjournment. But this was now and a trial bracketing the holiday was perfect. The jurors would relax. So would I.

"Your Honor," I said, "let the record reflect today the government provided thirty-five hundred material I am informed is complete. It consists of nine DEA-6s signed by Agent Scally."

"Thank you for the unnecessary commentary," Trieant said.

In the hallway, Kandi was talking to Scally. Over her shoulder, Scally flashed me a smile. Nearby, Nelson Cano was leaning against the wall, pretending to be absorbed in his device. But I knew he was also doing something else.

Watching me.

CHAPTER 80

I'd agreed to meet with Billy's public defender during lunch hour. We bought franks from an umbrella cart on Foley Square.

"The cops know it's a setup," she said bitterly. "They don't care so long as it closes the book on a case. Besides, they figure Billy must've killed someone, sometime." She was a small woman with kinky hair pulled tight into a tail. She'd never make it outside of the public defender's office, and I doubted she wanted to. She was an old-fashioned lawyer who liked nothing better than a cause to fight for. Right now, it was Billy. I wanted to tell her that—particularly given the inevitability of several African Americans and Latinos on the jury—she would do better than I.

"They made an offer," she said. "The usual."

"Murder two?"

She nodded. "Twenty-five to life."

Just as I'd figured, but it was a gut punch. I tossed the rest of my frank away. "I'm right he won't take it?"

"Why should he?" She squeezed my bicep. "Superman's gonna save him."

We spoke a few more minutes. I'd been right that no pretrial work was necessary. This was strictly an eyeball case. Five guys who'd swear they'd seen Billy shoot a girl to death. I'd been thinking Bolivar was going to be my swan song, but it would be Billy for whom I'd be floating like a butterfly and stinging like a bee. An eyeball-only case was a spontaneous brawl in which anything can happen.

But nothing I could do about that yet. And I had other problems on my plate.

I'd put off discussing Robinson's offer to Bolivar until getting the 3500 material. It wasn't very likely, but I'd thought, hoped, it might include a game-changer.

It didn't. Instead, it made everything painfully clear.

If Bolivar turned the offer down, we'd go to a trial I most probably couldn't win *unless* Traum's crooked fantasy came true, in which case I'd waltzed into a conspiracy. For the rest of my life, I would fear it circling back and biting my ass.

But if Bolivar lost and cooperated on his people and the Russians, sooner or later one or another of these vindictive psychos would surely take me out.

Whichever my fate, it was Bolivar's choice.

Later that day, I went to visit him.

The visit room was crowded with lawyers and defendants, mostly drug cases, except the one in the big conference room, again occupied by lawyers and defendants seated amid a maze of discovery cartons. Plitkin looked up, then quickly away as we exchanged gazes.

Bolivar appeared shortly after my arrival, bony in his oversize orange SHU jumpsuit. We went into a glass-walled visit room. He sat across from me without offering his hand. I set down the DEA-6s, and Bolivar's eyes moved across each page like a typewriter reaching a margin, then returning to the next line.

"My old friends have good memories," he said.

"According to Special Agent Chaz Scally."

He looked up. "What about Scally?"

"He memorialized the DEA sixes. People say the same things differently, but the statements Scally quoted are nearly word-for-word identical. Which opens the door to my attacking Scally's credibility, insinuating that he put his words in their mouths."

"So, then, we win?"

I evaded the question. My strategy wasn't original, but it was all I had. Sharing it with Bolivar was a downer. I didn't want the jurors seeing him mopey. "Let me put it this way," I said. "It's a big thing for us."

"You're a fucking con, Bluestone."

"So are you, Bolivar."

We shared a laugh.

Then I said, "Something new came up. Now that you know what you're up against, think it over." I paused, making sure I had his full attention. "A prosecutor offered a deal. Not Kauffman; a prosecutor from the Southern District. He says if you cooperate, you'll be on the street young enough to still get it up."

"Yeah? How about you, Bluestone? You young enough? Bet you are with the blonde you're always asking me about. Jally, Jolly, whatever."

"You said you don't know her."

"I don't. But you keep mentioning her name. She must be young and juicy, just the way guys your age like 'em."

I let the provocation slide. I'd already made Bolivar and Jilly as a couple; there was no reason to discuss the accompanying details. Like, who killed Sholty? And did Jilly have a role in hooking up Natty and Kursk with *Sombra*, the Shadow King of the Jungle?

"Why cooperate now?" he said. "Maybe we win. Even if we lose, Kauffman will be interested in what I have to say. This other prosecutor, what does he want?"

"He said you'd know what it was."

"What does he bring to the table?"

"Honesty. Kandi's a liar."

"You told my friends?"

"Of course not."

"Doesn't matter. They're not stupid. They know if I lose the trial, I'll sit on them. That's why they'll do anything to get me out. Why they paid you to do whatever it takes to do it. Why are you looking at me like that?"

I'd been staring. Willing him to close his big yap. Talking walk-the-line shit was only done in whispered, coded conversations. What if the visit room were wired? No one's ever proven it, but I'd bet my ass it happens in cases involving national interests. The kind of cases that include both CIA and foreign intelligence organizations. Cases involving international cartels opening a second front in the war against drugs.

"What shall I tell the other prosecutor?"

"Nothing. He'll also be hungry if we lose."

He stood and crossed to the door. He'd been a singularly handsome man less than a year ago. Now he'd morphed to a feral creature intent only on escaping his cage.

"Anything else?" he said.

"All done for now."

"What's next?"

"Trial."

"Tell my friends to pray it turns out well."

I nodded but no way was I passing that message. On my way out, I had to wait in the air lock until CONTROL buzzed me through the lobby door. Never had jail felt so oppressive.

What do I do now?

Ten days to go. I'd already prepped for the trial until I was blue in the face—no pun intended. Right now I desperately needed to take a break before it began.

Elsewhere.

CHAPTER 81

At three in the afternoon, church bells pealed. I was sitting atop the castle wall of an old Spanish fort, shaded by a big tree inhabited by small green parrots screeching at one another. In the near distance, sunlight glittered off a tropical sea whose tranquility was occasionally disturbed by a pelican diving for lunch.

I sat, waiting, as I had for three days now.

I didn't mind waiting. I was in Viejo San Juan, and my cares and woes were two thousand miles away, in New York. In another week, I'd have to return to do whatever was necessary to free Joaquin Bolivar. I had a bad feeling about that. But that would be then, and this was now, and there was something I needed to do.

At seven, the bells pealed again.

Across the water, the sky was streaked with all the colors of the spectrum, the low sun refracting through the fine Sahara dust atmospheric winds carried across the Atlantic to the Caribbean.

I continued waiting, occasionally looking around.

Behind me, houses were still shuttered against the day. Far below the seawall, people were walking along the *paseo* that ran along the harbor. But not the person I was looking for. Not a problem. I'd wait as long as it took.

My first day, I'd rented a car and driven to the nearby town of Bayamón, made my way through its sleepy streets, gone through an untended gate, and slowly driven through the Puerto Rico National Cemetery. One hundred ten acres of razor-cut, rolling lawns beneath which were interred 150,000 Puerto Ricans who'd served America. I parked and walked a marble path that wound between bronze plaques, most slightly sunken and too tarnished to read, but here and there shining like a newly minted penny. Beneath one of those lay Mady's brother.

It was the anniversary of his death, the day Mady always visited.

She wasn't there. Perhaps she'd come and gone. Perhaps she would come later. There was a grove of trees nearby, and I sat in their shade. Overhead, the sky was deep blue, but to the south, dark clouds were rising above the central mountains. In the far distance, lightning crackled; long moments later, thunder rolled overhead. Boomers. Maybe it would rain, or maybe the clouds would retreat to the high mountains and try again tomorrow.

Mañana.

The way of the tropics. Not now, later. Patience.

The clouds neared. The sunlight now shafted between them, reflecting off the long rows of graves. So many men still boyishly thin and brimming with laughter in the moment before death . . . so many good husbands and sons whose dreams were not to be.

I'm not a sentimental kind of guy, but I wiped a sleeve across my eyes. The fucking injustice of life. Uncle Sam's boot on Puerto Rico's neck. *Sorry, we won't admit you as a state, but not to worry, you can be a, ah . . . commonwealth.*

Translated: colony. As in, an occupied country where the natives are deemed inferior. *Nothing personal, some of my best friends are, uh . . . Spanish.* Motherfucking politicians. Man, I do love the United States, but my country does some very fucked-up things.

The second day I waited outside Mady's house, but again, she was a no-show.

At sunset on the third day, I saw her.

Standing alone at the end of the pier jutting from the old city gate into San Juan Bay. I went downhill past La Fortaleza and through the gate to where the *paseo* offered entrance to the pier. I was about to go onto it, but the way Mady stood there made me think she wanted to be alone.

Again, I sat, waiting for her.

People passed. Young and old lovers and families with lots of kids. Waves beat softly against the seawall. There was laughter, the throb of salsa, gulls squawking.

Mady started from the pier.

I stood to meet her. As she neared, her face lit up, and I let out the breath I'd been holding. I didn't know how she'd react at seeing me, but her smile said it all—

Only it wasn't meant for me.

It was directed at the tall, silver-haired man behind me. The man Mady had been with on New Year's Eve. As she hugged him, I turned to leave, but too late—

"Benn? What are you doing here?"

For once in my life, I was tongue-tied. I fumbled in a cargo pocket and took out two things: the acrylic slab encasing a golden horseshoe, and an envelope. I thrust both at her.

"For you. The good-luck charm you gave me."

Curious, she held the horseshoe, then smiled. "Oh, I remember this . . . but why?"

"It's a housewarming present. Open the envelope."

She opened it and saw inside the deed conveying *Casita Azul* to her. She cocked her head and studied me in a way I recalled, her eyes gazing through mine, into my thoughts. "You could have mailed it."

"Could've, would've, should've. Wanted to make sure you got it."

She tilted her head the other way. "Are you okay?"

"Sure," I said brightly. "Never better."

343

"You keep this," she said, returning the horseshoe. "Benn, this is Father Enrique Morales."

Father Enrique? It wasn't until he pumped my hand that it dawned on me that the man wore a Roman collar.

"Good meeting you," he said. "Wish I could chat, but I must be off. Vespers."

He pecked Mady on the cheek and left. His absence left a void. After a moment, Mady said, "Leaving New York to come to Puerto Rico. Must have a big case here, I bet."

"I escaped New York. I'm done doing that work."

"You came all the way here to tell me that?"

"To say I'm sorry. And goodbye."

"Where are you going?"

No need to burden Mady with my problems. I didn't want to lie, but my only truth was that, win or lose, I would be done lawyering. After that, I'd either be in the slammer or the wind.

"Don't know. Someplace the weather's good."

She chewed her lip thoughtfully. "Like here?"

It wasn't a question. "Like here."

"Benn?"

"What?"

"Why don't you . . . fly a kite."

With that, she spun on a heel and walked off.

I slumped to the bench. *How had I ever let it come to this?* Bad enough we were history; now she was dumping on me. *Go fly a kite?*

Then I remembered something.

About flying kites.

CHAPTER 82

As we'd done many times, Mady and I bought a kite from a stand outside the great lawn of *Castillo del Morro*. We assembled the kite and cast it aloft where it joined dozens of others, specks swirling in the offshore breeze from the Atlantic, which boiled against the rocks below the great old stone bastion.

Through the spool, I felt the kite darting, straining to be free. Mady took the spool. She let it run to the end, and the kite flew out to sea.

"Freedom for all," she said. "You got a problem with that?"

"No problem. So long as you don't punch me."

"Why on earth would you think I would?"

"You used to, when you were angry."

"We were together then."

I raised my chin. "Punch me. I'm dreaming."

She balled a fist, touched it to my jaw.

"Almost but not quite," I said.

"If at first you don't succeed."

I nodded, and we both smiled.

I wouldn't exactly call that exchange the beginning, more like the beginning of the beginning. A few more days passed, and we both knew *we* were coming back together. But two dark clouds on the horizon threatened to come between us.

The first had been there all along: I had to return to New York for the trial. I figured I'd tell Mady I had to go to New York briefly to tie up some loose ends. If things worked out, I'd catch the first flight back. If they didn't, well, at least I'd done my best to do right, and I wouldn't darken her door again.

The second was a tropical storm. I'd been following it online for a few days. The forecast said it would be near Puerto Rico later tonight; one of its predicted tracks was directly across the island. As a precaution I had booked a seat on an afternoon flight, to be sure I wasn't stranded if the electrical system went down.

I was staying at El Convento. I went down to the city gate to meet Mady.

During the years we'd been apart, Mady's mother had died, and her ashes had been scattered from the pier. While ill, she'd been cared for by the sisters of *Servicio de Maria* convent, whose Moorish walls overlooked the pier. Truly one of the most beautiful spots in all the world. The reason Mady had been so intent on having *Casita Azul* in her name was because when she passed, she wanted to leave the house to the nuns who had taken care of her mother.

Today was the anniversary of her mother's death, and Mady was spending a long time on the pier. I sat on a bench and looked at my device, hoping the storm would miss the island, allowing me a few more days with Mady before I returned for the trial.

No such luck. Not only was the storm on a direct path to the island; it was expected to become a hurricane and had picked up speed, due to hit earlier than expected. Already, flights were being canceled. If it were severe, flights could be canceled for days. I had to leave the island now.

I called the airlines. Too late. My flight was already canceled. I had no choice but to stay on the island and hope that the damage was minimal and that flights would resume as soon as the storm passed.

We dined that evening in a restaurant overlooking the water. The place was usually packed, but not this night. People were home, securing shutters, preparing. Every few minutes, foghorns blared. Below the seawall, cruise ships were leaving port to ride out the storm at sea, away from the eye. There was a feeling of expectancy. A *waiting*. We were still eating when the waiter brought the check.

"Sorry," he said. "We're closing early."

The wind hit us as we left. The sky looked ominous. In the fading light, rain bands veiled the far side of the bay. Mady took my arm.

"I don't want to be alone tonight."

"You won't," I said. "I'll be with you."

I still hadn't been inside *Casita Azul*. It was the last wall standing between us, and the first place we would be alone.

"It took me a long time to get over you, Benn. Finally, I got happy again, but then you came back. Now I don't know what to think. I mean, I know what I *want* . . . Promise me something."

"Anything. I'll even give you Arpege."

"No jokes. I couldn't be more serious. I need to hear something from you. A promise that you really have changed. No more getting wasted. No more running around. Most of all, no more criminals. Not ever. *Never*. Promise me that, Benn."

"I promise," I said.

It was the strangest moment of my life. I'd never been happier and never more frightened. Happy because the love of my life was back; frightened because I didn't know if I'd be able to keep her.

We walked hand in hand. As we rounded a corner, the wind nearly took us and we laughed. Her laughter was genuine, but mine was forced. I escorted her to *Casita Azul*. Told her to start securing things; I was going to the hotel for my stuff. I'd return in fifteen minutes.

She kissed me on the mouth. "Hurry, Benn."

I hurried. The city was empty. No vehicles, no people. I went up *Caleta de las Monjas*. Not a soul in sight; even the ubiquitous stray cats were sheltering. The street lamps flickered. The Convento was battening down. I went to my room, stuffed things into my bag. As I hurried back down the *Caleta*, I sensed a presence behind me.

I turned—something struck my head.

And I tumbled into darkness.

CHAPTER 83

I was at the bottom of a well. I tried to climb out, but the walls were too smooth to grasp. I tried and tried again, each time slipping back into blackness . . . then, briefly, I saw daylight—

But only for a moment before I was shoved into the trunk of a vehicle. The hatch slammed shut. Darkness again. Abrupt movement. Gravitational pulls. The vehicle bounced through a pothole, and the trunk popped open a few inches. I tried opening it the rest of the way, but the handle was secured by a rope to the bumper. Rain slashed within the trunk. The wind keened. I saw angels dancing atop pins . . .

True. We'd come to a place I'd often strolled below Morro: the seaside cemetery of Santa María Magdalena de Pazzis, where stone-carved angels cavorted beneath eternal lights, oblivious to the screaming wind and roar of the sea. Through the rain stood the blurred, dark mass of Morro—

The trunk opened.

"Do what I say," a man said, his voice familiar. A gun jammed against my side. I frog-marched ahead of the man, through the deserted cemetery, toward Morro. I knew it, too, would be deserted. On its promontory, it was exposed to incoming storms: no watchmen would stand guard on this night.

The man wanted to be alone with me.

We climbed stone steps leading to the top level of the fort—the enfilade wall, notched with cannon emplacements. The storm was furious here as it came wheeling in from the sea, but the man guided me into the lee of the fortifications, where it was relatively calm—

I saw his face: broad, under a balding pate. His gap-toothed smile. Traum had been a cop for a long time. He knew how to handle suspects. A few deft pokes and kicks moved me face-first against a wall, my arms akimbo, legs splayed. My face was turned toward the cemetery, its bright angels dancing in the fury.

"I don't understand," I said. "I thought we had a deal."

"Twenty mil's chump change. The score's the gold."

"What gold?"

"No more games, Benn. Scally traced the bitch's money. The Russians got most of her cash, but not before she put a big chunk of it in gold. Where is it? Tell me, or you're meat."

"I don't know."

"Benn, I *know* you know. Borg told us he quit Jilly, and you took over as her lawyer."

I understood now. Traum had hooked up with Scally to get the gold. They wouldn't believe my denial. I needed to buy time.

"It's in New York," I said. "I can take you to it."

"You lie. It's here. It's why you came to PR."

"I'll deal. I have a piece in my pocket."

Traum was good. His gun stayed hard against me as he patted me down and undid a cargo pocket and took out the acrylic-embedded golden horseshoe. Out of the corner of my eye, I saw it in his hand.

"What is this thing?" he said.

"Look in it. *Inside* it."

"I don't see anything."

"It's *gold*. A sample."

"The fuck you talking?"

"I'll show you. Let me move my arm. Let me hold the thing, and I'll show you. I just want out of this deal. I'll take you to the gold if you let me walk. It's the same gold as in the slab. I'll show you."

The slab moved into my vision, and I gripped it. The lit angels refracted through its scratched, acrylic surface, the golden horseshoe within gleaming dully.

"See," I said. "*See?*"

He sighed in a way I recognized as the wheeze of pure greed. Ugly sound. Been there, done that myself the first time I saw a fortune, my entire consciousness contracting to the object of my desire.

Happened to Traum, too. The gun eased.

"Isn't it beautiful?" I said.

"Beautiful. How much—"

I slammed the slab against his cheekbone. The wind smothered the sound of the blow, but I was sure I felt bone crunch. The gun left my body, and Traum hunched, holding his face.

For a millisecond, I hesitated: Fight, or flight?

A no-brainer. Run, and Traum and Scally keep on looking for me, and I keep on looking over my shoulder until sooner or later, they find me again. No. I needed to end it now and forever. The realization was like pouring gasoline on a fire: a sudden flare.

Kill him.

I raised the slab and brought the edge down atop Traum's head—hard. He crumpled to his knees, dropping the gun. I struck him again, and again and again, until his head was pulp and he lay still—

Something jittered in my pocket. My cellular. I took it out. I recognized the caller. Mady. I answered, but the call was lost. I clicked her number to call her back, but the signal was gone. Better not waste time here. Better I hustle to *Casita Azul*.

But first . . .

Traum lay with his face in profile, one wide-open eye staring at me. I bent and gripped his arms and dragged him to the cannon notches. The wind screamed; below, the sea crashed.

I pulled and pushed him through the notch.

Watched him fall into the dark maelstrom.

I'd killed again. No regrets. Again.

CHAPTER 84

The old city was deserted, eerily still. Stars twinkled in the clear sky above, but the horizon in all directions was dark, veined by lightning. It was like being beneath a doughnut hole. The hurricane's eye.

I felt as if I were floating over the blue cobblestones. My present was past. I lived for my future. For the first time, I knew what it was.

A woman.

Not poor, lost Jilly, whom I no longer desired.

Not Laura Astorquiza, lost wanderer in a world of evil.

Only the love of my life. Madaleina Andaluz. Waiting, for me . . .

Casita Azul was dark, shuttered. I rapped on Mady's door. Nothing. I called her name. No reply. I tried calling her. The line was still dead. The wind began howling again.

When I hadn't returned promptly as promised, Mady might have thought something had happened to me. Maybe she had gone looking, and something had happened to *her*.

I started running again. The streets were empty. I had no idea where Mady might be, nor where I was running. The storm was in full fury when I staggered into the lobby of Convento. The staff was gone but for a single bellhop. Diego? The one who'd outed my New Year's presence to Mady.

"Is my wife . . . Mady, is she here?"

"No, sir. Hey, don't go outside . . ."

The police station was closed. Not a shop was open. No people. The wind was a torturous scream in wires hanging from twisted posts. I ran and walked and ran in the storm until it had passed and then some. Desperate. Delirious. Hallucinating that there was a world in which I belonged. There wasn't.

I was the last zombie.

The next morning, wooden shutters were splintered and some streets flooded, but otherwise, Viejo San Juan was intact. The Spanish had built low, thick-walled structures that had survived many hurricanes over the centuries: this one would be a mere footnote in its meteorological history.

I returned to her house. On her corner, a few early risers were gathered where cop cruisers straddled the street. An ambulance rolled down from Morro. I stood there, watching, as innocent as the next man.

"They say a man fell," someone said.

"An American," another man said.

"Named Traum," said a third.

I felt eyes on me. When I looked up across the street, I saw Mady watching me.

I went to her. Her eyes were red-rimmed, her face pale. I went to hold her, but she interposed a hand. "No, Benn. Just listen. Please . . ."

"I'm listening."

"When you didn't show up, I thought you were hurt. I went looking for you, up and down the streets. Until just minutes ago, I was so worried. I heard a man had been found. I thought it was *you*." Tears filled her eyes.

"No, I'm—"

"I saw the dead's man's face. It wasn't you . . . but it *was* you. Please, don't explain. I don't know or care what happened. It's enough knowing who you were with. I never liked that man. But everything for a reason. His death made me realize I don't like you, either. I love you and I always will, but it's tomorrow that counts. Who and what you are then. But Benn, my beautiful boy, Benn, you are always going to be you and do what you do, and there's nothing else to say."

"Mady, please listen to me."

"If you care, leave it at that."

"I care too much to leave it."

"No more, Benn. It's over."

She walked to *Casita Azul* and entered. The door closed with a thud of heavy tropical hardwoods. I stared at it. The seventeenth-century crucifix above the door. The fan palms bordering the walkway. The blue stucco facade and lantern-lit windows. Mady's life. No room in it for me . . .

Leave it at that.

CHAPTER 85

Wednesday, July 1. My neighbors had evacuated to the Hamptons, and the Upper East Side was a ghost town. But when Val drove into Brooklyn, the city came alive. Parks and avenues were crowded with citizens like those I'd be selecting for Joaquin Bolivar's jury. The anonymous population that would produce a panel that would come to a verdict that would determine the course of many lives: mine, Bolivar's, maybe Jilly's, and those of countless others, known and unknown. Big cases tend to shake up the status quo in the drug hierarchies. Lots of people disappear. Others wind up splashed on front-page accounts of turf wars or government sweeps or guerrilla attacks. This case, which was so much more important, would most likely be tried in an empty courtroom.

My shoulders were loose, my mind clear. I was moving on the balls of my feet. Ready to rock and sock. I was the man with the golden tongue.

I sat alone at the defense table. Across from me, Kandi Kauffman was pretending absorption in her trial loose-leaf. Cano was texting. Scally winked hello.

I blew him a kiss. Weird Benn. Let the opposition think I'm off my rocker. I am, anyway. After spotting Cano tailing Traum, I'd dismissed Scally as Traum's source. But now I knew they'd been partners.

So maybe Cano had tailed Traum to make sure he was being righteous. For sure, Cano had a piece of the action.

Kandi's eyes flicked sideways. An instant later, Bolivar sat beside me. Scally and Cano sat with Kandi. Two bent cops. Fortunately, they couldn't connect me to Traum's death. Traum had failed, but soon enough, Scally would come to me.

Gold. Tons of gold.

Had Rafe, playing with Jilly's money while high, succumbed to gold fever? Surely, Jilly hadn't bought the gold herself; she probably couldn't balance a checkbook—

"All rise!"

And so began what I knew—no matter the outcome—was going to be my last trial.

Jury selection in federal court is fairly brief. In the state courts, lawyers often take days to select a jury, but in federal court, only the judge decides whether a prospective juror should be disqualified for cause.

Besides disqualification for cause, prospective jurors could be removed simply because either the defense or the prosecution didn't like them. These removals were known as strikes. Both sides had the same limited number. Getting an impression of a prospective juror was limited to a quick read: trying to discern whether blue collars didn't conceal rednecks or bearded old hippies weren't really closeted Fox News addicts.

For some lawyers, federal jury selection is an art form. They hire jury-selection experts. Psychologists. Number crunchers. I just go with my gut. Occasionally, if a prospective is attractive, I trust my dick. None of it means a thing. You can't read people's heads by what they do or look like. When it comes to exercising power over another person's future, there's no telling what privacies influence which mind.

My only other rule about jurors is to ignore them. Make believe they're not there. Work as if they're an unseen audience, the fourth wall.

By early afternoon, sixteen jurors—twelve on the panel and four alternates—had been selected and sworn in: the usual mix of citizens from all walks of society. Right now they were ciphers, but after a few days of observing body language and covert glances, I'd have myself a good idea which were leaders and which were followers. Not that I'd have the slightest notion which way the leaders were leaning.

The close of jury selection meant the trial had officially begun. Which in turn meant that the deadline had passed for Kandi to turn over 3500 material.

Trieant told the jurors to report at nine in the morning of July 6. When the jurors left, Trieant glared at Kandi and me. "Anything to discuss?"

Usually at this point, there are many evidentiary issues to hash out, but this case was procedurally simple. Law enforcement and forensics would testify about the seizure and composition of the weed, then Scally and the four coconspirator witnesses would testify as to their knowledge of events.

"Nothing from the government, Your Honor."

"Nothing from the defense, either," I said.

"All rise!" Judge Trieant doddered out.

"I'm *so* gonna enjoy this," Kandi said.

When she was out of earshot, Bolivar whispered, "I need for you to visit me before trial. I'll tell you when. You got that? You hear me?"

"I heard you."

"Then say so."

When I got into the Flex, I was about to tell Val to take me back to the city, but decided I wasn't in the mood for a solo lunch in an empty restaurant. It occurred to me this was not only my last trial; it very possibly was the last time I'd have downtime in Brooklyn.

I told Val to drive around, and we traveled through side streets lined with brownstones shadowed by old trees and tenement blocks where people were dining on fire escapes. I told Val to take a left here, and a right there, and as purple twilight fell, we were back in Manhattan. Just as Val was about to turn off Fifth into my block, he pulled to the curb and sat with his eyes on the rearview mirror.

"What?" I said.

"I thought maybe a car following, but now it gone."

"Again? The Mercedes?"

"Not a Mercedes."

"The customized limo—the bulldog?"

"Not bulldog. Ordinary car. American. Black. Very long antenna. What you call, I don't know."

"Unmarked," I said.

CHAPTER 86

Thursday morning, the city was so quiet, I could hear a bird singing in the lesser billionaire's hidden garden. Probably imprisoned in a gilded cage.

Like me.

I wasn't going out. Because Cano and Scally were shadowing me. Or maybe it was SOD agents. Or Russians or Colombians. All of them watching, waiting for me to do something, or for something to happen to me. But I wasn't playing fisherman, and I wasn't baitfish. I was just staying home, chilling.

Ignoring whoever was out there, watching, waiting.

Fuck them. Time to work. Four days to trial.

Not that much time, but not a problem. As I'd told Bolivar, his old shipmates told the same story in essentially the same words, to a man nailing him to the cross. The case hinged on their credibility, or lack thereof. I'd crossed coconspirators so many times, I could recite my boilerplate questions chapter and verse:

Isn't it true that you're not testifying because it's the right thing to do, but because you're hoping to get a sentence reduction?

Working backward: Sunday, I'd rest.

Saturday and Friday, I'd review my cross-examinations of the four cooperators. I'd guide them into agreeing with my simple questions, honing their answers down to a simple yes or no, then suddenly coming at them from another direction . . . like reading a statement from another defendant's six, then asking him if it was true.

"Yes."

"And you stated it."

"Yes."

"And signed it?"

"Yes."

I'd ask permission to approach the witness, and Trieant would begrudge it, and I'd show the six to the witness. "That's your signature right there?"

"Yes . . . I mean, no, it's . . ."

"Your codefendant's signature?"

"Yes."

"No more questions."

A nice little catch, but disposable after one use, because surely Kandi would warn the other cooperators not to fall into it. I'd come up with variations. I always do.

Okay. That left today open. Probably the only Thursday I've been home alone in years. A day during which I'd think of nothing as a prelude to waking with a clean slate on Friday. Today, maybe I'd work out a little. Definitely write Billy a cheer-up letter. But first, I was hungry, so I dialed up a Greek diner on Lexington and ordered a big breakfast.

Half an hour later, Viktor buzzed. My food had arrived. I told him to send the delivery guy up. When the elevator door opened, the guy held out a bag. I smelled a ham-and-cheese omelet and toasted bagel. I went to pay the delivery guy—

He was Agent Nelson Cano.

"I come in peace," he said.

"What?"

"Never mind. Take your freaking food, will you?"

I took the bag.

"This, too," he said, handing me a large envelope I figured was another subpoena.

"Listen, *papi*," Cano said. "I was never here."

"What do you mean?"

Cano smiled. "I dunno. I guess sometimes a guy has to do the right thing. Be well, Counselor."

The door closed. I opened the envelope. It held a sheaf of papers. Photocopies. Each sheet bordered by black around an image from a lined notepad covered with writing whose top edge was frilled with some kind of spiral. It took a moment, then I realized what it was.

Copies of the pages of the late Officer Pimms's notepad.

For all his lies, Traum had told a truth. Kandi had held back 3500 material. But why had Cano delivered it to me?

Sometimes a guy has to do the right thing?

What the hell was going on?

Pimms's handwriting was old school, as easy to read as print. Like most old-fashioned cops, he organized his notes to form a timeline of sorts.

On the night of July 4, he had been summoned from home when the billionaire who owned the Southampton beach mansion lodged a complaint about his lady friend going out to a sailboat on a Zodiac with a pot dealer. Couldn't blame the man, losing a looker like Jilly. After paddling out to the sailboat and realizing the situation wasn't just a minor misdemeanor but beyond his capacity, Pimms had called for assistance.

I flipped to the next page. It was blank. All of Pimms's stuff I already knew. So fucking what? I turned another page, and the notes continued.

So fucking what turned out to be the arrival of two federal agents who'd been in the area: Chaz Scally and his late partner, Vince Mongello.

When Pimms and the agents went to the sailboat, the crew was observed escaping in a Zodiac, except for one man who swam ashore.

The only person left on the boat was the woman, who seemed dazed. Or high. *Oh, Jilly.* She was taken into custody. Pimms had personally driven her to the agents' Hampton Bays motel room, ostensibly to be questioned, and had left her there with the two federals. The narrative ended there, mid-page.

It resumed on the next day, July 5, with a cryptic note:

Agt. Mongello dead in motel. Suicide. Girl?

That was all he wrote. But it was enough.

Suicide. Girl? The puzzle was finally coming together, like filings inexorably drawn to a magnet, revealing previously invisible force fields.

Jilly had been in the motel room when Mongello was shot.

Suicide? Maybe. Murder? Maybe.

Either, but not surprising. Put two bad cops and a case of beer in a room with a beautiful, stoned woman, and something had to give.

I tried to reconstruct what really had happened. My guess, Scally realized he was in a ton of trouble and rearranged the scenario. I closed my eyes and conjured up a hypothetical:

Jilly had been raped. Afterward, she'd flipped out, grabbed Mongello's sidearm, and shot him. Scally had wrestled the gun from her. Put the weapon in Mongello's hand and then driven Jilly back to Southampton, warning her that if she told anyone what happened, she'd be looking at a murder rap. Twenty-five to life.

Now, six years later, Scally was willing to ruin his own career, using Traum as a cat's paw to get at my fee and Jilly's gold. Could even be that Scally never had any intention of tanking the case; perhaps that was just a ruse to keep me close, so as to find the gold.

But now that Traum was dead, what was Scally's next move?

And what role did Cano have in whatever played out?

I thought about this. Then I went into the kitchen and shouldered the refrigerator a few inches aside. Just enough for me to reach beneath the adjoining cabinet and remove an object taped there.

It was a small, dull-gray .380 handgun. A Colt Mustang XSP designed as a concealed-carry weapon. I didn't have a carry permit. Years ago, feeling threatened by a disgruntled client, I'd applied for one, but instead was only granted a license for a weapon that could not leave the confines of my home. Basically useless, but the disgruntled client was shot to death by an equally disgruntled coconspirator, and I hadn't bothered to renew the license. Still, for no particular reason, I'd kept the gun.

I had good reason now.

Blunt and ugly, it sat on my kitchen table as I ate the breakfast Nelson Cano had hijacked from the delivery guy, at the same time reading my favorite news.

Nothing unusual on my regular sites, but *Radio Free Bogotá* was blogging again:

> Citizens, the hour draws close. Will *Sombra* put an end to our long suffering, the decades of narco-domination? Or will he continue his greedy ways, thereby continuing our national pain, and guaranteeing his own eventual, violent death? Pray for *Sombra* to do the right thing. Viva Colombia!

I stared at the screen for a very long moment.

This time I *knew* Laura was talking to me.

Telling *me* to do the right thing.

Or be bound for violent death.

Again I looked at the street.

They were hidden.

They.

CHAPTER 87

On Friday I reviewed the nuts and bolts of my trial strategy. Its cornerstone was the similarity of Scally's DEA-6s. My argument? Chaz Scally had threatened and cajoled Rocky, Fuji, JD, and Teddy to testify according to his version of events.

Undoubtedly, when Scally testified, Kandi would roll out his long, successful DEA career, underlining his integrity and truthfulness. Knowing Kandi, she'd go a bridge too far, but I wouldn't object. When it came time for me to cross-examine, I'd decline.

I had more in mind for Scally.

After the government rested its case, I'd call him as *my* witness. Bring out that he was nearing retirement and wanted to close the door on an old unsolved case. Then, just as I had done with the crew, I'd bring out the near-duplication of the four DEA-6s he had written, suggesting that the words were his, not theirs.

He'd deny it. Skillfully, considering his experience.

I'd replay the voice tapes in which each newly arrested crew member had phoned another crew member, offering to repay an old debt related to the monies they'd been promised for the *Swan*'s voyage, a repetitious daisy chain bringing dead conspiracies back to life. These conversations were also nearly identical, and I'd underscore that by establishing

Scally's presence when the calls were made and his instructions to the callers as to what they needed to say, and so on.

Then I'd get Scally to admit that none of the calls had mentioned Bolivar by name. He'd reply that drug conversations always omit names.

"Are you telling us that these criminals omit names for their own security?"

That's exactly what I'm telling you, Counselor, he'd say.

"Based on your experience, no other reason, Agent?"

He'd say none, and I'd say, "Based on your common sense and experience, did it occur to you that another reason could be that they didn't know one another's names, because none of the conspirators believed Bolivar was involved until you so informed them—"

Here, Kandi would object: "That's two questions, Judge."

"Withdraw both, Your Honor. One last question. It was light out when you and Agent Mongello reached the *Swan?*"

"Yes."

"That's when Mr. Bolivar jumped boat and swam ashore?"

"Yes."

"In all your notes and all your sixes, did you make a single reference to Mr. Bolivar's physical description?"

"At that moment I didn't."

"Did there come a moment when you did have the time?"

"I don't believe that information was included."

"Correct. Thank you. No more questions."

That left one issue unaccounted for. Explaining why Bolivar had agreed to accept an old debt. In my closing argument, I'd point out that fact last, almost as if an afterthought:

"Ladies and gentlemen, the government contends the phone calls were about collecting a drug debt, which is the basis for the conspiracy to have been deemed as continuing. But it occurred to me—I checked it last night, and you're free to do so during your deliberations—that there was no mention of the debt being for a drug deal, but rather a vague reference to an old loan."

Then I'd turn and point at Kandi.

"Fair or not, in our system, the prosecutor gets to speak last. Therefore, since I, like you, won't have the opportunity to do so, on all our behalf, I'm going to ask Ms. Kauffman to explain why such a basic fact as confirming a *drug* deal was omitted."

Okay. I was ready. A good night's sleep away.

But that night I had bad dreams again.

The volcano erupted. But instead of lava, torrents of ice rushed from the crater. I ran but soon found myself waist deep in a vista of white ice. As I struggled to free myself, I saw structures nearby: weathered plank buildings surrounded by wire whose barbs were star-shaped, enclosing miniature hammers and sickles. I heard Traum's hollow laugh, but it was lost beneath a screaming wind, and the ice became a boiling sea in which a fishing boat bobbed, and then the boat became the *Swan*—

I bolted awake and saw daylight.

Saturday, the Fourth of July.

A bell tolled—*for me?*

CHAPTER 88

It took a moment before I realized the bell was an incoming message on my device. The CORRLINKS icon was blinking. A message from Bolivar:

URGENT YOU VISIT TONIGHT AFTER THE COUNT. REPEAT: AFTER!

If Bolivar wanted to see me on the eve of trial, that was his client-given right, although I didn't appreciate his rudeness. I was about to send an affirmative response when Bolivar sent another message, a single word:

CONFIRM!

It annoyed me that Bolivar felt a need to remind me . . . then again, he was on the inside facing the trial of his life. So I replied that I'd be there. Three times. But his insistence was worrisome:

Was I about to discover *whatever was necessary?*

I felt tense. Physically so. Stiff and achy. Fuck it. I was as sharp as I'd ever be. I needed to loosen up, get outside. I put on sweats and sneakers and hit the street.

Brassy sun, cloudless sky. No suspicious vehicles in sight. The natives away, the tourists still asleep. I trotted along a leaf-shaded path, meandering the hills and dales of Central Park. For a mile or so, I hurt, but then got oxygenated and zoned out until I exited the park, slowed to a walk, turned up my street. Fifty feet from my building, the bulldog pulled to the curb, Kyril behind the wheel. The rear door opened, and Evgeny Kursk got out, smiling.

"Good morning, Mr. Bluestone."

I looked around. All I needed now was feds observing me with Kursk during a period when I'd said I was weighing an offer to my client to cooperate. The street was empty.

"When you visit Bolivar?"

I wondered how Kursk knew I was visiting Bolivar. By CORRLINKS? "I'll be going soon."

"We drive you."

"I have a driver."

"I insist. On the way, there are things to discuss."

"Why don't you tell me these things now?"

"You *will* drive with us."

"I don't think so."

His mouth twisted, and color patched his pale cheeks. "I don't like lawyers. I especially don't like lawyers who interfere with my business. Those that do so come to bad ends. Like Raphael Borg. Do not follow his example. We will be waiting for you when it is time to go."

He sat back and closed the door, but the big car remained where it was. I walked to my building. Viktor flicked his butt into the gutter and opened the front door for me.

"That's some weird car," he said.

"You have no idea," I said.

Back inside my apartment, I looked at the street. Kursk's bulldog was still there, like a *Star Wars* beast lazily taking sun.

I stood in the shower with my eyes closed and water drumming on my head while trying to get a handle on why Kursk wanted to drive me to jail. Possible he had another destination in mind? Was I the next Raphael Borg?

No. That would delay Bolivar's case.

Perhaps Kursk's insistence originated with Bolivar, so intent had he been about my visiting *after* the late count. Had Kursk come to make sure I did so?

Whichever, I'd go. But not with Kursk.

It was one o'clock. The late count ended around 5:00 or 5:30 p.m. I doubted there'd be traffic on the way. Then again, people would be coming home from the beaches, so the Belt Parkway and all of south Brooklyn might be jammed. A safer bet if I left my place by four; I'd be ready to go into the MCC when the count ended.

I fixed myself a tuna sandwich and washed it down with iced black coffee. Caffeinated, I lay on my bed, looking up at the ceiling while I devised a plan.

At 2:00 p.m., I looked outside.

The bulldog was still there. Where were Scally and Cano? The SOD agents? The CIA people? Had everyone given up on me? Or were they watching Kursk watching me?

I made two phone calls, putting things in motion.

I took another shower, shaved, donned fresh civvies. I regarded the .380 Mustang for a long moment, then jacked a round into the chamber. I made sure the safety was on, then jammed it into my waistband, and put on a blazer.

I went down to the lobby. Behind the front desk, Viktor was reading the *Post*. I stood at the street door. The bulldog squatted fifty feet away. It was 2:55 p.m.

At 2:59:30, Val's Flex pulled to the curb. I left the building, walked ten feet, and slid into the back seat. As soon as my door closed, the Flex burned rubber.

The Madison Avenue light was going red as we blew past it and turned uptown. Val jumped the next light and quickly caught up with the changing pattern. I looked back but didn't see the bulldog. Then it appeared from behind a bus and ran a red light, four, five blocks behind.

"Turn east," I said.

Val tapped the brakes, turned, heavy-footed the gas. "Where to?"

"Bloomingdale's."

But we hit traffic, and the bulldog closed fast. Too fast. Even as Val pulled over in front of Bloomie's Lexington Avenue entrance, the bulldog cut in front of us, its passenger door opening, two men getting out. One was ferretlike Kyril, approaching the Flex. The second was a bullet-headed lug who blocked the store entrance.

I was about to tell Val to back up and go around the bulldog, but then a yellow cab pulled over behind us.

Trapped!

"Listen up, Val," I said. "When I get out, stay here. Keep your hands out of sight, and stare at the two guys at the entrance."

"That's all?"

"Just stare until they leave."

I moved my gun around to the front of my waistband. I unbuttoned my jacket so the gun was visible as I got out of the Flex.

Kyril started toward me. I gripped my gun.

"I'll kill you first," I said. "I'm going shopping. You and your pal wait outside, or my driver will drop you."

Kyril glanced at the Flex. Val looked ready to bite Kyril and his partner. As I'd instructed, his hand hovered just below the door, as if concealing a gun. Kyril stepped aside.

I pushed through the revolving door. Once inside the big store, I raced across the first floor like a mad track star and burst through the Third Avenue doors. I got in a cab and gave the driver directions to where I keep the Mini garaged.

As per my earlier call, it was waiting for me.

CHAPTER 89

Traffic was light. I emerged from the Battery Tunnel at 3:25 p.m. Just a five-minute drive to the jail. Where Kursk likely would be waiting for me. If I went there now, I'd be stuck outside—*exposed*—until the count cleared. No. Better I start doing drive-bys at five—not a problem, they'd be looking for the Flex—and, soon as the count was clear, fast park by the entrance and hustle inside. Leaving the bastards no way of using me to get to Bolivar . . . *Not unless they broke in to jail to catch me.*

Funny that I was feeling funny. Not in a nervous way, either. Or to keep my mind off the dark side. Just straight-up funny, maybe with a dash of irony. Olives, not onions. That left a half hour to kill, preferably in a fun place.

I came up with a beaut.

Instead of continuing beneath the Gowanus Parkway span, a few blocks before the Gowanus Canal Bridge, I turned into Red Hook and rumbled through its potholed streets and finally stopped on a cobblestone lane that separated New York Harbor and a nineteenth-century warehouse that had been converted to subsidized housing for artists. I got out of the Mini and leaned on the hood, looking at the warehouse, thinking . . .

There but for the grace of God I might have wound up.

An artist. Poor but creative. Compared to the path I chose, I'd have certainly been poorer, definitely quite a bit wiser, very possibly happier. On the flip side, I'd have also missed out on some wild times and remarkable women. Another which-would-it-be, I'd never know. Now there was only one thing worth knowing:

I had to get through the weekend, and the long week of the Bolivar trial, and whatever ordeals followed it.

The harbor sparkled in the sun. A mile across it stood the concrete block that was MCC. By design, isolated from the rest of Brooklyn. All alone on a few acres of land jutting into the harbor; its land side hard up against the de facto wall that was the Gowanus Expressway. A jail within a jail.

4:45 p.m.

A speedboat appeared, its motor a distant hum. Same boat four thousand miles south would be crammed with kilos. Here, it carried party people. It left a white wake like a demarcation line between me and the distant jail. The wake slowly faded until the water was again smooth, unbroken. Nothing between me and jail now.

Despite the heat, I gave a little shiver.

4:50 p.m.

I got into the Mini and drove to the MCC.

The bulldog wasn't there. Only a handful of cars in the visitor spaces. No activity at the entrance, so the count was still on. I U-turned up 29th Street and drove onto the pier and stopped there, looking at the brackish-green water beneath which rotted evidence of the last of Jilly's inherited fortune.

Which made me wonder again:

Gold? How much? Where?

I drove back to the jail. No one was allowed in or out during the count, but now a lawyer was emerging, so the count was clear. I'd seen the lawyer before: one of those from Plitkin's stable representing Natty Grable's codefendants. He got in his car and drove away. I took the

Mustang from my waistband and shoved it under my seat. Then I parked the Mini in the spot he'd vacated and hurried into the jail.

Bonesy was grinning. "The lawyer that just left? Said he couldn't take it anymore. Was going home to kill his wife."

"What're you talking about?"

"You'll see."

I filled out a visit form and stashed my keys in a locker. I went through the metal detector, and Bonesy stamped my hand. The legal-visit book was turned to a new page. Blank. When I signed in, I started paging back to see who'd been visiting whom, but Bonesy slammed the book cover down hard.

"I'm caught letting you do that, I'm in trouble," he snapped.

"Sorry." He was right, of course. Which was why my snoopings were always surreptitious. But this time, I'd done so openly. I'd been sloppy, inexcusably so. Time to stop the funny business and get serious.

I entered the air lock and put my hand beneath the black light. The daily password was a smear of green fluorescence. I stood there waiting for CONTROL to verify me. Behind its dark glass, I could see instruments glowing, the dim profile of a guard seated at a console, a bank of screens. I coughed loudly. No response. A minute or three passed. I tapped on the dark glass. No response. I was being reminded that I might be a rich lawyer, but that he was CONTROL.

This was a big reason why I hated jails so much, the total dependence on others: Bonesy, CONTROL, the entire damn correctional cadre. Another long minute passed. Another . . .

"Go," CONTROL finally said.

When I entered the visit room, a few guards clustered around the high desk were laughing. They went poker faced when I approached. I handed up my visit form.

"Your guy's already down, Counselor," said a guard, pointing at the visit rooms.

Fucking CONTROL had kept me waiting so long, Bolivar had gotten there before me.

I walked past empty visit rooms. One of Plitkin's flunky lawyers carried a vended coffee into the last visit room at the end, where he sat with another lawyer. Obviously, they and the lawyer who'd just left had stayed over the count. *Hmm.* Natty Grable's trial wasn't coming up soon, and I wondered what was so important that they were working over the holiday.

In the smaller adjoining room, Bolivar was seated with his back to me.

He turned when I entered. And I stopped short, staring at him.

He'd transformed for the worst yet again: his hair was now shaved to his skull, his posture stooped.

"You all right?" I said.

He made a dismissive motion. "I'm hungry. Get me something from the machines."

"How about a chicken sandwich?"

"Whatever. Get something *now*."

I felt like decking him, but the man was in bad shape. Looking into his future and not liking the view. I went to the machines like the good boy I wasn't. While I fed bills into slots, I looked into the big visit room. Two inmates and the two lawyers were drinking coffee and nodding while looking at a third lawyer who was obscured by the cartons. The way they were sucking up made me think it was Morty Plitkin himself. *Working on the holiday?*

I carried food and drink back to Bolivar.

He ignored it. "Who's out there?"

"Codefendants and lawyers next door."

"Besides them?"

"No other visits. A bunch of guards up front, laughing about something. Aren't you going to eat?"

He glanced at the greasy food and wrinkled his nose. He said, "What time it?"

"We got maybe another five minutes. If I hadn't got jammed in the air lock, I'd have been here earlier. What's on your mind?"

He snorted, then made a face as if doing so was painful. Probably it was. I thought his eyes would be glazed, but they looked hard as petrified rocks.

"You know what my friends are thinking?"

I did: that if he lost, he'd rat on them. A subject I didn't care to discuss. I'd given all the advice I had, and what came next was Bolivar's choice.

"Tell them whatever happens, I'm cool," he said. "Tell them to have faith in The One Who Knows Most."

I nodded. Codes. Crimes. Betrayals. I wasn't having any of it . . .

Bolivar was looking past me. I turned and saw the codefendant meeting in the big visit room had ended: the lawyers and inmates were passing by our glass wall. Bolivar stood and went to the glass and peered down the visit area until they disappeared by the front guard's desk.

"What's happening?" I asked.

He remained silent.

I got up and joined him at the glass. As when I'd entered, guards were clustered at the front desk, surrounding a person I couldn't see. One guard motioned the two codefendants toward the inmate door. It opened. They went through; it closed. The departing lawyer waited at the air lock door. Another guard motioned, and he left.

Bolivar hesitated, listening. Then came the echoed sound of the air lock door closing. Now, he opened our door. "Too claustrophobic here. Come."

The big conference room was marked off-limits to those not connected to the gas-tax case, but Bolivar was already entering it. Up front, the guards were still chattering happily, so I figured no one would make a fuss. I followed Bolivar inside, and we sat amid the stacked cartons.

The space was even more claustrophobic than the smaller room, a point not worth discussing. It smelled stale . . . of men and old cardboard.

"I left your food next door," I said.

"Fuck the food. Sit down."

I held my tongue and sat. From my seat, I could look down at the visit area. The guards were now turned in my direction, watching someone my angle precluded me from seeing. Then the person appeared on the other side of the glass wall.

It was Jilly.

CHAPTER 90

Now I understood the show Bonesy was talking about—why a lawyer would want to kill his wife—and who had the guards' rapt attention.

Jilly entered our room looking more beautiful than ever. Tall, blonde, curvaceous. Sheena in a concrete jungle. A wild thing who ignored rules. Her being in a room with an inmate other than the inmate she was visiting was a gross violation of BOP rules. And she couldn't be legally visiting Bolivar because, as his lawyer, I decided who his paralegal was.

Yet Jilly seemed strangely unperturbed. Her eyes were fixed on Bolivar, as if she was a puppy waiting to be cuddled. I wondered what kind of drug her Alpo had been spiked with.

I said, "Jilly, you can't come—"

"I left my briefcase," she said.

So she'd been with Bolivar before I arrived. I didn't want any part of this. "Find it, and get out. *Now*."

"Shut up," Bolivar said to me.

"That's it," I said. "I'm done."

Sombra or not, he was just a drug dealer who was going to be locked up for a long time. Much as I'd been paid, it didn't buy his disrespect. I'd prep the case without him.

I gathered my file and stood to leave.

"Sit, motherfucker," Bolivar said.

"Be nice, Joaquin," said Jilly.

"Shut up, bitch," Bolivar said.

"See you Monday," I said.

My chair was wedged between two rows of cartons, and I had to step between them to get around the table. I was doing so when a hand snaked around my neck and clamped my mouth, and something sharp pressed against my throat.

A man spoke into my ear: "Sit back down, boy."

Natty Grable. He must have attended the codefendant meeting but remained in the conference room, hiding between the stacked rows of file boxes.

I said, "You're making a mistake—"

The pressure against my throat increased, and I froze. I felt blood running down my neck. I heard a zipper opening, felt Natty moving. His trousers flew past me to Bolivar, who had unbuttoned his prison jumpsuit. Quickly, Bolivar stepped out of it and put on Natty's pants. Natty's shirt came next. Bolivar caught it, put his arms through its sleeves, and buttoned it up quickly.

"Briefcase?" he snapped at Jilly.

Jilly smiled vacantly. "Don't worry, I brought it, honey."

"I know *that*," Bolivar snarled. "I'm asking where the fuck is it?"

Jilly pointed to a briefcase on the floor, and Bolivar bent to it.

I felt Natty moving behind me as he tossed his loafers to Bolivar, who kicked off his jail sneakers and stepped into the loafers, then tossed his jumpsuit and sneakers past me. As Natty caught them, his movement increased the sharp pressure against my throat, and I gasped.

"So sorry," Natty murmured. He yanked me farther back between the stacked cartons. I felt him moving and twisting behind me, then we faced each other in the narrow space. He had on Bolivar's orange SHU jumpsuit. It hung from his skinny frame, and with his shaven head and white skin, he looked like a skeleton. He slipped off his eye patch. The eye beneath bulged whitely, its pupil the size of a match head.

He tossed the eye patch to Bolivar, who put it on.

I understood now. It was such a simple plan.

Natty tossed his yarmulke to Bolivar, who placed it atop his shaved scalp. I was impressed. Their newly exchanged identities were convincing. At a glance, each looked exactly as the other had moments ago. And a glance was all the guards would get, what with their preoccupation with Jilly—

The PA squawked: "Visiting ends in two minutes."

Natty spoke into my ear. "So do you, boy."

From the briefcase, Bolivar took a plastic vial of liquid and a cotton swab. He opened the vial, wetted the cotton, then dabbed it on the back of his hand. I caught a whiff of the liquid. The same chemical odor as that of the invisible ink with which Bonesy applied the day's password: the final touch for a paint-by-numbers escape.

The PA squawked: "One minute."

Bolivar looked at Natty. "Done?"

Natty nodded. "Kiss my brothers for me."

Bolivar snapped his fingers at Jilly. "Ready?"

She nodded dreamily.

Bolivar opened the door. Jilly went out first, and he followed behind, concealing himself in the penumbra of her radiance—

Natty yanked me deeper between the cartons. For a brief moment, his weapon left my throat, and I saw it was a sharpened comb handle, plastic so as to pass through the metal detectors. Then it touched my throat again, and Natty whispered:

"A little longer, boy."

CHAPTER 91

Keeping the point against my throat, Natty shifted, peering down the visit area to the visitor's exit. I looked, too.

The air lock door opened. Jilly and Bolivar went through it, and the door closed.

"Count to sixty, boy," Natty said. "Another minute until they're passed through the air lock. Then all over for you."

"Kill me, and you'll never get out," I said.

The comb point jabbed deeper. "Get out? *Look* at me."

He allowed me to turn slightly in his arms so I could see him, and I realized just how ill he was. My revulsion must have showed, for he laughed.

"I have a spider in my brain. It devours me. I have a week, a month perhaps, but no more. The Colombian means nothing to me, but to my brothers from Murmansk-54, he is the key to everything. His life is my gift to them."

"A gift they will never receive," I said. "The police are outside, waiting for Bolivar and the girl."

His good eye narrowed. "You lie, lawyer."

"It's true. Kursk and Kyril were arrested."

"No!" He gave a little start and—

I grabbed his wrist.

For a moment, we struggled. Despite his condition, he was strong. He pulled me toward the sharpened point of the weapon held between us. I used the momentum to head-butt his face. I felt cartilage crunch; blood jetted from his nostrils. He tottered, opened his mouth to speak, but no words came out, and he slumped.

I didn't know whether my blow was fatal, if it had driven shattered bone into his brain or simply rendered him unconscious. I didn't wait to find out.

I stood, gathered my file, and left the visit room. Blood trickled into my eye. I ducked into the restroom and splashed water on my face. My mirror image was a person I'd never seen before: a conspirator, a criminal, a killer. I left the restroom.

One guard remained at the desk. "Where's your client?"

"My client? I dunno. I was in the bathroom. I believe he already went upstairs. At least, I think."

I feared the guard would go to the room and find Natty, but he was too busy peering through the exit-door wire-glass into the air lock.

As I had been earlier, Jilly and Bolivar were stuck in the air lock, waiting for CONTROL. Jilly's hand was under the black light, her body bent, perfect ass jutting.

The guard sighed, appreciatively.

I was about to blurt out what was happening, but paused. If I foiled Bolivar's escape, the Russians and Colombians would compete for the pleasure of killing me slowly. As weak as the explanation seemed, I could claim I was in the bathroom when the switch and Natty's beating took place—

As if Jilly somehow sensed my presence, she turned and looked at me, her expression fearful, anxious, as if begging me not to ruin the escape. Her lips moved, but the door was wire-glass. I couldn't read her lips, but her face was soft when she uttered them. Soft as the Florida night when she'd offered herself to me. I'd refused then. Now?

"She don't look so happy," the guard said. "Probably ain't getting any. I'd sure like to help her out."

CONTROL's voice was muffled. "Next."

Jilly stepped aside as Bolivar put his hand beneath the black light. I wondered if his smeared password would fool CONTROL. It must have, for the outer air lock door opened, and Jilly and Bolivar walked through it.

A moment later, the inside door unlocked. I entered the air lock and put my hand beneath the black light. *Please don't make me wait, please—*

But at least two minutes passed before CONTROL said, "Go."

The outer door opened, and I entered the lobby.

Empty except for Bonesy. He shrugged sheepishly. "Sorry I went off on you, but this job gets to a person. Except for nights like tonight. Some kind of show. You missed the final act."

"What?"

"The one-eyed Russian guy puts the blonde into the back of this weird stretch limo with a front grille looks like teeth. Mexican guy, or some kind of Indian, at the wheel. Another woman inside, dark hair. The blonde takes one look at her and gets out, screaming at the Russian."

"About what?"

Bonesy shrugged. "Something about him lying, I think. Whatever it was, the blonde was freaking hysterical. She runs away. The limo does a U and starts after her, but by then, the blonde's at the car of this lawyer for the Russians who just walked out . . . you following me?"

"Yeah, yeah. So then?"

"She opens his car door and yanks him into the street—the sucker's so surprised, he lets her do it—and she gets behind the wheel and burns rubber. The limo takes off after her."

"Which way?" I figured Bolivar's original plan was to head for the pier, where a boat would transport him to a ship anchored in the harbor. But Jilly had clearly thrown a wrench in the works.

Bonesy pointed up the street toward the Gowanus Expressway. "She ran a red light under the highway. The limo ran the light, too, but she had a head start. Hey, where you—"

I didn't hear the rest of what Bonesy said, because by then I was in the Mini, replicating what Jilly and the bulldog had done: accelerating through the red light beneath the Gowanus Expressway and racing into Sunset Park.

I didn't know if the bulldog would find Jilly, but I was damned sure that I would.

I knew where she was going.

CHAPTER 92

The main entrance to Green-Wood Cemetery is a pair of massive iron gates hung between two ornate towers that house offices and security. On either side of the gates stand ten-foot-tall spiked fences that run the length of the avenue. The gates were locked. Security was unlit. I drove past the entrance and down the avenue a quarter mile before turning up a side street bordering the cemetery. Here, the fence was chain link. I slowed so as to study it.

A smart guy named Wolfe once opined that only the dead knew Brooklyn. True as to those sleeping in Green-Wood. Me, I grew up in the last great years of the borough, after the Johnnies marched home from 'Nam, before their kid brothers shipped to a who-cared place called Iraq. I was a street rat whose pack prowled obscure places. How we cavorted. Life was a rave. What was considered harmless trespassing then triggered jail time now. Wolfe was wrong.

Not only the dead knew Brooklyn.

My eyes scanned the gate. There'd be other gates. Small entrances for workers. Side gates. Locked? Maybe. A side gate was just ahead. I stopped and got out.

The gate was locked.

Not. The gate was hasped but unlocked. I went through it, found my bearings, then headed uphill.

In the purple twilight the cemetery was still. I went around bend after bend with the lights of Brooklyn unraveling below. Finally the Mini crested the high point where Val had told me the Revolution had been saved. Battle Hill.

I, too, wanted to be a savior.

By saving Jilly, I might save myself. She could truthfully testify I was duped into the escape. She'd be incriminating herself by doing so, but she was already in so deep, there was no way out. An insanity defense, maybe. Jilly, victim of a Svengali who'd programmed her to flirt with the guards. Hmm. It might work. At the very least, it could enable a compassionate plea to a lesser charge—

Jilly . . . who, on another Fourth of July six years ago, had bitten an apple, leaving tooth marks that matched her slightly crooked front tooth, the less-than-perfect flaw that made her perfect . . . before she'd been transformed from a vital beauty to a broken spirit by two bad cops in a cheap motel room. Had she blacked out during the rapes? No one would ever know. Nor did it matter any longer.

No one would ever know. Nor did it matter.

No doubt she remained a victim of the trauma of killing a man to defend herself. Poor Jilly was the kind of woman who escaped one problem only to find herself a worse one. Like when, years later, with her life finally stabilized . . . along came Joaquin Bolivar again.

He'd murdered her husband and conspired with Kursk to take her inheritance and invest it in Murmansk-54, a shell corporation intended to finance exporting cocaine via the unguarded polar route to Murmansk and northern Europe.

Much of her vast fortune was gone, but she'd purchase $150 million in gold. An investment recommended by her financial guru, Raphael Borg?

The tragedy abruptly ended when Jilly was coerced into assisting in Bolivar's escape. During it, I was certain she was stoned, hallucinating a nonreality. Only then to abruptly suffer the ultimate betrayal: Bolivar joined by an unexpected person or presence in the bulldog limo.

And so Jilly had fled to her one true love: Filly, entombed in a faux pyramid.

Fascinating story. What a closing punch. Jilly was nuts. Have pity.

Or so I'd argue. The prosecution would claim she'd murdered Mongello, helped murder her husband, knowingly participated in the escape.

I didn't know what the real truth was. Or care.

I was thinking like a lawyer again, remember?

I thought all this in the few seconds between cutting the engine and retrieving the Mustang from beneath the seat. I jammed it into my waistband, then got out and walked to the edge of Battle Hill. And looked down.

Filly's pyramid was outlined against the near-dark sky. A car was parked nearby, driver's door askew. I went down the path.

Light faintly flickered from the side of the pyramid. It came from a small rectangular opening. Maybe two by three feet. Enough for someone to crawl through. Clearly, Jilly had. Big question was whether anyone else had followed.

Only one way to find out.

I made my way to the side of the pyramid, grabbed hold of the edges of the opening, and levered myself into cool dimness without a sound.

There, I heard a sound:

A muffled sob.

Jilly.

My eyes adjusted.

What light there was came from a small candle set before a raised casket with a glass lid. Probably hermetically sealed, because the woman lying in it was as perfectly preserved as Vladimir Lenin. She wore a gold-flecked gown and gold jewelry. Her eyes were heavily mascaraed, her lids painted bright blue.

Filly Randa. Jilly's mother. In life she had played a servant girl; in death she'd become a leading lady. An Egyptian queen.

From the other side of the sarcophagus, another sob.

Jilly sat against the casket. Mascara streaked her cheeks. The top buttons of her blouse were undone, and she gripped her golden ankh tightly, as if it were a crucifix, its chain necklace dangling. Her voice was a strangled whisper.

"You were right," she said to her mother, again and again.

I went to Jilly. Even in extremis, she was radiant. A mad beauty. Unaware, or uncaring, of my presence, she reached within her blouse and undid a safety pin on her bra and from it took a twenty-dollar bill.

"See, Momma? Just like you told me. Always keep emergency money. That way, if it comes to put out or get out, I can leave. Just like you told me . . ."

"Jilly," I said quietly.

"Soon, Filly," she said.

Soon? I flashed on the film Filly had never quite been in: the pharaoh's diabolical method of sealing himself and his treasure . . . forever. I looked back at the opening, so small in the heavy stone wall.

"Jilly," I said. "Let's go."

She spoke, but not to me.

"I'm staying with you, Momma. I don't care what he says. Mr. Joaquin Himself can keep that other woman. I'll bet you a Lincoln penny he'll come crawling back, begging forgiveness. But no way I'm going off with him again. We had ourselves a couple or three nice times, and thanks for the memories, but one thing we didn't and won't ever have is love. And I'm done looking in all the wrong places. So here we are again. The two of us. Just like before."

I knelt by Jilly and took her hand in mine.

"Hello," she said.

But I doubted she recognized me. She'd been heavily stoned in the jail, and God knew what else she'd ingested since. I had to convince her to leave of her own volition; no way could I force her through the small opening.

Since there was no reasoning, I spun a lie. "Joaquin's waiting outside. The other woman's gone. He loves you."

She shook her head with the vehement denial of a child. "Please, tell them that I didn't mean to kill him."

She'd shifted time and place incoherently, talking now about her dead husband, Sholty Chennault III.

"It's okay," I said. "Everyone knows you didn't mean—"

"I couldn't help it . . . they wouldn't stop pounding atop me . . ."

They? Then I got it. She wasn't referring to her husband's murder, but to the motel room in which she'd killed Scally's partner, Vince Mongello.

"Pounding, pounding. They took turns pounding . . ."

I tried to move her, but she wouldn't stir. What to do? Then I remembered her fascination with the woman who'd posed for the golden statue atop the Municipal Building.

"Listen to me, Jilly. If you stay here, you'll end like poor Audrey Munson. You're not a forgotten statue like Audrey: you're a winner, a star."

Light sparked in her eyes. "I'm a star. Like Filly said."

"That's why you need to come with me. Now."

Again, I tried moving her, and this time she stood—

A sound. I turned and saw a man entering through the opening. In the flickering candlelight, his cheeks were shadowed with pits.

Scally. With a gun in his hand.

"Sit with the bitch," he said.

CHAPTER 93

After registering Jilly's mental state, Scally turned to me. "Where's the gold?"

"I have no idea," I said.

Scally held his gun at her head. In the dimness, she was pale as plaster. She clutched the golden ankh tight against her breast.

"Tell me, or I'll kill her," Scally said.

I said, "Tell you, you'll kill us both."

"A deal. The gold, you live. Five seconds you got to decide. One, two . . ."

Something sparked in my mind. A realization. "I'll give up the gold. But you'll have to let us go in order to get it."

"After I get it, you go."

"Not possible." I tapped Filly's sarcophagus. "The gold's here."

"Hidden inside the coffin?"

"No. It *is* the coffin."

"What are you talking?"

"This room. The coffin, and the platform, and the floors and inner walls are solid gold. Tons and tons of gold. A hundred fifty million dollars' worth of gold. But the only way to get it out of this tomb would be if Jilly applies for a court order to do so legally. If I tell her to, she'll do it."

Scally frowned at the dull finish of the sarcophagus. "Prove it."

"I'm going to put my hand in my pocket. Slowly. Okay?"

The gun's muzzle became a dark eye, staring at me. I put my hand in my pocket and took out a quarter. I held its serrated edge atop the sarcophagus, applied pressure, scraped . . .

If, as I suspected, the gold was hidden beneath the matte finish, then Scally would have no choice but to deal. Not that I could trust him if and when, but the first order of business was getting out of the pyramid before Jilly carried out what I now knew was the final act of her plan.

The coin scraped the sarcophagus's surface with a metallic sound that sounded like a scream in the small space. When I lifted my hand, the sarcophagus was scratched, revealing the dull, yellow glow of gold beneath.

Scally whinnied a laugh. "We're in business—"

A flash of gold as Jilly swung the ankh at Scally's skull. *Thunk!* He fell, and his gun bounced across the floor.

"He's one of them who hurt me," Jilly said.

Scally propped on his elbows—

Whack! Jilly dealt him another blow to the skull with the ankh. Scally fell hard and didn't move.

"See, Filly?" she said. "Like you taught: if a man gets fresh, slap him."

I took Jilly's hand. "Come on."

"No."

Again, she raised the ankh. I went to block her but no need. I wasn't her target. I heard glass shatter and realized Filly's Hollywood role had come to life. In *Land of the Pharaohs*, the mad ruler constructed the last opening to his treasure chamber so that tons of stone rested on sand-filled glass tubes that, when broken, would drain, allowing the final slab to lower, sealing the tomb for eternity.

Already sand was spilling from the glass tube, and I heard the faint rumble of the slab beginning its descent. Scally was stirring again, trying to roll over. I stepped over him and went to grab Jilly, but she danced from my reach.

"Please come, Jilly," I said. *"Please . . ."*

But she backed away to the opposite wall, ankh in hand, her eyes focusing on nothing and on everything at once. Behind me, the exit was narrowing. Too late for her now . . .

I dived toward the open space—

But I managed to get only halfway through because Scally gripped my leg, trying to escape with me. I fumbled in my waistband for the gun, pointed it behind me, pulled the trigger.

The shot was deafening. I felt Scally's grip shudder, saw his shoulder bloom red, yet he held on, dragging me back inside.

I pointed the gun again, but he swatted it down, and it fell inside the pyramid.

Deadlocked. Despite the blows to his head and the gunshot wound, Scally had strength enough to hold me in place. And the slab was low now, touching my jacket. If I remained in place, it would crush me.

Another gunshot rang out, and I felt Scally's grip loosen. Behind Scally, I saw Jilly pointing Scally's gun at him. Another shot, and Scally let go. The slab was pressing down on me. I scrabbled, pushed, and pulled myself through the opening.

Behind me, the pyramid was almost sealed.

My last glimpse within was of Scally's malevolent face . . . for an instant, his image changed to George Maledon, the executioner.

Let no guilty man escape.

I heard a shrill cry. Jilly. A laugh or a sob? I'd never know. The slab closed with a thud. I'd killed again; again without regret.

Exhausted, I lay still on the grassy embankment below the pyramid. Gradually, I became aware of headlights and the sound of a car approaching. I didn't get up. No point in doing so: too late to run, no place to hide. The headlights grew brighter, closer. I turned toward them and behind their glare saw the chrome teeth of the bulldog, growing closer—

But then the lights paused.

And I heard other sounds:

A siren, growing louder.

A car door opened.

A gunshot echoed.

The door closed.

The bulldog's headlights swept past me as it turned around. There was a crunching sound, and the bulldog was gone.

I remained still. The grass smelled sweet. Above me, the pyramid's face was strangely turning colors: red, white, blue . . . and I became aware of the distant *whumps* of fireworks.

I stood and walked to the top of Battle Hill and watched the July Fourth fireworks illuminate the big city I loved and—in one way or another—was about to leave forever.

That wasn't all that had changed. I'd crossed a red line and become one of *them*. One of those who killed. Traum, Scally, probably Natty. I could justify the killings as self-defense, but the truth was that I had no regrets.

The siren was close now.

CHAPTER 94

Bubble lights reflected off the mausoleums. A second car appeared. I'd thought it would be feds, but it turned out to be a blue-and-white NYPD cruiser. Two uniformed cops got out.

I kept my hands in plain sight.

"You drunk, pal?" the first cop said.

"Not drunk," I said, realizing cemetery security had called them; apparently, they had no idea of what had transpired at the jail.

"Cemetery's private property," the second cop said.

"What's that?" The first cop shone a flashlight on the ground nearby.

The beam played over a body. A man lay on his back, his face a mash of flesh and bone caused by the tires of the vehicle that had driven over it. The bulldog.

One cop went back to the cruiser and got on the radio.

The other stayed with me. "You know this guy?"

I shook my head, although I recognized the clothes Natty had worn to the jail, and his eye patch and yarmulke. Natty's things and Bolivar's corpse. It made me wonder:

Why had they—whoever *they* were—killed Bolivar? Because he'd threatened to cooperate if convicted? Because he was *Sombra* and they wanted to depose him? Was the dark-haired woman in the bulldog Laura?

"You're under arrest for trespassing, and maybe a lot more to come."

The least of my worries. I stayed mute as the tombstones around us.

They cuffed my hands and sat me in the cage in the back of the cruiser while they waited for backup. But before any more NYPD arrived, a pair of white federal cop cruisers did.

I saw the feds talking with the local cops, apparently as to who had jurisdiction and custody. Then more NYPD showed, and the conversation grew heated. Through the grimy window of the cruiser, I watched the last Fourth of July fireworks spark out, then sat there, waiting . . .

About an hour later, a midsize sedan appeared, and Kandi Kauffman got out. She conferred with the feds, then with the locals, then approached the cruiser and opened the rear door.

"Poor Benn," she clucked. "You really stepped in it this time. Don't suppose you want to talk with me? Like, *cooperate?*"

I just smiled. "I'm already lawyered up."

"You dumb fuck. Your attorney?"

"You're looking at him."

"Only a fool . . ."

"Why do fools fall in love?"

"You really have lost it."

"Why do birds sing so gay?"

"Keep on laughing, sucker. I could let the locals pull you in, but why waste time and money on a state misdemeanor charge when you're looking at a bunch of federal felonies?"

"Why indeed."

"Your participation in Bolivar's first escape attempt was a coin toss, but after tonight, the case against you is a slam dunk. Soon as the marshals finish their forensics—not just for the dead man here, who I have reason to believe is Bolivar, but for another dead man in the MCC visit room . . . but I guess you know about that."

"My client takes the Fifth."

"Soon as the marshal reports are in, I'll be presenting the matter to a grand jury. Tell your client to prepare to be indicted."

"I take it that, until that happens, he's free."

Kandi nodded. The cops unhooked me.

I got in the Mini and left Green-Wood.

CHAPTER 95

Monday morning, I went to Judge Trieant's courtroom for the resumption—and end—of Bolivar's trial. I had a nodding acquaintance with the clerks and the steno, but none of them would look at me. I figured the word was out: a dirty lawyer was going to the cleaners. Kandi was already there, dressed to the nines, perfectly coiffed. I'd assumed Nelson Cano would be present, but there was no sign of him. Probably there was no need for him to be there, because Bolivar had been ID'd and the case was over.

"All rise!"

Judge Trieant entered, sparrow-size in a black robe. The son of a bitch had to know what had occurred, but he looked at the empty space next to me, and oh-so-innocently asked where my client was.

"I don't know," I said, which was technically true.

"You're aware of the penalty for perjury?"

"I am. But thanks for asking."

Trieant's face became flushed, as if he were verging on a stroke. Made me think that even in the worst of times good things can happen.

Kandi stood. "If I may make a statement for the record, Your Honor?" She proceeded to state that the defendant was deceased. She allowed a small smile, looking at me pointedly, as she continued. "At this time I am not free to state the particular circumstances of his death, but in the very near future, the government will be making the, ah, *matter* public."

I remained expressionless. It wasn't easy. The copy of Pimms's memo pad was in my bag. If I presented it to the court as deliberately concealed 3500 evidence, Kandi was fried. And since she was the guiding force behind my investigation, no other prosecutor would pick up the torch.

Trouble was, I'd have to explain how I got the 3500 material, which meant a good cop named Nelson Cano would be ruined as well.

Trieant's gavel banged. "Case closed."

Outside the courthouse, several jurors were clustered, saying good-byes to one another. All they knew was that the case was concluded, and they glanced at me curiously. I smiled, mouthed, *Innocent*, and went on walking.

Once in Val's Flex, I opened my bank app. The $20 million was still there. Inwardly, I was both exhilarated and frightened about it.

"Everything okay, Mr. Benn?"

"Fine. Let's go to the office."

Midday traffic on Fifth Avenue was horrendous, so rather than circling around, I told Val to drop me on the corner of Madison. As I neared my office, a man suddenly emerged from a parked car and blocked my path. He was bronzed and muscular and had Indian features. The Logui who'd guided me down the mountain. From his pocket—*It's a hit*, I thought—he gave me a flash drive, the same brand of thumb as I'd gotten twice before in different versions:

The first, given me by Mondragon, ostensibly to assist Rigo's cooperation, had shown Rigo bribing General Uvalde. I'd passed it on to AUSA Barnett Robinson.

The second, left for me by Stefania before she was murdered, was a continuation of the video of the bribe, but including Bolivar and Laura Astorquiza in the room. I'd disposed of it.

The Logui drove off. In my office, I inserted the third thumb in my computer.

Another video. Yet another version of the bribe. Sort of a middle between the first two: it included Rigo, Uvalde, and Bolivar but cut out before Laura.

Clever Rigo. He'd given the version just showing him and Uvalde but held back the uncut video. Partly because he preferred negotiating piecemeal, partly to keep Mondragon from knowing he was unmasking Bolivar as *Sombra*.

I went to the web and read a new blog I'd expected to find:

> ### Radio Free Bogotá
> Countrymen, rejoice, for at last we are free. The bandit known as *Sombra* is dead, and General Uvalde, his partner in crime, has finally been exposed as a corrupt traitor to the nation. Viva Colombia!

Laura was some piece of work. Possessed of a pure brilliance. Obviously, she'd been Bolivar's partner—and probably his lover—from the start, which was why she'd attended the bribe meet with General Uvalde, way back when the *Sombra* DTO was just a start-up. Its founding members were Uvalde for security, Rigo for financing, and she and Bolivar as the hands-on doers.

A risky business, but she'd made it through and afterward wisely stayed in the background. She'd even created another persona: Laura Astorquiza, archenemy of narco-traffickers and corrupt cops. Which further unbalanced my state of mind.

I knew Laura was complicit. So why didn't she kill me, too? Was she after my $20 million? Or did she plan to let me keep the money as a quid pro quo for what she'd stolen, *and* for my silence about her?

I didn't know. It didn't matter yet. Something else had to be dealt with first. I knew what it would be and how I would respond.

So I leaned back and kicked my feet up and waited for my phone to ring.

It wasn't a long wait. I let it ring three times before answering, as if I hadn't a care in the world. "Benn Bluestone."

"Barnett Robinson here."

"Just thinking of you, Barnett."

"We need to meet."

"We just did."

"Again."

"Sure. When?"

"Today."

CHAPTER 96

Before meeting Robinson, I went to Rikers. Billy had on an oversize orange jumpsuit. He saw me looking at it and shook his head. "I'm in the SHU on suicide watch. Can you believe that? Me, the man who has everything to live for?" He tried to laugh but began to weep.

I sat with him awhile longer. When I went to shake hands with him, Billy collapsed into my arms. To my surprise, but apparently not to his, I stroked his head and kissed his cheek, then winked and left.

I had uglier fish to fry.

The conference room of the SDNY International Narcotics Bureau was occupied by the same cast of characters as before—Richard of CIA, the INB chief, AUSA Barnett Robinson, the SOD agent from DC, and the Russian spy posing as an attaché.

"Read any blogs today, Bluestone?" the chief said.

"I might have," I said. "Any one in particular?"

"Cut the crap. You know what we want."

"Could be. Do you know what I want?"

Pregnant pause. Robinson averted his eyes as if wanting to avoid watching me hang myself. The INB chief grinned as if he'd enjoy handing me the rope. But I had no intention of doing myself in. At worst, I was in for a licking, but I was going to keep on ticking.

"You're in a world of trouble as it is," said the chief. "Grief happens when you withhold evidence from federal authorities."

"Grief's good," I said. "Cleanses the soul."

Robinson said, "What do you want, Benn?"

"Long list. Let's see. I want . . . not to be indicted. I want . . . not to be disbarred. I want . . . not to have to forfeit anything."

The chief's laugh was a sneer. "You're not getting anything, and in the end, you *will* confirm that Bolivar was *Sombra*."

I said, "I'm a big believer in everything being negotiable so long as the deal is fair. The deal I have in mind is more than fair. In return for no indictment, no disbarment, no forfeiture, I might be able to help you out."

"It's true?" Robinson said. "Bolivar was *Sombra*?"

"My impression is he . . . might have been."

"Shove your *impression*," the chief said. "We have reason to believe Rigo gave you a full version of the bribe video."

"He did not," I said. This was true. Stefania had given it to Prince Boris, who had given it to me.

The chief snorted. "You *might* be able to help us out? Without the video, you can't help yourself out."

"Actually, I can," I said. "Way back when you were worried about getting into law school, a drug dealer named Noriega ran Panama . . . with the approval of the United States, because he kept things in line. Only Noriega got too greedy, so he was informed that he had a choice: he could take his ill-gotten gains and skip, or we were going to invade. He thought we were bluffing. We weren't. We invaded Panama, and Noriega spent the rest of his life behind bars."

"So fucking what?" the chief said.

"So a few years later, the same scenario occurred with the drug dealer who was president of Haiti. But he'd seen what happened to Noriega, so he took his loot and skedaddled to Gstaad. At the time, I had a client who had a ton of evidence against the Haitian, but since the problem ended peacefully, my guy received zero credit. He got shafted because the government didn't want to publicize dealing with the corrupt general. To keep my client from shooting his mouth off, they isolated him in a SHU in a level-five penitentiary. He was unprotected there. Two years later, he was stabbed to death by a North Valley Cartel *sicario*. I still have the affidavits and videotaped statements of Colombian and Haitian authorities and conspirators. Confirming they stifled an indictment of a presidential family and its hangers-on for political expediency."

The chief pointed a finger at me. "You're accusing employees of the United States Department of Justice of breaking the law?"

I pointed a finger back at him. "Fucking-A, I am."

The chief's face reddened. "Watch your words."

"If you don't like 'em, don't listen." I turned to Richard, who until then had been expressionless. "In fact, one of the criminals still works in the Eastern District of New York. A certain, what's the word? Prosecutoress?

Robinson said, "I assume your client was Maximilian Barrera?"

"Max. Brother of Nacho, CFO of the Cali Cartel."

"Ancient history," the chief said.

"History repeating itself," I said. "Dated or not, the Haitian proof is going to the media, *together* with the *timely* video of Rigo bribing Uvalde, the esteemed Colombian antidrug czar our government recently made an honorary member of the DEA. The American public will see that we *still* let drug dealers operate, so long as they don't make waves. The too-big-to-fail syndrome. Nice story, don't you think?"

"So you have the video," the chief said. "You just obstructed justice, asshole."

I said, "The only obstructed asshole is in your cheap suit."

"Nice try, but no cigar. No one will buy it," said the chief.

"No one will have to pay a penny," I said. "It's going to be free. It's going to be turned over during a news conference during which I am going to allege that the government made a deal to let Uvalde walk with our money so long as he keeps mum."

The chief said, "You're making your situation worse."

Again, I addressed Richard, who seemed slightly amused. "Tell your colleague to shut his face, because he's making *his* situation worse."

Heads turned as the Russian barked a laugh.

"Why is he still here?" said the chief to no one in particular, none of whom replied.

The SOD agent harrumphed. "We don't take kindly to threats."

"Please wait outside, Mr. Bluestone," Richard said.

I waited outside the conference room. A little later, the Russian emerged. He winked at me as he left the waiting area. I wasn't surprised Ivan was no longer included in the loop. Probably he'd been invited to participate because *Sombra*'s polar route skirted Russian territorial waters. But now his presence was no longer necessary, and the government—meaning Richard—had decided that Ivan had seen enough federal inner workings.

Another few minutes, then Robinson emerged.

"Here's what we can do for you," he said.

"No. First, tell me what you want."

"We get the Haiti material, along with your sworn statement that you will never reveal any of it. We also get the video that includes Bolivar, aka *Sombra*."

"Now, what can you do for me?"

"No prosecution for the escape and the events surrounding it, but you resign from the bar. You forfeit your fee for Bolivar."

"Maybe. I'm still waiting to hear from her."

"Who?"

"The fat lady. I hear she has a nice voice."

"Don't screw around, Benn. This isn't negotiable."

"Everything's negotiable, Barnett. Let's go inside."

The analyst was sitting in the lead chair where the INB chief had been. The chief was now exiled to the far end of the table, looking miserable.

"Your deal is rejected," I said. "I repeat my offer. No prosecution for anything. I keep my ticket to practice. I keep my money. Before you reply, another factor to consider: There's a congressional hearing on drug-war funding next month. You want to close the door on *Sombra* and tell the legislators how the forces of justice have once again prevailed. But the video just showing Rigo and Uvalde doesn't do that. Neither does the video including Bolivar, because that doesn't prove he was *Sombra*."

"Go on," Richard said.

"You need confirmation to prove Bolivar was *Sombra*. Like a statement by another participant that they knew Bolivar was *Sombra*. Trouble is, no way Uvalde will say so. But Rigo might."

"On tape?" asked Richard,

I shook my head.

"In writing?" asked the chief.

I shook my head.

The chief shook his head as if he'd never encountered a schmuck like me. But Richard was still interested. "What do you have, Benn?"

"Maybe Rigo's statement was recorded."

"Maybe? Okay. How is his voice verified?"

"Softball. Rigo's made personal calls from jail. I know and you guys pretend not to know that when it comes to big guys like Rigo, all his calls are recorded. Compare his personal calls with his recorded statement, and you'll get a voice match."

"You have a statement?" asked the chief.

I ignored the chief. Looked at Richard. "Deal?"

"I'll have to make some calls," said Richard. "Excuse us, please."

This time my wait was longer. Finally, the conference-room door opened, and Robinson motioned me within.

I went to learn my future.

CHAPTER 97

"The government requires you to agree to strict confidentiality," said Richard.

"Agreed," I said.

"Eastern District AUSA Kandice Kauffman," said the chief. "An ambitious prosecutor, you'd agree?"

"I'll give her that. With an asterisk."

"Care to tell us about her?"

"Tell you what? That I don't like her, don't respect her, don't trust her. Never have and never will. Enough?"

"Specificities?" said the chief.

News flash! So politics were in play. By lucking out with the North Valley Cartel takedown, Kandi had established herself as a star prosecutor. Along the way, her imperious manner had rankled a lot of people. The SDNY feds were team players who didn't like stars. They wanted Kandi out of the picture. They wanted *Sombra* to be *their* takedown.

I wished I could help them. Reveal that Kandi had withheld the Pimms discovery to ensure convicting Bolivar, who'd in turn flip. I guessed Kandi wasn't sure Bolivar was *Sombra*, but she was positive Bolivar could give up *Sombra*.

It was so tempting.

Divulging Kandi had again withheld discovery material would end her career. Deservedly so. But how to dishonor Chaz Scally and get Kandi booted without throwing Nelson Cano to the wolves?

As if reading my mind, the SOD agent said, "What about Agents Cano and Scally?"

I shrugged. "What about them?"

"They were working the Bolivar case. No secret they were investigating you as well. Scally's disappeared."

A chill went down my spine. Scally had bullets in him that had been fired by my Mustang—which lay next to his body. If Filly's pyramid were unsealed, I was consigned to history. But if that were in the cards, it would have happened already, and I'd be having this interview with my hands cuffed behind my back.

"Check the drunk tanks," I said.

The agent showed me a photograph of the bulldog. "Recognize this car?"

I nodded. "It resembles a car used by a man named Nathan Grable."

"Care to comment about Natty?"

"Not part of our understanding, is it?"

"What about Jillian Sholty?"

I shrugged.

Richard said, "Evgeny Kursk?"

I shrugged.

"One more question, Mr. Bluestone," the SOD agent said. "Agent Scally was last seen on the afternoon of July Fourth. He was with Agent Cano."

"Is that a question?"

"Getting there. Like Agent Scally, Agent Cano then went missing. Unlike Agent Scally, Agent Cano was soon found. He was shot to death. Your thoughts on that?"

Whoa. I had plenty of thoughts on that. Cano hadn't been a player in the game until he'd turned on Scally and Kandi by giving me the

3500 material. The only person who had motive and opportunity to kill Cano was Scally. But Kandi was as guilty as Scally. If she hadn't conspired with Scally to hide the 3500 material, none of this would have happened.

Richard said, "Was Cano dirty, Benn?"

"Nelson Cano was cleaner than anyone in this room."

I looked around at the assorted suits: some honest and some not so honest, all engaged in a war that couldn't be won and shouldn't be fought. I thought of Groucho Marx's joke about not wanting to join the kind of club that would accept him as a member.

Everyone was waiting on me.

The SOD agent was a high-ranking cop, with the good intentions and failed oaths that entailed. The INB chief was an ambitious asshole who would climb the Main Justice ladder. AUSA Robinson would put in his five or six years as a keeper of public morality, then go off to a big firm to defend Wall Street thieves and corporate polluters. Richard was a cold-blooded bastard who toyed with people's lives, trading and sacrificing them without a second thought.

That left me.

I had blood on my hands and blood money in my bank account. My whole life had revolved around a dirty war that had cost so much in lives and treasure, a futile chase-your-tail exercise during which I'd lost my one true love.

I was as guilty as Scally, or Bolivar, or Kursk.

But with a difference: I could redeem myself, and in the process honor a good cop named Cano. *But going that route meant losing all.* It had been my obligation as an attorney—an officer of the court—to reveal I possessed the 3500 material as of the moment it was given to me. My secretly holding on to it was a violation of that obligation, as well as an obstruction of justice. If I admitted it, I'd lose my leverage and torpedo my deal.

This was my moment to choose.

Who am I?

I looked out the window. The view was of 500 Pearl and the MDC and the upper-story pedestrian bridges that connected them, architectural contrivances I'd always thought of as rat mazes, funneling cooperators from jail to inquisitions to ultimate fates. What a fucking system I'd been a part of.

The time had come for me to decide: *Stay, or go?*

"Gentlemen," I said, "let's renegotiate."

* * *

The renegotiation went smoothly. When I explained what my new proposal entailed, the government took the old deal off the table. The new deal was simply a matter of give and take.

I gave them Rigo's taped statement that *Sombra* was present at the bribe, the version of the video that put Bolivar—but *not* Laura—at the scene, the Haiti material and a sworn statement never to divulge it, and the 3500 material Kandi had withheld.

Additionally, and most reluctantly, I gave up the $20 million I'd received for Bolivar's case. This requirement came from Richard, and my first instinct was to bargain. But I didn't. Strangely, I felt . . . *relieved*.

The final part of our agreement sprang from my verbal request. I whispered it to Richard. He nodded agreement. I wasn't surprised, although what I asked was out of line and illegal. But I knew if the price were right, everything was for sale.

Just follow the chains of command and demand:

Richard's boss calls a senator who calls the New York County District Attorney who notifies a line prosecutor that a certain homicide indictment is to be dismissed, forthwith.

Half an hour after Richard and I finalized things, Billy's public defender called me, sounding shell-shocked. Given that her name was foreign sounding—Latifa Mohammed—and that she represented petty criminals, many of whom were aliens, she probably didn't have many cases that ended happily. "They just offered Billy a disorderly conduct. An offense with no criminal record. Sentence is time served."

"Tell him Benn said to take it."

The final touch was that I was given the right to resign from the bar rather than be publicly disbarred, and I received blanket immunity from any prosecution having to do with Bolivar's escape, or Natty's death. And, best of all:

Kandi's investigation of me was terminated.

Of course, there were collateral consequences. Although they didn't affect me personally, I was greatly pleased.

One week after my deal was finalized, Kandi Kauffman left government service. I wasn't surprised when a month later, she reemerged as a defense attorney.

Another month later, General Uvalde abruptly retired.

Nelson Cano was accorded a memorial ceremony and posthumously promoted, and his wife was awarded a pension for life. For once, Richard—I assume it was him—had done a decent thing, for an anonymous someone had me invited to the ceremony.

As for me? I was broke but not busted and for once not disgusted.

Incredibly, for the first time in years, I found myself happy.

SIX MONTHS LATER

BENN

I moved to a small apartment in a marginal Brooklyn neighborhood. The very same hood in which I'd grown up. At first, I wasn't a happy camper, but slowly I accepted coming home. I'd deal with its short-comings. I still knew people who knew people. Things would come my way. Call me Mr. Patience. With nothing but time on my hands, I walked the city. Saw it from a different perspective. Upside down and sideways now. Like, standing in the cold rain, gazing through steamed-over windows into a splendid restaurant that shortly ago I'd dined in several times weekly.

One day on the Brooklyn Heights Promenade, I bumped into a lawyer I somewhat knew. I remembered him as another anxious face rushing through the city. We'd never spoken but after a few years had graduated to nods in passing. For years, it seemed. Then he'd disap-peared from my life, or maybe I'd disappeared from his, but what the whatever, here we were.

Just two guys, recently retired.

He'd aged poorly. I remembered him as sleek, a sharp dresser with a magic mouth and a knack for making money. Now he moved as stiffly as a fat man wearing tight shoes, although his slit eyes darted like a pigeon searching for a morsel.

"Jesus," he said. "The years went fast. You good?"

I wondered how he viewed me. *Please God, not as his contemporary.* I gave him a nod, like: *Are you kidding?* I was touchy about people knowing I was down-and-out. I shunned company and didn't want sympathy.

He sighed. "Boy, those were the days . . ."

I nodded. Across the river, lower Manhattan was as beautifully unreal as a movie set. It was nice sitting there, facing it with the breeze in my face; besides, the guy had a need to talk and just maybe I had a need to listen to a human voice.

He paid lip service to his wife and kids and grandkids, and then shoptalked: relating some weird case, ranting on this fucking dumb judge, admiring that prosecutor with the great ass, who was doing what to whom and why.

Two tidbits made me smile.

One was that Morty Plitkin was under investigation in connection with the July Fourth escape from the Metropolitan Detention Center.

The second was that Kandi Kauffman and William Dreidel had partnered up and already were co-representing a big guy. A doomed partnership, I knew. You can get away with some things, but uncool avarice is fatal. Gets the client to thinking: *My fucking whole life is falling apart, and all this fucking lawyer wants to talk about is his fee.* So the new partners would make some scores until their old character weaknesses emerged; then they would be the broken dream team.

"What's their client's name?" the lawyer wondered aloud. "On the tip of my tongue. Ah. Fernando Ibarra, aka Fercho."

I shrugged and gave him a friendly pat on the shoulder. "Nice seeing you again."

Unbelievable. Me, a smiley face. My body had changed, too. Instead of nursing my joints, I took to jogging, and lo and behold, my aches and pains receded.

One evening, I was running along Prospect Park Drive when I became aware of a car directly behind me. I left the roadway for the grassy shoulder, but the car still followed.

I ran into the trees. Behind me, I heard the car's door open. I burst from the trees onto a lawn sloping upward. I ran hard, but when I glanced behind, the man in the trees was gaining on me. I cut back onto the roadway—

Another car cut me off. A guy got out, blocking my way. The guy behind caught up. They looked like each other. One was hardly more than a boy; the other, a man in his prime. Loguis? Probably. Experienced hunters. Spook me from behind and into a pincer maneuver. I was their prey.

I froze. *My turn now?*

The older Logui was the one who'd escorted me to and from *Sombra*'s mountain stronghold, the same who'd brought me the third thumb drive

He had something else for me. From a pocket, he drew and fanned three photographs. Held them in front of my eyes. Three close-ups of dead men, each with a bullet hole placed between eyes wide open. I recognized them all.

General Uvalde.

Evgeny Kursk.

Enano.

The Logui put them away. Looked at me, brow arched.

"I understand," I said.

He did not acknowledge me. Just stood there for a long moment with his head cocked, as if he were having a conversation with himself.

Then he and the younger man drove off.

But did I understand? Those who'd known *Sombra*'s identity were dead. Yet *Sombra* was dead, and his identity was public knowledge on both sides of the law.

So, why the murders?

I walked the park. The Long Meadow was deeply shadowed. On the far side a few cars were on the roadway, behind the roadside fence their lights just winks in the darkness . . .

I flashed on the night I'd first met Laura Astorquiza.

And what a night it was. Benn's last party. Money and women. Jilly's exquisite beauty. The extraordinary Laura; she and I in sync, one-upping wordplay. What did my middle initial *T* stand for? Nothing. A letter like the *S* in Harry S. Truman.

Laura hadn't believed me. She said *T* was short for a name.

She'd been right. I'd been lying for no reason except that I never used my middle name. *T* was short for Ted. An obscure fact no one knew except Mady . . .

And one other person.

I'd thought all of Nacho Barrera's family had been murdered. I'd thought wrong. One relative had survived that awful night of the long knives:

Nacho's daughter. Sara.

Sara with the large, dark eyes of a child in a Keane painting; the same eyes as Laura Astorquiza. The child Sara Barrera had grown into the woman Laura Astorquiza.

How could I have not known?

My eliminating Laura as a possible *Sombra* had largely been because no Colombian mafioso would take orders from a woman. But there was always another way into a locked place. The Logui were the key to this lock, for they were the buffer between Laura and the macho narco-trafficking world. The Logui loved Nacho Barrera. And worshipped his daughter.

Meaning Laura was *Alune*.

And *Alune* was *Sombra*.

Laura had been her father's constant companion when she was little Sara. Possessed of the patience of a natural leader. A master who saw the moves ahead and deployed her pieces accordingly. I was just a pawn, and yet . . .

She had spared my life. And now only I can tell the tale.

As I said at the very beginning of this tale, a person needs but four things to tell a story:

A beginning, a middle, and an end . . . Also, you can't be dead.

I have no illusions. I know why I'm alive and talking.

Because Laura doesn't know that I know who she is.

ALUNE

Benn doesn't know I know he knows. He doesn't know the real reason he's still alive is because, in all the world outside Anawanda, I trust only him. Not only because of our shared past, but because he is like family now. I think one sister has a crush on him. I don't blame her. I do, too.

Because he has become one of Those Who Know More.

I have big plans for our future . . . together.

ACKNOWLEDGMENTS

My ultimate thanks to Gracie Doyle and the team at Thomas & Mercer for their trust.

A benediction for Soraya, without whom this book would have never been written.

A big shout-out to my agents, David Hale Smith, and Liz Parker at Inkwell.

My endless gratitude to Ed Stackler, editor nonpareil.

And of course, to my readers: thank you.

Benn Bluestone hopes to return soon.

ABOUT THE AUTHOR

Photo © 2017 Luis Alicea Caldas

In his thirty years as a criminal attorney, Todd Merer specialized in the defense of high-ranking cartel chiefs extradited to the United States. He gained acquittals in more than 150 trials, and his high-profile cases have been featured in the *New York Times* and *Time* magazine and on *60 Minutes*. A "proud son of Brooklyn," Merer divides his time between New York City and ports of call along the old Spanish Main. *The Extraditionist* is his first novel.